"Why are you here?"

Imoshen's hands trembled as she pushed the hair from her face, muttering under her breath. Tulkhan didn't need to understand High T'En to know that she was cursing him.

Spinning on her heel, she stalked off, all wounded dignity despite her nakedness. He was on his feet before he knew it, lunging forward to catch her around the waist. She arched against him, her body an exclamation of silent fury.

Anticipating her attempt to drop out of his grasp, he lifed her off her feet, still writhing. Then he spun and threw her over to the bed. A shiver of instinctive awe rippled through him in response to her Otherness. She scurried across the bed, but he tackled her before her feet could hit the ground on the far side.

It struck Tulkhan that she did not mean to harm him. She used her strength only to repulse him, forbearing to deliver the killing or maiming blow to his eyes or throat.

By the time she lay beneath him, panting, he too was panting, their faces only a hand's breadth apart.

"This is a lie," he said and lowered his head to inhale her scent. It hit him like a physical thing. When he went on, his voice was hoarse. "You could have blinded me and escaped. Or using your T'En gifts, you could have struck me in some way I can't imagine, but you didn't.

"You are here beneath me because it is where you want to be."

Also by Cory Daniells

Broken Vows

DARK DREAMS

Book Two of
THE LAST T'EN TRILOGY

CORY DANIELLS

Bantam 🦋 Books

New York Toronto London Sydney Auckland

DARK DREAMS

A Bantam Book

PUBLISHING HISTORY
Bantam mass market edition / July 2001

ISBN: 0-553-58100-7

Published simultaneously in the United States and Canada

Bantam Books are published by Bantam Books, a division of Random House, Inc. Its trademark, consisting of the words "Bantam Books" and the portrayal of a rooster, is Registered in U.S. Patent and Trademark Office and in other countries. Marca Registrada. Bantam Books, 1540 Broadway, New York, New York 10036.

PRINTED IN THE UNITED STATES OF AMERICA

OPM   10   9   8   7   6   5   4   3   2   1

To my editors,
thank you for your patience
and dedication

DARK DREAMS

One

ONCE THE PALACE of a thousand chambers had overwhelmed Imoshen, now she strode its corridors as
the uncrowned Empress. But her position was as
precarious as General Tulkhan's. He and his Ghebite army
were the minority overlords of a conquered people who remained loyal to the old empire. Every day the palace servants
deferred to Imoshen, when in reality she was the General's
captive. Every day the Ghebites flaunted their barbarian splendor, carelessly insulting her people.

Imoshen smiled grimly; she would not be ground down.
Though she had been forced to surrender her family's
Stronghold to the Ghebites, and had seen her island conquered, General Tulkhan had claimed her for his own which
gave her great tactical strength. Much had been achieved
in the twelve weeks since Harvest Feast. Only last night
Tulkhan had signed the document recognizing Fair Isle
Church Law, returning to her all she had lost and more. For
on their bonding day she would stand before her people as
co-ruler, the first pure T'En woman to take a bond-partner
in six hundred years.

At the screech of metal on metal Imoshen froze, wary as
a hunted woodland creature. She had become intimately ac-
quainted with fear, and the knowledge that her life hung by
a thread shadowed her every move. Heart hammering, she
followed the razor-sharp sounds to a balcony where half a

dozen servants were avidly watching a confrontation in the courtyard below. One glance told her the General and his men were at sword practice. Relief flooded her.

"Get back to work, the lot of you!" she hissed, dismayed to see the Ghebite fascination for violence infecting her servants. They made guilty apologies and hurried away.

In the confines of the courtyard the swords' song resonated harshly. As Imoshen remained in the balcony's shadows, watching unseen, she could not but admire the Ghebite's skill, though she deplored their love of violence.

Once past boyhood, a Ghebite warrior practiced with battle-ready weapons, scorning the use of blunt swords. They were feared for their ferocity across the known lands, and Tulkhan embodied the Ghebite Ideal. For at only nineteen he had assumed command of the Ghebite army, leading it south, creeping inexorably across the mainland. In eleven years no kingdom had managed to withstand the General's onslaught, and it had appeared he would conquer the known world.

But instead of attacking the last of the southern kingdoms he had turned his eye on Fair Isle, making a surprise assault. Betrayed by her allies, unprepared for war on her own shores, Fair Isle had crumpled in the space of one spring-summer campaign.

General Tulkhan was renowned for his tactical skill and physical bravery. Given that, why was he taking on three swordsmen while his Elite Guard watched? What was he trying to prove?

Suddenly Imoshen understood; once her position as co-ruler of Fair Isle became known, his men would believe she had emasculated their General. They might even suspect he had been ensorcelled by his captive. Some of them still refused to meet her eyes, believing the rumors of treacherous T'En powers. No wonder Tulkhan wielded his sword with such intensity that his trusted commanders could barely defend themselves.

Metal grated, setting Imoshen's teeth on edge. She gasped as one man gave a guttural cry, dropping to his knee. At the last moment Tulkhan turned his sword, striking with the flat of the blade. The Ghebite sprawled on the slippery stone.

No one moved.

Imoshen took a step closer, drawn by the charged atmosphere. She could taste their intoxicating blood lust in the air.

The sound of the men's ragged breathing was magnified, trapped in the snow-bound inner courtyard. It was not unknown for Ghebites to take a fatal wound in practice. In the brilliant early morning light two remaining swordsmen faced Tulkhan over the body of their barely conscious comrade, steam rising from their skin.

General Tulkhan's naked back glistened with sweat as he stood poised to strike. He was magnificent and undeniably dangerous. Something tightened deep within Imoshen. With bittersweet self-knowledge she recognized the sensation. She had known Tulkhan's body only twice but her need for him was so strong it made her vulnerable.

Moistening her dry mouth, she watched mesmerized as the confrontation unfolded. Swordsman Jacolm stood over his fallen sword-brother, bristling, ready to die for the man who was bound to him by the Ghebite warrior code. No wonder their army was invincible, when its individuals shared such an unbreakable bond and welcomed death in battle. Fallen Ghebite soldiers were ensured a place riding at the side of their warrior god. Imoshen's lips curled with contempt.

Then the grizzled veteran, Peirs, deliberately lowered his weapon. Turning his shoulder to Tulkhan he helped the injured man to his feet. Following his lead, Jacolm sheathed his sword.

The General gave a disgusted shrug, though whether he was annoyed with them or himself, Imoshen could not tell. With a word he dismissed the others.

From her vantage point she saw the Elite Guard and Tulkhan's trusted commanders leave the courtyard. The General walked toward her. He scooped up a handful of the snow which had been swept into the deep drift, rubbing it vigorously over his face.

"General?" Imoshen's heart raced as she stepped into the patch of sunlight which illuminated the balcony rail. Startled, Tulkhan looked up, his expression guarded.

She recognized that battle stance. "Only me."

"Only?"

Imoshen smiled. She liked Tulkhan best when they were alone, when he did not have to play the public role of General Tulkhan, nor she the role of T'Imoshen, last princess of the T'En.

With a tug Imoshen pulled the brocade tabard over her head, casting it aside so that she stood dressed only in her loose-fitting trousers, thin undershirt, and soft-soled boots. "Teach me the use of the Ghebite sword."

The General's eyes narrowed.

The women of Tulkhan's homeland never touched weapons. They hardly dared raise their eyes to a man, let alone a sword. Imoshen knew she was breaking Ghebite law, which was why she had waited until the others had left.

Before the Ghebites invaded last spring she had taken for granted the ways of Fair Isle. Now she felt that her island was a beacon of enlightenment in a sea of barbarism. Everything she believed in was under threat but she was determined the Ghebites would not erode the position of women in Fair Isle. If this meant confronting Tulkhan and constantly forcing him to question his assumptions, then so be it. There was an ancient T'En saying which translated, *"Truth is a precious but often bitter seasoning."*

Imoshen swung her legs over the balustrade and dropped two body lengths into the heaped snow near Tulkhan. Aware of the General's keen, dark eyes, she straightened, wiping crusted snow from her buttocks and thighs.

"What now, Imoshen?"

Holding Tulkhan's gaze, she tried to gauge his mood. For a Ghebite, the General was a reasonable man, but he was also a proud man. "I began instruction with the T'En sword the year before you attacked Fair Isle. But the Ghebite style is different and I may need to defend myself, so teach me."

He prowled around her. "How casually you insult my honor."

"All I ask is to be able to defend myself." She kept her tone reasonable. "Where is the dishonor in that?"

"Truly, you do not see. In Gheeaba a man is expected to defend his wife. His honor rests on—"

A surprised laugh escaped Imoshen. She caught herself, aware of the slow burn of his anger. "I mean no insult, General. But I fail to see how you could protect me unless I never left your side and even then, wouldn't you rather have me at your back with a weapon in my hand, than clinging to you and encumbering your sword arm?"

Her question drew a reluctant grin and she smiled in return. She was not his *wife* yet and she never would be. Bond-partners of Fair Isle stood shoulder to shoulder.

Tulkhan lifted his hands. "In Gheeaba my wife would be safe within the walls of my estate. You would be escorted to events of importance, protected by the Elite Guard of my house-line. You would never set foot outside alone, you—"

"How boring. How could you live like that?"

Tulkhan grimaced. "You willfully misunderstand me, Imoshen."

"Yes."

"You are a trial!" His hands flexed as if he would like to use them on her.

Imoshen's heart rate lifted another notch. "All I ask is to learn to use the Ghebite sword."

He glanced up at the balcony where she had been watching. "So that is your excuse for spying?"

"Spying? If you call watching your men wield those ploughshares spying, then yes, I was spying."

She saw a flash of amusement in his obsidian eyes. Sweat glistened on his coppery skin.

"For a woman to touch a man's weapon is death in Gheeaba, Imoshen."

She stiffened. "This is not Gheeaba. And I will not be limited by your . . . by Ghebite attitudes. Teach me."

Tulkhan's eyes narrowed. "Very well, I will enjoy teaching you your place."

He turned and walked to the courtyard door, calling to someone in the passage beyond. Satisfied, he returned his attention to her. "My servant is bringing you a ploughshare."

Imoshen inclined her head, aware that she might have overreached herself this time. Her skills with the T'En sword were basic. The Ghebite weapon was much heavier and used in a different manner. As a Throwback to the T'En race which settled Fair Isle, she was taller than an average True-man but Tulkhan stood half a head taller again, and even a T'En female did not have the muscle bulk of a male.

Imoshen knew she had no chance of beating the General. Her goal was to create a bridge between them. If he taught her to use the Ghebite sword, he would be one step closer to accepting her as his equal.

The courtyard door opened and a nervous servant handed Tulkhan a second sword. The General dismissed the youth and weighed both weapons in his hands, observing their blades.

"I suppose you would rather fight with a toothpick and a knitting needle?" he challenged. "Catch."

Instinctively she caught the sword by the hilt, gauging its weight and unfamiliar balance. At that moment she wished for a sharp, short dagger and a tapered sword such as she had been training with. The T'En blade would have given her the advantage of speed and length of reach against the Ghebite sword's greater weight. Already she felt clumsy, and guessed that before long her wrist would be aching.

If she were using T'En weapons and this were a fight to the death, her only chance would be to strike fast before Tulkhan could use the advantage of his heavier blade and greater strength.

Like all pure T'En, Imoshen was left-handed. She turned her body side-on to the General to present as small a target as possible. Tulkhan took up the same stance. Because he was right-handed the two of them faced the same side of the courtyard, instead of opposite sides. It might have unsettled the General but only for a moment.

"At least the T'En way offers precision and style, instead of brute strength!" she told him.

"You're holding it all wrong."

"Show me."

When he stepped around behind her she felt the heat radiating from his skin. His hand closed over hers and she forced her arm to relax, letting him lower the sword.

"Not high like that. Hold the sword more naturally."

She swallowed, wondering how he could not be aware of her body's reaction. Concentrating, she met his eyes as he resumed his place opposite her.

"In my lessons I was taught to use my wrist to deflect the attacker's sword," she said. "But after watching your men at practice I see the Ghebite style is more—"

"Crude?" he suggested with a hint of anger.

"I was going to say that you appear to bring the whole weight of the body behind the blade, in slashing motions as opposed to lunges."

"Hmmm." Tulkhan's black eyes studied her. "If you were a youth with those scrawny arms, I'd advise you to use a two-handed grip. These are hand-and-a-half grips, designed for two-handed fighting if necessary."

Imoshen bristled. "I am stronger than I look."

"Really? Defend yourself."

He struck, telegraphing his intention but not restraining his speed or force. Imoshen barely had time to bring her weapon up. She took the impact of his strike on her blade, ready to deflect it with a twist of her wrist. But the force jarred her arm right up to the shoulder, numbing her fingers. Only by an effort of will did she maintain her grip on the weapon and divert the blow.

"Wrong technique, Imoshen." Tulkhan's white teeth flashed against his coppery skin in a wolfish smile, startling her. "These are not T'En weapons."

She darted forward, aiming for his throat, knowing that he would deflect her strike. With a laugh, he caught her blade, using the force of his swing to throw her off balance. She danced out of range, recovering in an instant.

"You are as light as a cat on your feet. It's a shame you're a female. You'd make a fine swordsman. I mean *woman*. If only you had the strength in your arms and shoulders. Try the two-handed grip."

"Wouldn't that limit my range of movement?"

"Always an answer. Pity your tongue isn't a sword!" He advanced. "Defend yourself. This time divert my weapon past your body. Yes."

He struck, she diverted. The shock of it ran up her arms to her left shoulder. He struck again on the other side and she realized Tulkhan was right, she should hold the sword double-handed. But there was no time to change grips.

Backing away with each strike, Imoshen barely maintained her guard. She suspected he was playing with her, and her suspicions were confirmed when he struck, skidding up over her weapon in such a way that she knew his energy hadn't been directed into the first strike. His sword passed inside her guard, striking her ribs under her left breast with the flat of the blade. The blow knocked the air from her lungs.

"That was a death blow," he told her. "Had enough?"

Each breath seared. She gritted her teeth. "Teach me that trick."

"It isn't trickery. It takes years of practice." He punctuated his phrases with strikes, the blows coming faster and faster. "Maybe one day I will show you the battle sword I inherited from my grandfather. Now there's a beautiful weapon!"

The force of his blows jarred her sword arm, numbing her fingers. It was all she could do to block his attacks.

Imoshen knew she did not have the strength in her upper body to wield the sword properly. She barely had the skill to defend herself. Backing across the slippery stones, she realized it was only a matter of time before her boots sank into the heaped snow and she lost the ability to maneuver.

Each screech of the blades echoed around the courtyard, pounding in her head till she could hear nothing but the reverberating ring of steel on steel.

"I don't expect to become an expert overnight, General." She grunted with the effort it took to hold him off. "You said yourself I am light on my feet and willing to learn."

"Why bother? By spring you won't even have that. You'll be heavy with child!" He was barely sweating. "That is why men fight and women don't. Only in Fair Isle is the natural balance disrupted."

Anger flooded Imoshen. "I won't be heavy with child forever, so your argument doesn't stand up!"

The familiar taste settled on her tongue, warning her that her T'En gift threatened to surface, but she refused to call on her powers to cloud his mind or distract his aim. To use her innate ability against the General now would negate everything.

Absorbed in her silent inner battle she gave ground. Her heel sank into the snow. Her guard wavered.

The General struck. She blocked.

The force of his blow tore the hilt from her useless fingers, sending her weapon spinning across the courtyard to clatter against the stone wall and drop blade first into a snow drift.

Silence hammered loud in the palace's inner courtyard.

Tulkhan smiled. It pleased him to have Imoshen at his mercy. She stood panting. Two spots of color flamed in her pale cheeks. Damp with sweat, her thin undershirt clung to her breasts as she struggled to regain her breath. He was reminded of the first time he'd seen her, restrained by five of his Elite Guard but not defeated. She had been injured defending a library of knowledge, crimson blood trickling down her white throat over her high breasts. He craved her then just as he craved her now.

She glared at him. Her distinctive T'En scent, at once so familiar yet alien, drew him. It tempted him to forget all reason.

He needed to make her admit that she wanted him. At the same time he despised himself, despised his hunger for her. How could he want her, the antithesis of a Ghebite woman? There she stood, defiantly tall and strong limbed, refusing to admit his mastery.

Unlike Ghebite women, Imoshen used no feminine wiles to arouse and entice him. Instead of diminutive womanly curves, delicate coppery skin, and deferent dark eyes, he faced those accursed T'En eyes. Rich as ruby wine held to the candle flame, they blazed with keen intelligence.

He had grown up hearing tales of this legendary race and their ability to enslave a True-man. But in Imoshen he had found a much more dangerous enemy—a living, breathing woman whose fierce pride and passion called to him against his better judgment.

His body urged him to ignore the stricture which forbade physical contact before their formal union. His blood was up. He saw the comprehension in her eyes, saw a flush of anticipation race across the pearly skin of her throat, and felt his own body respond. By the gods, he was but a breath away from taking her here in the snow. And who would know? Who would dare raise voice against him if he did?

Silently, she straightened. Dropping the defensive stance of a fighter, she inclined her head acknowledging him the victor. A ragged cheer echoed across the courtyard, startling Tulkhan. He spun to see a dozen of his men, the three commanders amongst them, standing under the arch on the far balcony.

He grinned reluctantly and marveled that they did not demand that Imoshen be punished for daring to raise a weapon against him. Then he returned his attention to her. She had fought as well as any untrained man, and she had fought in the knowledge that she was outclassed.

He raised the sword point to her throat and she lifted her chin to avoid the blade.

"The Ghebite sword is not meant for a woman's hand. Kneel and concede me the victor," he ordered in a voice meant to carry, then added more softly, "Kneel, Imoshen. Do not insult me before my men."

"And you do not insult me?" Her voice was breathy with anguish and exertion.

He frowned, surprised that she would see it this way. As he watched, the feral light of battle faded from her eyes. She swallowed. He saw her wince and recalled the blow he had delivered to her ribs. He knew that her every breath must hurt, yet she did not complain. Unlike Ghebite women she made light of being pregnant and did not hesitate to ride.

"You fight well," he said, recalling another time when she had stood at his side and faced death. Curse his weak-willed half-brother, Gharavan. Curse the Vaygharian's sweet, poisoned tongue for planting the seeds of betrayal in Gharavan's mind. The youth had been king only one summer when his advisor's words of treachery overrode Tulkhan's years of service. Tulkhan would have served his half-brother as loyally as he had served their father but he had not been given the chance.

He had been arrested in Imoshen's Stronghold, and together they had been thrown into her dungeon on false charges of treason. Only her maid's bravery and Imoshen's T'En trickery had saved them. "You were not outclassed when you faced the Vaygharian, Imoshen."

"That night I fought for my life against an enemy I despised. Besides, the Vaygharian did not seek to kill me, his aim was to escape." Imoshen's gaze flickered past him to their audience on the balcony. When she spoke her voice was low and intense. "General, why won't you trust me?"

A bitter laugh escaped him. Trust one of the T'En, a *dreaded Dhamfeer* as the saying went in his own language? Everything he had ever been taught went against that concept. "Kneel and acknowledge me the victor."

She hesitated.

Shouting down from the balcony, one of the Ghebites advised the General what to do with this recalcitrant female. Even though he spoke Gheeaban, his meaning was clear enough to make Imoshen's nostrils flare with fury.

Tulkhan smiled ruefully. He had been a heartbeat away from acting on just that advice.

Imoshen's eyes darkened to mulberry black, glittering dangerously as she dropped to one knee and slowly bent her head. The men cheered loudly. But when she raised her mocking gaze a jolt of understanding hit Tulkhan. She might be on her knee to him, but in her heart she would never kneel.

His mouth went dry. Her defiance goaded him. He wanted to lose himself in a battle for mastery. Only when she was in his arms, under him, could he appease his passion for her. But if he guessed correctly, every touch, every look weakened his resolve, laying his mind open to her T'En gifts.

Bed her? Yes. Trust her? Never!

"I yield to you, General," she said, but her expression denied her words.

Tulkhan grimaced. Just as Imoshen had been forced to surrender her Stronghold to him, he vowed she would ultimately admit him the master. Then Fair Isle and all it contained would be his. It was imperative he held Fair Isle, for he could not return to his homeland.

Imoshen had advised him to kill his half-brother, but he could not execute the boy he had taught to ride. Gharavan's betrayal still stung, for Tulkhan had loved him, even though his half-brother's birth had been his disinheritance.

Years of devoted service had earned Tulkhan the respect of his men and the command of the Ghebite army, but they could not make him the son of the king's first wife. He had planned to kneel before his father as conqueror of the legendary Fair Isle. For hundreds of years the island had been growing rich on the trade routes between the mainland and the archipelago. Protected by its vigorous merchant navy, Fair Isle was the envy of the bickering mainland kingdoms. And Tulkhan had meant to present this jewel in the crown to his father.

But the invasion had gone sour. His father had fallen on the battlefield leading a secondary attack on the island. Far in front of the larger army, Tulkhan had given Gharavan his fealty and continued the campaign, ultimately winning Fair Isle for the young Ghebite King.

And how had he been rewarded for his loyalty? Tulkhan skirted Gharavan's treachery like an open wound, returning to practical, tactical matters. After his half-brother's betrayal, Tulkhan had banished the young King and claimed this island for his own, effectively exiling himself and his warriors from Gheeaba forever. He and the men who had remained loyal to him were outcasts, Fair Isle their only home. Yet he could not hope to hold the island without Imoshen's support.

Tulkhan stepped back, sheathed his sword, and offered Imoshen his hand. With a tug he pulled her lightly to her feet. In that instant he saw the hunger she felt for him before she could mask it. An answering need moved him. It was there between them, this primal pull, body to body.

He'd been a fool to think casual bedding would be enough. He licked his lips. Their bonding day could not come soon enough.

Behind him, unaware of the undercurrents, his men signaled their approval with the Ghebite battle cry.

Imoshen glanced at them then back to Tulkhan. "Thank you for the lesson in swordplay, General." Once more the T'En royal, she gave him a graceful obeisance between equals, inclining her head and raising one hand to her forehead.

When she met his eyes he thought she seemed pleased. Why?

"Now I must issue invitations for the celebration tomorrow night. The townspeople will have heard that you signed the document acknowledging Church Law, but when they see you sitting down with the head of the T'En Church they will really believe it." She turned away from him.

Bemused, Tulkhan watched her leave the courtyard. Imoshen had deliberately humbled herself before his men, yet she had done it on her own terms. The old wives' tales were right, truly the Dhamfeer were a devious race.

Imoshen returned to her chambers where she discarded her soiled shirt, wincing as she peeled down her trousers. Confronting Tulkhan was worth the pain. Her mother had often said she was a willful creature.

Imoshen faltered, but there was no time to mourn her family, lost on the battlefield. If they had agreed to take her with them, she would have died fighting by their sides; but no, they said she was too young, at seventeen. Yet they had left her to run the family Stronghold, where she was responsible for the lives of a thousand people. Her great-aunt had been her sole support.

Hot tears of anger stung Imoshen's eyes. Even in death her parents had not wanted to acknowledge their Throwback daughter. She brushed the tears away roughly, glaring at the marble bathing chamber. A bitter laugh escaped her. Soon she would be bonded with the General, co-ruler of Fair Isle. Her parents could never have foreseen that.

But her great-aunt had. The only other member of their family to be born pure T'En, her great-aunt had devoted her life to the service of the Church and on her hundredth birthday had been rewarded with the title of "the Aayel." She had advised Imoshen to surrender the Stronghold and accept terms. Even so, their lives hung by a thread. As the last remnants of the old royal line their very existence would foster insurgence. They needed a lever on their captor. The Aayel had used her mind-reading gift to discover the General's secret fear and most fervent desire. In Gheeaba, a man's virility was judged by how many sons he produced. Tulkhan's only arranged marriage had been annulled after his wife had not produced a child within three years. The Aayel's advice for Imoshen had been to seduce Tulkhan, and ensure that she conceive a boy.

It had seemed an impossible task, yet when it came to consummating the Harvest Feast the General had played into Imoshen's hands. Every year the fertility of the land was ensured with a ritual consummation. Usually a young man and woman from one of the local villages were chosen, but that year the General had claimed Imoshen. She had told him the moment she felt his son's life flare into being.

However, she would not have lived to conceive this child if the Aayel had not saved her life by sacrificing her own.

When an assassination attempt on Tulkhan had failed, he had ordered the execution of the last of the old royal line as punishment. The Aayel has chosen to assume blame, absolving Imoshen, and had then taken her own in an abbreviated form of the T'En ritual suicide.

Grimly Imoshen stared at herself in the silver-backed mirror. She hoped that if she were ever faced with such a choice, she would be as brave.

Tentatively she touched her still-flat belly, shaking her head in wonder. Her child broke with six centuries of tradition. She shuddered. Her pregnancy made her feel vulnerable. Pure T'En women were supposed to be chaste, devoting themselves to the Church. To take a lover was to court death.

Yet she should not feel as if she was committing a crime, for before the invasion, the Empress had granted dispensation for her to break with custom and bond with Reothe.

Imoshen swayed, sinking to her knees. She must not think of Reothe and what might have been. When she had surrendered her Stronghold to the General she had believed Reothe dead. As last surviving member of the extended royal family, her duty was to help her people recover from the Ghebite invasion. For this purpose she had gone to Landsend Abbey only to be confronted by Reothe. Slipping unseen into her chamber, he had intended to complete their bonding vows, escape with her, and retake the island.

Imoshen's left wrist tingled and she lifted it to her mouth. Licking the bonding scar, she urged it to fade. To remember was to feel, and she did not want to recall Reothe's arms around her, or his determination as he cut his wrist, then hers to mingle their blood. She had not wanted to refuse him but she could not sanction more bloodshed. Reothe represented her lost dreams and now her loyalty must be to the people of Fair Isle and the General.

She looked down at her left wrist where the scar was now all but invisible. So much rested on her. She had to believe she had made the right choice.

"How can I be your maid if you won't let me serve you?" Kalleen demanded, running into the room.

With a relieved laugh Imoshen came to her feet. "Soon you will be the Lady of Windhaven and have servants of your own."

The girl used a choice farmyard word. "I'm not the Lady of Windhaven yet."

"It is only right that your loyalty and bravery be rewarded," Imoshen said. She suspected there would be many who resented seeing a farm girl elevated to nobility. But it was due to Kalleen that she and Tulkhan had ended Gharavan's brief reign.

Kalleen gasped as Imoshen turned. "That bruise on your ribs! Did the General do that because you dared lift a sword to him?"

Imoshen sighed. "Does *everyone* know?"

"The Ghebites are saying that if you had been properly disciplined you would know your place. They say the General should beat you every day until he breaks your spirit."

Imoshen cursed softly under her breath.

"Should I unpack the Empress's formal gowns for tomorrow night?" Kalleen asked, practical as always.

Imoshen thought of the fearful town dignitaries, of the General's wary eyes and of the Beatific, leader of the T'En Church, who remained an enigma.

Imoshen sighed. Her only experience of the Empress's court had been a visit the summer before Tulkhan attacked. At the time the subtleties of the power interplay between the Church and the Empress had not interested her. She had simply accepted that the Church venerated the T'En gifts and in return the T'En served the Church. But since entering the capital as Tulkhan's captive she had sensed a wariness in the woman who should have been her closest ally.

Imoshen turned to Kalleen. "For the celebration, I must remind them of the old empire. I must be T'Imoshen, the last princess of the T'En. Yes, unpack the formal gowns and jewelry."

"It is lucky the Empress was nearly as tall as you," Kalleen said as she left.

Imoshen sank into a warm bath with a sigh of relief. The General might mock Fair Isle's aristocracy, grown complacent after six hundred years of uninterrupted rule, and he might scorn the highly ritualized behavior of the court, but he could not fail to be impressed by hot, running water.

Dimly she heard Kalleen's raised voice from the room beyond.

"My lady's in the bath, General Tulkhan!" Kalleen snapped, darting forward as if she intended to restrain him. "You can't go in."

"Then you'd better tell Imoshen to come out because I want to speak with her!"

Radiating disdain, the maid bundled up Imoshen's clothing and retreated to the bathing chamber.

Tulkhan heard their voices. He imagined Imoshen, her pale flesh glowing from the hot bath as she dressed indignantly. He smiled to himself. Confronting Imoshen was always invigorating, any excuse would do.

Already once today she had stood before him, disarmed but not beaten. He should have refused to let her touch the Ghebite sword yet he could not resist her challenge, and because of this he'd just broken up a fight between the palace stable workers and his own horse handlers.

"General Tulkhan?" Imoshen greeted him, weaving the ends of her long silver hair into one thick plait.

He turned, aware of her frank gaze. Clearly it did not trouble Imoshen that she had just stepped naked from the bath. The knowledge that they were soon to be married and then he would have the right to join her in the bathing chamber made Tulkhan short with the maid. "You are dismissed, Kalleen."

Instead of obeying him she looked to Imoshen, who nodded. This irritated Tulkhan. The palace's army of servants were always deferring to Imoshen.

"You wanted to speak with me?" she asked.

"I will assign several of my Elite Guard as your private escort when you leave the palace."

"I have my own Stronghold Guard," Imoshen said. "Besides, I can look—"

"Hear me out. By raising a sword to me you have broken Ghebite law—"

"Hear *me* out, General. This is not Gheeaba. And tomorrow night we celebrate yesterday's signing of the document which recognizes the Church Laws of Fair Isle. In this land anyone can bear arms in defense of themselves and their loved ones."

"Don't lecture me, Imoshen. My army is quartered in T'Diemn. They hear garbled stories of how you insult me by taking up arms against me. The customs of Fair Isle confuse them. Every day they see women walking about the streets, running businesses, sitting in tea houses and taverns, laughing and talking."

"So?"

Tulkhan repressed a wave of frustration. "In Gheeaba a woman covers her face to walk out in public. Don't look outraged. It is just the way things are. My men don't know what to make of women who look them in the eye and laugh."

"It'll do them good!"

"Imoshen. Be serious!"

She bit back a smile. "I am listening, General. Surely in the years you've been on campaign your men have seen how other countries live."

"Less than you'd think. We traveled as an army and camped as an army. They are good men but simple. Even our bone-setter, Wharrd, is wary of you, and he has worked at your side helping with healings." He could tell his arguments had not convinced her. "By the gods, Imoshen, I am trying to honor you. If my Elite Guard escorted you, it would be the same as if I was at your side. It would look right to my men."

She sighed. "That may be, but it would not look right

to the people of Fair Isle. Your Elite Guard would offend them. They expect the Empress to be approachable. And even though I do not claim this title, it is how they see me. From the poorest homeless worker to the master of the greatest guild, I must be accessible to them, so I will decline your offer. And now, if you'll excuse me, I have work to do."

"Wait." He caught her arm as she brushed past. "I broke up a fight in the stables. Some hotheads were brawling over your honor. This time there was nothing worse than a few bloody noses, but I cannot be at your heels every time you step out of the palace."

She laughed, flicking her arm free of his grasp with one easy movement. "I am not so useless that I need protecting from my own people or yours. Now I must send these invitations."

"Imoshen!"

She waited, regal and amused.

"All it takes is one zealot with a knife. You could be killed!"

All amusement left her face. She held his eyes, hers as sharp as garnets. "It is the same for every ruler. I have faced death many times since I surrendered my Stronghold to you, General Tulkhan. You of all people must be aware of that. But this has not stopped me performing my duty."

He wanted to deny that he had been ready to order her death on more than one occasion but could not.

She leant closer and raised her hand in what he thought would be a caress, but instead she plucked a straw from his temple plait and tossed it into the fire. "Don't worry, General. I will be on my guard."

As Imoshen collected the official invitations, she was aware of the General's displeasure. Since they had arrived in the capital, she had watched Tulkhan study the palace and its people. He was quick to learn and adapt. He would not insist on assigning an Elite Guard to her if she could convince him otherwise.

She paused at the entrance to her chambers where one of her people stood and smiled at the youth, remembering

how twenty men and women from her Stronghold Guard
had accompanied her to the capital at an hour's notice.
When Tulkhan had banished Gharavan, he had needed to
move quickly to seize power. He had moved so swiftly that
he had laid claim to her by announcing their betrothal the
first night in the capital. Her guard and a single chest of belongings were all that were truly hers in this great palace. It
would impress the town dignitaries and Church officials if
their invitations were delivered by the leader of her personal
guard.

"Where is Crawen?"

The young man flushed, lifting T'En eyes to Imoshen's.
They shared a common ancestry, though only Imoshen carried all the traits of the pure T'En, the six fingers, the silver
hair, and the wine-dark eyes. Since her people had settled
Fair Isle, they had interbred with the locals until the pure
T'En had all but died out. Her birth had been an unwelcome surprise for her family, both a curse and a blessing.

"Crawen is practicing T'Enchu in the ballcourt."

"Thank you." Imoshen turned to Tulkhan. "I trained
under Crawen from the age of ten. Come see my people's
skill at unarmed combat, then tell me I cannot defend myself." She led the way but they did not reach the ballcourt.
Raised voices greeted them even before they entered the
connecting passage.

". . . her place!" Harholfe's words became clear to
Imoshen.

"Her place?" Crawen repeated softly. "You insult—"

"She insults our General. In Gheeaba a woman would
not dare touch a weapon!" Jacolm said. "In Gheeaba she
dare not raise her eyes to a man who is not her husband or
blood relative."

Imoshen would have rounded the corner to confront
them but Tulkhan caught her arm, his expression urging her
to listen. If he could listen, so could she.

"You Ghebite bar—"

"Quiet," Crawen ordered her companion, her tone sharp
but level. "This is not Gheeaba, Commander Jacolm.

T'Imoshen is second cousin to the Empress and skilled enough to teach the art of T'Enchu. Once True-men and women did not raise their eyes to the T'En, but we have come a long way since then. One day Gheeaba may—"

"You call yourself a leader? Yet you fetch and carry these fairground disguises!" Harholfe kicked an arm-guard which bounced off the wall and skittered around the corner landing at Imoshen's feet. She picked it up automatically.

Again Crawen's companion would have protested but she cut him short.

"It is said in Fair Isle that the higher we rise the more we serve. The Stronghold Guard is an ancient, honorable—"

"What kind of guard accepts women into its ranks?" Jacolm sneered. A charged silence followed.

"Your men are deliberately baiting my people, General!" Imoshen mouthed.

"What do you expect?" He held her eyes. "You bait me, they are only—"

Furious, Imoshen turned the corner to find Jacolm and Harholfe and three of Tulkhan's Elite Guard facing three of her Stronghold Guard. Crawen and her two companions stood with their backs to a decorative arched niche. Behind them was a scene from the Age of Tribulation painted with lifelike accuracy. The first two hundred years of T'En rule in Fair Isle had been spent containing bloody uprisings. As Crawen had said, Fair Isle had come a long way.

Imoshen faltered. Was the shedding of blood the only way to resolve ideological conflict? Was threat and might the only thing the Ghebites respected?

"Crawen," Imoshen greeted them. "Jacolm, Harholfe. The General and I wish to stage a Tourney." She caught Tulkhan's eye as he joined her. He cloaked his surprise and, with a gleam of annoyed amusement, folded his arms, leaning against the wall. She realized he had abandoned her to sink or swim. She plunged on. "When the Age of Tribulation ended, our people kept their martial skills alive with competition and display. I propose the Stronghold Guard stage a martial display of T'Enchu and T'En swordsmanship on the spring fairground east of town." Imoshen turned to Tulkhan. "Would your men like to stage a display of their own?"

He straightened. "When?"

Imoshen glanced from the belligerent Ghebites to her beleaguered guard. "This afternoon?"

Two

A S THE TWO columns of Ghebite horsemen circled, Imoshen marveled at their precision born of discipline and ceaseless training.

Spellbound, the silent crowd watched the Ghebites' horses pound over the field, kicking clouds of snow and dirt high in the air. Taking up position opposite the painted hide target, the two columns paused, one to Imoshen's right, the other to her left.

On the far side of the field parents hurriedly herded children away from the target and there was a moment of hushed expectation. Uttering the eerie Ghebite battle cry, the first archer urged his horse to a gallop, charging diagonally at the target.

Before he had even let his arrow fly, the alternate rider surged forward. Standing in their stirrups, both archers approached the target. One instant's misjudgment and the riders would collide, going down beneath sharp hooves.

First one then the next let his arrows fly, alternating like the rug maker's threads, weaving a craft of whistling death. The bolts flew true, striking the center of the target. No wonder the Ghebites had swept all opposition before them.

Their display finished, the Ghebite cavalry made a triumphant circuit of the field. As the people of Fair Isle cheered their conquerors, Imoshen repressed a bitter smile. Even though she had been the one to suggest the Tourney, the crowd's response rankled her.

The mounted men wheeled and saluted the far side of the field, where their general appeared on his black destrier. Imoshen caught her breath.

Tulkhan wore no armor, nothing but boots and breeches. His long, black hair hung free around his broad shoulders and he rode at one with his horse. To Imoshen he was the physical embodiment of his Ghebite heritage, of those fiercely loyal tribesmen of the harsh plains who counted their wealth in horses.

A buzz of speculation spread through the crowd. Tulkhan circled the field at full gallop, then stood in the stirrups. Without warning he leapt to the ground, running beside the flashing hooves of his horse, hands on the saddle pommel. The crowd gasped. Imoshen glanced to the cavalry who watched their general proudly, and she understood he was repeating the deeds of his ancestors, men who rode bareback as boys, men who worshipped bravery and skill. With a leap, Tulkhan regained his seat, rising to stand on the horse's back. Arms extended, knees flexed, he balanced above his galloping mount.

When Tulkhan finally dropped into the saddle Imoshen let out her breath. He pulled his mount short, walking it backward. With a flourish he urged the horse to rear. It danced on its hind legs to everyone's applause. Tulkhan's teeth flashed white against his coppery skin, triggering a tug deep inside her.

Imoshen smiled. The General claimed to hate pomp and ceremony, but the barbarian in him loved this kind of display.

A servant ran onto the field to present Tulkhan with his round shield and sword. The cavalry had discarded their bows, taking up swords and shields.

Tulkhan signaled that the bout was to begin and Imoshen tensed as the men charged, striking right and left. Horses wheeled and went down screaming. At first she thought the Ghebites had gone mad. Their swords were battle-ready, wicked weapons half as tall as a man. Then she realized the men were turning the flat of the blades on each other; even so, some would pay with broken bones.

One by one the Ghebites conceded defeat, leaving the field dazed and bleeding. At last, only one horse and rider remained. General Tulkhan.

The crowd roared.

Tulkhan stood in the stirrups, black eyes flashing. Damp hair clinging to his broad shoulders, he took a victory lap. He was the perfect Ghebite warrior, fearless and terrifying. On the battlefield he was a brilliant tactician, able to weigh the alternatives and make the intuitive decisions which led his men to victory even against great odds. But it was his integrity and personal bravery that had earned him his men's devotion. They would die for him.

Imoshen studied Tulkhan. True, he was the perfect war general, but could he hold Fair Isle? The skills of a general were not the skills of a great statesman.

By claiming her he had consolidated his position, and by agreeing to honor the laws of the Church, he had earned the support of this powerful body. The Beatific sat in the row behind Imoshen, flanked by her priests, lending the Church's sanction to today's display. But Tulkhan no longer had the backing of the Ghebite Empire, and he held Fair Isle with only his loyal commanders and army. They were a formidable force, yet spread over the population of Fair Isle they were like pebbles on a sandy beach.

Then there was Reothe, once the late Empress's adopted son, now rebel leader. The whole island knew he bided his time in the impenetrable Keldon Highlands with his ragtag rebel army, awaiting the moment to strike.

To retain Fair Isle, Tulkhan had to win the support of its conquered people. Imoshen knew her people. If only Tulkhan would trust her enough to heed her advice. Irony warmed her. Since when did a Ghebite listen to a woman? She was not even a True-woman, but a T'En, "Dhamfeer" in their language. And when they called her by that name they made it an insult.

Her hands tightened with repressed anger as she poured

wine into the victory goblet and raised it high to the applause of the crowd.

This martial display had not only given her Stronghold Guard an opportunity to display their skills to the Ghebites without bloodshed, but it had reassured T'Diemn's townsfolk. As word had spread across the capital, shopkeepers had locked up and harnessed their horses, piling children, blankets, and food in carts. Quick-thinking bakers had thrown hot buns into calico sacks, and by noon everyone had marched out to the field where the annual spring fair was held.

Determined to remind Tulkhan that she was not one of his slavish Ghebite women, Imoshen had taken her place in the T'Enchu display. She was wearing the traditional loose-fitting trousers, and her pure white tunic proclaimed her skill equal to that of a teacher. T'Enchu was an unarmed combat which had evolved in the early years of the T'En settlement when many of their small band had been without weapons. The artform had been maintained and polished because T'En warriors never knew when they might be caught unarmed. It was said a T'Enchu master could defeat an armed opponent and Imoshen knew many techniques for disarming an attacker. T'Enchu also placed males and females on a more equal footing because it relied on speed and using the opponent's strength against him.

Imoshen delighted in the precision needed to pull her attacks so that she left no mark. Blows which could break bones merely brushed her sparring partner's tunic. Because this was a display match and she fought a partner of equal ranking, they wore no protectors.

But when it had come to the T'En swordsmanship bout, she had bowed out after the first round, having only just begun her training last year.

Heart racing from the exertion, she returned to the hastily erected dais to take her seat beside the General. As the display bout continued, Imoshen could not resist leaning closer to Tulkhan to say, "See what a skilled sword player can do with a knitting needle and a toothpick!"

He had the grace to grin.

Having disarmed the last opponent, Crawen approached the dais to accept the victory cup. She dropped a little wine on the ground, an old custom which acknowledged the Ancients, then drained her goblet. The Beatific frowned. Worship of the Ancients was regarded as primitive and by this action Crawen had revealed her peasant roots.

When the Stronghold Guard's piper saluted the victor, Imoshen had felt tears of pride prick her eyes. Her people had given a good account of themselves. Perhaps now Tulkhan's men would not be so quick to cast aspersions. But having seen the Ghebite cavalry, she had to admit they were impressive.

Now as Tulkhan rode towards her, his men chanted a paean to the great Akha Khan. It was said that in times of danger the greatest of their gods took on a physical form. In some tales he appeared as a black stallion; in others he was a hybrid creature, half stallion, half man; and on rare occasions he took the form of a man, a giant in stature with brilliant, black eyes. It was not surprising that Tulkhan's men regarded him as the embodiment of their god.

Triumphant, Tulkhan remained astride his destrier to accept the victory goblet from Imoshen. When he tipped a little of the wine onto the ground his gaze held Imoshen's, as if to say, see I honor your customs even if I don't believe in them.

She gasped. As formidable as the General's physical presence was, it was not his most dangerous attribute. She must never underestimate his perceptive intelligence.

"A most impressive display of skill, General, but how many of your men nurse broken bones?" She made her voice rich and mocking. Her Stronghold Guard had suffered nothing worse than bruises.

Tulkhan's eyes narrowed. A frisson of danger made Imoshen's breath catch.

The General drained the goblet then tossed it to Wharrd. He offered Imoshen his hand. "Trust me?"

"In matters of warcraft? Yes."

His eyes narrowed. "Then take my hand and I'll show you *real* skill."

Imoshen stepped onto his boot and astride his thighs. The horse surged forward and she felt the solid wall of Tulkhan's chest at her back. When he turned the destrier, she faced the ranks of his men dressed in their purple and black cloaks.

"Bring me three short spears and a target," Tulkhan ordered.

Two men raced forward with these.

Tulkhan took the spears and handed Imoshen the target. "You don't ask what I do?"

"You seek an opportunity to strut like the barbarian warrior you are!" she could not resist prodding, but he only laughed, then urged his horse towards the edge of the field where canny shopkeepers had set up portable ovens. The scent of roasting cinnamon apples hung on the air, making Imoshen's stomach rumble.

He halted the horse beside a waist-high tree stump. "Stand here."

Imoshen slid off his thighs to stand on the stump.

He showed her how to thread her arm through the target's support and warned, "Now brace yourself, and when this is over mock me no more."

As she spread her weight Tulkhan wheeled the horse, galloping across the field. The crowd fell silent. The steady thud of the black horse's hooves echoed Imoshen's heartbeat.

The General selected his first spear, then with a shout spurred the horse on. The black destrier surged forward, guided by the pressure of his rider's knees.

Tulkhan raised the spear.

Imoshen braced her shoulders, centering the target which barely covered her chest. One misjudgment and she would be dead, a spear through her head or belly. One calculated mistake and Tulkhan would be free of her.

Imoshen gritted her teeth.

Tulkhan rose in the saddle, slewing the horse sideways. Even as the first spear left his hands, he plucked the second and threw; then the third, moving so fast that all three were in the air at once.

With a thud, the first spear struck home, numbing Imoshen's arm. Two more followed in rapid succession. The impact rocked her and she had to fight to regain her balance. The cheering of the General's men drowned out the rushing in her head.

Suddenly Tulkhan was beside her, hand extended. His eyes blazed with triumph, reminding Imoshen that the savage in him was very close to the surface.

Accepting his hand, she leapt up behind him. Aware that the Ghebites loved display, she took her cue from Tulkhan's earlier horsemanship exhibition. Planting her feet on the horse's broad rump, she steadied herself with one hand on Tulkhan's shoulder and held the spear-impaled target above her head. The crowd's loud acclamation made her heart race and she felt the heady rush of battle fever. This must have been how Imoshen the First's T'En warriors felt when they subdued Fair Isle centuries ago.

When they reached the dais Imoshen tossed the target aside and jumped to the platform, where she signaled that the display was over. The court heralds sounded the closing notes while the General's black destrier pawed the ground restlessly.

Imoshen caught Tulkhan's eye as she collected her cloak. "Night comes early this close to midwinter, General. I will ride back to T'Diemn with you."

As Tulkhan extended his hand, he wondered why Imoshen had chosen not to ride her own horse. She leapt up before him, settling across his thighs. When he wound one arm around her waist, strands of her silver hair tickled his face and he inhaled her scent like rare perfume. She might be pure Dhamfeer, but she was all woman in his arms. The blood sang in his veins and suddenly he threw back his head and laughed.

Imoshen twisted round to look up at him, searching his face. In Gheeaba an unmarried woman would not dare look a man in the eye. But then no Ghebite woman would have done what Imoshen had done today, turning what could have degenerated into a vicious fight into a celebration of martial skill. When Imoshen had taken part in the unarmed combat display, his men had muttered as though they expected him to rebuke her. But Imoshen was not a Ghebite woman. If he questioned her bravery he would not have offered his challenge.

"You did not doubt my spear's aim?" he prodded, full of admiration for her.

Her lips quirked as she gave him a knowing look. "You are a great tactician, General. If you had wanted me dead you would have chosen a less public way of doing it."

Anger replaced admiration, making his body tighten. The horse responded to the pressure of his knees, increasing its pace as the General turned his mount towards T'Diemn.

Weary shopkeepers packed up their stalls and children cried sleepily for their dinner. In the clear, winter twilight, a long line of carts and walkers snaked down the road to the capital, making way for General Tulkhan's black destrier and their escort, the Elite Guard.

Silhouetted against the setting sun's glow, the palace towers and Basilica's dome dominated the old city. But T'Diemn had long ago outgrown its defenses, and the city sprawled outside the old walls, prosperous and exposed.

"I must design new defenses and repair the old," Tulkhan said.

"And I must oversee the restoration of the palace."

The General grimaced. The capital had suffered when it surrendered to his half-brother. King Gharavan had slaughtered the town officials and executed guildmasters. His soldiers had camped in the palace, destroying what they did not understand and looting what they coveted.

Imoshen had been quick to point out that Gharavan's legacy of cruelty threatened to undermine any trust Tulkhan had established with her people. Conquering was one thing, holding was another. A conqueror had to win the people over or constantly fight rebellion.

"General, what do you think of combining your Elite

Guard with my Stronghold Guard and giving them a new name like . . . oh, the T'Diemn Palace Guard?"

"You ask the impossible. My men would never accept women in their ranks."

"But you saw Crawen's skill with the sword. Though the people of T'Diemn cheered you today, they are still uneasy. To restore their confidence we must be united."

"You push too hard, too fast, Imoshen. I have signed an agreement to honor the laws of the Church and that is enough for now." It was more than enough. He needed the support of the Church but he dreaded the reaction of his men when they realized he meant to acknowledge Imoshen as his equal. It was a delicate balance. Somehow he had to appease the people of Fair Isle, yet retain the respect of his men.

Imoshen radiated impatience but she held her tongue for once. A small mercy. Their escort was pressed close about them and it annoyed his men when Imoshen debated his decisions.

She rode before him, brooding in silence as they reached the outskirts of T'Diemn. Mullioned windows glowed with welcome and the rich smell of roast meat hung on the winter air, making Tulkhan's mouth water.

Suddenly Imoshen stiffened in his arms. "Stop."

A plump woman thrust through Tulkhan's Elite Guard to clutch Imoshen's hand.

"You must come, Empress. This way." She ran off as though Imoshen's agreement was a foregone conclusion.

Tulkhan halted the horse. "What is it?"

"Down the lane, General," Imoshen said, her face tight with foreboding.

Tulkhan turned his mount.

Wringing her hands, the woman waited outside a modest two-story house which bore the Cooper Guild's symbol of two half barrels.

"The new-life garland hangs on the door. The woman of the house must have given birth within the last small moon." Imoshen raised her voice. "What is—?"

Before Imoshen could finish a man threw the door open and staggered out, his face a mask of grief, a hat clutched in his hands.

"His hat bears the new father's badge," Imoshen whispered. "I dread . . ." She dropped to the cobbles. "You, cooper. What is wrong?"

He cast aside his hat as he made a deep obeisance, lifting both hands to his forehead. By this, Tulkhan knew he accorded Imoshen the honor of Empress, just as the woman in her distress had given her this title. Old habits died hard.

"T'Imoshen?" The cooper used the royal prefix. "You must help me."

"Of course." Imoshen threw Tulkhan one swift glance as she disappeared inside.

Responding to her unspoken plea he swung down from his horse. "Wait here," he told his men, tossing the reins to Wharrd. He paused long enough to retrieve the man's hat. Only in Fair Isle would a man don a badge of fatherhood and decorate his house with a garland so that his neighbors could celebrate the birth of his child.

The plump woman watched Tulkhan anxiously as he ducked his head to cross the threshold. The man's voice carried down the stairwell to him. ". . . Larassa delivered our daughter this time yesterday. I offered to stay with her but she urged me to go." A groan escaped him. "Why did I listen?"

Tulkhan hung the hat on the hall peg and took the steps two at a time, but slowed as he came level with the landing. A young woman lay in a pool of blood.

"No one stayed with her?" Imoshen asked, incredulous. "Right after birthing a woman is—"

"I know. But all our relatives died in the war and we know few people in T'Diemn. I should not have left her!"

Imoshen knelt to touch the woman's neck. When her eyes met Tulkhan's, he knew there was no hope.

"A woman walks death's shadow to bring forth new life," Imoshen whispered. "Sometimes . . ."

The cooper dropped to his knees, rocking back and forth. "I failed her. I must not fail her soul. You must say the words over my Larassa. Send for your T'Enchiridion and say the words for the dead."

"I know the passage by heart," Imoshen said. "But you should send for the priests to do this."

As she rose, Tulkhan noted Imoshen's strained face. She carried his son. Was she thinking that soon she would be facing the trials of childbirth? The thought of Imoshen lying dead in a pool of blood stunned him.

"My daughter." The cooper sprang to his feet, darting through a door. He returned with a babe so tightly wrapped in swaddling clothes that only her face was visible. "Does she live? I cannot tell."

Imoshen took the baby from him, pressing her fingers to the infant's temples. "Alive, yes . . . but her life force flickers like a candle drowning in its own wax." She frowned at the father. "Didn't the midwife deal with the afterbirth?"

"She did, but . . . You must call on the Parakletos to escort Larassa's soul through death's shadow. I have heard how mothers who die in childbirth refuse to be parted—"

Imoshen hissed, pressing the baby closer.

"T'Imoshen. I beg you." The cooper fell on one knee. Taking her left hand he kissed her sixth finger. "You are pure T'En. The Parakletos will listen to your voice above all others. You *must* do this. Please."

Imoshen closed her eyes. For an instant Tulkhan thought she would refuse. Then she took a deep breath and looked down at the man. "Prepare Larassa. Place her on your bonding bed while I watch over your daughter."

Tulkhan would have helped the man, but Imoshen drew him aside. "None but a blood relative or bond-partner must touch the dead one's body. Come." She studied the baby. "So cold and pale. We are lucky the babe still lives. The mother has been dead for hours." She sniffed the air, her garnet eyes narrowing. "But her soul still lingers."

Tulkhan shuddered. "I don't understand. How could the dead mother take the baby? Who are the Parakletos?"

"Guides between this world and death's realm. When the priest says the words for the dead, the Parakletos answer her summons, escorting the soul through death's shadow. I have never sensed them but the danger to this baby is very real. New life is always fragile." She frowned on the silent infant. "Considering how the mother died, this little one would be vulnerable even with the proper words over the afterbirth."

"I still don't understand."

"How could you? As a trained midwife I learned how the soul of the baby is formed in the afterbirth, just as the babe's life force is housed in the growing body. At birth the soul transfers to the baby's body, animating the life force. The proper words must be said and the afterbirth disposed of safely to ensure the baby's soul is securely bound."

"But my people don't . . ." Tulkhan hesitated. A Ghebite man avoided his wives when they were due to give birth.

"How often are Ghebite babies born dead or die unexpectedly? The new soul can drift, leaving the baby alive but its mind unformed. Sometimes this does not happen until the person is grown. Have you seen people whose minds wander, people who kill and have no memory of it? This is what happens if the soul is not properly fixed in the body. This little girl is barely one day old. The bond is fragile and the mother—"

"I am ready. Come quickly," the cooper beckoned.

They ducked their heads to avoid the lintel. Wrapped in a rich cloth, the woman was laid out on the bed. Candles glimmered in the four corners of the room. The single mirror had been covered and the window was opened so as not to impede her soul's passage.

"My daughter?" The cooper peered anxiously at the pale little face.

"We must move quickly." Imoshen put the baby in his arms. "Hold tight to your daughter, fasten her soul and life force with your will. I'm sure Larassa would not wish to kill her baby, but the time immediately after death is very confusing. A soul which has been parted from its body by violent death often lingers for a day or more before beginning its journey through death's shadow, and this is a tragic death. Larassa will not want to leave you and the child." Imoshen gave him a compassionate smile. "Remember there is an honored place in death's realm for women and babies who die in childbirth, a place alongside warriors who die defending their loved ones."

Tulkhan frowned. In Gheeaba fallen warriors had the honor of riding with the great Akha Khan, but priests taught that women did not possess true souls. Once dead, their life force dissipated. They were mourned but only as one might mourn the death of a favorite dog. When told of his mother's death Tulkhan had felt nothing, though the knowledge that she had died alone and untended troubled him.

Imoshen's voice came to him speaking High T'En, then alternating with the language of the people. She called on the Parakletos by name, begging them to hear her plea, binding them to their task.

As she spoke, Tulkhan heard the people in the street outside singing a dirge.

Imoshen's voice faltered. Tulkhan's gaze flew to her face. Her brilliant eyes were fixed on something he could not see, the whites showing all around. A metallic taste settled on his tongue. He grimaced, recognizing that sensation. How he despised the taste of T'En power!

Tendrils of Imoshen's long, silver hair lifted as if they had a life of their own. The room grew oppressively cold, filled with palpable tension.

The cooper held his daughter to his chest with fierce determination. He repeated Imoshen's last words as she recovered, continuing the passage.

Had it been possible, Tulkhan would have left the room to escape witnessing this T'En mystery, but his body was not his to command.

The words flowed from Imoshen's tongue, but although he could see her lips move, he couldn't hear a sound for the pressure in his ears. Suddenly there was a perceptible lightening and the cooper's legs gave way. He sank onto the chest under the window. Burying his face in the baby's blanket, he wept softly with relief.

Imoshen gasped, dropping to her knees. Tulkhan caught her as she pitched forward. He expected his skin to crawl with the physical contact, but she felt as warm and yielding as a True-woman. "Imoshen?"

She moaned, her open eyes unseeing. "This time I *felt* the words. The Parakletos came at my call. May I never . . ." She shuddered and pushed him away, pulling herself upright using the bedpost. She looked from the dead woman on the bed to the grieving father with his baby daughter. "I have done what I can—"

Shouts came from the street below, a combination of Ghebite soldier cant and the common trading tongue delivered imperiously. Tulkhan strode to the window.

"What now?" Imoshen asked.

He had to smile. "We are honored. The Beatific herself is here."

Imoshen's heart sank. Since entering this home she had been laboring under the dead mother's despairing heartbreak which hung, thick as a blanket, on the air. The effort of controlling the Parakletos when they answered her call had drained all her reserves. She did not have the strength for a confrontation with the Beatific.

Several pairs of boots sounded on the stairs. The door swung open and a priest announced the leader of the T'En Church. The Beatific swept into the room, still dressed in the rich fur mantle she had worn to the display. Her elaborate headdress brushed the doorjambs.

Taking in the body on the bed and the four candles, she turned on Imoshen. "What have you done?"

"I have done nothing but serve my people," Imoshen replied carefully.

The Beatific's mouth thinned with anger. "You overreach yourself."

"It was necessary. I could not refuse—"

"No? You have not given your Vow of Expiation. By what right do you perform this holy office?"

"By right of birth." Imoshen lifted both hands, fingers splayed like fans before her face. Looking over the twelve fingertips, she held the Beatific's eyes until the woman's gaze wavered, then she let her hands drop. "I trained at the Aayel's side. Many times I have said the words to bind a baby's soul."

"That may be so," the Beatific conceded. "But the words for the dead are powerful tools. You should have sent to the Basilica for—"

"T'Imoshen saved my daughter's life." The cooper lurched to his feet. "I begged her to say the words."

The Beatific ignored him. "You said the words without your T'Enchiridion, Imoshen? Or do you have it with you?" She looked pointedly at Imoshen's empty hands. "What were you thinking? The Parakletos are not to be called lightly. One wrong word and they could take the soul of the caller!"

Tulkhan cursed. "You risked yourself?"

Imoshen stiffened, meeting his eyes. "I am a healer. I could not let the infant die. And I did not need the book because the Aayel made me memorize it." She faced the Beatific. "If we had sent for help, it would have been too late. The baby's life force was ebbing, its soul lured by the mother's restless—"

"You are not qualified to speak of such matters!" There was a fraught silence. Then the Beatific massaged her temples, sighing heavily. "You thought you were acting for the best, this I understand, but the sooner you take your Vow of Expiation the better."

Imoshen dropped to one knee, both hands extended palm up, offering the obeisance of a supplicant. "Wise Beatific, hear me. I was ready to take the vow on the seventeenth anniversary of my birthing day, but Fair Isle was at war and I could not travel to the Basilica. I am ready to take the vow—"

"Of chastity? Are you ready to follow the true path for a

pure T'En woman, the one dictated by your namesake, Imoshen the First?"

Imoshen looked up startled.

"I have claimed Imoshen." Tulkhan strode forward. "She ca—"

"I cannot take the vow of chastity," Imoshen spoke quickly before Tulkhan could reveal that she carried his child. She came to her feet. "Once I would have taken that path willingly. But I was granted dispensation even before the Ghebites invaded Fair Isle. Now I must serve my people in another way." She felt for Tulkhan, who took her arm, linking it through his. He was reassuringly solid. She drew on his certainty.

"In other circumstance I would have called on the Church to say the words for the dead, and I concede it is wisest to speak those words from the T'Enchiridion." Her mouth went dry as she recalled her discovery that the Parakletos were not merely an abstract concept. Even worse, they were not the benevolent beings of the Church's teachings. She shuddered, forcing herself to go on. "This is no longer the old empire, Beatific. We must bend before the winds of change or be uprooted."

The True-woman's eyes narrowed.

Imoshen had not meant it as a threat. They were all vulnerable, none more so than she.

"What is this Vow of Expiation, Imoshen?" Tulkhan asked.

But the Beatific replied for her. "Before they can be accepted into society, all pure T'En must give the Vow of Expiation to the church, offering themselves in its service."

"Imoshen can give this vow when we make our marriage vows on Midwinters Day, that is less than six weeks away," Tulkhan announced, sweeping the problem aside.

Imoshen caught the Beatific's eye. Bonding was nothing like a Ghebite marriage.

Tulkhan continued, "No harm has been done here today and a life has been saved. My men wait outside in the

cold, grumbling for their dinner. Come, Imoshen." He gave
the Beatific a nod, insulting in its brevity.

"Beatific." Imoshen offered the leader of the T'En Church
the proper bow and waited for her to leave first. Imoshen knew
General Tulkhan would have simply marched out, leaving
them to trail after him. Every day was filled with a thousand
small insults, salt in the wound of Fair Isle's surrender.

Three

THE RIDE BACK to the palace was swift, but not swift enough. The cook had prepared an old empire meal which had to be served the moment it was ready. Imoshen had just left the royal kitchen after soothing the cook's feelings when a young boy ran into her.

"What's so important that you cannot walk the palace corridors in a civilized fashion?" Imoshen asked, hauling him to his feet.

He rolled his eyes. "The Ghebites—"

What now? Distantly she heard their raised voices. "Take me to them."

The boy led her through a connecting passage to an old wing dating from the Age of Tribulation. Curious servants clustered in doorways, pointing and giggling.

A dozen of Tulkhan's commanders and Elite Guard marched past Imoshen. Some held candles and wine flagons, others carried massive oak chairs between them, all sang at the tops of their voices. There was much laughter and they stopped every few paces to share the wine casks.

Imoshen experienced a strong sense of dislocation. In the old empire, ritual and protocol guided every moment of the day. This bizarre Ghebite parade was so out of place it left her disoriented and bemused.

As the song ended Tulkhan's voice echoed down the passage ordering them to take care. Imoshen edged past the men, brushing against wainscotting and ancient weaponry. She entered a disused hall where she found fourteen men staggering under the weight of a feasting table. Leaping candle flames cast frantic shadows on distant walls but could not illuminate the high ceiling.

"What are you doing?" Imoshen demanded of the nearest man.

He blinked owlishly, realized who she was, and made the Ghebite sign to ward off evil, fist before his eyes. She frowned.

"Imoshen?" Tulkhan located her. "Is our meal ready?"

"Not yet. The cook is trying to muster up enough cold meat and cheese to feed forty people. Her spoiled masterpiece will be fed to the pigs."

"Then we have time to get these tables and chairs upstairs. Come on, men!"

They launched into a roisterous drinking song as they manhandled the solid oak table out of the room. Imoshen winced when one corner chipped the doorway.

"Take care!" Tulkhan bellowed, then tilted a flagon across his forearm and drank deep. "Take it up the marble staircase. Should be wide enough."

Imoshen caught Tulkhan's arm. "But why? What's wrong with the tables and chairs that we've been using?"

"Too small. I'm tired of sitting on chairs that protest every time I move. This furniture's more to my liking. A man can get his knees under this table!"

"That table was built at T'Ashmyr's command nearly five hundred years ago. He was the first Throwback emperor of Fair Isle!"

Tulkhan stared at her.

Imoshen realized the General was not drunk at all. "You can get your knees under that table because it was designed and built for a pure T'En leader who could have looked you in the eye. In the parts of the palace built during the Age of Tribulation all the furniture is T'En size. You might be a giant amongst your own kind, but you would have fit right in with my people."

Wax from Tulkhan's candle fell on his wrist. He grimaced then shrugged. "Well, at least I'll be comfortable." And he strode after his men.

Imoshen lengthened her stride to keep up with him. They entered the royal wing where upper echelon servants clustered in statue niches, pointing and whispering. Tomorrow the tale would be all over T'Diemn, how the barbarians marched roughshod over palace treasures.

In the long gallery they found the elegant gilt-legged, red velvet chairs piled carelessly high on their matching table. Anger and dismay flooded Imoshen but she did not reveal this; turning instead to the servants, she directed them to clear the furniture away and store it. "We will have our meal now."

Tulkhan offered Imoshen his arm. When they walked into the formal dining room the Ghebites gave a cheer. Raising their drinks they indicated the new table and chairs. Well pleased, Tulkhan took his place at the head of the table and Imoshen joined him. None of them seemed aware how incongruous the heavy dark furniture looked set against the pale splendor of the room's mirrors and gilt-edged plaster work.

"Wine?" Tulkhan offered to pour Imoshen a glass. She declined. He took another mouthful from the cask, then appeared to recollect that he was not on the battlefield and poured a generous glass. The fine T'En crystal looked fragile in his hands. "A toast to the greatest army in the known world!"

The men echoed his sentiment, downing their drinks lustily. Crystal goblets slammed emphatically on the tabletop as soon as they were emptied; most survived this rough handling.

A memory of the Empress graciously finger-clicking her approval for a pair of dueling poets struck Imoshen with renewed pain—the old empire was truly dead, supplanted by these vigorous barbarians. How would the remnants of the T'En nobles react when they saw this kind of behavior?

Imoshen caught Tulkhan's arm, dropping her voice so

that only he could hear. "General, the nobles from the Keldon Highlands will be here soon. They have not formally surrendered and you have every right to expect an oath of loyalty. But—"

Servants entered with trays of cold meat and cheeses, presented in patterns which were works of art. The Ghebites fell upon them with gusto, grabbing chicken legs and tearing into the white flesh.

"Don't wrinkle your nose like that, Imoshen. The men are hungry. They've been out in the cold all day doing a man's work."

"I suppose I am lucky they will even eat with me. Men don't share the table with women in Gheeaba, do they?"

He put his glass down. "Business and battle plans are discussed at the table. These are not for women's ears. In the privacy of his own home a man might invite his favorite wife to eat with him. But this is not Gheeaba and my men have not been home for eleven years." He gave her a shrewd look. "We've seen all sorts of customs in mainland palaces. Eating with women is the least of it. Why, I remember one banquet which was served on the naked bodies of nubile virgins." His dark eyes challenged her. "They were sweet!"

Imoshen refused to rise to his bait. "The southern nobles are a proud lot. They were the last to adopt T'En rule. It was only at the beginning of the Age of Consolidation that the locals truly accepted their T'En nobles, and by then those T'En had grown away from their cousins in the north.

"The Keldon ravines might be rich in precious metals but they don't provide an easy living. 'Scrawny sheep and stiff-necked Keld,' as the saying goes." She smiled at the expression. "I'm asking you to go slowly with the Keldon nobles. In a week or so they will come to the capital to give you their oath of fealty because they must. But they—"

"They shielded the rebel leader while they smiled and gave me false welcome," Tulkhan growled. "I hunted Reothe in those ranges. I know how wild and unforgiving they are."

Imoshen nodded. "The land shapes the people. The Keld

are few and fiercely loyal. They cannot hope to stand against your army, but they are quick to take offense and slow to forgive. Unless you want to split Fair Isle with civil war, you need to win them over." She felt General Tulkhan watching her curiously. "Yes?"

"You advise me against your own people?"

"I advise you for the *sake* of my people. The fields lie blackened from T'Diemn to the north of Fair Isle. This a fertile island. Once her towns had great stores of grain but your men raided these—"

"An army on the move needs to eat."

Imoshen sighed. "We have had this conversation before and I argued for cooperation then. I don't want to see this spring's planting ruined because of more fighting. I cannot watch my people starve."

"What do you care? They are True-men and women, not even of the same race as you."

Even though she knew Tulkhan was baiting her, Imoshen could not hide the heat in her cheeks. "I belong to Fair Isle. In the centuries since the T'En took this island, my race has interbred with the locals. The blood of T'En, True-man and woman alike has enriched the soil. Only the land endures."

Tulkhan grimaced. He could not argue with Imoshen's logic, but he sensed she was intimating more. How long before his Ghebite army was absorbed into the larger population of Fair Isle? Would they one day cease to be Ghebites? Would his grandson don the badge of fatherhood and invite everyone to celebrate the birth of a daughter? In Gheeaba, the father did not even bother to name a daughter, that was left to the mother.

"What is wrong with Jacolm?" Imoshen asked abruptly.

Before Tulkhan could stop her, she hurried down the long table and ordered Jacolm to his feet. The man stood resentfully, favoring his right side. His thick eyebrows pulled together as Imoshen told him to open his shirt.

The room fell silent. Tulkhan tensed. Jacolm was

renowned for his hasty temper. Yet he stood at this woman's command and bared his flesh to her eyes.

Imoshen ran her hands over the man's torso as he gaped, too stunned by her temerity to react. "Just as I thought, a cracked rib. Let me—"

Jacolm stepped back. "I will not be tainted by the touch of a Dhamfeer."

Tulkhan saw Imoshen's face grow pale with the pain of rejection, but he also understood his man's reaction. Imoshen, however, was too much the statesman . . . stateswoman, to respond with anger.

"Let me heal your rib," she offered. "It must be painful."

But Jacolm's answer was to lace up his shirt. His swordbrother came to his feet in a gesture of solidarity.

Imoshen glanced at Tulkhan, who could only shrug.

She lifted her hands and turned them over for all to see. "I see no taint on these fingers." She met Jacolm's eyes. "True, these are T'En hands with six fingers, but they have healed many a True-man and woman and it mattered not whether they came from Fair Isle or Gheeaba." Gracefully she took three steps back and gave them the T'En obeisance among equals. "I bid you sleep well."

As Imoshen sailed out of the room, Tulkhan considered following her, but his men would not be impressed if he ran after *"that Dhamfeer bitch,"* as they called her none too quietly behind her back.

When the door closed on Imoshen, there was a long moment of silence, then Harholfe made a jest about what would help him get to sleep and the men laughed. But they spoke too loudly and laughed too long, anxious to ignore the issues Imoshen had raised.

Tulkhan could not ignore those issues. He poured himself another glass of wine and drained it grimly.

As Imoshen walked the long gallery, she sighed. Jacolm's rejection stung, particularly when she had offered nothing but help. It was always two steps forward and one step back with Tulkhan and his Ghebites.

She made her way to her bedchamber where as usual one of her Stronghold Guard stood at the door. The young woman straightened when Imoshen approached. All twenty of Imoshen's Stronghold Guard could not hope to save her if Tulkhan's Elite Guard planned her murder. But it was the symbol which carried weight. These people were as loyal to her as the General's guard were to him, and they had done her proud today.

Imoshen entered her room where she found the fire had been built and candles prepared. She lit a candle, going through to the bathing chamber beyond. Wearily, she checked that the burner was working and let the water flow. Alone at last, Imoshen dropped her guard. As she sank onto a low stool she shuddered, recalling the death ceremony. In the future she would leave such things to the Church priests trained for the task.

Many times she had stood at the Aayel's side while her great-aunt said the words for the dead, and not once had she sensed the Parakletos. Was it because her T'En senses had been less mature? Her gift had always been healing and this came more easily to her now.

Instinctively she knew she had to hide her growing gifts from the True-people, particularly the Ghebites. The enormity of her position stole her breath. One wrong move and she would be dead, assassinated by enemies or even executed at the General's command.

Though she suspected Tulkhan would regret ordering her death, she knew he would do so if he thought it necessary. She'd heard how he had suppressed the defiant mainland kingdoms in the early days of his career and knew he could be utterly ruthless. Yet when Tulkhan looked at her, really looked into her eyes, she sometimes thought she read. . . .

Anger fired Imoshen. She rose and prowled the chamber. A metallic taste settled on her tongue. With a start, she recognized the first signs of the T'En gifts moving unbidden, and unwanted. Dismay flooded her. If only she knew how to harness her gifts. If only her great-aunt had lived long enough to instruct her.

Shortly before the Aayel died she had revealed that Imoshen's parents had forbidden her to instruct Imoshen in her gifts. All those years she had walked at the Aayel's side, learning herb lore, memorizing the T'Enchiridion, watching her great-aunt serve the people, she might have been learning about her heritage. Instead she was ignorant.

Imoshen grew utterly still. The Aayel hadn't lived to teach her, but the palace library was even more extensive than her Stronghold's. The library was sure to contain learned discourses on the T'En gifts. It might take all winter, but she would sift every ancient document.

If only she didn't have to organize the feast to celebrate Tulkhan's signing of the Church agreement. She had never wanted to play a role in court life, yet now she had the responsibility of running the palace. How her sister would have envied her!

Imoshen's eyes filled with tears. Now her sister would never mix in the Empress's inner circle; her brother would never compete at the Midsummers Feast for the dueling poet's crown of fresh flowers. All her kinsmen and women had died in a futile attempt to halt the General's advance. How could she discard them so easily to plot for her own future?

Imoshen hardened her heart. To survive she had to look to her future. She would not let the General relegate her to the position of a Ghebite woman—a piece of comfortable furniture to be used when needed then put away in a gilded room. She would be the architect of her future and the future of Fair Isle.

Imoshen tested the water and turned off the spigot. She sank into the bath, feeling her muscles relax. She might have saved the life of the cooper's child, but she had offended the Beatific, who should have been her ally. After all, the Church retained its position as arbiter of law only because Imoshen had convinced Tulkhan to sign the document.

Between the Church and the proud Keldon nobles, the

conniving mainland ambassadors, and the arrogant Ghebites she must somehow keep the peace while consolidating her position with General Tulkhan, and his position with the people of Fair Isle.

Satisfied with the menu for this evening's feast, Imoshen left the kitchen wing. She had only just entered the main gallery when raised voices echoed through the great marble foyer. The palace's main entrance had been built during the Age of Consolidation and it had been designed by her ancestors to impress their subjects with huge marble columns, a grand divided staircase, and a painted ceiling which appeared to open up to the heavens.

Imoshen peered around a marble column and cursed softly. A party of Keldon nobles had arrived sooner than expected and Lord Fairban was busy identifying himself and his three daughters to the flustered palace footman.

This meant more places to set at the feast tonight, more volatile tempers to soothe. Because the Keld had not formally surrendered or offered fealty to General Tulkhan, the situation was delicate.

What must her southern cousins think of her, aiding and abetting the invader? She hoped they realized she had to choose the path of least resistance to ensure her survival, just as they must give lip service to the Ghebite General to avoid having their lands and titles forfeited.

What good was honor if you were dead?

Below her, the master of the bed chambers hastened to greet Lord Fairban, and Imoshen smiled. Let this palace dignitary earn his keep. He could escort the new arrivals to their chambers while she spoke with the master of ceremonies and adjusted the seating.

But after this was done, Imoshen decided to deliver the dinner invitation to Lord Fairban's daughters in person. It went against the usual palace formality but she would need the support of the Keldon noblewomen in order to civilize the Ghebites.

Imoshen plucked her metal comb from her key chain and scratched briefly on the door tang. To her trained ear, every comb had a different sound. She could identify a servant, or a noble, by the note their comb made when run across a door's metal tang. The Ghebites habit of thundering on doors grated on her nerves but it certainly identified them as a race.

Discarding protocol, she entered the suite's outer chamber. A maid gave a muffled shriek and ran off to get her mistresses. The Fairban women entered, followed by curious maids laden with clothing and jewelry.

Trying to hide their surprise, they gave the obeisance appropriate for the Empress. But the Empress would not have slipped unannounced into their rooms. The younger two Fairban women exchanged stiff smiles and Imoshen recognized that tolerant, half-embarrassed look. They could not ignore her height and her coloring. She was so obviously pure T'En. Even her own family had found her an embarrassment.

But she was not going to apologize for her existence. Instead Imoshen studied the Fairban women. Would they suit her purpose? The two younger girls were very like their father, small, fine-boned, and truly of the people; but the eldest, who now stepped forward graciously, was nearly her own height.

"I greet you, T'Imoshen," Lady Cariah said formally.

In her bearing, Imoshen recognized the polish of the old empire. The woman was several years older than her, in her early twenties.

A pang of insecurity stabbed Imoshen. How she longed to have that air of effortless elegance. Again she was reminded of the painfully self-conscious sixteen-year-old she had been on her first visit to the palace less than two years ago. Just finding her way about the endless rooms had been a challenge then, without having to try to unravel the politics of the court. But she was no longer that child. She had a role to play and needed their cooperation.

Resolving to win the Keldon noblewomen's support, Imoshen took Cariah's hand, returning her formal greeting.

Imoshen couldn't help admiring her hair. It fell around Cariah's shoulders like a shawl of burnished copper. Good. All three of the Fairban women were beautiful enough to arouse the interest of the Ghebite commanders.

"I am honored to greet you and your sisters. We need the civilizing influence of your presence at . . ." Imoshen's fingers curled around Cariah's, the invitation on the tip of her tongue, but all thought fled as she registered the oddity of the hand held in hers. Lord Fairban's first daughter had six fingers.

Startled, Imoshen's gaze darted to Cariah's face. She read tolerant amusement in the older woman's eyes.

Heat flooded Imoshen's cheeks. She was no better than the younger Fairban women. Why did they find her T'En characteristics disturbing when their own sister carried T'En blood? Perhaps it was because Imoshen confronted them with something they wished to deny.

"Our mother had the eyes as well as the six fingers," Cariah explained, seeing Imoshen's confusion.

"Y . . . Your mother?" Imoshen faltered.

"Long dead. Father would never bond again."

The conversation was much too personal for old empire protocol, but then Imoshen always had trouble containing her unruly tongue. Her own mother had despaired of her.

The enormity of her loss hit her.

"My mother is dead, too. They are all dead!" Even as tears threatened, shame flooded Imoshen. But she could not contain the soul-deep sobs which shook her. She had not let herself grieve. There'd been no time, and now it was as if a dam had broken. Unable to contain the fury of her tears, Imoshen turned away, covering her face in despair. Surely this worldly woman would despise her.

But Cariah slid her arms around Imoshen's shoulders, offering unconditional comfort, and for a few moments Imoshen knew the peace of compassion as she weathered the storm of her loss. Then she pulled away.

Ashamed to have revealed her weakness, she walked to a mirror. As she composed herself she was acutely aware of the noblewomen and their maids reflected behind her.

"Forgive me." Imoshen turned to face them, giving the lesser bow of supplication. "I am here to invite you to the celebration tonight."

"You honor us," the Lady Cariah replied, and though Imoshen searched that beautiful face, she could read no mockery.

Imoshen took formal leave of them and even as the door closed she could hear the buzz of comment behind her. Her cheeks flamed with humiliation.

Though they were stubborn Keldon nobles, poor cousins of the prosperous T'En court, they were still steeped in its traditions. Grief, love—all strong emotions had been highly ritualized in the court.

Imoshen castigated herself. To weep in the arms of a stranger was unheard of. The Keldon women would think her as uncouth as the Ghebite barbarians. How could she look the Lady Cariah in the eye tonight?

But she had to. Somehow she would hide her discomfort, for she could not leave the General to host the evening alone. But first she must reorganize the menu to include Keldon delicacies.

"T'Imoshen? Where is the Empress?" an anxious voice called.

The cook looked to Imoshen, and she summoned a smile, even though the sound of running feet made her stomach cramp with fear. Hopefully it was simply a crisis of protocol precipitated by an unthinking Ghebite.

A youth thrust the door open and stood there panting. By his dress he was one of the outdoor servants, and by his state, he had searched the endless corridors of the palace for her.

"I am here." Her voice sounded calm. Only she could feel the pounding of her heart. Absurdly, her first thought was for Tulkhan's safety.

"The Ghebite priest has gone mad!" the youth announced. "He's destroying the hothouse!"

This was the last thing Imoshen had expected. A laugh almost escaped her. The hothouse supplied the palace with year-round fresh vegetables. Why would that pompous, self-important priest object to fresh vegetables?

"Why—"

"Come and see!" Even in his agitation, the youth did not dare touch her.

Imoshen left the amended feast menu on the scrubbed tabletop and marched out of the kitchen, followed by the kitchen staff. Human nature being what it was, they welcomed any excuse to put their work aside, and this promised to be entertaining, for no one liked the Cadre.

She smiled grimly but the smile slipped from her face when she heard the sound of smashing glass. Even in T'Diemn, glass was valuable, especially glass crafted for large windows.

She caught the arm of the nearest scullery maid. "Fetch General Tulkhan."

The girl gave the old empire obeisance and hurried off.

With the youth dancing in front of her like an agitated puppy, and a growing crowd of spectators following her, Imoshen approached the large hothouse. Several anxious gardeners ran up to her, their voices strident with outrage as they told her how the priest had marched into the hothouse raving about blasphemy. It made no sense. No sense at all.

When Imoshen thrust the door open, the heat hit her, followed by the rich smell of fecund earth. Tray after tray of sprouting seeds stretched before her. Inoffensive tomato seedlings lay bruised and trampled.

Unaware of his audience, the Cadre swung the rake at another window. The sound of shattering glass threatened Imoshen's composure. She tasted the forewarning of the T'En gift on her tongue, aroused by the excitement and her anger.

"Cease this destruction immediately!" Her voice rang out as she strode through debris.

But the priest was too intent, deafened by his own actions, to hear her. He positioned himself before another window and raised the rake. Imoshen came up behind him, tore the rake from his hand, and tossed it aside. She caught him by the scruff of his neck, swinging him off his feet.

Empowered by her fury it took little effort to hold the Cadre off the ground. The startled priest shrieked and clutched frantically at his collar which had risen up under his chin.

"What is the matter with you?" Imoshen shook him as a dog shakes a rat and said the first thing that came into her head. "Do you hate fresh carrots?"

The absurdity of it made the servants laugh. She suspected they were as relieved as she was to find the threat was not armed Ghebites slaughtering innocents.

The priest clawed at his throat, his face going red.

Imoshen opened her mouth to speak but General Tulkhan forestalled her.

"What's going on here?" His deep voice cut through the nervous giggles, silencing everyone.

Imoshen dropped the priest in disgust, indicating the destruction. "Isn't it obvious? Your priest objects to fresh vegetables!"

General Tulkhan contained his annoyance. Summoned by a frantic palace servant, he had been expecting something far worse than this. "Explain yourself, Cadre."

Glaring at Imoshen, the priest rearranged his elaborate collar ruff and dirt-stained surplice. "It is an abomination!"

"Since when is fresh food an abomination?" Imoshen snapped.

"What is this place?" Tulkhan demanded.

"The hothouse where the palace's fresh vegetables are grown," Imoshen explained. "You wouldn't need this in Gheeaba. During our long, cold winters, the windows capture the heat of the sun."

"It is an abomination in the eyes of the great Akha Khan!" the Cadre insisted. Quick as thought, he darted past Imoshen to pull a plant out by its roots, shaking it fiercely so that damp earth flew everywhere. "This is the abomination, this and all its brothers!"

Imoshen wrinkled her nose. "You object to a cup of herbal tea?"

Tulkhan felt a smile tug at his lips but kept his voice neutral. "This is a tea plant?"

"We dry the leaves, boil water, and make an infusion which we drink," Imoshen explained. "It is one of many teas sold in the teahouses throughout—"

"Tell him what it's used for," the priest insisted, his eyes gleaming triumphantly.

"Women drink it to control their fertility," Imoshen replied.

"Exactly!" The priest stepped forward, waving the plant under General Tulkhan's nose. "This is the root of the evil in Fair Isle. This plant is an abomination. No wonder the women of this island know no shame. No wonder their men are emasculated!" Spittle flew from the Cadre's lips. "It is a woman's lot to bear children. She is the property of her husband, and the sons she produces are his heirs. The more sons the better to make a strong house-line!" The Cadre glared at Imoshen. "To interfere with a woman's natural bearing of children is an abomination, an affront to Akha Khan. Think of all the Ghebite sons who would never be born to take up arms if this plant were used in Gheeaba!"

Imoshen made a rude sound. "I should prepare a shipload and send it—"

"You dare to mock me, Dhamfeer bitch?" the priest rounded on her. "You are twice over an abomination!"

The palace servants gasped, turning fearfully to Imoshen. She towered over the priest, her brilliant, wine-dark eyes flashing dangerously. Even from half a body length away, Tulkhan could feel the overflow of her T'En gifts rolling off her skin.

"Leaving aside my race—" Imoshen's control was more frightening than rage. "Leaving aside the fact that Ghebite men don't think their women possess true souls but are only one step above the beasts of the field, I would like you to explain to me what is wrong with preventing unwanted children? Surely it is better for a family to be able to feed the children they have than to breed irresponsibly?"

"See how she twists everything?" the priest demanded. "Cunning Dhamfeer! Listen to her long enough and you'll believe black is white, General. You must protect yourself from her. You must protect your men from the women of Fair Isle. These women would emasculate our men, play them false with their vile herb! What man does not want sons? What man would not believe himself a lesser man if his wife did not produce a babe every year, or at least every second year?"

"Like a prize pig?" Imoshen asked, her eyes glittering.

Tulkhan was aware of her fury but he was also aware that a Ghebite warrior who had risen high enough to afford to keep three or even four wives expected to see them all heavy with child. Thirty, maybe even forty, children was not unheard of. Hopefully, half would be male. With all those sons to further the interests of his house-line, while his daughters married to consolidate alliances, he would be considered a rich man. However that was back in Gheeaba and this was Fair Isle.

The priest flung the herb to the cobbles and ground it under his foot. "General, you must order all these plants destroyed. Send your men throughout the island to collect them. Pile these vile herbs in every village square and burn the lot. It is the only way to teach the women of Fair Isle their place!"

Imoshen felt her world tilt on its axis. General Tulkhan's Ghebite features gave nothing away. Surely he could not be considering this? The priest would undo six hundred years of T'En civilization and reduce the women of Fair Isle to slaves like their Ghebite counterparts.

She covered the distance between them, instinctively taking the General's arm, seeking contact with his mind. In the moment before he raised his guard, she sensed his reluctance to shame the priest.

Her fingers tightened. "Every woman of Fair Isle grows

this herb in her garden. Every woman decides when to have a child. Would you deny her this? Would you make her fearful of physical love? As a healer, I know there are women who cannot carry a baby. It would kill them." Imoshen searched Tulkhan's face but his features remained impassive. How could she convince him? Suddenly, she recalled his one secret fear and understood the moment had come to use this knowledge. "There are other women who have trouble conceiving children. They use a variety of this herb to bring on fertility. Would you deny those women and their bondpartners the joy of their own child?"

She saw a muscle jump under the General's coppery skin.

"Cadre," Tulkhan's voice was explosive in the strained silence. "An agreement with the T'En Church has been signed."

Imoshen took a step back, releasing the General's arm.

"By the terms of this agreement," Tulkhan continued, "we will not interfere with their worship and they will not interfere with ours. I charge you not to force your beliefs on the people of Fair Isle. This law you propose would be impossible to enforce. Any plot of dirt or windowsill pot can be used to grow this herb. Would you have my army reduced to gardeners, rooting out unwanted weeds?"

Put that way it did seem absurd. When the palace staff tittered, the Cadre glared at Imoshen. She held his eyes. He had brought this ridicule upon himself.

"Take care of your soldiers' souls, Cadre," Imoshen advised, linking her arm through Tulkhan's once again. Whatever dissonance there might be between them personally, before his men and her people they had to present a united front. "And leave the temporal lives of the people to us. Come, General."

They left the Cadre fuming and walked towards the hothouse door. There Tulkhan turned to Imoshen, deliberately removing her arm from his. "Don't think I don't know what you are about."

Imoshen stiffened. "General, what is at stake here is much larger than you or me. It is the fate of the women of

Fair Isle. Would you see half your subjects reduced to wife-slaves? Would you be the cause of a generation of unwanted children left to roam the streets, begging or stealing their bread, as I have heard they do on the mainland?"

"T'Imoshen?" a gardener spoke, hovering at a polite distance.

Imoshen searched the General's face. He was a clever man, but he was also steeped in the culture of his people. How far could she push him before he pushed back?

"I have work to do," Tulkhan ground out, according her the barest nod of civility.

Imoshen gave him the obeisance between equals, the significance of which would not be lost on her servants and, knowing how sharp he was, it would not be lost on the General either.

Imoshen dealt with the gardeners, assuring them repairs would be carried out in time for the seedlings to reestablish. But her mind was on the General. Tonight, the two of them must sit side by side at the feasting table without revealing their differences.

Four

TULKHAN WATCHED IMOSHEN step lightly through the patterns of a complicated dance. Three pretty noblewomen made up the corners of the intricate pattern as they partnered four town dignitaries. His commanders watched, waiting for a Ghebite tune so they could break in and claim the women.

Imoshen moved with a casual grace which could not be taught. She wore a deep plum velvet gown. It was the same vivid color as her eyes were when she was thoughtful and it made her pale skin look even paler. Her hair was loose, confined only by a small circlet of electrum, inset with purple amethysts. When she turned, her hair fanned out over her shoulders like a rippling sheet of white satin. She came to the end of the dance, her hair and skirt settling around her long limbs. Tulkhan swallowed. He wanted to run his fingers through those long pale tresses, to lean close and inhale her heady scent. Just watching her made him ache with need.

"T'Imoshen dances well," observed his table companion.

He turned to the Beatific. In Gheeaba, she would not dare to speak to him. An unmarried woman, or a married woman past childbearing age, was thought fit only to mind the small children or feed the animals.

"You seem distracted, Prince Tulkhan."

"I am not a prince." He balked at explaining the complicated family structure of his people. "As first son of the

King's concubine, I was not given a title. I earned my position through merit and years of service in my father's army. I prefer to be called by the title I have earned."

He caught her clever, hazel eyes on him. Pinpoints of golden candlelight danced in her pupils. He reminded himself that he must not underestimate her simply because she was a woman. Imoshen had taught him that.

"And soon to be King of Fair Isle," she agreed smoothly. "I must congratulate you on your forthcoming bonding, General."

The words were innocuous enough, but there was something in her tone which warned him to be on his guard. Did he detect a trace of mockery? Did these people think him presumptuous to crown himself king? Of course they did. He was a mere three generations removed from his nomadic herdsman grandfather who, through his great strength and stature, had united the Ghebite tribes.

"Thank you," Tulkhan said, turning to watch Imoshen, who was making the robust Ghebite dance a thing of precision and grace. How could he wait another six weeks?

"T'Imoshen is very . . . beautiful isn't the right word. The T'En are too dangerous to be merely beautiful. They have a kind of terrible beauty. You never met the rebel leader, T'Reothe?" The Beatific paused, making it a question.

Tulkhan shifted in his seat, trying to appear only mildly interested. He neither denied nor admitted meeting Reothe. Deep in the Keldon Highlands, Tulkhan had inadvertently called on the Ancients by spilling blood on one of their sacred sites. Attracted by this surge in power, Reothe had appeared before him. The rebel leader had laughed when he had realized who Tulkhan was, then he had cursed him. Quoting a line from an ancient T'En poem, Reothe called him a dead man who walked and talked, and had claimed he was destined to kill him. Reothe's words had often returned to haunt Tulkhan's darkest hours.

The Beatific's words recalled Tulkhan. ". . . surprised when the Emperor and Empress approved Reothe's betrothal to Imoshen. By custom she would have taken the vows of chastity at seventeen when she made her Vow of Expiation. Instead, the Empress informed me I was to witness the historic bonding of the last two pure T'En. They were to be joined this spring, did you know that?" But she did not pause for him to reply. "Reothe could have looked to almost any woman for his partner, any woman but a Throwback. He went to the Emperor and Empress for special dispensation. By the time I learned of it, they had already agreed, and I had to witness the decree. It was so unexpected. The custom has always been to marry out, T'En male to Truewoman. Imoshen the First made it mandatory. Do you know much of the T'En history?"

Tulkhan no longer pretended only polite interest. He spoke slowly. "There are rumors of great gifts."

She nodded. "T'En gifts can also be a curse. The first Imoshen and her shipload of refugees fled their homeland to escape persecution. She ordered the ship burned."

"But I was told Imoshen the First was an explorer."

"With small children and old people?" The Beatific smiled. "No, she rewrote our history for her own purposes."

Tulkhan met the woman's eyes frankly. "How do you know this?"

"I have access to the journals of our early Church leaders. When the first Imoshen set out to take this land she was utterly ruthless. She had about her a band of devoted T'En warriors—the legendary Paragian Guard—who had sworn an oath to serve her. Those who died in her service were destined to serve beyond death, bound by their oath. They are the Parakletos." She made a furtive sign before resuming. "It was only through the dedication of this Paragian Guard that Imoshen the First was able to subdue the people. But once the island was taken she disbanded the Paragian Guard and ordered her own kind to mingle with the locals.

"She took a vow of celibacy and all pure T'En females since have followed her example. Her only surviving daughter became Beatific. Imoshen the First bonded her pure T'En nephew, Aayel, to the old royalty, just as you are doing. But she did it for an even stronger reason."

Tulkhan contained his impatience, very aware that this woman enjoyed playing him like a fish on a line.

"Pure T'En are unstable. Even amongst Imoshen the First's people, there were not many pure T'En. Throwbacks like Imoshen and Reothe can have great gifts, but they are also cursed."

"Explain."

The Beatific smiled. "Well, even the royal family was wary of Reothe. They were happy when he absented himself on long sea voyages of exploration and trade."

"Piracy, you mean. I have heard about his exploits."

The Beatific held his eyes. "Reothe was acting under a charter from the Empress herself. His task was to harry the trade of Fair Isle's enemies on the high seas. A small wealthy island such as Fair Isle must protect her trading interests or the greedy will think her weak. Reothe was a great sea captain. He also explored the archipelago and opened new trade routes." She shrugged. "However, the pure T'En males are a danger to themselves and to those around them. Who knows what mischief Reothe might have caused if he had remained at court. As it was, the Empress had to remove one of her other adopted sons to preserve the peace.

"The Empress loved Reothe. She reared him from the age of ten, but as he matured so did his gifts. They first began to manifest at puberty. The pure T'En have a range of gifts, from the ability to scry and manipulate the minds of others, to the more practical gifts, like healing. In the females the gifts are weak, but in the males they can be quite powerful. It was expected Reothe would be strong in one area, but none of us knew the extent or specialization of his gift. The T'En have ever been a secretive race and Reothe was true to his blood."

She lowered her voice. "Why, the Emperor himself confided in me that he feared Reothe might supplant his own children. And then there is the question of why the Emperor and Empress granted Reothe dispensation to bond with Imoshen. I advised them against it, but they were fixed on the idea, even though it flouted six hundred years of custom." Her brilliant eyes held his. "I often wonder whether Reothe used their trust and affection for him to sway their judgment."

Tulkhan's hand tightened on the goblet's stem.

The Beatific sat back. Languidly she selected a cube of diced fruit, slipping the choice morsel between her lips. She dipped her fingers in the little bowl provided and wiped them fastidiously. "I can only speculate as to why the first Imoshen led her shipload of refugees from our homeland. But it has long been the role of the Church to limit any damage the T'En might do. When the remaining Paragian Guard were disbanded they chose to serve the Church. They formed the T'Enplars, warrior priests sworn to uphold the sanctity of the T'En gifts, but it was from their very ranks that the first T'En went rogue.

"Sardonyx led the revolt of sixty-four. His own cousin, Empress T'Abularassa, joined with the first Beatific to contain him. They created the Tractarians to balance the power of the T'Enplars. Balance, that is what *En* means in High T'En. After Sardonyx's death, T'Abularassa built a tower in his memory; Sard's Tower. Since then the families of the rogue T'En have commemorated their loss with a tower of tears, and the Beatific has been empowered to declare one of the T'En rogue if there is enough evidence of treason against the Church and the Empress. For over five centuries the Tractarians have hunted down rogue T'En. You have heard of the stonings?"

"It's been over a hundred years."

"I know. There has not been the need. After the last stoning, no pure T'En males were born for seventy years, and the Tractarians withered. But since Reothe came to maturity, they have been revitalized under the leadership of Murgon." She gestured without actually pointing. "That's him at the next table, third from the left. Tall thin man with the T'En eyes." She saw Tulkhan's surprise. "Those of part blood are particularly sensitive to the use of the gifts."

"Would it not be simpler to kill all pure T'En babies at birth?" Tulkhan asked coldly.

"We are not barbarians!" Disgust made the Beatific's voice sharp.

"I meant, why wait? Why not contain the threat?"

Her eyes narrowed. "Not all T'En go rogue. They, like all nobles, are taught that their duty is to serve Fair Isle. The T'En gifts can serve True-men and women. Look at Imoshen's ability to heal. The people love her and she is a visible symbol of our past. We revere the T'En!"

"In abstract?"

He surprised a smile from her but she did not acknowledge his question.

"General?"

Tulkhan looked up to see Imoshen's flushed, smiling face. Guilt stirred in him. On Imoshen's advice, he'd signed the document that enabled the Beatific to retain her position of power, and now the woman was undermining Imoshen. Politics! Disgust filled Tulkhan. He much preferred the knife-edge life and death decisions of the battlefield. At least when death held a blade to his throat, it did not smile and whisper words of comfort.

Imoshen gestured to the small man at her side. "Let me introduce the first of the Keldon nobles to accept our hospitality. Lord Fairban."

Tulkhan came to his feet. "So we meet again, my lord. This time in my Keep."

"No one can say the Keld dishonor the laws of hospitality," Fairban bristled.

Tulkhan smiled grimly. "I'm sure you will find my hospitality everything yours was and more."

Silence hung heavy between them as Imoshen glanced from Tulkhan to Lord Fairban.

"General Tulkhan spent a night at my holdings while he was hunting rebels," the old lord answered Imoshen's unasked question.

Imoshen's eyes widened.

"How are your beautiful daughters, Lord Fairban?" the Beatific asked.

Under cover of their conversation, Imoshen turned to Tulkhan. "Come dance with me, General?"

"No." Dancing was not something a general needed to be proficient in. Yet he longed to take Imoshen in his arms in front of everyone, to know that when he put his hands on her, she was his.

But what was he thinking? The Beatific had told him the T'En were unstable, a danger to others and themselves. Was Imoshen exerting some kind of mental pull on him?

"General?"

Looking up into her teasing face, Tulkhan could not believe she was consciously manipulating him. The only power she had over him at this moment was the pull of his body to hers. But that was powerful enough and that was too much.

"You mock me, Imoshen." He made his voice hard and contemptuous as he sat down. "What time does a general have for dancing? Go ask someone else."

She hesitated, her features briefly registering the humiliation of his rejection. Then she stepped closer, her voice dropping. "Since you don't know the T'En dances, General, I could have the minstrels strike up a Ghebite dance."

Just for a moment he thought he read something in her face beneath the teasing, a need. Perhaps she wanted him to step away from everyone else to be with her and her alone. He hesitated, surprised by how much he wanted to believe this. Shaking his head in disbelief, he chastised his weakness.

A formal mask settled over Imoshen's face. Twice he had rejected her before the Beatific whom he was sure was listening in on their conversation. He suddenly wanted to recall his hasty words but Imoshen was already moving gracefully aside. Only he had seen her quickly veiled disappointment, only he knew the hurt she hid as she stepped lightly to join the others.

Or did he? Perhaps he was just a lust-crazed fool projecting these finer feelings on a manipulative Dhamfeer. He craved her, yet he knew she was his by necessity not by her own choice. True, she had agreed to bond with him when he publicly claimed her. But what real choice had she had?

Imoshen took several steps from the table, not really aware of where she was heading. Only pride made her approach a group on the dance floor. Unshed tears stung her eyes.

The General had not seen the malicious gleam in the Beatific's gaze. That was good, she told herself, at least now she knew where she stood.

"T'Imoshen?"

It was Cariah. Imoshen's heart sank. Had she seen General Tulkhan reject her? Imoshen turned to face the woman's contemptuous gaze but found in it understanding instead.

"The Ghebites want to start a fresh dance circle," Cariah said, slipping an arm through Imoshen's. "And I need another female to make up the numbers."

"Then how can I refuse?" Imoshen replied with a grateful smile. "When the rest of the Keldon nobles arrive we will have the numbers for the formal dances." And more tempers to soothe. But she did not add this.

Cariah met her eyes, a rueful smile lighting her face. "The Keld can be quick to take insult."

Imoshen blinked. Had Cariah simply anticipated her, or did she have a little of the T'En gift for skimming thoughts? There was nothing in her expression to suggest it was anything more than a lucky guess.

"True, they can be touchy," Imoshen said, "but then the Ghebites are so good at giving unintended slights."

A chuckle escaped Cariah.

Imoshen slowed her step before they joined the circle. Instinct told her to trust this woman. "Cariah, I am all alone with no one to guide me in court protocol. Will you help me ease the transition of power? I need to find common ground for the Keld and the Ghebites."

She saw her request had surprised Cariah, who hesitated midstep, then continued smoothly, "Commander Jacolm, your partner."

It appeared to be an unfortunate choice. The man's heavy black brows drew down, making it clear he would have preferred Cariah's company. Imoshen's stomach clenched, yet another rejection. Then she turned to see Cariah take her place in the dance circle with her father, Lord Fairban.

Cariah's answer had been to act on her request.

When the music started Cariah caught Imoshen's eye and for the first time since the Aayel's death, Imoshen did not feel cast adrift. Then the dance swept them apart as they circled their partners before moving to the next. If Cariah was prepared to do her part, Imoshen must do hers. As they changed partners she determined to be charming.

Tulkhan watched Imoshen take Lord Fairban's hand. The top of the man's grey head came up to Imoshen's chin, but Tulkhan could tell she was charming him with a word, a teasing smile. When she moved away to join the women who circled the men, Lord Fairban's eyes followed her.

"That is another of their tricks." The Beatific gestured briefly to the dance floor. "When they choose, the T'En can be delightful companions. The males make notoriously good lovers. But it is said they can only know true release in each other's arms. Of course, with the women's vow of celibacy, that is impossible."

Tulkhan was aware of the Beatific sipping her wine thoughtfully, though his gaze never left Imoshen.

"Discarding her vows of celibacy does not seem to trouble Imoshen," the Beatific observed casually.

Tulkhan snorted. He could not believe he was having this conversation with the leader of the T'En Church. In his own country there were no females in the Church hierarchy and the priests were celibate. Recalling the earthy Harvest Festival at Imoshen's Stronghold, something told him celibacy was not a prerequisite for the priesthood in Fair Isle.

Did the Beatific have her choice of lovers? Turning to study her mature, sensual beauty, he could well believe she did.

Imoshen laughed and his gaze was drawn irresistibly back to her. She looked over the heads of those around her to him and met his eyes. He realized she was willing him to share her amusement. An unexpected longing took him. He wanted to share her quick understanding, to know they had a special affinity.

The path he'd chosen would be a difficult one, but he would not relinquish Fair Isle and Imoshen at any price. If she were at his side and they were truly united in purpose, then it was not an impossible dream. He could have it all. He could hold Fair Isle and savor Imoshen's willing companionship.

Second wife's son, second best, supplanted heir. He desperately wanted the supremacy of Fair Isle. And Imoshen was the key. Politically, he had to take her to his bed, but gut-deep he knew he would have to have her even if it were political suicide.

What was he thinking?

If the Beatific was to be believed, a True-man could not even satisfy a female Dhamfeer. And he had arranged to marry the last pure T'En female in a "bonding" ceremony which would make her his equal in the eyes of the law, a law she had maneuvered him into recognizing. Yet he was not fool enough to let his lust rule his head. He did not doubt Imoshen's devotion to Fair Isle, it was her commitment to him he doubted.

Perhaps she was merely buying time for Reothe to rebuild his forces. Unlike her pragmatic acceptance of him, Imoshen had discarded a life of celibacy to take Reothe as her betrothed. Cold suspicion shook Tulkhan. Were the last two T'En in league against him?

The dance finished and Imoshen returned to the seat on Tulkhan's right.

Her smile faltered when she met his eyes. "What is it, General?"

Her hand lifted to touch his arm but he recoiled. She had used just such a touch to pluck the image of his mother's death from his mind and use it against him. The old woman had died of the fever, alone and uncared for, while he was on campaign. As a woman past child-bearing age she had been worthless in the eyes of Ghebite society, yet even now her lonely death stung him. "Don't touch me!"

Imoshen's expression hardened into a beautiful mask. Once again she was that alien, unknowable creature, the Dhamfeer.

Pulling her hand away from the coppery flesh of Tulkhan's arm, Imoshen clasped her fingers tightly beneath the table, hiding her tension. She didn't need to touch the General to read his emotions. At this moment the Ghebite feared and hated her.

Why?

She detected a slight movement to his left. The Beatific was devouring the succulent white meat of a roasted bird with dainty but decisive bites. Immediately, Imoshen knew this woman had been planting seeds of doubt, poisoning Tulkhan's mind.

Drawing a quick breath, Imoshen searched for a neutral topic of conversation to restore communication. "With Lord Fairban's arrival, we can expect to see the rest of the Keld soon. It would be best to hold off awarding your men their estates until the nobles are here to witness the ceremony."

Tulkhan's wary eyes met hers.

She lifted a hand to deny any ulterior motive. It was simply good politics to assuage the older nobility's feelings when investing new nobility.

"Very well," Tulkhan conceded. "We'll give them a week."

Imoshen had to be satisfied with that. He had said *we*, not *I*. Once they were bonded and Tulkhan lay naked in her arms, she knew there would be no cause for mistrust. How could there be when they shared their bodies and their minds?

Beckoned by Wharrd, Tulkhan left her. She watched as he spoke with his bone-setter. Both men wore the dark breeches and boots of the Ghebite soldier. Tulkhan favored a red velvet thigh-length shirt. A heavy belt, worked with gold filigree inlaid with niello, was slung low on his narrow hips. He wore his thick, straight hair loose on his shoulders, while two long plaits threaded with small gold beads fell from his temples. By old empire standards, he wore too much vibrant color and too much gold ornamentation, yet he looked utterly at ease in his barbarian splendor, dwarfing and over-whelming the more soberly dressed males of T'Diemn.

"The General struts like a peacock, yet he puts our men to shame," the Beatific remarked.

Startled, Imoshen met her eyes.

"I must be growing used to the Ghebite love of display," Imoshen said to fill the silence. Alone with the Beatific, now was her chance to find the woman's Key. Other than healing, Imoshen's gifts were weak. The Aayel had been good at reading people to discover their secret fears and desires, but though Imoshen had attempted this many times, it was only on first meeting General Tulkhan that she had successfully plucked the Key image of his dying mother from his mind.

Since coming to the palace, she had been forced to de-velop her ability to read people. Every day, she soothed tem-pers and assuaged hurt feelings. Everyone had a weakness, everyone could be reached.

Imoshen offered to refill the Beatific's wineglass. "A toast to preserving the dignity of Fair Isle's women," she said, then filled her own.

They exchanged looks across the rims of the glasses. At least in this they understood each other.

Imoshen savored her wine. "Signing the document was an important step, but every day in subtle ways they grind us down. It will be a long battle, I fear."

"A battle we must win." The Beatific put down her glass.

Imoshen placed her hand over the other woman's. "I need your help in this." But when she gently probed for the Beatific's Key, she discovered the woman's mind was sealed against her. Not only that, but she was very much aware of Imoshen's attempt to trawl her thoughts.

"Remove your hand!" The Beatific enunciated each word individually. "In the old empire that would have been unpardonable!"

Heat flooded Imoshen's cheeks. None of the palace servants or guildmasters had been aware of her subtle mental touch. "Forgive me, I—"

"Indeed?" True-woman eyes narrowed. Then the Beatific smiled, but it was hard and patronizing. "It seems I must forgive you, for how could you know better? Your parents deliberately kept you in ignorance of your T'En heritage. If you had been born in the Age of Consolidation, when you were ten one of the pure T'En would have been nominated as your mentor. This T'En would have trained you in your obligations to Fair Isle, preparing you to take the Vow of Expiation at seventeen. But there was no one who could—"

"The Aayel could have."

"No. She too was untrained. When T'Obazim went to her parents offering to mentor her, they broke with tradition and refused. He appealed to the Church. For two years it went through different appeals, with a final submission to the Empress. But before she could give her decision, Obazim went rogue, demanding the girl be given into his care against her family's wishes. The Tractarians hunted him down and he was stoned."

"I know. The Aayel told me." Imoshen shuddered, recalling how her great-aunt had described witnessing, at twelve, the rogue T'En's death. The Aayel had lived the rest of her life in the shadow of that memory. Imoshen had not forgotten her great-aunt's ambiguous comments about the Church's motivations either. "The Aayel told me that T'Obazim captured her mind so that she experienced his death with him."

The Beatific looked grim. "That was cruel. Did the Aayel also tell you that Reothe's parents approached her to mentor him? No? She turned them down. Shortly after that they committed ritual suicide."

"I never understood how they could abandon him."

The Beatific looked upon her with cruel pity. "I believe they could not face the terrible grief of building a Tower of Tears for Reothe."

"No." The denial was instinctive. "Reothe has served

Fair Isle on the high seas and here at home. He had the love of the Empress, some say T'Ysanna's love too. With the protection of the Empress and her heir he would never have been declared rogue. Not that he would ever go . . ." Under the Beatific's frank gaze Imoshen ran down.

"Your great-aunt was investigated but exonerated of any responsibility for the deaths of Reothe's parents."

"I did not know." Imoshen was shocked.

"How could you? Your parents refused to admit your T'En nature. Before you turned ten my predecessor asked that you be gifted to the Church, but your parents refused."

Imoshen was glad. It would have been terrifying to have been cast adrift at so young an age in a great building like the Basilica, surrounded by unfriendly True-men and women. Poor Reothe. On the death of his parents, the Empress had become his guardian and he had been thrown on the tender mercies of the royal court.

"I see you are troubled." The Beatific deliberately covered Imoshen's hand with hers.

Fighting a sense of entrapment, Imoshen understood that the Beatific felt secure enough in her defenses against the T'En gifts to touch her.

"Let me advise you, Imoshen. You find yourself in an invidious position, forced to accept this Ghebite General as your bond-partner, forced to host this parody of a royal court. I know palace protocol and I have the experience of nearly seven years as Beatific behind me. I was the youngest person ever to be awarded this office. I can advise you."

"I must admit I am out of my depth." Imoshen felt relieved when the woman released her hand. She resisted the impulse to rub away the imprint from her fingers. It would not hurt to appear to accept the Beatific's offer. There was much she could learn from this woman. "I thank you for your offer."

The Beatific smiled like a contented cat, and Imoshen knew she must walk a dangerous path if she did not want to become the mouse.

Imoshen's fingers stroked the cover reverently. "So this is the oldest book in the palace library?"

"The T'En Codex of the Seasons." The Keeper of the Knowledge undid the clasp.

"Beautiful," Imoshen whispered. She marveled at the workmanship, but it was not what she wanted. She had not dared to tell the Keeper she needed information on how her T'En ancestors controlled their gifts; instead she had asked to see the rarest and oldest books in the library, hoping they would contain what she needed.

"But it is not the original. That was destroyed in the revolt of sixty-four when the palace library burned. We lost much during the Age of Tribulation." The Keeper shook his head sadly. "This reproduction is a labor of love. Each page is made of a wafer-thin sheet of wood. The words are incised with a delicate touch, and each drawing is a work of art. See how the phases of the moon are illustrated, two small moon cycles to each large one, and the twin full moons on the season cusps. Perfect *En*.

"There is a page for each season and its ritual celebration is described here. See the two full moons of autumn's cusp, and the instructions for the Harvest Feast?" He turned several pages. "And here is midwinter—small full moon, large new moon—and the blessing for the new year."

"T'Imoshen?" A plasterer appeared at the library door, her clothes dusted with white powder. "The Masterbuilder would speak with you in the Age of Tribulation portrait gallery."

Imoshen sighed. Brief though their reign of terror had been, Gharavan's Ghebite soldiers had done much damage. They had taken particular pleasure in defacing the portraits of her ancestors and right now the gallery was in the process of being restored. She thanked the Keeper and followed the plasterer.

The palace was a warren of wings, stairs that led nowhere, even rooms within rooms. It was built on the site of the original palace, which had been burned to the ground. This was when Imoshen the First's very own T'Elegos had been lost to posterity. Imoshen felt its loss keenly. How she longed to read the history of the T'En journey from their homeland and the trials of subduing Fair Isle. The T'Elegos had been written by her namesake in the autumn of thirty-one, just before she died, and unlike the Codex of the Seasons, it could not be replaced.

"T'Imoshen." The Masterbuilder held a branch of candles, which Imoshen thought odd since it was only late afternoon. Tools lay discarded in the empty passage and the smell of fresh sawdust was the only evidence of the workers.

"This way. I thought the proportions of the gallery strange," the craftsman said. "Your ancestors were great ones for building. Sometimes they pulled down the work of the previous generation, sometimes they just built over things. When we removed the damaged wainscotting, we discovered this."

He paused before a dark passage. Musty, stale air greeted Imoshen. The candles flickered.

"A secret passage." She smiled with delight. The palace was supposed to be riddled with secret passages but she had never seen one. "Where does it lead?"

"I'll not go in there." He handed her the candles. "Anything that old has the taint of the pure T'En, if you'll pardon my plain speaking."

Without another word he left. Imoshen peered into the darkness, her heart racing with excitement. Lifting the candles high she ducked her head to enter.

Tulkhan opened the door, letting Lord Fairban and his daughters enter. Several of his commanders vied none too subtly for the attention of the young women.

"And this room has just been restored. Unfortunately my half-brother's men could not resist looting it." Looking around he could just imagine his countrymen's reaction. Late afternoon sunlight poured through a single circular window in the center of a dome. The room needed no more illumination, for every surface other than the black marble floor was golden. The dome was lined with beaten gold, impressed with intricate designs. The walls alternated gold-embossed panels with amber-lined niches which housed statuettes of pure gold.

No wonder the Ghebites had been consumed with gold lust. Fair Isle was renowned for its wealth, but this was almost beyond belief.

"Imoshen insisted the room be restored precisely as it had been," Tulkhan said.

Lord Fairban nodded. "Very proper. After all, it is part of Fair Isle's heritage, even if it is in bad taste."

Wharrd caught Tulkhan's eye.

"Bad taste?" Tulkhan asked.

Cariah nodded seriously. "This whole wing dates from the Age of Consolidation." She picked up a golden statuette of a couple amorously entwined and held it up for them to see. "Too much decoration and ostentatious display, particularly during the middle period. In this, the Age of Discernment, we can look back on these rooms and their contents and appreciate them for their heritage, if not their artistic value."

Tulkhan's men looked stunned. He hid a smile.

When Cariah returned the statuette to its niche, Harholfe stroked its sensuous curves. The T'En claimed to be highly civilized, yet they thought nothing of portraying the naked body in varying stages of arousal. The Ghebites found the sculptures and frescoes disconcerting to say the least, and if Tulkhan was not careful Harholfe would make some crude joke and offend Lord Fairban.

"Let me show you the old portrait gallery," Tulkhan said quickly. "The actual portraits are away being repaired and repainted while the gallery itself is being restored."

A little crow of delight escaped Imoshen. The steps had led into a passage, down more stairs, and finally through an archway out of the secret passage into a long corridor. Someone had wedged the panel open with a broken tile. Imoshen left it wedged in place, not trusting that the old mechanism would still work.

Raising the branch of candles high, she turned a full circle, marveling. With its rendered stonework and buttresses, this corridor must date from the Age of Tribulation. She was standing in history. This had to be part of the palace rebuilt after Sardonyx's revolt.

She closed her eyes, inhaling air redolent with great age, and opened her T'En senses to the past. If only she could have lived in a time when the T'En were revered and accepted.

She opened her eyes and gasped with surprise as a boy wandered past her, his hands extended like a blind man's. He was pure T'En, and though he stood nearly as tall as her, she knew by his smooth chin that he was not yet in his teens.

"Who are you?"

He didn't hear her. Perhaps he was deaf and mute as well as blind.

Imoshen hesitated. There were no pure T'En left, save herself and Reothe. Perhaps someone had hidden the birth of a T'En baby, keeping him locked away in these passages. How cruel. Who would feed and care for him?

Imoshen stopped as the boy turned toward her, hands extended. Eyes blindly staring, he felt his way along the corridor. Gently, because she did not wish to frighten him, she lifted one hand to touch his arm, but her fingers passed right through him.

Imoshen gasped, sagging against the wall. The boy's ghost continued on. Was she watching some long-lost ancestor or someone from the future? His clothing was the simple breeches and shirt which could have been worn at any time in the last six hundred years.

Imoshen took a deep breath to slow her heart rate. Though he was blind the boy seemed to know his way around. He appeared to be counting the archways until he found the one he wanted. There he ran his fingers over the stonework, triggering a hidden panel which opened onto a narrow stairwell. He wedged the panel open with one shoe and went down the steps.

When Imoshen looked down to see a real shoe wedged in the doorway, dusty with age, she realized she was seeing an event from the past. She hurried down the steps, anxious not to lose the boy. They were below ground now, in the catacombs deep under the original palace. She shivered with awe as the branch of candles illuminated the wall niches where the dead lay, their forms carved on the stone lids of their coffins.

As a child she had listened to her older brother and sister whispering stories late at night of how T'Sardonyx had gone slowly mad. According to legend he would creep into the palace catacombs to lie on the marble slab destined for his body and commune with the Parakletos.

Imoshen shuddered. After the revolt it had become mandatory to burn the bodies of pure T'En and sprinkle their ashes on the sacred garden of their estates.

The boy felt his way until he missed a step and fell forward onto the ground where he lay weeping softly in despair. Imoshen hastened to his side but her words of comfort could not reach him.

Setting the branch of candles down she sat back on her heels. Maybe if she could reach him with her gift. Lifting her face she closed her eyes and concentrated. This was not a healing so she did not know how to begin, only that she must seek the familiar tension of the T'En powers. The metallic taste settled on her tongue, making her mouth water.

Ready to attempt contact she opened her eyes and saw the ceiling of the catacomb's barrel vault above her. Dismay made her groan. Staring down from above were paintings of the T'En martyrs, the Paragian Guard who had died in the service of Imoshen the First.

Men and woman stood dressed in early T'En armor, their hands on their sword hilts. Their garnet eyes were alive in their pale faces as they watched her. These were the T'En warriors who had given their lives to secure Fair Isle, the ones Imoshen the First had commemorated in the T'Elegos.

When Imoshen read the high T'En name of the one directly above her she recognized him as one of the Parakletos. She bit her tongue, wishing the words unthought. Unbidden the words of the death-summoning came into her mind and she resisted saying them aloud. But it appeared that thinking them was enough, for a great oppression settled on her, filling her ears with roaring silence so that the sound of her ragged breathing faded.

The Parakletos were coming for her soul. Panic engulfed her, froze her to the spot. Her heart faltered. Time stretched. She could sense them approaching, eager and vindictive, questing for her. Soon they would fix on her and when they did she would not escape.

She must act now. Propelled by terror she broke the trance and, with one last frantic effort broke free of her paralysis. Snatching the candles, she ran. The flames winked out one by one so that by the time she reached the top of the stairs only one candle remained alight. She tripped and fell full length on the stone, skinning her hands. The last candle rolled away, winking out.

Fear stung her. Suddenly the candle flared back to life and she scrambled to her feet, careful to shield its precious light.

Panting with fear, Imoshen found she could hardly think. Which way?

"Why aren't your people at work?" Tulkhan asked the Masterbuilder who stood in the entrance to the old portrait gallery.

"We uncovered an old passage. T'Imoshen is exploring it."

There was a buzz of excitement from Tulkhan's companions.

"Show me," the General ordered.

The craftsman led them down the gallery and stopped before a dark opening to light a branch of candles, handing it to Tulkhan. "You will need this."

"Let's go!" Lord Fairban's youngest daughter exclaimed.

"There might be ancient treasures," Cariah whispered.

"More gold?" Jacolm asked, nudging Harholfe.

"No." Cariah laughed. "Much more valuable. Lost knowledge."

Jacolm frowned.

"Wait, General," Lord Fairban began, but Tulkhan had already ducked his head and stepped into the steep stairwell. He heard the others following him, complaining that there was only one branch of candles.

The steps led into a passage, down more stairs then through an archway.

"General, I—" Lord Fairban began, then pointed, muttering something in high T'En.

Suddenly light appeared at the end of a long corridor. The single candle's flame illuminated only the figure's face so that it appeared as though a disembodied T'En wraith was gliding toward them.

"Imoshen?" Tulkhan called uncertainly. She looked up. For a fleeting instant he read terror in her features.

Then she smiled and raised her voice. "I did not expect all of you to come looking for me."

"I was showing Lord Fairban and his daughters the restoration," Tulkhan explained, holding Imoshen's eyes for a moment longer than was necessary. The candle flame trembled and he took them from her. The metal was so cold it burned his skin. Something had terrified Imoshen. "What is it?"

"Yes. Where have we come out?" Cariah asked.

"Only a long passage and old storerooms. Nothing more exciting than rat holes, I'm afraid," Imoshen shrugged. She took the unlit candles and lit them, handing them out. "Take these. We don't want to break our necks going up the stairs."

"Yes, but what about exploring?" Jacolm asked.

"Nothing but rat holes and musty storerooms," Imoshen repeated. Tulkhan felt a thickness in his head. "Let's go."

A sense of urgency filled him. He wanted to get out of the confined passages.

Muttering under their breath the others turned and shuffled up the stairs, their candles casting myriad shadows on the walls. Imoshen right behind him, Tulkhan found himself stepping out of the secret stair into the portrait gallery where the Masterbuilder waited for them.

Imoshen turned to him. "You were right. Nothing of interest lies down there. Replace the panel and continue the restoration." She collected the candles from the others. "It must be time for the evening meal."

Linking an arm with Cariah, she began to stroll out of the gallery. The others followed her.

The Masterbuilder met Tulkhan's eyes and his expression was grim. Tulkhan handed the other candle branch to him, then hurried after his men. Imoshen's words carried to the General as he caught up. To his ear her tone was a trifle forced.

"Lady Cariah, I wish to speak with you about tomorrow's entertainments. General Tulkhan and I will be doing a tour of the hospices and Halls of Learning. Will you be hostess in my place?"

"I would be honored."

Imoshen stopped at the foot of the stairs. "Oh, I forgot. There is one more thing I must tell the builder. You go on ahead."

Tulkhan strode up the stairs with the others, ignoring their idle chatter. Something felt wrong. He paused on the landing. Wharrd met his eyes.

Tulkhan shook his head. "Go on, I'll catch up."

Careful to move quietly, he retraced his steps to the entrance of the portrait gallery where he could observe Imoshen unseen. She stood halfway along the gallery in a pool of light, holding the candles high so the Masterbuilder could position the new wainscotting.

"Make certain it is sealed. And tell your people there was nothing but old storerooms." Imoshen ordered.

The builder replaced the skirting board then left by the servants' exit.

Tulkhan waited in the shadows until Imoshen walked past him, her head down in thought.

"Imo—"

She spun, a knife appearing in her hand, her eyes glittering dangerously.

Tulkhan lifted both hands in a placating gesture and she slowly dropped her guard.

"What was down there?" he asked.

"Nothing."

"Since when were you frightened of nothing?"

A half-smile lifted Imoshen's lips. The flames reflected in her garnet eyes and their flickering points of light lured Tulkhan to forget everything.

"Well?" he prodded, refusing to be distracted.

"Nothing . . ." Imoshen whispered. As she replaced the knife under her tabard, he caught a glimpse of pale thigh. "Nothing you want to know about."

"Let me be the judge of that."

She shook her head silently.

"Imoshen?"

"This is better left undisturbed. Trust me."

"How can I trust you when you hide things from me?"

"In this you must trust me." She took his arm and he felt the insidious lure of her T'En gifts urging him to lose himself in her alien beauty, to trust, to devote himself to her.

He flicked free of her touch. "Don't play your T'En riddles on me!"

"I did not mean to." Her lids flickered down, hiding her eyes. "I only—"

"You seek to hide something. I will have it from you or I will tear the wainscotting off and go down there myself!"

"Fool!" Imoshen hissed. "Nothing could induce me to go down to the catacombs again. If I can't face them how can you?"

"Who?"

She laughed bitterly. "I see you will not let it rest. Very well, General. Far below us lie the catacombs of the original palace built over six hundred years ago. There the bodies of the pure T'En were laid to rest to protect them from grave robbers. You would be surprised how much gold the left sixth finger of a pure T'En would bring on the mainland. But I digress. Among them lie the legendary Paragian Guard, who after death became the Parakletos." Her voice dropped on that word, growing breathy and urgent. "I used to think them nothing but legend, pretty stories peddled by the Church to keep the farmer folk in need of their services, but you were there in the cooper's house with me when they came at my call. And tonight . . . tonight I barely escaped them. They sought me, hungry for—"

"I don't want to hear."

She stepped away, giving him an ironic obeisance. "I will see you at dinner, General."

Imoshen removed one candle from the branch and gave it to Tulkhan, leaving him alone in the dark with a single candle and his doubts.

Five

IMOSHEN WINCED AS Kalleen did her hair. Apart from the one day they had spent touring the Halls of Learning and the hospices, the General had avoided her, occupying himself with riding the outlying reaches of T'Diemn with his engineers.

". . . and who's to say what those Ghebite commanders will do once they get their hands on their new estates?" Kalleen asked, pulling vigorously on Imoshen's hair. "Only yesterday when I was in the market I overheard an old farming couple. Talk about moan! You'd think they faced the loss of their livelihood and their rights when the new Ghebite lord takes over the estate where they live. I told them it is a noble's obligation to protect their people. At least, a noble *should* take care of. . . ." Kalleen frowned. "Who knows what these newly ennobled Ghebite lordlings will do."

Imoshen twisted from the waist to face Kalleen. Naturally the country folk would fear their new Ghebite overlords.

Kalleen was experimenting with an ornate old empire hairstyle. She gave a sharp tug. "Hold still. I can't get your plaits straight!"

"I'd be just as happy with a simple twin-plait."

"Well I wouldn't. You should hear them in the servants' wing, talking about how I turn you out."

"What do you care? Tomorrow you'll be Lady Kalleen of Windhaven with a maid of your own." Imoshen grinned.

Kalleen was still acting as her maid because she had refused to relinquish the position. "I hope she snaps at you and pulls your hair—"

"I never . . ." Kalleen looked horrified, then contrite.

Imoshen smiled, holding her gaze in the mirror. "Only a little. But you've given me an idea. I must go to the library to check on early T'En investitures of nobility."

General Tulkhan came to his feet impatiently. The performance had been obscure at best.

Imoshen appeared at his elbow. "General?"

He didn't remember her sitting through that interminable monologue yet here she was, ready to be sociable. He should take a leaf from her book.

"Walk with me?" Sliding her arm through his, she guided him towards the windows overlooking the courtyard.

Tulkhan frowned at the many small panes of glass. One good swing with an axe and the enemy would be into the vulnerable underbelly of the palace. It was typical of the T'En to build for effect, not defense. Still, it could be argued that if the enemy had made it as far as this private courtyard, the palace was already taken.

Then he realized that this was the courtyard where he had seen his half-brother's men burning books, destroying everything that offended the Ghebite Church's dictates.

"Was the performance so bad?" Imoshen teased.

Tulkhan schooled his features and tried for a light tone. "I've never heard such a long death-bed eulogy. I thought the poor fellow would never die."

"I'll have you know that was one of the great tragic moments of T'En literature, portrayed by one of the greatest actors of the Thespers' Guild."

But he could tell she sympathized with him. For a rare moment they were alone, removed from the Keldon nobles and Ghebite commanders in the room. He took her hands in his—her palms were soft, unlike his callused skin. She was representative of her people, of the old empire grown complacent. Contempt flashed through him. He had walked the original fortified walls of old T'Diemn and seen where new buildings had weakened the walls' defenses. Too much peace made a people weak.

When Imoshen looked up he could not fail to recognize the intelligence in her sharp eyes.

"Yes?" he prompted.

"Tomorrow you reward your faithful men with lands and titles."

"There's no need for more delay. The nobles from the Keldon Highlands have arrived."

"There is some resentment—"

He snorted. His men had been restrained in claiming their rights as the conquering army. He opened his mouth to say as much but Imoshen anticipated him, or did she skim the surface of his thoughts? Frustration fired him because he could not tell.

"True, to the victor go the spoils, but we are trying to smooth the transition, General." A rueful smile tugged at Imoshen's mouth. "I have been researching T'En investiture. I think it would help reconcile the people if we were to use the old formalities when your people are ennobled."

"Good idea," he agreed swiftly, her talk of research reminding him of something. "I heard some tale of the river being diverted from its original bed, past the walls of old T'Diemn. Surely it is only a tale?"

"Not at all. T'Diemn used to flood, so T'Imoshen the Third's brother diverted the River Diemn to run on three sides of the walls of old T'Diemn. Scholars have pinpointed the day he became Emperor as the beginning of the Age of Consolidation. Much was achieved. They built the locks, and the port facilities were improved by dredging." Imoshen's bright eyes fixed on him. "But that's enough of a history lesson. If I have your agreement I'll organize the investiture and ensure the ribbons of office and deeds are ready."

"A T'En investiture rather than a Ghebite?" Tulkhan muttered. "Very well. I would have the men swear on something other than my faithless half-brother's kingship."

Imoshen's fingers tightened on his arm. "Honor knows no nationality, General. Your men serve you because they respect you."

Her words warmed him. "You are right, a man's honor knows no—"

"You mistake me," Imoshen corrected gently. "The full quote translates as, *'Honor knows no nationality or gender.'*"

"I should have known," Tulkhan muttered. "You never miss a chance to remind me that you are heir to so much T'En culture and learning. Divert the River Diemn? What next, flying machines?"

Imoshen's eyes flashed as she opened her mouth to reply.

"General Tulkhan?" a voice interrupted. "Would you take a partner for a game of chance?"

He forced himself to turn. "Sahorrd, what game?"

The tall commander grinned. "Something T'En. Lady Cariah is organizing the teams. Jacolm and I agreed to play as long as the loser does not have to compose a rhyming couplet!"

Tulkhan had to smile. He remembered his own dismay when he had discovered the variety of forfeits T'En games entailed.

Imoshen slid her hand from Tulkhan's and lowered her voice. "Join the game. I have much to do before the investiture. When I find the plans for old T'Diemn I will show you. Locks, river dredging, and more besides. Then mock the T'En if you can!"

She gave him the formal bow of leave-taking which was at variance with the challenge still ringing in his ears. He'd noticed Imoshen was always careful to accord him the honor of his uncrowned position when others were there to observe, but she was quick enough to forget it when it suited her.

Tulkhan eased his toes in his new formal boots and grimaced. He'd had no time to break them in before the investiture of his commanders. A small boy fidgeted as he waited at Tulkhan's side with the first of the ribbons and deeds on a silver platter.

Imoshen signaled for silence in the great hall. She was dressed in white samite, the heavy silk threaded with silver. A small skullcap of woven silver formed a net over her hair, ending in delicate chains tipped with rubies which caught the light as she turned her head. A single ruby hung in the middle of her forehead, echoing the color of her eyes.

As she lifted her arms the pale winter sun broke free from the clouds and a finger of multicolored light pierced the nearest stained-glass windows illuminating her. The air was heavy with expectancy; everyone who could wrangle a place from guildmaster to noble, soldier to entertainer, and T'En Church official was present.

The small boy by Tulkhan's side made a strangled sound in his throat then sneezed loudly. An agonized blush flooded his smooth cheeks. As Tulkhan gave the boy's shoulder a re-assuring squeeze he met Imoshen's smiling, sympathetic eyes.

First to be ennobled and receive his estates was Wharrd. That Imoshen had given this honor to the veteran bone-setter pleased Tulkhan.

Wharrd strode up the two steps onto the dais. Even on the same level he had to look up to Imoshen. Tulkhan waited ready to receive the oaths of service. There had been time for only a quick explanation of Imoshen's new part in the cere-mony. Pomp and ceremony had always bored him and his thoughts returned to the challenge of making T'Diemn im-pregnable, until Imoshen's words pierced his abstraction.

". . . are being raised to this position so that you may serve the people of Fair Isle." Imoshen went on to list the re-quirement of his position. Tulkhan listened with growing surprise as Wharrd promised to rebuild his estates' hospices and schools where none would be turned away.

Now he understood Imoshen's maneuverings. Anger stirred in him. The last princess of the T'En was educating her barbarian conquerors.

Wharrd signed his name to the land deed. Unlike many of Tulkhan's men, the bone-setter could read and write. In the Ghebite army, verbal oaths were sworn before witnesses for few of his commanders could read and write more than their own names. At this rate a farmer who worked a noble's fields would have more education that his liege lord.

Once the document was signed, Imoshen picked up the three ribbons. She draped the first across Wharrd's chest.

"In accepting the ribbons of office you accept what they signify. White for purity of purpose, to serve selflessly." Her voice carried throughout the silent great hall as she draped the red across his chest. "Red to signify the blood you have shed and are willing to shed to protect your people and all the people of Fair Isle." When she took the third ribbon, a black one, Wharrd looked at Tulkhan questioningly. But the General had no answers.

Imoshen continued inexorably. "Black to signify death which comes to us all, no matter how high we are raised in this world."

Wharrd's mouth opened in silent surprise. Ghebite ceremonies did not mingle a man's inevitable death with promotion. This was a strangely humbling ceremony.

"Now give your oath to the General," Imoshen whispered to Wharrd who was fingering the three ribbons.

Recollecting himself, the veteran stepped sideways to drop to one knee before Tulkhan. He gave his oath of allegiance then hesitated, on impulse Tulkhan drew his sword, folding both hands over the hilt.

Wharrd touched the embossed seal-ring Tulkhan wore on his right hand. It carried his father's symbol of a rearing stallion. There were only two such seal-rings in existence and the other was on King Gharavan's hand.

Following Ghebite custom Wharrd kissed the sword's blade. When the man rose, Tulkhan could tell it had been the right gesture.

Kalleen stepped forward as Wharrd retreated. Tulkhan cursed as he realized Imoshen meant to reward Kalleen before his men. They would see it as a calculated insult. Tulkhan caught Imoshen's eye sending a silent warning. Two bright spots of color blazed in her pale cheeks.

"Step forward, Kalleen," Imoshen said. "Your personal bravery saved my life when King Gharavan would have had me executed. Before everyone here I acknowledge that debt and honor my obligation. If you or yours are ever in need I can be called upon."

Then to Tulkhan's surprise Imoshen repeated exactly the same formalities with the farm girl who had once been her maid. In the eyes of T'En Church Law and state, Kalleen was Wharrd's equal.

A finger of multicolored sunlight moved across the dais as the ceremony wore on. At last Tulkhan sheathed his sword and offered Imoshen his arm. She took it, casting him a swift glance to gauge his mood. He smiled grimly. She had orchestrated the contents of the oaths for her own purposes. The war swords had been sheathed when she surrendered her Stronghold to him but the battle continued, only now she fenced with protocol.

Much later, as the tables were removed and the musicians in the high gallery began a tune, Imoshen looked for Kalleen.

"My lady?" Lifting one hand to her forehead, Imoshen gave her former maid the correct T'En obeisance for an equal, then straightened to meet Kalleen's gaze.

Excitement and disbelief danced in the girl's hazel eyes. Imoshen smiled. It was like one of the epic poems. The farm girl had risen to become Imoshen's maid and then Lady Kalleen of Windhaven. Kalleen's delight, however, was tinged with sadness. On arriving in T'Diemn, Imoshen had sent a rider to contact Kalleen's family to share her good fortune, but they had been unable to find anyone who had survived the invasion.

The little maid flushed, stroking her ribbons and the seal. "If only my family had lived."

"We are each other's family now." Imoshen hugged her.

Kalleen bit her bottom lip and brushed angrily at her tears, giving a shaky laugh. "No one in the servants' wing will talk to me after this. They'll think I've grown too grand!"

"What do you care? From this day forward you'll live in the nobles' wing." Imoshen took her hand. "You must promise never to tell me what I *want* to hear, only what I *need* to hear."

"Spoken like a true Empress," Cariah said as she approached.

"Now you are telling me what I want to hear!" Imoshen chided.

Cariah laughed.

Imoshen grew serious. "I'm concerned about the General's lord commanders. They will need guidance when they take control of their new estates."

"Why not appoint a Church official to advise them?" Cariah suggested.

Imoshen frowned. She did not want to give the Beatific any more power than she already had.

Tulkhan watched Imoshen's expressive face.

Lord Commander Jacolm nudged his General's elbow. The man's heavy eyebrows lifted suggestively and he gestured toward the trio. "A woman like that redhead makes a man glad he's not a eunuch!"

Tulkhan grinned.

"It's the Lady Kalleen for me," Wharrd admitted. "It has been since we first took the Stronghold. I'd have married her without the Windhaven estate. As far as I'm concerned, our bonding day can't come too soon."

He said this with such relish that Tulkhan smiled. If only he could look on his and Imoshen's approaching bonding with the same unreserved enthusiasm.

"I usually like them with a bit of meat on their bones," Jacolm remarked as if he were talking about a brood mare. "But that head of red hair promises a fire a man could warm himself in!"

Wharrd chuckled. "Beware you don't get burnt!"

But Jacolm insisted he knew how to handle himself and their banter turned crude even by soldiers' standards.

Tulkhan studied the three women. Little Kalleen was a lively thing and the Keldon noblewoman was a beauty, but neither of them stirred him like Imoshen did. He wondered what three such disparate women could possibly be talking about. Clothes, men?

At that moment Imoshen and her two companions turned and glanced in Tulkhan's direction, their expressions disconcertingly intense.

Imoshen's perceptive eyes met his and he felt a tug. Tulkhan found himself walking towards her, wending his way through the revelers.

Imoshen stepped away from her companions, her gaze fixed eagerly on his face. "General, I want to speak with you about your lord commanders. They—"

"In time," Tulkhan said. He turned to the redheaded beauty. "Lady Cariah, you know my finest swordsman, now Lord Commander Jacolm." As he suspected, the man lost no time asking her to dance.

Wharrd then spirited Kalleen away, which left Tulkhan alone with Imoshen. It was the outcome he had both wanted and dreaded.

Imoshen's hand closed on his forearm and he responded immediately. Surely she must feel it too. Was he an open book to her, so transparent that she laughed at his hopeless, helpless craving for her?

He slipped her hand from his arm, intending to put her away from him, but instead he pulled her closer. "Let's dance."

"I thought you said you couldn't dance."

"I lied."

Imoshen laughed and shook her head.

He stared down into her upturned face, feeling a smile on his own lips. If only he was a soldier and she a camp-follower. He would simply lead her away to a secluded corner and seduce her. Already he felt his body reacting to the thought of her uninhibited response.

Tulkhan knew Imoshen wanted him. He could feel it now in the way she melded against him. How could he wait until their official bonding day, when his body raged at him to claim her?

"Only five weeks till midwinter," Imoshen whispered.

Furious, Tulkhan stepped back. She had done it again, skimmed the surface of his mind.

"What is it?" Imoshen hissed, intently watching his face.

She looked so innocent. Was she unaware of what she was doing even as she invaded his privacy? "I have no time for this. I have matter of state to deal with."

Imoshen watched the General stalk off, his back stiff with tension. What possessed him? Here she was trying to help his men assume control of their estates and he would not even listen to her.

Annoyance flashed through her, but it was tinged with regret. She had to admit she'd felt a heady rush of desire when he held her. And now her body thrummed with a need that made his rejection of her doubly cruel.

Impatience drove Imoshen as she glided across the empty anteroom to the door of Lady Cariah's private bedchamber. She scratched on the door tang, her comb sending its delicate clear notes ahead of her as she pushed the door open. "Are you feeling better, Cariah?"

It was nearly time for the noon meal and Cariah had retreated to her bedroom, complaining of a headache. Imoshen hated to disturb her, but already a day had passed since they had spoken of the General's lord commanders and their new estates. Imoshen was concerned for her people. They needed someone to explain their customs and beliefs to their new overlords.

"I have a tisane for your headache, Cariah," Imoshen called.

The woman's tousled head thrust through the bed curtain and she laughed. "A moment."

Cariah reappeared a few heartbeats later, slipping through the closed bed curtains dressed in a simple undershift.

"I made you this." Imoshen offered the prepared draught.

"The Aayel always gave it to me if my head ached. And I wanted a chance to talk to you about—"

"Wait. We must be alone." Cariah put the tisane aside and raised her voice. "Jacolm, get dressed. I will see you tonight."

Imoshen's face stung with heat as she realized she had interrupted their lovemaking. There was a muttering and rustling from inside the closed bed before the man climbed out, still lacing his breeches.

"Cariah, I—" Imoshen began, but the woman gestured for her to be silent.

Jacolm glared at the pair of them from under his heavy black brows, then recollected himself and made a perfunctory Ghebite bow before hastening away, shirt tails flapping.

When the bedchamber's door closed Imoshen sank onto a seat, covering her hot face. "Oh, Cariah!"

But she was laughing. "Hush. The wait will make our joining all the sweeter tonight. Jacolm is oversure of himself anyway." She sat down next to Imoshen, taking her hand.

Imoshen felt the warmth of Cariah's skin, noting the sensual flush in her face. Without wishing to, she registered the subtle change in Cariah's scent. She glowed with life and passion, making Imoshen feel inexperienced and gauche.

"I am sorry." Imoshen could not meet Cariah's knowing eyes. "I forget the ways of the high court. I only visited once. For the most part my family kept me secluded even from my own relatives."

Cariah squeezed her hand. "You wanted to speak with me?"

Imoshen bit her lip. Naturally Cariah did not want to hear how she lived as an outcast. The T'En traits Cariah bore were subtle enough to let her pass amongst True-people. A flash of resentment stung Imoshen but she put it aside as unworthy.

"Of course," she said. "I have been thinking and I don't want to send priests as advisors with the new lord commanders. I'd prefer to send lesser masters from the Halls of Learning," Imoshen smiled, "as interpreters."

Cariah laughed. "How could they refuse?"

Relief flooded Imoshen. "Then I must select the most tactful of lesser masters for these posts." Again she hesitated. "The General might not believe this necessary but if it is already arranged—"

"Use my chamber to interview them."

"And then?" Tulkhan asked, his voice as cold as the ache in his chest.

The little man flinched at his tone but continued. "As she has done for several days, your betrothed entered Lady Cariah's bedchamber. The princess was in there from one bell to next. After she left three men slipped away."

Tulkhan winced. The thought of Imoshen's quicksilver passion being ignited by another man's touch was abhorrent to him. Nausea roiled in his belly. He could not believe it of Imoshen.

"Leave me!" He dismissed the man, a trusted Ghebite who had spied for him on other occasions.

Tulkhan rose, knowing he should be preparing for the hunt. It was one of the few pastimes both his own people and the Keld enjoyed.

He knew he should expose Imoshen, yet . . . With bitter insight he understood he feared to confront her because he did not want to discover the truth.

"He comes," Kalleen hissed, then hurried past Imoshen, disappearing around the corner.

Imoshen straightened, her heart thumping. This was ridiculous, but every time she had tried to speak with the General he had been too busy to see her, forcing her to rely on this little ruse. She had asked Kalleen to watch for him and warn her of his approach.

She heard the thud of his booted feet. Good, he was alone. It was much harder to speak when his commanders were with him.

Imoshen stepped out of the doorway and collided with him as he rounded the bend.

"General?" she gasped.

"Imoshen." He accorded her a cold welcome.

She ignored it and plunged on. "I'm glad to see you. I promised to show you the plans of old T'Diemn. Come this way."

For a moment he looked blank, then he nodded grimly. It did not bode well. She was hoping that if she lured him away from his men and showed him something of interest, his manner might change.

They made their way to the palace library in silence. As the Keeper of the Knowledge scurried off to get documents, Imoshen cleared her throat.

"I'm glad you asked me about the River Diemn. I was able to hunt up . . . Ah, here it is." She thanked the old man and spread the large tome on the table, opening it at the right page. "T'Diemn was originally built on several hills, with the river skirting their bases. Every second year it would flood with much loss of life and livelihood. T'Imoshen the Third's younger brother diverted the river, taming it so that a small portion flowed through T'Diemn, bringing fresh water, while the rest flowed around the city walls. That was when he designed the palace's ornamental lake—"

"The lake is not natural?"

"No. Neither is the forest. Then he improved on the original design of old T'Diemn, which was laid out in concentric circles with streets running directly from the south to the north gates and from east to west. He built the ring-road within the city walls so that reinforcements could be rushed to the defenses if the walls were breached. He designed the fortified bridge we crossed to enter the old part of the city."

"That bridge? But you can't see daylight for the shops and homes."

Imoshen nodded. "They are more recent additions. Originally it was built for defense. You know where the bridge ends in an L-shaped bay before the outer and inner gates of the old city? If attackers managed to cross the river, they would be pinned there, by the defenders on the gate towers."

Tulkhan shook his head. It never ceased to amaze him. The T'En had created great feats of engineering and built fortifications more sophisticated than any he had come across elsewhere, then they had let it all go in their complacency.

"I thought you might like to see this." Imoshen's smile warmed him.

Still, he was surprised when she opened the last pages of the book to reveal intricate faded drawings of complex machines.

"Imoshen the Third's brother attempted to build a flying machine. But he couldn't get a person off the ground for more than a gliding flight. And this—"

"Some kind of siege machine?" Tulkhan studied the drawing. "The wheels would only work over smooth ground. The metal plates would stop defenders from setting fire to the machine, and protect the men crouching behind it, but it would be very heavy, hard to transport."

"I don't think it was ever built. Reothe lived at the beginning of the Age of Consolidation, when Fair Isle no longer faced internal threat. The T'En—"

"What did you call him?"

Imoshen stopped, took a slow breath, and raised her eyes to his. "He was T'Reothe the Builder. My kinsman Reothe was named after him, just as I was named after T'Imoshen the First. They are common names."

Tulkhan stared at Imoshen. It was always there between them, her cultural heritage, her T'En traits, and her broken vows to the rebel leader.

"Here." She pushed the old volume aside and selected another, opening it. "If you follow the family lines you will see the same names turn up again and again."

Tulkhan stared at the indecipherable High T'En script. He couldn't even read the dates. "More chicken scrawl."

"It is our family tree. Here is Reothe the Builder, my ancestor." Imoshen smiled as she turned the page. "He heralded the Age of Consolidation, which lasted around three hundred years. The Age of Discernment began with the stoning of the last rogue T'En a hundred years ago." She turned two more pages, tracing the line, and pointed. "Here I am. Imoshen the Last."

Then she blinked in dismay, as if hearing her words.

But Tulkhan had no sympathy for her. He found it hard to credit what he saw before him, six hundred and sixteen years of births, deaths, and marriages. The written records of his Ghebite royal family went back only as far as his grand-father's time. Before that the histories and traditions of his monadic people had been remembered by the tale-teller of each tribe.

Nomads did not carry heavy items like books. It was only when Tulkan's father was a boy and his people moved into the palace of their first conquered kingdom that they begun to write down their oral histories, transposing a tent culture to a more permanent home. Strictly translated they were not house-lines, as he had told Imoshen, but tent-lines.

He felt her watching him now and tapped the page. "In this book you have six hundred years of blood lines, father to son?"

Imoshen laughed. "You're thinking like a Ghebite, General. This book itself was begun four hundred years ago at the dawn of the Age of Consolidation, transcribed from fragmentary older records. But yes, it traces the royal line from empress to daughter for just over six hundred years. The males only inherited, as in Reothe the Builder's case, if the empress had no daughters. Emperor Reothe bonded with his second cousin to consolidate the royal line."

His eager gaze returned to the book of war machines. "I want to study this, particularly the parts referring to the defense of old T'Diemn. Have it sent to my bedchamber."

"You can take it now if you like."

"No. I'm late already. I'm supposed to view the Passing Out Parade at the Halls of Learning." He could not hide his reluctance and saw her answering smile. "Could you trans-late those passages for me by tomorrow afternoon?"

"I can't. I have an engagement."

Anger hardened in him. An engagement with her lover? "Break it."

"I can't. Like you I have responsiblities."

Was Imoshen betraying him? True, their vows had not been given, only a commitment to marry. Tulkhan frowned. Broken vows meant nothing to Imoshen.

"I must go." He stepped back.

"I will have the book sent to your bedchamber."

He wanted to tell her to bring it herself or not to bother. But he did not know what he would say if he opened his mouth, so he strode out in silence, leaving Imoshen looking confused and hurt.

How could she look so innocent if she was taking lovers? If his men believed he was being cuckolded, they would expect him to salvage his honor with her death.

Six

IMOSHEN STOOD BY the balcony door, tracing the lines of the beveled glass. Tulkhan had not returned from the Halls of Learning. It was one of those clear, crystal cold nights of winter and she longed to escape the confines of the palace. Opening the door she stepped out onto the balcony which overlooked the city. She wished she was an apprentice being granted her year's service, or a student of the Halls of Learning accepting her passing out for the year.

Soon it would be Midwinter's Day, and the scholars had agreed the historic bonding of the last T'En princess with the Ghebite General would determine the end of the Age of Discernment and the dawn of a new age.

She had spoken only yesterday with the engravers at the royal mint to approve the design of the new coin they were producing to celebrate her bonding with the General. Resentment warmed Imoshen, for Tulkhan had been too busy to accompany her.

She turned, resting her elbows on the balustrade to survey the palace, its windows blazing in the night, its towers dark against the stars. A movement on Sard's Tower caught Imoshen's attention. She frowned. It looked for all the world like the Keeper of the Knowledge struggling with a bulky object. Curious, she darted inside and retraced her steps to the long gallery before making her way to the tower.

By the time she found him, the old man had set up his

equipment and was seated on a stool with a blanket wrapped around him, studying the stars.

"I thought so!" Imoshen crowed. "Can I have a look?"

He stood up with good grace.

She took his place, peering through the enlarged farseer. "Amazing. I can see patterns on the large moon!"

"Mountains."

"You think so?" She studied it.

"Take a look at the smaller moon. I think the concentric circles are artificial constructions, primitive fortifications perhaps."

Imoshen was not so sure. She pivoted the instrument to study the spires and rooftops of T'Diemn, looking for something she could recognize. A gasp escaped her. "What's that glow? Something's burning."

Leaving the farseer on its tripod, Imoshen went to the edge of the tower, and the Keeper of the Knowledge joined her there.

"Look." She pointed. "A building's burning within the old city walls."

"That's the Caper Night bonfire in the main square of the Halls of Learning. They'll celebrate, paint their faces, and don their masks. Before long they'll be roaming the streets looking for mischief."

"I've heard they fight pitched battles in the streets."

He laughed. "Last Caper Night they caught one of the guildmasters, stripped his shoes off him, and painted his feet bright red. There's no harm in it. There's always been rivalry between the Greater and Lesser Guilds and the students from the Halls of Learning—battles with brooms and paint brushes, guild symbols painted out, white-washed hall ensigns. Why, I remember the Caper Night I graduated . . ."

Someone suddenly burst through the open trapdoor.

"Imoshen!" Kalleen snapped. "I've searched half the palace for you. There's a messenger waiting and it's urgent."

"Urgent?" Imoshen's stomach clenched in fear for the General.

Imoshen's soft slippers flew over the polished wood of

the palace corridors. When she opened the door to her chamber and saw a familiar face, relief flooded her. "Healer Rifkin. What is it?"

"T'Imoshen," he greeted her formally. "Dockside Hospice calls on your healing expertise this night."

As patron of the Healing Guild she had an obligation to help, but it went deeper than that. She could not turn away someone in need. "Kalleen, my cloak."

It was lucky Kalleen did not know T'Diemn well enough to realize how dangerous it was to venture out on Caper Night. No harm was meant, but decent folk stayed indoors and barred their windows.

The girl returned with both their cloaks.

"Don't bother with yours. No need for you to have a late night too," Imoshen told her. "The healer will guide me."

Kalleen looked dubious.

"I'm sure I saw Wharrd at the entertainments. Why don't you rescue him from the dueling poets?"

Kalleen smiled. "You should take an escort."

Tulkhan had said the same, offering her the use of his Elite Guard. But she did not want Ghebites hounding her every step. "I know. I'll take Crawen, she's at my door tonight."

General Tulkhan was glad he had missed the dueling poets. Their ability to wrest a rhyme from thin air and wield it like a weapon unnerved him.

Kalleen and Wharrd were occupied in the far end of the room but he saw no sign of Imoshen.

Cariah swept forward to greet him. Instinctively he bristled. Was this woman providing a cloak for Imoshen's infidelity?

"General Tulkhan. Would you like to hear a reading?"

Anything but that. He never knew when the thing was over. According to the T'En nobles, the pauses were as significant as the words. Clapping was considered gauche and finger-clicking your approval in the wrong place brought embarrassed silence.

"Where is Imoshen?"

"I don't know. She was here a little while ago."

Nicely evasive. Perhaps she was with a lover right now. A rush of fury coursed through his veins like liquid fire. He stalked past Cariah to join Wharrd and Kalleen.

"Where is Imoshen, Kalleen?" Would the girl lie too?

Kalleen stiffened, responding to his unspoken threat. "Doing what she must to serve her people."

"Just what does that mean?"

"She's been called away to help in a healing. She may be on her way back already."

"Back?" Tulkhan barked.

"From the hospice."

Tulkhan's body tightened. He'd heard all about the excesses of tonight's celebrations from students at the Halls of Learning. "Imoshen has left the palace on Caper Night?"

Kalleen nodded. "A healer from the Dockside Hospice came for her. Where are you going?"

"To escort her back to the palace."

Tulkhan didn't want a large group to accompany him, that would attract attention. Luckily Sahorrd and Jacolm were nearby and they caught his signal, following him out of the chamber. As he left he was aware of many curious eyes watching them.

Kalleen bustled after him like an officious little bird. "T'Imoshen is—"

"Out alone on Caper Night!" He seized Kalleen's small wrist. "What if someone with a grudge against the old empire catches her?"

"She took one of her Stronghold Guard," Kalleen said.

"Who?"

"Crawen."

Tulkhan cursed. "Stay here. If Imoshen returns alone, tell her I would speak with her." He did not wait for an answer.

·   ·   ·

A single candle burned in the hospice's empty foyer, symbol-izing welcome for anyone in need.

Imoshen left her cloak on the peg. "I don't know how long I'll be, Crawen. The kitchen is down the back."

Rifkin lit a second candle and led Imoshen up a set of narrow stairs to a small door. He scratched softly before standing aside.

Imoshen entered a small room, closing the door after her. A candle burned beside numerous glass jars of dried or pulverized herbs stacked on a narrow table. The room's only occupant was a beggar, huddled on the low bed. She smiled to herself. It seemed right to her that the highest should be called upon to serve the lowest. It represented all that was good in the old empire.

Imoshen lifted the candle and approached. "How may I help you, grandfather?"

The beggar looked up and stood slowly, seemed to keep rising so that he grew taller than her. Suddenly the hood fell back from his beggar's cloak to reveal silver hair, sharp cheekbones, and T'En eyes.

"It is I who have come to help you, Imoshen."

"Reothe." The word was torn from her. Her breath caught in her throat. The healer had betrayed her. No. Rifkin had probably seen what she first saw—a lowly beggar.

The rebel leader stepped forward, his eyes glittering in the shuddering candle flame. Every time she saw Reothe she was reminded of her own T'En traits and of how the True-people must see her. Tonight he was austere, inspired by an inner fire like a legendary warrior from the T'Elegos.

"I heard that the General has claimed Fair Isle and forced you to accept him," Reothe whispered tensely. "These Ghebites have no respect for T'En women, for any women. Come away with me, Imoshen."

"I can't."

He caught her free hand, bringing it to his lips. She felt the warm rush of his breath on her knuckles.

"Why not? You refused me last time for fear of pointless bloodshed. But now that the General has been betrayed by his own people, he cannot call on the resources of Gheeaba to resist us. Join with me tonight and we will sweep him from the island by midsummer and fulfill our betrothal oaths."

"No."

"Think, Imoshen. Joined we could be so much more than apart," Reothe pressed.

His intensity made her body resonate. Imoshen's sight blurred with the visions conjured by his words. Fair Isle restored, Reothe as her bond-partner. Suddenly it seemed not just possible but the only viable alternative.

"Don't do that!" Imoshen hissed, twisting her hand free from his. "I won't let you use your gift to influence me. My decisions must be based on cold hard logic!"

His garnet eyes narrowed. "Logic tells me General Tulkhan cannot hold Fair Isle without Gheeaba's support. Logic tells me that the people will unite behind us, if we are united. Would you side with a Ghebite invader against your own blood kin?"

Imoshen's head reeled.

He caught her hands in his. "We can do it, Imoshen. Come to me, this very night."

Reothe's fierce will illuminated his features. She could drown in his eyes. Worse, she suspected he was right.

"The Ghebites were in the wrong to invade our peaceful island," Reothe whispered, his thumbs caressing the back of her hands. "They stole our future. This spring we should have made our bonding vows before your family."

Imoshen moaned.

Tulkhan strode the streets of T'Diemn with Wharrd and Jacolm on either side of him and Sahorrd at his back carrying a single lantern. The larger thoroughfares were lit at night but down by the docks it would be pitch-black.

When they crossed the fortified bridge the shops and

homes perched precariously on its sides were closed and boarded shut. Their upper storys almost met in places, excluding the light of the waning larger moon.

"Dockside Hospice is in the roughest area, catering to the merchant sailors," Wharrd said as they passed under the bridge tower. "There have been strangers in the dockside taverns asking questions about you, General. Gharavan won't rest—"

"You think this could be my half-brother's idea of revenge? But why? He has the rest of the Ghebite Empire. All I took was Fair Isle—"

"And his pride. You humbled him before his followers, sent him packing!"

Tulkhan shook his head. He still had trouble reconciling his half-brother's actions with the boy he'd known.

Just as they came out of the tower's archway, a dozen apprentices ran around the corner, jostling them. They laughed, waving torches and paint-sodden brooms. Six young people danced around Tulkhan, singing a doggerel which praised the Silversmith Guild and made jest of others. Paint slopped on his boots.

Suddenly another band of apprentices in different masks charged out of the laneway opposite, waving brooms and brushes. Tulkhan lost sight of his men in the crush.

Laughing faces with masks awry tried to stop him but he forged through, anxiety for Imoshen gnawing at him.

Once free of the crowd Tulkhan broke into a run, one hand on his sword hilt to steady it. Having studied T'Diemn's layout, he knew he could find the hospice. His long legs ate up the distance. He ran down narrow lanes towards the smell of the docks. Several more turns and he saw the open hospice door, dimly lit by its welcoming candle.

Perhaps he was wrong and this was a perfectly innocent call for Imoshen's healing gift. He heard laughter coming from behind a closed door and marched down the hall. Throwing the door open he found Crawen and a healer sharing warmed wine and hot cakes. So much for guarding Imoshen.

"Where is T'Imoshen? I am here to escort her back to the palace."

"This way." The healer hurriedly put his wine aside.

Crawen came to her feet with a hand on her sword hilt.

"Don't bother," Tulkhan snapped.

"Don't speak of my family!" Imoshen closed her eyes to shut out Reothe. With a great effort of will she pulled her hands free of his. "Don't speak of what might have been. The Ghebites are here. Fair Isle has surrendered. What you ask would bring more war to our people, Reothe, more bloodshed."

"Death in a righteous cause. It would not be the first time the T'En gave their lives. The Paragian Guard laid down their lives to secure Fair Isle. Surely we—"

"Reothe?" Imoshen clutched his arm. She longed to tell him of her meeting with the Parakletos in the catacombs but was too ashamed to reveal her cowardice. "I performed the ceremony for the dead. I called the Parakletos. When they came, they. . . ." She shuddered. "They are not the benevolent creatures the Church claims."

He laughed grimly. "Cruel bluff. They have no power in this world except when summoned, and then the words bind them. But you and I must be especially wary. The barriers between this world and the next are much frailer for pure T'En and the Parakletos are malicious creatures. They will try to drag you into death's shadow with them." A haunted expression shadowed his eyes. "I've walked with them in their world and—"

"But I thought no one could escape?"

He focused on her and fear prickled across her skin because his eyes were windows to death's shadow, then the moment passed and he smiled grimly. "Most of what the Church teaches is distorted or simply not true."

"I suspected but . . . I can't believe—"

"Believe me. There is much I could show you." His

voice grew intimate. "No one can give you what I can, Imoshen."

She could not break his gaze.

"This is our chance. We can influence events this very night. My rebels are hidden in the city awaiting orders. I could get us into the palace, into the Ghebite General's bed-chamber. By dawn he would be dead, his Elite Guard captured, and the palace would be ours." Visionary fervor illuminated Reothe. "Think of it, Imoshen. With General Tulkhan gone—"

"But that is murder!"

A short bark of laughter escaped him. "And this is war!"

Imoshen turned away, her mind filled with a vision of Tulkhan murdered in his bed. His blood staining the sheets, all his dreams and passion extinguished.

Tulkhan! Even now she thought she heard his voice. Startled, she darted to the door and swung it open. She was amazed to see him approaching with the healer. The General's broad shoulders filled the hall almost as if he had been conjured by her thoughts of him.

Rifkin greeted her. "Your escort is here, T'Imoshen. How fares the beggar?"

Her heart sank.

Already, Rifkin and Tulkhan were waiting for her to step aside and let them enter. The General thrust the door open, peering past her into the room. Shadows clung to the far corners but no one hid in them.

"Gone." Imoshen's throat was so dry she could hardly speak. She gestured to the table with its equipment. "I was just cleaning up."

Tulkhan thrust past her and strode to the window, looking down.

"He wouldn't leave that way," Rifkin said. "There's only the river below. He must have slipped out while I was with Crawen."

Imoshen realized Reothe had leapt into the river. In his beggar's guise, he could only have carried a knife, and for all he knew Tulkhan might have been accompanied by a dozen of his Elite Guard.

"Then you are free to go?" Tulkhan rounded on Imoshen. She shuddered. Would she ever be free of the expectation of others? Tulkhan thrust the candle into her hand, drawing her out of the room.

Imoshen shielded the flame as they sped down the steps to the entry where Crawen awaited them. Tulkhan barely allowed Imoshen time to bid the healer goodbye before they were out on the street, their single candle casting a small pool of light.

"I don't know what possessed you to come out alone on this night of all nights, Imoshen!"

"I had to answer a call for help."

"What if it had been a hoax?"

"I took my own guard. Besides, I trusted Healer Rifkin." It would not do to reveal how her trust had been betrayed.

Armed men with a lantern rounded the bend. Imoshen tensed.

"General!" Wharrd exclaimed. "You should have waited for us."

Raucous laughter echoed down the street, drowning out the General's reply.

"Here." Tulkhan snatched the candle from Imoshen, pinching it out. He took Sahorrd's lantern and thrust it into her hands. "You carry the lantern to free up his sword arm. Come."

Shame stung Imoshen. The meaning was clear. Tulkhan thought she was useless, capable only of carrying a lantern, and he ignored Crawen altogether.

As several laughing apprentices charged around the lower end of the street, Tulkhan grabbed Imoshen's free arm. Dragging her with him, he strode up the hill.

The General moved so swiftly that she was hard pressed to keep up with him. Only the taverns and less reputable teahouses were open, their lights and patrons spilling into the streets. Snatches of song and laughter rang out on the

otherwise quiet night air. Imoshen lost track of where she
was. Then suddenly she recognized a shop front. Two more
bends and they would approach the fortified bridge. Soon
they would be in the better lit streets of old T'Diemn.

But before they could enter the bridge, a dozen or more
revelers, students by their cloaks and masks, charged out of
the laneway and cannoned into them.

"Run, Imoshen!" Tulkhan sprinted ahead.

She ran at his heels, half stumbling to keep up, the
lantern swinging awkwardly. From the shouts and laughter
behind them she could tell the others had been waylaid.
They were probably having their faces or some other part of
their anatomy painted.

Imoshen's booted heels struck the bridge's stonework
with a hollow sound which echoed off the closed shop faces.
She took the chance to catch her breath as Tulkhan slowed
to a fast walk. A group of masked revelers left the dark entrance of a shop and wove drunkenly towards them.

When Tulkhan cursed, the revelers' appearance suddenly turned sinister. The General caught her arm again.
She'd have bruises tomorrow. She strained to see the lower
half of the faces of those approaching them.

Three steps, two . . .

The rasp of weapons being drawn made her mouth go
dry with fear. Tulkhan's sword was already in his hand. She
didn't remember him drawing it.

"Get behind me." He shoved her into a doorway.

Imoshen unsheathed her knife, but it didn't have the
reach of a sword and if she risked a throw she would leave
herself disarmed.

A figure lunged. Tulkhan parried and struck. There was
no time for finesse. Laughing, mocking masks were set above
grim tight mouths, their attackers danced around them ready
to deal death.

Imoshen feinted with the knife at an overeager attacker,
then lashed out with the lantern to defend Tulkhan's unpro-
tected left side. The attacker's return blow tore the lantern

from her fingers, and oil spilt, carrying little blue flames which clung greedily to the man's clothes.

"*Fire!*" Imoshen screamed. That was guaranteed to bring the bridge's inhabitants out. The shops and houses were built of wood. "Fire!"

Tulkhan kicked the nearest attacker in the thigh and darted out into the center of the bridge.

"Now, Imoshen, run!"

Her line of sight free, Imoshen threw her knife at the third attacker. Tulkhan's assailant rolled to his feet. Imoshen tore off her cloak and flung it in his face before fleeing. The heavy thump of Tulkhan's boots told her he was at her heels.

Down the length of the dark bridge she ran, heading for the pool of light beyond. Moonlight illuminated the courtyard, and beyond that a narrow passage led through the gates of old T'Diemn—the perfect place to be ambushed and killed.

Skidding on the cobbles, she looked back the way they'd come. Their attackers were closing in, and behind them were more figures. She could not tell if they were the other Ghebites or students.

"Quickly!" Tulkhan dragged her into the dark passage. Running blind she paced him, heading for the crescent of light at the end of the tunnel.

They hesitated under the streetlight. Before them were two paths, one into the ring-road which ran around inside the walls of the old city, the other into a square where she could see glimpses of jostling bodies and torches.

"This way." She made for the square.

"No, Imoshen."

She ignored him.

Frustration and fear surged through Tulkhan. He didn't want to enter a square full of potential killers, masked enemies who hid behind laughing young men and women. In that crowd someone could get close enough to sink a knife between his ribs or Imoshen's. But their attackers had almost caught up and his own men were nowhere in sight. Cursing Imoshen's impulsiveness, he charged after her.

She entered the square three long strides ahead of him,

her silver hair glistening in the torchlight. Without missing a beat, she broke into a line of dancers and tore a burning torch from someone's hand.

A torch was as good a weapon as any under the circumstances. Tulkhan shouldered a youth aside and darted forward to join her, also grabbing a torch. But the dancers had stopped. They stared and pointed as Imoshen leapt onto the rim of the fountain.

"T'Imoshen!" Their cry went up.

Joyously the revelers surged forward, dragging Tulkhan with them. Arms reached for Imoshen. As he watched, they hoisted her off the fountain and carried her high on their shoulders. Cheering, leaping people surrounded him. He saw Imoshen search the crowd for him and waved. She returned his signal.

"To the palace!" Imoshen gestured, pointing the torch.

Relief washed over Tulkhan as the crowd took up her cry. They broke into stirring song and surged through the streets towards the palace.

Studying the merry faces around him, the General strained to identify the masks of their attackers. Pressed amidst the bodies, he could not maneuver, could not even use his drawn sword, but at least they were being escorted back to safety. The singing, laughing crowd carried Imoshen right across the square and deposited her on the steps of the palace, where they began another song, linking arms and swaying.

Tulkhan forced his way to the steps to join her. He saw surprise register on the unmasked faces of those nearest. When Imoshen drew him to her side and kissed his cheek, several tore off their masks and tossed them in the air.

Imoshen lifted the burning torch high, her voice meant only for him. "Smile, General. Caper Night has saved your life."

"My life wouldn't have been at risk if you hadn't gone off alone!"

She tossed her head, eyes glittering with anger.

He wanted to shake her, to make her realize how close they had come to death.

"You should trust me, General."

Light spilled down the steps of the palace as the doors to the grand entrance opened. Imoshen slipped away from Tulkhan to speak with the bewildered servants then returned to his side, taking his hand in hers. "Sing, General. They are singing of their love for Fair Isle."

He realized what he thought was a rowdy drinking song was really a tribute to their homeland. By the time they were ready to repeat the chorus he was able to join in.

The last notes drifted away and the crowd looked up at them expectantly. Tulkhan tensed. Crowds were unpredictable animals. Then he heard noises behind him.

"Right on time," Imoshen muttered with relief. She dropped his hand to direct the servants. "Go out into the crowd and serve them."

Tulkhan watched as a long line of servants moved past him, carrying trays laden with food. The revelers cheered and waited with surprising courtesy to be served. The people of Fair Isle would never cease to amaze him.

"We can slip away now," Imoshen whispered, retreating up the steps.

He followed. Their footsteps echoed in the marbled foyer. Drawing her into an antechamber he snatched the torch from her hand and flung it in the unlit fireplace along with his. "If those attackers on the bridge weren't waiting for us, who were they after?"

"Thieves looking for a party of drunken revelers?" She shrugged. "How should I know? What does it matter? We escaped them."

The wood in the grate burst into flame. Imoshen stepped closer and extended her hands towards the warmth. A shudder gripped her.

Of course she was cold. She had thrown her cloak at their attackers to buy him time. She had faced death at his side. Admiration stirred in Tulkhan. He knew of no Ghebite woman who would have stood by him like that, or would have been capable of thinking on her feet as she had. "Imoshen?"

When she looked up at him her eyes were haunted by the danger she had passed through. Before he could stop himself Tulkhan opened his arms and she went to him. True, she was Dhamfeer, the people's revered T'En, but she was also Imoshen and not half as sure of herself as she pretended.

"Imoshen? You are unhurt?"

With a half-sob she turned her face into his neck, her hot breath and damp tears warming his throat.

"How many times must I walk through death's shadow?" she whispered.

Tulkhan had no answer.

Tulkhan had joined with the Keldon nobles and Ghebites to watch a T'En display match. It was staged in a hall built specifically for this purpose with tiered seats on three sides.

The match was yet another example of T'En absurdity, played with flat paddles and rag balls and following obscure rules. There was much explanation of points taken and loud guffaws from his own men who found the niceties of the game beyond them.

Tulkhan stiffened as Imoshen received a message from a servant. Was she leaving to go to her lover?

When she slipped away, Tulkhan decided he must discover the truth. His hand settled on his sword hilt as he stalked down the long gallery to the bedchamber wing. Imoshen was a distant figure ahead of him, sailing noiselessly through the fingers of afternoon sunlight which pierced the narrow windows. Even in this small connecting gallery the T'En had indulged their love of beauty. Lifelike paintings of vistas containing fantastic mythological figures filled each niche.

Imoshen entered the wing of bedchambers and he waited before following. If she was being unfaithful, he wanted to catch her in an incriminating situation, something she could not talk her way out of.

Heart pounding, he marched up the stairwell after her, dreading what he would discover, for he could not live with the dishonor of her betrayal. He would kill her and then himself.

As Imoshen entered Cariah's bedchamber, three young men turned to face her.

"I have their recommendations," Cariah said.

Imoshen took the letters, saying, "The post of interpreter will not be an easy one. The Ghebites—"

The door burst open, crashing against the wall. In the reverberating silence General Tulkhan stood in the entrance glowering, naked sword blade raised.

Imoshen's heart plunged. What was he doing here battle-ready, weapon in hand? Surely he had not imagined her in danger, not in the palace itself? Perhaps there was some heinous plot she knew nothing about. Imoshen's skin grew cold as she realized the door had been ripped off its hinges. Tulkhan must have thrown his whole body behind it, must have feared for her life.

The General observed the room's occupants then sheathed his sword. "What are you doing, Imoshen?"

"Interviewing prospective interpreters."

"In Lady Cariah's bedchamber?"

Foreseeing trouble, Imoshen turned to the young men. "Leave now. I will contact you."

One of them plucked his recommendation from her hands. "I was mistaken. I could not work with . . ." He glanced to Tulkhan then scurried out, followed by the others.

The General strode across to Imoshen taking the letters from her. While he frowned over them she cast Cariah a pleading look.

But Cariah tilted her head as the Basilica's bells rang. "Is that the half-hour bell already? I must go. I am late to meet Sahorrd."

"Sahorrd? I thought it was Jacolm?" General Tulkhan muttered, but Cariah had already departed.

"I can't keep track of her lovers," Imoshen said.

He sank onto the chair. "What are these are letters of recommendation for?"

"I was trying to find tactful interpreters to assist your lord commanders when they take over their estates."

"Is that what you have been doing these afternoons?" he demanded.

She hesitated, surprised by the urgency of his tone. "I did try to speak with you the night of their investiture, but—"

"Why didn't you tell me?"

She recognized the pain in his voice. As a healer her instinctive reaction was to offer comfort. She searched his upturned face. "Surely you did not think I was in danger here in the palace itself? Have you had word of a plot against my life?"

"A plot?"

"You burst in with your weapon drawn . . ."

He stifled a bitter laugh.

She stepped back unnerved. "I . . . I don't understand, General."

Cursing, he sprang to his feet and marched towards the door.

As Imoshen watched his departing back anger overrode her confusion, driving her tongue. "In the old empire we did not reward kindness with boorish behavior!"

He turned. "Is that how you see us? Barbarians who need nursemaids?"

"No!" The cry was out before she could stop it. "This was for my people as much as yours. Your men are loyal and skilled commanders but they are not like you."

"And what am I, Imoshen?"

Heart hammering, she dragged in a ragged breath. This was her chance. She had wanted to speak with him free of hangers-on and court protocol, but suddenly she found his intense dark gaze frightening.

"What am I to you, Imoshen?" he asked, striding back to search her face.

Resolutely she met his eyes. If there was going to be

anything between them it had to be built on honesty. When she spoke, her words sprang from a deep need to believe this was the truth; for if it wasn't, all her hopes and plans were laid on a foundation of shifting sand. Swallowing her trepidation she closed the distance between them. Splaying her hand across his chest, she said, "You are a fair and good True-man who seeks to do what is right for all of Fair Isle, not just for your own Ghebite soldiers."

Something like a groan escaped him as he caught her in his arms.

A rush of warmth filled Imoshen. She could feel his great heart hammering under her palm which was pinned against his chest. For a moment she wanted nothing more than to be held like this.

But Imoshen had to have answers. She pulled away. "Why have you been so cold to me, General? What aren't you telling me?"

His lips found hers, drowning her questions, drowning all coherent thought. Desire ignited her. She wanted to forget everything in this moment. Only this was real, this passion and this man.

She felt tears escape her closed lids and did not care. Everything weighed upon her—the resistance of the Keldon nobles and their unspoken condemnation of her. Then there was the knowledge that her every action was being watched by foreign ambassadors while they debated whether to support the rebel T'Reothe or the Ghebite general. Rights and wrongs did not bother these pragmatic brokers of power, only results. Yet she could bear all this if only she knew she had the General's trust.

As his lips covered hers, Imoshen gave herself up to the hunger of his kiss. She knew they should not be touching like this, not when they were to be bonded soon, but she needed to feel his desire for her. His hands cradled her head and his thumbs brushed her cheeks.

"You're crying?"

"No." She shook her head and would have pulled away,

but he caught her arm, making her wince. Her split-sleeve parted to reveal livid bruises.

"I hurt you last night?"

She shrugged, not meeting his eyes.

"Forgive me?" he asked, voice thick with emotion.

A laugh escaped Imoshen. "For what? How could I be so mean-spirited when you were only thinking of my safety?"

He shook his head, drawing back a little. "I judged you by Ghebite standards. I listened to evil advice."

"From the Beatific?" It was out before Imoshen could stop herself. When he pulled away sharply she ground her teeth in frustration.

"I told you to keep out of my head."

"I wasn't in your head! I have eyes. I can see and I'm not stupid, although your Ghebite men treat me as if I were!" She lifted trembling hands to her face, brushing the hated weak tears from her cheeks. "Oh, General, is there any hope for us?"

"Us?"

Imoshen faltered. "Fair Isle. The peace is so fragile. The Keld watch your men like hawks, looking for any slight, imagined or real. Your commanders seem to seek ways to flaunt their rise in status. A hundred times a day Cariah and I have to soothe ruffled feathers."

He snorted. "I have seen the way Cariah soothes ruffled feathers. Which of my commanders hasn't she bedded?"

"Peirs, I think. And Wharrd," Imoshen replied automatically, then wondered why Tulkhan glared at her.

"In Gheeaba a woman of good standing would never take a lover!"

"In Gheeaba a woman is the *property* of her father, husband, or son. No wonder she has no love for men!"

Tulkhan shook his head despairingly, but Imoshen thought she detected a faint gleam of amusement in his obsidian eyes.

"Ah, Imoshen, you have no idea!" he told her.

Relief warmed her but she stifled it, hardening her

resolve. To need his approval weakened her. "Then explain what I don't understand. Perhaps I don't know a great deal about your culture, but I can learn. To keep me in ignorance demeans us both!"

He sighed. "The Cadre would argue to keep a woman in ignorance is the only true kindness for she does not have the ability to cope with the same intellectual complexities as a man."

Imoshen laughed outright. "That Cadre is a prime example of his own argument. Because his mind is closed, he cannot see the Beatific for what she is. She sits in the Basilica and weaves her web of power!"

Tulkhan gave a snort of laughter then rubbed his chin ruefully, watching her intently.

"What?" Imoshen asked, feeling strangely lighthearted.

He shook his head, offering his arm in a formal gesture. "T'Imoshen?"

She laid her arm along his and closed her fingers over his hand. Regally, she inclined her head. "General Tulkhan?"

"I believe there is an entertainment being performed in the forecourt to welcome the newly arrived nobles and ambassadors from the Amirate," he said. "Our presence is expected."

"If we are lucky it will all be over before we get there," Imoshen whispered, falling into step with him. She darted a quick look up at him and caught his grin.

"You are terrible, Imoshen."

She sighed elaborately. "Yes. My mother despaired of me. She said I was too wild for the high court."

He squeezed her hand. "You will have to prove your mother wrong."

A little ball of sorrow formed inside Imoshen. It was true. She longed for her simple life at the Stronghold, now irrevocably lost. But she would have to succeed in the elaborate game of court life, for the fate of Fair Isle lay amidst its seething factions.

She frowned. Would Reothe dare to move against

Tulkhan without her support? Because of the formality of the old empire, she had not come to know Reothe as well as she now knew the General, but she had to acknowledge the powerful pull she felt towards him. They shared the same T'En heritage but the affinity went deeper than that. She feared it was intrinsic.

Seven

TULKHAN PUT ASIDE his plans for T'Diemn's defense, irritated by the scratching on the door. Damn these
palace servants with their little metal doorcombs,
creeping about in their silent slippers, obsequiously bowing
to him while smirking behind his back. "Enter."

Imoshen strode in and placed a sheaf of papers on his
desk. "I have selected fifteen interpreters for you to make the
final selection from."

Tulkhan was not convinced his men would accept the
advice of Fair Isle interpreters. He missed Wharrd's counsel.
Following custom, after bonding Kalleen and Wharrd had
left to visit their estates.

Every day Tulkhan watched Imoshen win over ambassadors from both the mainland and the archipelago, securing
her position. If only he could be certain of Imoshen's motivation.

Tulkhan read the top letter. The man could read and
write in three languages. The General fought a surge of despair because few of his commanders could do more than
sign their own names. If he foisted a Fair Isle scholar on
them they would be sure to take insult.

"You'll note I chose only men so as not to offend your
commanders," Imoshen said, eager to convince him but
Tulkhan looked up at her dubiously. "Believe me, General,
in all of Fair Isle you have no more loyal supporter!"

"For the good of Fair Isle," he said, his Ghebite features impassive.

"What? Yes, for the good of my people—and yours."

"And if you thought that T'Reothe stood a better chance of holding the island, would you throw your support behind him with as much ingenuity and vigor?"

She gasped, instant denial leaping to her lips, but he spoke quickly, overriding her.

"Think long and hard before you answer that, Imoshen," he warned, "because I can smell a lie!"

She swallowed, resentment flooding her.

"He was your betrothed," Tulkhan continued. "You broke your T'En Church vows of celibacy to—"

"I had given no vows of celibacy. I wasn't old enough!"

"It was expected." The General's expression was implacable. "You thought little enough of your honor to break your vow to your betrothed."

Fury consumed Imoshen. "You stood at the gates of my Stronghold with an army. You threatened to put my people to the sword. What would you like me to have done, sacrifice their souls for my personal honor?" She drew in a shaky breath. "I took the path of peace."

"So, from your lips I hear it. You support me out of necessity." He smiled grimly. "Do you wonder that I question your loyalty?"

"You twist my words," she snapped, holding his eyes. "Whatever my reasons, I stand at your side now. The worm of doubt is in you, General, not me."

When he did not respond she gave him the formal T'En obeisance and turned to go, sadness welling in her.

"I heard from Wharrd. He and Kalleen plan to be here for our bonding," Tulkhan said to her retreating back.

Imoshen hesitated then turned to face him. He sat sideways at the table, his long legs thrust out toward the fire. Even seated, he dominated the room and not simply with his size. It was the force of his personality.

Their bonding . . .

He was deliberately flaunting their imminent intimacy.

She felt her cheeks grow hot. It was impossible to hide her reaction when her skin was so fair. She saw his features tighten.

Daring him to comment, she held his gaze. The silence stretched. She sensed that he wanted something from her, but was unable to determine what.

Suddenly he pushed the letters back towards her. "Take these. When my men assume control of their estates I will not send your watchdogs with them."

Rejection made her stomach clench. She picked up the sheaf of papers, straightening them. "The farmer folk speak their own language."

"They'll find someone who can speak the trading tongue."

"But—"

"Enough!" He sprang to his feet, striding to the door. "My men would have nothing in common with your over-cultured scholars!"

Deeply troubled, Imoshen returned to her room and left the letters on her desk. If her judgment was wrong in this, how could she trust her instincts? A wave of despair swamped her. She needed Cariah's cool-headed counsel.

Heart thumping, Imoshen paused by the open doors of the crowded gaming salon. Slowing to a casual stroll, she wove through the tables.

Catching Cariah's eye, Imoshen used old empire signals to let her know that she wished to speak privately. With in-nate elegance Cariah made towards a door which led to the withdrawing room.

"Lady Cariah," Jacolm called. "Stay and give me good luck. Sahorrd and I are losing hand after hand."

"Later," Cariah answered as she joined Imoshen.

"Why doesn't he ask you to advise him on what cards to play? At least then he might win a game!" Imoshen mut-tered.

Cariah bit back a laugh. "Imoshen, you know he thinks the complexities of a card game too much for my feeble mind!"

"How can you bear it? Prove him wrong!"

Cariah's lips parted in a smile sensual as a cat's. "When I am ready. Not everything can be achieved by direct confrontation. Now, what troubles you?"

Through the withdrawing room window Imoshen could just make out the shapes of a formal garden with knee-high hedges and topiaried trees—a classic example of T'En order and formality.

Jacolm and Sahorrd laughed raucously, crowing their victory over a turn of the cards. The sound rubbed on Imoshen's raw nerves, fraying the edges of her control. She felt the T'En ability move in her, shifting like a restless, eager beast. It was more than she could bear.

"Do you fear your T'En heritage, Cariah?" she asked abruptly. "Failing—"

"Hush!" The woman closed the connecting door then returned.

A dim light filtered through the stained-glass window, illuminating Cariah's features as she spun to face Imoshen, her eyes luminous. "How can you speak of failure? Soon you will be bonded with General Tulkhan, soon you will be co-ruler of Fair Isle. You are on the brink of achieving everything. Why, you even carry his child."

"How did you know that?"

Cariah blinked. "Kalleen told me. Forgive me if—"

"Kalleen did not know."

"She suspected. So I . . ."

"You what?" Imoshen pressed.

Cariah silently lifted her hand and placed it palm down over Imoshen's flat belly.

"I felt the growing life," Cariah told her. "This child is historic . . ."

Imoshen covered Cariah's hand with her own and opened her T'En senses, willing herself to feel that same fragile life. Her heart rate lifted and that recognizable taste settled on her tongue, sharp enough to sting.

Cariah gasped, pulling her hand away.

"What?" Imoshen asked, seeing Cariah's startled expression. "You felt my T'En gifts?"

Cariah nodded. "I've never come across it so strongly before. But then you are the first pure T'En I've known. T'Reothe's voyages coincided with my times at court so I never met him. Though I did hear rumors." She shuddered. "You made my skin crawl."

Imoshen laughed. "If I don't cloak it, even General Tulkhan knows when I use my gift on him and he is pure Ghebite! I wanted to feel my child's life force stirring. Was I going about it the right way? Show me."

Cariah shook her head slowly. "I am not tutored in the gifts, anything I know I deduced myself." She caught Imoshen's hand and placed her palm open on her belly. "By accident I felt the life force moving in you when we touched."

A strange tension gripped Imoshen, a skin prickling awareness of . . . "You do have the T'En gifts!"

"No! Only a little. Don't tell anyone, I—"

"Cariah!" Imoshen dropped to her knees, clasping Cariah's hands to her face, kissing her palms. Tears of relief tightened her throat. "Teach me what you have discovered. Together we can make sense of this. I have been so alone, so frightened. The Aayel died before she could instruct me. I feel the gifts stir in me. I fear what I cannot control."

"Hsst! You must not speak so." Cariah sank to kneel with Imoshen, casting a swift look towards the closed door. "*They* must never suspect."

"Suspect? They know I am a Throwback cursed with these gifts. How can they not suspect?" Imoshen demanded. Then she saw Cariah's expression and with an unwelcome jolt she understood her duplicity. It was Cariah's own gifts the woman did not want revealed. Until this moment Imoshen had assumed only the pure T'En were gifted. It was said their part-T'En cousins were more aware of the use of the gifts, but . . . "You live a lie, Cariah. You deny what you are!"

"Don't be so quick to condemn me, Imoshen!" Her

beautiful face twisted with emotion. "I saw my mother sicken and die, locked away in the tower of my family's Stronghold because as much as my father loved her, he feared her more. I will not be an object of fear and hatred!" Her face hardened. "At best I could coach you in hiding your gifts and you already know how to cloak them."

Guilt lanced Imoshen. How many times as a child had she longed to be accepted? What would she have done if she could have hidden her heritage? She could not judge this woman.

"I'm sorry. Forgive me, Cariah," she whispered. "I did not think of your position."

Tears spilled over Cariah's lower lids, chasing each other across her cheeks. She fought to hold back a sob.

Her pain touched Imoshen. Lifting a hand she smoothed the tear track from Cariah's soft cheek. "Forgive my cruel words."

"Life is cruel!" Cariah turned her face away, wiping the dampness from her cheeks impatiently. The bitterness in her voice surprised Imoshen. "We must take what we can, while we can."

"I don't believe that." Imoshen took hold of Cariah's shoulders, turning her, willing the woman to meet her gaze.

Cariah shook her head pityingly. "You are so young. One day you will see."

"No. I have to believe there is hope," Imoshen whispered, fervently. "If I did not, I could not bear to live. My family are all dead. The Aayel died so that I would live. I must believe we are capable of greatness—"

Cariah kissed her.

The gesture was so unexpected Imoshen froze, experiencing those soft lips on hers, salty with tears. The gentleness of the caress was unmistakable. Cariah offered love.

Imoshen gasped and pulled away.

Cariah sank back onto her heels. Her mouth trembled, unshed tears glistening in her pleading eyes. "Don't reject me, Imoshen."

Stunned, Imoshen stared.

Cariah's hand lifted imploringly.

"I . . ." Imoshen floundered.

Abruptly, Cariah rose and stood before the mirror over the mantlepiece. In the dim light she made a great production of straightening her hair and smoothing her face to remove all traces of emotion.

"I surprise you. You are unsophisticated. This was the way of the old empire," she explained with brittle casualness. "T'Ysanna was my first lover. She shared her men with me, taught me to enjoy them for what they could give but to look elsewhere for true love."

Imoshen could hear Cariah distancing herself, denying what had passed between them.

With a smile Cariah returned to face Imoshen, offering a hand to help her rise. "Come, tidy your face. They will be watching us."

Imoshen stood stiffly, clasping Cariah's hand. She refused to release it, instead she lifted it to her lips, kissing the soft skin. "Don't draw away from me, Cariah. I am out of my depth. I need your counsel."

"You deny me in one breath, then in the next . . ." Cariah stiffened. "What you ask is cruel."

Pain twisted in Imoshen. "I'm sorry if I am cruel in my need."

"Here we are. Just for you!" The Keeper of the Knowledge beamed at Imoshen as he unwrapped the first of two packages. "You would not believe what I went through to hide these from King Gharavan's men!"

Imoshen gasped. She had never seen anything like it. The edges of the pages were thick with gilt, but it was the cover and spine which astounded her. She stroked the plush velvet, her fingers tracing the inlaid jewels. "This must date from the Age of Consolidation!"

"Middle period." The Keeper nodded and gently opened the tapestry pouch removing the second volume. "This one is even more magnificent."

"Pure gold?" Imoshen laughed.

"It is exquisite work," he snapped. "See the filigree, the granulation. This is real craftsmanship!"

Imoshen had to agree. "May I?"

He hesitated, unwilling to let the book pass from his hand to hers.

"I will take care," Imoshen promised. "You know how much I value knowledge."

At last he left her alone to search the book's indexes, but she was disappointed. Though the books themselves were valuable works of art, they contained nothing more unusual than a collection of poems and a study of Keldon Highland customs. Still she would read them, searching for a clue to her T'En gifts, even a reference to other sources was helpful.

Imoshen sighed, replacing the volumes. She felt so alone. Cariah had drawn away from her and Imoshen could not blame her. Cariah helped with the entertainments, but instead of sharing her private time with Imoshen she spent it with her lovers. Imoshen tried not to begrudge this. Lady Cariah Fairban was enough like her sisters to be accepted. When she sang beautifully and danced with the Thespers' Guild, no one acknowledged that it was her T'En heritage which enabled her to move them to tears of joy. Imoshen tried not to resent this ambiguity.

In the days leading up to her bonding with General Tulkhan, Imoshen had walked the corridors of the palace with no one to call friend, cut off from Cariah and cold-shouldered by the General.

She desperately missed Kalleen who had left with Wharrd after their bonding. It had only been when Kalleen asked for formal blessing from Imoshen that she made the connection between touching the tip of her little sixth finger to the center of Kalleen's forehead and the origin of the old empire obeisance. When people raised their hands to their foreheads they were acknowledging the T'En blessing. Old customs were deeply ingrained.

Imoshen smiled, recalling how the people of her

Stronghold had stroked her sixth finger for luck. A wave of homesickness swept over her.

Food had no flavor and her life was as grey as the ever-shortening winter days. By the cusp of spring the babe would begin to show and everyone would see how she had flaunted tradition.

"Finished already?" the Keeper asked. "If you told me what you are after . . ."

Imoshen shook her head. She did not dare reveal her real purpose. "Just curious. I am content to wander the library. You may go."

She knew the old man liked to spend his days in the kitchen, sipping mulled wine near the ovens where the heat warmed the ache from his bones. There he enjoyed the company of the cook and bored the scullery maids with his stories.

He nodded and smiled, bright old eyes fixed on her. "He was very like you, earnestly studying the old tomes."

Imoshen's mouth went dry. Only one other person was like her. "Reothe?"

"He was a pleasure to teach."

Imoshen did not want to hear tales of Reothe's boyhood. She did not want to dwell on how lonely he must have been. Knowing the high court, he would have lived as an object of pity and ridicule. Her heart went out to that boy, but Reothe was no longer a defenseless child and she would do well to remember that. "You were his tutor?"

"Yes, before he went to the Halls of Learning." The Keeper's face glowed with pride. "I have a copy of the treatise on philosophy he wrote when he was fifteen. He argued—"

But Imoshen had no time for philosophy; she dared to ask, "Was there anything on the T'En that he particularly liked to read?"

"Everything. He devoured everything we had on the T'En, then he moved on to the great library in the Halls of Learning. He was disappointed because they don't study the T'En there, but his debates were legendary. When he took his place on T'Ashmyr's stone there was standing room only around the library stoves!"

Imoshen tried not to show her disappointment. "Can you show me the books about the T'En?"

The old man laughed. "Every book mentions the T'En."

Imoshen looked down. She longed to trust the Keeper. But what would he say if she revealed she wanted to harness her gifts?

"No matter how high he rose, Reothe never forgot his old teacher," the man continued fondly. He pulled something from inside his vest and unwrapped it. "When he returned triumphant from his first voyage to the archipelago he brought me this."

"What is it?" Imoshen asked. "A religious artifact?"

"A shrunken human head."

Imoshen shuddered. How primitive the dwellers of the archipelago were. Fair Isle was literally an island of culture in a sea of barbarism. She could not, would not let the heritage of her T'En culture sink into darkness.

Tulkhan rubbed his eyes wearily. Despite its subsequent alterations, he believed the old city of T'Diemn could be made secure again. If he could have devoted all his time to the problem of fortifying the new city he would have come up with a solution by now. But he had to greet ambassadors so he could observe the interchange between them, particularly the triad of prosperous mainland kingdoms which he had not conquered.

He focused on the map of T'Diemn and its surrounds. Every street, every gate and spring was marked. It was all to scale with the highest points in gradients of color so that when he looked on it, it seemed three-dimensional. There was no point in building fortifications around new T'Diemn if he did not include that hillock to the south. Any general worth his salt would mount an offensive from that hilltop, yet it would mean taking the fortifications out to the hill since the outlying market gardens only reached its base, or pulling back and being prepared to sacrifice those people and their livelihood. Every decision was a compromise.

The door to his maproom flew open. Imoshen stood there in nothing but a thin nightgown, her feet bare, her hair loose on her shoulders. Her cheeks were pale and her chest rose and fell as if she had been running.

"You could not leave well enough alone, could you?" she demanded. "You thought you knew better!"

Tulkhan put the scriber down with exaggerated patience. "I have no idea what you are talking about."

Her eyes widened with fear.

Tulkhan felt a prickling sensation travel across his skin. "What is it?"

She took a deep breath. "You had better come."

When Tulkhan collected his sword from the back of his chair she made a noise in her throat.

"What?"

"Cold steel will not help," she whispered, then hurried off.

He followed, lengthening his stride to keep up with her as he buckled his sword belt. "Should I call out my Elite Guard?"

"Not for this."

The evening's entertainments had finished long ago and the servants had cleared away. Only the occasional sconce of candles lit the way.

Tulkhan fought a sense of foreboding as Imoshen glided down the steps to the Tribulation Portrait Gallery and stopped at the entrance to the gallery. It was deserted and unlit except for a branch of candles which sat on the floor about halfway along, before a gaping hole in the wainscoting.

"The secret passage has been forced!"

"He fled," Imoshen whispered. "I don't blame him."

"Who?"

"The servant who found this." Imoshen spoke over her

shoulder as she hurried down the hall. "He was taking a shortcut through this gallery to meet his lover!"

Tulkhan picked up the branch of candles and peered through the splintered wainscoting into the secret passage. The stale smell of dusty air made him grimace. He straightened and looked at Imoshen. "What would you have me do? How do you even know it is my people? It could be some of your builders."

"My builders would not be so stupid. They know better than to disturb the past. And they would not be so crude. If they wanted to explore the passage, they would remove the skirting board and wainscoting, then replace it afterwards, not bludgeon a hole with a battle axe. No. It is one or more of your men. My guess is Harholfe and his friends."

Tulkhan frowned. "They've gone looking for gold."

"Isn't the gold room gold enough?"

"It's the challenge." He grinned then sobered. "What do you expect me to do? Go after them like misbehaving boys? Likely as not they'll find nothing down there but storerooms and rat holes just as you said—"

"That was not all I said."

"No." Tulkhan had not forgotten, merely tried to deny what he did not wish to face. He shook his head. "We must bring them out."

He ducked his head and stepped through the jagged gap. He'd taken four steps when he realized Imoshen was not following him. Turning on the stair he looked back up to her, her face framed by the splintered wood. Six candle flames danced in her fixed eyes.

Tulkhan's body tightened, responding to her fear. His free hand went to his sword hilt. But Imoshen had said cold steel would not help him against what lay below.

He cursed under his breath. "They are my men and your ancestors. You can't turn your back, Imoshen!"

He saw a flare of anger displace her fear. Still she hesitated.

"If you expect my respect you must earn it," he told her. "A good general has a responsibility to his people."

"A good leader does not attempt the impossible."

"What? What is so impossible?"

"Tulkhan, I am out of my depth!" Her hands lifted in a silent plea.

He did not let himself feel compassion. "Please yourself."

Turning his back, he walked down the narrow stair. Though she moved soundlessly, he knew when she caught up with him because he could feel the skin-lifting tension of her T'En gift. It made his temples throb and left a metallic taste on his tongue.

When he came to the long passage, Imoshen caught his arm. "They brought this on themselves by forcing entry to the secret passages. If they have gone down into the catacombs, we must seal the door and leave them there."

Cold horror closed like a vise around his chest. He hardened his voice. "You know I cannot do that."

She stared at him, her face pale and set. Suddenly with a string of high T'En curses, or perhaps it was a prayer, she darted around him. Still muttering, she plucked the candles from his hand and went ahead.

Tulkhan smiled grimly to himself. But the hand which gripped his sword hilt was slick with sweat as he followed.

Imoshen went unflinchingly down another staircase. At the base he noticed the exit panel was wedged open with a broken tile. They stepped into a long narrow gallery. The candles could only illuminate the nearest walls and part of the vaulted ceiling. Their lowered voices echoed.

"See the style of vaulting? This dates from the Age of Tribulation. This way." Imoshen spoke as if she was conducting a leisurely tour of the palace, but her eyes never ceased searching the shadows.

Tulkhan followed, his senses on alert. The tension which rolled off Imoshen's skin was not so bad now. She had to be controlling it, because she had not relaxed.

"How far along was it?" she muttered. "All these archways look the same."

A man's raw scream cut the air. Imoshen went utterly

still. Tulkhan strained to hear as the echoes of the cry faded. He was just about to speak when the clatter of boots reverberated on the stonework.

"This way." Imoshen ran, trying to shield the candle flames.

Tulkhan pushed past her. He could see light and leaping shadows coming from a narrow opening. He stopped as Sahorrd and Jacolm stumbled out.

"General?" Jacolm raised his candle.

"One of them. Behind you!" Sahorrd warned, lunging forward, his sword drawn.

Tulkhan spun, unsheathing his blade. Sahorrd aimed for Imoshen's throat. She parried with the candle branch, disarming him even as Tulkhan struck using the flat of his sword. The man went down with a grunt of disbelief.

Jacolm swore. "The Princess."

"Who did you think it was?" Tulkhan hauled Sahorrd to his feet. The man rubbed his head, avoiding Imoshen's eye as she handed him his weapon.

"Much good it would have done you, if I'd been who you thought I was," she hissed. "Let's get out of here. But first I must seal the catacombs."

Jacolm stepped between her and the open passage. "Harholfe's still down there, General."

Anger flashed through Tulkhan. "You left him down there?"

"He was right behind me!" Jacolm bristled.

"Harholfe had the battle axe," Sahorrd said. "He used it to pry the lid off the coffin."

Imoshen gasped. She made the sign to ward off evil, raising her left hand to her eyes then over her head. "May their eyes pass over me, over all of us."

"Your long dead T'En warriors?" Tulkhan asked. "The Para—"

She hissed, cutting him short.

Tulkhan looked to her for an explanation.

"Names have power." Imoshen's voice quavered. "We invoke them by name to serve us."

"But what of Harholfe?" Jacolm ground out.

"We will go down," Tulkhan said. "You two stay here, cover our retreat."

He caught Imoshen's eye. She wiped her mouth with the back of her hand, then moved into the narrow stairwell. He stepped down after her, aware that Jacolm and Sahorrd were following despite his orders. He was not surprised. No matter how deep their terror, they would not abandon their brother-at-arms. To display cowardice would mean ostracism.

Imoshen waited at the base of the stair, holding the candle branch high to illuminate a long barrel-vaulted catacomb. Heavy stone coffins lay in wall niches.

Silently Imoshen pointed upward. Above them were life-size paintings of the legendary Paragian Guard in full armor. The inlaid gold and silver flickered in the candlelight.

There was no sign of Harholfe.

"This way, General." Only the glisten of Sahorrd's fearful eyes betrayed his dread as he led them to the right, where a waist-high stone coffin rested under a High T'En inscription.

"Imoshen?" Tulkhan indicated the words.

She raised her candles.

" 'Here lies the Aayel, First of the Last,' " she translated.

"What does it mean?" Tulkhan asked.

Her awed eyes met his. "It is the sarcophagus of Imoshen the First's own nephew, Aayel, First Emperor of Fair Isle. After he abdicated in favor of his half-T'En daughter, Abularassa, he served the Church and the people of Fair Isle. The title *the Aayel* was created to honor him. He was the first to serve in this capacity and the last pure T'En male to be born in the old country. Only children, those born on the long journey and those too young to remember, were left." She touched her forehead giving the deep T'En obeisance to the first Aayel. "This is almost worth the—"

"But where is Harholfe?" Jacolm took two impatient paces past them then stopped. Holding his candle high he looked back, radiating furious fear. "Come on."

Imoshen ignored him, studying the lid of the sarcophagus instead. Tulkhan joined her. The lid was decorated with a raised stone carving of a very old T'En male. He was richly dressed in clothes of state and carried no weapons. The individual hairs of his plaited beard had been delineated in stone, then silver thread.

"For Akha Khan's sake, can we move?" Sahorrd hissed. "The coffin is just around the corner."

"The one you were foolish enough to open?" Imoshen snapped.

He did not meet her eyes.

"You desecrate my heritage," she told him. "These are the T'En of legend and you—"

"Imoshen!" Tulkhan barked. "We must find Harholfe and get out of here."

As he strode past Jacolm, he sensed the man's terror and knew he was not far from violence. Tulkhan's small pool of candlelight moved forward with him and soon he identified another stone block. The lid was off, tilted against the side.

"So small," Imoshen whispered.

"It contains a child," Sahorrd explained as they came abreast of it. "The carving on the lid was inlaid with precious metal and jewels. That's why we—"

Imoshen's whimper cut him short. She swayed as if she might faint. Tulkhan steadied her; her skin was ice cold and her body felt stiff.

He peered into the opened coffin expecting a skeleton. Instead he saw a perfectly preserved ten-year-old child. She was richly dressed in red velvet embroidered with gold thread. Jewels were sewn into the broad yoke collar that lay across her shoulders. Her eyes were closed and he could see the individual lashes, the soft curve of her top lip. A single ruby lay on her forehead.

"Why didn't you plunder this one?" Tulkhan asked.

Sahorrd and Jacolm stared down at the child, their weapons forgotten.

"I don't understand." Panic edged Sahorrd's voice. "The ruby . . ."

Tulkhan felt a sense of time stretching out so that he could hear his own heart beating in his ears, echoing hollowly in his head, drowning all sense of urgency.

"Imoshen?" He had to force himself to speak.

She left his side, walking around the stone block to read the inscription on the lid which rested against the sarcophagus.

" 'Here lies Ysanna. Killed by rebels.' " Imoshen touched the date. "In the early years of Fair Isle's settlement. She was six years old. I've never heard of her."

Imoshen looked across at him her eyes were awash with tears. "My daughter . . ."

"You have no daughter."

Tulkhan glanced into the coffin again and felt himself falling away. He forced his numb tongue to work. "What T'En sorcery is this and where is Harholfe?"

"He claimed the big ruby," Sahorrd said.

"But he's put it back for some reason," Jacolm muttered. His hand darted forward as if to take the precious stone.

"No!" Suddenly Imoshen's fingers were between his and the stone, holding it in place on the child's forehead. She glared at him, her features austere, her eyes flickering red in the candlelight.

"Curse your witchy eyes, woman!" Jacolm spat, his sword lifting threateningly.

"Enough," Tulkhan snapped. "Where is Harholfe?"

They looked around but there was no sign of him, only empty stone walls.

"Tell me what happened," Tulkhan ordered.

"They came for us when he took the ruby." Sahorrd shuddered. "Three Dhamfeer dressed in warrior's armor appeared from the shadows. The priests say a True-man should turn his eyes from the black arts and now I know why. These beings made the blood run cold in my veins. I've never known such terror. . . ." He looked down in shame, then met their eyes resolutely. "I fled."

Jacolm indicated back the way they had come. "When we ran for the stairs I swear Harholfe was right behind me."

"Then where is he?" Tulkhan turned to Imoshen only to discover she was standing absolutely still, the big ruby pressed to the center of her forehead between her closed lids. She opened her eyes and replaced the ruby. When she met his gaze, her garnet eyes were cold and contemptuous.

"I thought you didn't want the grave desecrated?" Tulkhan fought down a surge of fear when she merely looked at him in silence. "Where is my man, Harholfe?"

Closing her eyes, Imoshen lifted her left hand. Her splayed fingers seemed to feel the air.

"What is left of him is just beyond the next coffin propped up against the wall." Her voice was rich and strangely intimate.

Jacolm cursed. He darted away, candle held high, weapon drawn. They followed him.

"Nothing. I see nothing but his battle axe." Jacolm spun around, gesturing to the dressed stone walls and floor which were bare except for the discarded weapon. "Here is the stone coffin, but where—?"

"Where is the body, Imoshen?" Tulkhan went to catch her arm but before he could touch her he felt a sharp blow as though someone had given him a resounding slap. The flesh under his nails throbbed painfully. He cursed.

Imoshen pointed to a blank wall, lifting her candles high. "There."

The reflection of the flickering flames glistened on the stone's slick surface, glistened and coalesced into the outline of a man's body.

Sahorrd's indrawn breath sounded loud in the silence. "It is his shadow. I mean . . ." But he had no words for what he saw.

Like oil dropped into water, the outline of a man appeared on the wall's stone. Tulkhan could see Harholfe's expression of frozen terror. He felt cold to the marrow. As a general he had seen men die in many ways—in battle, in agony, raving with fever, even too weary to care. But he had never seen a man die of fear, leaving his last moment of terror imprinted on stone.

"Where is Harholfe's body?" Jacolm turned on Imoshen, sword raised. "His weapon lies at his feet unbloodied."

"Of course. Steel cannot kill those who are already dead." Imoshen held his eyes until he lowered his weapon. "Your companion broke the ward protecting the grave. His soul was forfeited."

"Don't play your riddles on me, Dhamfeer bitch!" Jacolm's voice vibrated with fear-laden fury. "Where is Harholfe?"

Imoshen's eyes closed. Tulkhan felt the overflow of her gift and took a step back, his fingertips still throbbing. Sahorrd and Jacolm made the Ghebite sign to ward off evil.

When Imoshen opened her eyes, they glowed with an inner radiance. "The Parakletos are escorting him through death's shadow into death's own realm."

"I thought you said . . ." Tulkhan stopped. Suddenly it struck him as odd that Imoshen no longer evinced any fear and seemed at ease with her T'En gifts. Her expression was unfamiliar and she looked on him as a stranger. His skin crawled with understanding; some long-dead T'En being was animating Imoshen. "I think it is time to go. Sahorrd, Jacolm?" He used the battlefield gesture to signal retreat. They moved to stand behind him, never turning their backs on Imoshen as they edged away.

"We can't leave," Jacolm protested. "Harholfe has not been properly buried."

Imoshen stabbed a finger at him. "You and your two friends trespassed on a sacred place and desecrated an innocent's grave. This Harholfe has paid. It is finished."

She walked past them unconcerned by their battle-ready weapons. To Tulkhan she seemed invulnerable, despite her bare feet and the thin nightgown which brushed her slender ankles.

He bent to retrieve the undamaged battle axe. As he stood, stone grated on stone. He heard his men's surprised intake of breath and spun to see Imoshen straighten, pivoting the stone slab into place.

The candle branch was on the floor at her feet behind the

coffin. It illuminated her from behind as she leaned over the stone statue to kiss the child's cold lips, whispering something in High T'En. When she wiped the dust off her hands, he glanced at the stone lid. It had taken three men to move it. He had fought with Imoshen, sword against sword. He knew she did not have the strength to move that slab.

Imoshen bent to retrieve the candles.

The moment stretched. She did not rise.

Dread made Tulkhan's movements stiff as he walked around the sarcophagus to find Imoshen sitting on the ground looking dazed. "General?"

Relief flooded him. He helped her to stand. Her skin was warm and soft.

"Come," he said.

"What of your man?"

"Dead."

She accepted this. In silence, except for the scuff of the Ghebite boots on stone, they hurried toward the first Aayel's sarcophagus. Jacolm and Sahorrd turned the corner, taking their light with them. The need to get out drove Tulkhan's legs, powering his muscles. Suddenly Imoshen stopped. She planted her feet, flicking free of his grasp to stroke the Aayel's tomb.

"What?" Tulkhan asked.

"My feet walk on history's path. Sardonyx used to come down here and lie on the stone slab meant for his body."

"We must go."

"They said it drove him mad."

Tulkhan took her hand even though it made all the hairs on his arm rise in protest. "Come."

"His own cousin and kinswoman condemned him to death."

Tulkhan tugged on her arm. "The others are waiting."

"My heritage is one of tragedy."

"Not now, Imoshen!" Tulkhan hurried her toward the steps, under the cold garnet eyes of the T'En warriors of legend and up the steps out of the catacombs to join his men who waited impatiently.

As they stepped out into the gallery, Imoshen shuddered. "Close the passage, seal the catacombs. No one must go down there!"

"How do I close the passage?" Tulkhan handed her the candles.

"The shoe." Imoshen pointed to an old shoe which was wedged into the door frame. "Long ago a boy used it to hold the door open."

"What boy?" Tulkhan asked.

"Some lost boy. I don't know any more."

Tulkhan sheathed his sword and worked the shoe loose. It came free with a tug and the panel slid into place, grating stone on dust. It did not close completely, remaining about a finger's breadth open.

He grunted. "That will have to do. Let's get out of here."

Jacolm and Sahorrd were already moving, but Imoshen pressed both hands on the stone trying to force the door.

"Leave it be, Imoshen," Tulkhan urged. "We'll seal the secret passage from above."

"No . . . Yes!" Regret and fear mingled in her features.

"What happened down there? Do you remember finding the child?"

Her eyes widened and she looked away, saying, "I'm not sure it is safe to leave the door like that."

"I'm not sure of anything. Not since I . . ." He had been about to say *not since I met you*. "Since I came to Fair Isle I doubt everything."

Her sharp eyes met his.

"General?" Jacolm called from the base of the stair.

"We'll seal the entrance at the portrait gallery. That will have to do," Tulkhan decided.

"What about Harholfe's body?"

Tulkhan realized she did not remember. "Harholfe has paid for his folly. There was no body." He wondered how he would explain Harholfe's disappearance to his men. "Come."

They hurried after the others and stepped through the shattered wainscoting into the portrait gallery. Grimly,

Jacolm and Sahorrd sheathed their weapons. Tulkhan knew by tomorrow night they would be boasting of this in their cups, denying their terror.

So much had happened since he had entered that secret passage, Tulkhan felt as though it must be nearly dawn.

Imoshen inspected the damage done by the battle axe. "I will have the Masterbuilder provide a stonemason. This will be sealed securely and the wainscotting replaced." She turned to Jacolm and Sahorrd. "You see there was nothing down there but storerooms and rat holes."

"But—" Jacolm began.

"Nothing but storerooms and rat holes," Imoshen repeated.

Tulkhan's temples throbbed and his head ached. He saw Sahorrd rub the bridge of his nose.

"But—" Jacolm frowned.

"Nothing," Imoshen urged. "Nothing worth a man's life."

"Harholfe!" Sahorrd moaned.

"Harholfe has taken a ship to the mainland in my service," Tulkhan said. There was no corpse to dispose of, no way to make his death public and honor him. "We will not speak of this to anyone."

Jacolm and Sahorrd exchanged glances.

Tulkhan dismissed them both. When they had gone he turned to Imoshen. "Well?"

"Well what?" she asked.

"What happened down there?"

She shrugged. "They disturbed a sacred site. One of them paid with his life. The T'En look after their own."

"What of the Para—"

"Don't . . ." She covered his lips, her fingertips gritty with dust. "At least not here, not now."

"You didn't look frightened." Tulkhan sheathed his sword.

"Nonsense. I was terrified the whole time."

"After we found the child's grave—"

"Do not speak of that."

Tulkhan frowned. "Do you remember the sarcophagus of the first Aayel?"

"Of course. And I would dearly love to explore the whole of the catacombs, but every time I think of it I am filled with such dread that I feel ill. Please speak no more of this. I will have the entrance sealed up first thing tomorrow . . . Today." She frowned. "I don't remember anything after Jacolm went to take the ruby. How do you know Harholfe is dead if you did not find his body?"

"We found enough." Tulkhan shuddered and shook his head uneasily. "Don't go down there again, Imoshen."

A bitter laugh escaped her. "You were the one who insisted I go. Believe me, nothing could get me into those catacombs again."

Tulkhan stared at her, not sure if she was being deliberately obscure. "Who was the child, Ysanna? You called her 'daughter.' "

She flinched. "Sometimes the gifts can be a curse." Her gaze slid past his and he knew she was going to lie, or at least avoid answering the question. "There have been many Ysannas. Most recently T'Ysanna was the Empress's only daughter and heir. Like all my other relatives she died defending Fair Isle. One by one they fell before the Ghebite army, choosing to fight to the death rather than be taken captive." Her face grew hard and proud, reminding him of how she had looked down in the catacombs. "Why do you look at me like that?"

"I am tired. Go to bed."

"That's where I was, in case you hadn't noticed," Imoshen told him.

"Oh, I'd noticed. You are wearing nothing under that nightgown. If I were to undo the draw-string and slide it off your shoulders you would be naked in my arms."

She lifted her chin. "I might be naked, General, but I would not be in your arms." She plucked a candle from the holder. "Goodnight."

He watched her go. The more he knew of Imoshen the

less he understood. And after tonight he was not eager to pry too deeply.

With a sigh he walked across the gallery and sat down with his back to the wall, holding Harholfe's battle axe across his knees. He snuffed out all but one candle then sat there watching the dark entrance to the secret passage.

He did not really believe anything was going to come up that stairwell. And if it did, he knew cold steel would not stop it. But he could not rest easy until the entrance was closed and the shades of the legendary T'En warriors sealed away from True-men.

Eight

RECOGNIZING THE OTHER occupants of the carriage as the elite of the Keldon Highland aristocracy, Imoshen hid her misgivings. They were leaders of the most powerful families, related by blood and bonding, and united, she suspected, in their plans for Fair Isle. What was supposed to be a tour of the sites of T'Diemn promised to be a grilling.

"T'Imoshen," they greeted her.

"Grandfathers, Grandmothers," she deliberately gave them the more intimate honorific than their titles. "What do you wish to discuss?"

"So impatient," Lady Woodvine, the iron-haired matriarch muttered.

Old, part-T'En Lord Athlyng shook his head. "In the high court the Empress—"

"The Empress is dead," Imoshen interrupted, "and the old empire died with her. The scholars are agreed that on the first day of the new year a new age will begin. We must make our peace with that."

The Keldon nobles exchanged glances.

"To the Causare," Lord Fairban told the driver.

Imoshen stiffened. It was in this building that the Causare Council of the old empire had met to debate policy. She had watched a meeting during her first visit to the capital. But the long-winded speeches bored her and it was much more fun to watch the spectators in the gallery. It had amused her when the nobles were unceremoniously bundled out on the bell of noon to make room for the other functionaries of the Causare, the traders.

From sun-up till noon, the building served the Council; from noon till dusk it served the traders. They were merchants, sea captains, guildmasters, anyone who thought they could turn an opportunity to profit. After the noon bell, the Causare became a place of furious buying and selling of fortunes as yet unearned. Traders bought and sold part-ownership of planned voyages to the archipelago or the mainland ports. It was said a canny Causare trader could turn a profit on a crop of grapes three times before it was sown, let alone harvested, crushed, and fermented.

Imoshen maintained her silence as the carriage passed through the streets of old T'Diemn. When the carriage stopped at the Causare she descended and sailed up the wide steps, through the double doors embellished with symbols of Fair Isle's prosperity in embossed bronze.

Once in the central chamber she hesitated. The Beatific, who was accompanied by four high-ranking priests, including Murgon, acknowledged her. Imoshen returned her brief nod. She had expected the rest of the Keldon leaders, and sure enough they were there, but accompanied by what looked like the elite of T'Diemn's traders. By their rich clothing and personal styles she identified merchants, bankers, guildmasters, and a few ship captains—an odd gathering considering it was not yet noon.

Lord Fairban caught up with her, leading her to the Empress's bench, which was no different from any other. In the Causare all voices were supposed to be heard with equal weight. But by custom this had become the seat of power. The Beatific left her companions and took the seat on Imoshen's left, claiming the highest precedent after the Empress. Fairban retreated to join his faction, and for several moments there was a general shuffling about as people found places in the circle of tiered benches.

The Beatific said nothing. Imoshen vowed that she

would not give her the satisfaction of asking what was going on. One by one, people settled and Imoshen waited, her features schooled.

In the ensuing hush, Woodvine came to her feet. "T'Imoshen. Unlike others . . ." the formidable Keldon matriarch paused to glare at certain people, "I will not call you Empress because you have not earned that title. We have two questions for you to present to the Ghebite General. First, when will the Causare reopen to serve the people of Fair Isle? And when it does, who—"

"Yes!" An eager merchant leapt to her feet. "War is bad for business. I lost a whole shipment of mainland fruit left to rot because—"

"And I have not seen the profits from my last voyage because the banks have frozen their funds!" another cried.

At this, a terrible clamor arose, as the bankers argued that if they had not frozen funds the panicked populace would have bankrupted the country, and traders angrily debated the efficacy of this policy. A smile tugged at Imoshen's lips. Trust the people of Fair Isle to be concerned about profits before power politics, or was it simply the other side of the coin?

The double doors flew open and General Tulkhan strode into the center of the Causare, his boots thunderous in the sudden silence. His Elite Guard marched in single file to take up position behind the highest seats, where they stood hands on their sword hilts. Half a dozen of the General's most trusted commanders formed a solid wall at the open doors.

No sound echoed in the great dome; no one moved. Imoshen feared the tiles would soon run with blood.

"What treason is this?" Tulkhan roared. He pointed to the Keldon nobles. "You swore an oath of fealty to me. And you!" He turned on the traders. "You also swore an oath. Yet you meet in secret!"

"General Tulkhan." Imoshen left the Empress's seat to join him. "No treason is being worked here. This building is the Causare. During the old empire the Council of Fair Isle debated policy here and traders met to arrange backing for their ventures." She took his hand, feeling the tension in him. "Come, hear them speak."

When Tulkhan allowed her to lead him, Imoshen felt almost light-headed with relief. He had entered the Causare as a war general, but it would take a statesman to resolve this.

"We must avoid bloodshed, General. Trust me," she whispered, sitting next to him so that he was between her and the Beatific. Imoshen signaled for silence, coming to her feet. "This is not how I remember the Council." Actually it was more like the energetic afternoon's trading. "You wish to know when the Causare will reopen? Well, today is that day."

The traders finger-clicked their approval, some going so far as to give the official traders' call of success.

"Pretty words." Woodvine stood. "But what of the Council? We have no say in—"

"What of the banks?" a merchant interrupted. "We are losing money!"

"We are saving your gold!" insisted a banker.

The Causare erupted.

Imoshen turned to the Beatific who appeared pleased, but it was Tulkhan's disgusted expression that made her smile. She sat next to him, close enough so that her lips brushed his ear. "The day-to-day business of Fair Isle has resumed but the larger ventures which risk great capital are all halted until the political situation regains stability. The merchants cannot undertake their ventures if the banks have frozen funds."

"What do you suggest, Imoshen?"

"Give the Emp . . . Give your royal seal to the banks. If they know they have the resources of the royal house behind them, they will release funds."

"But I am not officially ruler of Fair Isle until the coronation ceremony."

"The Causare will not meet again until the new year. Until then the traders can negotiate business in the taverns and teahouses, then get their agreements formally recognized when the Causare opens its doors." Imoshen hesitated, watching Tulkhan's features as he considered the ramifications.

The Beatific raised her voice over the din. "General, Fair Isle must not lose her position as center of trade."

"You both speak sense."

"And that surprises you?" Imoshen dared to tease. She sat back, pleased.

The Causare grew silent as people realized that the General was ready to speak.

"Hear this." Tulkhan raised his hands. "After the coronation ceremony I will underwrite the banks with the funds of the royal . . ."

Furious trading drowned out his voice as every merchant, banker, sea captain, and guildmaster touted their latest venture which would net anyone wise enough to invest in it enormous profits.

Woodvine left her seat to march across the floor towards Imoshen. She was joined by Fairban and Athlyng. Imoshen took the General's arm, aware that only part of the original question had been answered. She noticed the Beatific moved to stand on the General's other side.

Tulkhan shook his head, astounded by the sheer volume of noise. He eyed the belligerent Keld before him, ready to repulse their verbal attack, but they rounded on Imoshen instead.

"Very clever, T'Imoshen," Woodvine ground out. "You have cut our support out from under us by giving the traders what they want. But the Causare is not just a trading forum. We represent the old aristocracy, we have a right to sit on Council and direct the policy of Fair Isle. We will not rest until that right is acknowledged."

"All rights are earned, including the right to serve," Imoshen replied.

"Right?" Tulkhan repeated. The arrogance of these people astounded him. Though he had no proof he knew they gave aid to Reothe and his rebels. He would have been within his rights to confiscate their titles and lands. These Keld were lucky to be alive.

"General Tulkhan will hear your petition in the new year after the celebrations," Imoshen spoke quickly. "Until then the palace is packed with mainland nobility and ambassadors. We must present a united front."

"For Fair Isle's sake," the Beatific urged.

Tulkhan noted how Imoshen and the Beatific exchanged looks as the others agreed. He took Imoshen's arm, escorting her from the Causare. His men filed out after him.

Imoshen would have spoken but he signaled for silence, climbing astride his mount and offering his hand. She placed her foot on his boot and leapt up across his thighs where their conversation would not be overheard.

"The people of Fair Isle never cease to amaze me," Tulkhan muttered as the double doors closed on the noisy scene within. He turned his horse towards the palace.

"Why?"

He did not reply.

After a moment Imoshen cleared her throat. "I know you find the Keldon nobles' request to reopen the Causare Council a little—"

He gave a bark of laughter.

She hesitated. "When you are at war you consult with your commanders, you listen to the locals, you consider what you have learned, then you make the best decision based on all this. Yes?"

He nodded.

"Ruling Fair Isle is no different. You would heed the advice of your commanders. Among the Keldon nobles there are people who have seen eighty years of history unfold. Surely their advice is worth—"

"True, but are their goals mine?" Tulkhan countered grimly.

"There is a T'En saying that translates, *'A person who has nothing will risk everything,'*" Imoshen told Tulkhan, as they rode through the grounds to the palace stables. "Give your commanders and the Keldon nobles a say in the ruling of Fair Isle. As Fair Isle prospers under your rule they will also prosper, this way their goals become yours."

Tulkhan looked into her wine-dark eyes. "Truly the T'En are a devious race."

Imoshen slipped from his thighs, landing lightly on the stone paving. "There is another T'En saying, *Do not use a battle axe to kill a fly.*' " She grinned. "It is more poetic in High T'En."

He felt himself smile. "These are dangerous flies."

Imoshen gave him the lesser obeisance and walked off. Tulkhan swung his leg over the horse's back and dropped to the ground. Regretfully he watched Imoshen enter the palace. How he would welcome their intimacy if only she were not pure T'En. It appalled him to discover he craved her presence like a drug.

In the days leading up to their bonding, Tulkhan gave Imoshen's words much thought. While his father had been king he had gathered about him capable men, rewarding them to ensure their loyalty. There was merit in this but he did not see how he could implement it. His own men would not listen to the advice of a woman.

Now he hesitated on the brink of approaching Imoshen's card table. The older Keldon nobles had retired when the Beatific left, leaving only the younger members of the court. A buzz of conversation rose from the other tables, the players made up of visiting aristocrats from mainland kingdoms, politically minded Church officials, and several bizarrely dressed individuals from the islands of the archipelago. The evening's entertainment had continued later than usual, leaving Tulkhan bored and irritable. Imoshen never bored him.

Imoshen was involved in a six-sided T'En game of cards which elicited much comment and some laughter. In Gheeaba gambling was a serious business, a man's honor was at stake. If his luck ran out he could lose his estates and his wives. Suicide might be his only option.

Imoshen and her partner were teamed against Wharrd and Kalleen on one side, who had returned looking like sleek, cream-fed cats, and Cariah and Jacolm on the other. So far the luck had run Jacolm's way and he was not averse to letting everyone know.

"My 'Beatific' and 'Empress-High' outplay your hand of lesser nobles!" he crowed.

Tulkhan walked around the table to stand behind Imoshen so that he could see her cards. In the long winter evenings he had learnt the basics of this game and understood the system of playing alliances against alliances, while supporting your partner and undercutting the other teams.

He took the opportunity to observe Imoshen, drinking in the curve of her cheek, the line of her pale throat, the unconscious grace of her every movement. His mouth went dry with longing.

When the round finished, the cards were pushed Imoshen's way. Her partner Sahorrd reached for the pack but she was quicker. Tulkhan knew she was unaware she had insulted him as she collected the cards. Her fingers moved fluidly, shuffling and dealing. Watching the play he looked for a chance to advise her, for any excuse to touch her, even if it was in a room full of people. But she won that hand and the next three, playing with an uncanny ability to guess which alliances her opponents favored.

The shuffling and dealing made its way around the table again. Jacolm became progressively irritated, then belligerent as he received his new cards. At last he threw the painted paste-boards down in disgust.

Tulkhan stiffened. Was his commander going to accuse Imoshen of misdealing? In Gheeaba such an accusation would have occasioned a duel of honor.

Silence fell.

Imoshen laid her cards facedown. "Is there a problem, Lord Jacolm?"

"No problem. I should know better than to play a game of chance with a Dhamfeer!"

Tulkhan tensed. Those Ghebites within hearing went utterly still.

"If you have something to say, say it," Imoshen told him.

Tulkhan noted how Jacolm's sword-brother, Sahorrd, shifted in his seat, turning his shoulder away from his card partner. With this movement he withdrew his support from Imoshen.

"Well, Jacolm?" Imoshen pressed, one arm hooked elegantly over the back of her chair. Was she deliberately insulting him by omitting his new title?

The man's dark brows drew down as he flipped his cards over. "Look. It's been the same rubbish for the past four hands. Why, I even have the T'En rogue again!"

"The fall of the cards—"

"The cards fall in such a way that you win." Jacolm sat forward. "How else do you know what everyone holds in their hand?"

The spectators gave a collective gasp. Tulkhan sensed their speculative appraisal of Imoshen. Perhaps it was possible to use her gifts to manipulate the fall of the cards. He wondered whether he should intervene.

Several of his men looked past Imoshen to him, obviously expecting their General to respond. The day after tomorrow Imoshen would be his wife; any criticism of her character was a slight on his honor. His body tensed but he ignored the instinctive urge to declare her innocence.

If a man were accused of cheating in Gheeaba, it would be up to him to prove his honor, but Imoshen was a woman and so unable to accept Jacolm's challenge or offer challenge of her own. Tulkhan hesitated. There were no precedents to guide his actions.

"You are mistaken, Jacolm," Imoshen announced, her voice icy. "I would never use my T'En gift for such a paltry purpose."

Tulkhan saw the man flinch.

"So you say," Jacolm mocked.

Imoshen made an impatient noise in her throat. "Cariah, have I been using anything other than my wit and skills?"

Tulkhan saw the redheaded beauty swallow and lift her chin. He could tell she was preparing to lie.

"How would I know?" Cariah gestured as if bored by the whole thing. "I have not seen Imoshen do anything other than count the cards and anticipate what people have in their hands by what they have played."

"Thank you for your support," Imoshen said dryly.

Tulkhan knew by her tone that she was rebuking Cariah, but he did not know why. If Imoshen was not cheating, why was Cariah lying? Before Tulkhan could ponder this, Jacolm rose, telegraphing his intention to challenge Imoshen's word. To offer challenge to a *mere* female would demean Jacolm, but Tulkhan realized Jacolm's honor would not allow him to back down.

Everything slowed as Tulkhan stiffened. Cheating or not, he had to defend Imoshen's honor. He had to redirect the challenge.

Before Jacolm could speak Tulkhan stepped forward. "Are you offering insult?"

"There has been no insult offered," Wharrd interjected soothingly. This was strictly true; no formal challenge had been laid down because Tulkhan had intervened before it could get that far.

Imoshen ignored Wharrd. Coming to her feet she glanced from Tulkhan to Jacolm. "What goes on here?"

"I am merely asking this man if he offers challenge," Tulkhan ground out.

Jacolm's resentful eyes studied the General.

"If insult is intended it is to me, not to you," Imoshen snapped.

"Any insult offered my wife is an insult upon my name. A challenge," Tulkhan told her. Then he returned his attention to Jacolm, trying to read the man's next move.

Silently Sahorrd rose and moved around the table to stand behind his sword-brother.

With all his being Tulkhan willed Imoshen to remain silent. Anything she said now was bound to inflame Jacolm. Imoshen was but a heartbeat from death for Jacolm was one of his finest swordsmen. A muscle jumped in the man's cheek. Tulkhan sensed he was close to losing control. There was no chance of a formal duel here. Knowing Jacolm, he would favor the soldier's solution—challenge offered, accepted, and honor decided on the spot.

"There is no cause for insult to be offered. No need to challenge." Wharrd came to his feet. "I have been watching the cards. No one can cheat this old campaigner."

Imoshen drew a slow breath. "And I choose to take no insult. Jacolm does not know me. I would use my T'En gift to save a life, yes, but to win a game of chance, never!"

With a few brief sentences she had placed the man in the wrong and forgiven him. Tulkhan could sympathize with Jacolm as he bristled.

Cariah rose. "Supper is being served."

The sudden influx of servants carrying trays of food broke the stalemate. Imoshen turned her back on Jacolm with deliberate casualness, but her expression when she met Tulkhan's eyes was anything but casual.

She was furious. Not with Jacolm, with him.

Why? He had been about to defend her at the risk of losing one of his best men.

His body thrummed with unresolved tension as he escorted Imoshen to the sideboard where the servants had laid out the food. Every dish was a masterpiece of presentation, food sculpted to form animals, birds in flight, or intricate pieces of T'En architecture. Every morsel was a surprise to delight the palate.

Imoshen's fingers trembled ever so slightly as she poured wine for them both, but no one except Tulkhan saw this.

All around them people talked animatedly, but their chatter was too bright and their smiles forced. They skirted Tulkhan and Imoshen, while appearing to defer to them. At the same time the General knew that every ear was strained to catch their conversation and every malicious eye was trained on them to observe the undercurrents revealed by their gestures.

"Wine, General?" Imoshen offered him a crystal goblet.

His fingers tingled when they brushed hers and his temples ached as though a storm were about to break. Experience told him the power was moving within her.

"Since when did my honor cease to be my own?" She spoke softly so that only he could hear.

Her low, intense question startled him. "The day after tomorrow you will be my wife—"

"Bond-partner. *Equal!*" she hissed, turning her back to their audience. In a gesture that appeared affectionate she raised her hand and brushed a strand of hair from his throat.

His body responded to her touch, but he found it disturbing because her eyes, which only he could see, held ice-cold fury. She was lying with her actions to hide the content of their conversation from those who watched them. Again he had to admire her, desire her . . . and fear her.

"I will stand at your side, not behind you, General. If I am offered insult I will handle it, not you." Her garnet eyes glittered with suppressed fury. "I am not your lapdog to be petted and protected from the real world."

Her words hit their target. For an instant Tulkhan stood in her shoes. He saw her difficult position and empathized with her against his will.

With a nod of satisfaction, Imoshen turned away and moved gracefully along the length of the sideboard. She nibbled this and tasted that, pausing to speak with three minor Church officials then with Lady Cariah's two sisters and the young Ghebite commanders who rarely left their sides. Those she exchanged pleasantries with smiled and deferred to her, but when she passed on, Tulkhan saw their relieved expressions. Something twisted inside him. Suddenly he pitied Imoshen, destined always to be an outsider.

Amid the general conversation he caught the tone of

Jacolm's voice. His man was still angry. Sahorrd and a few others stood with him talking intensely, their gaze on Imoshen.

Wharrd approached with Kalleen at his side. Tulkhan greeted them and they both glanced over at the angry group.

"Jacolm's a hothead," Wharrd muttered. "He'll grow out of it one day."

"Or it will kill him," Tulkhan amended.

Wharrd met Tulkhan's eyes in silent acknowledgment.

"He's lucky T'Imoshen didn't take insult," Kalleen said.

Again Tulkhan felt that uncomfortable shift in his perception. To Kalleen that was the encounter in a nutshell.

Tulkhan was reminded how little he knew of this place and these people. A prickling awareness of menace moved across his skin. If sufficiently angered what was a Dhamfeer capable of? He had seen Imoshen furious and he had seen her frightened, but he had never seen her out of control. Or had he? He suddenly recalled a visual image so intense it seared his inner eye—two fighting birds exploding in a ball of fire.

Though Imoshen had refused to discuss the cockeral fight, he knew that she had been outraged by its barbarity. When she discovered his men betting on the birds' deaths, she had grown frighteningly still. He could see her now, standing across the pit from him, fierce eyes blazing. Then suddenly the birds had burst into flames.

Tulkhan wanted to find her, to warn her of Jacolm's hasty temper, to explain why honor was so important to his Ghebite commander.

Searching above the heads of those present, Tulkhan could not see Imoshen's distinctive silver hair. Impatience drove him. He took his leave of Wharrd and Kalleen and crossed the room slowly, forced to pause to engage in conversation several times. He realized he was projecting the same falsely casual air as Imoshen.

Deliberately stopping beside Jacolm, Tulkhan clapped a hand on the man's shoulder and passed a few innocuous words. They meant nothing. His real meaning was contained in the way he stood at their sides. He offered solidarity, and he saw his men understood as their expressions eased, conveying their relief.

Leaving the crowded room, Tulkhan entered the relative quiet of the hall, felt the cool air on his face. One of Imoshen's Stronghold Guard stood at the door. "Which way did Imoshen go?"

The young man stiffened and inclined his head to the left. Tulkhan set off, wondering what he had said to offend the youth.

He rounded a corner but did not see Imoshen. A servant approached. "Have you seen Imoshen?"

With a nod of his head he indicated the direction from which he had come. "T'Imoshen is with the Lady Cariah."

Tulkhan managed a smile. He told himself it was a good sign that the old man felt secure enough in his presence to reprimand him for not addressing Imoshen with sufficient reverence.

Keeping a tight rein on her anger, Imoshen had slipped from the crowded room at the first opportunity, intent on confronting Cariah. Rounding a corner she saw the other woman. "Cariah, wait."

From the way Cariah turned and met her eyes, Imoshen knew she had anticipated a confrontation. Imoshen nodded to an open door and the two women stepped into the darkened room.

The only light came from the building across the courtyard. It spilled through the room's floor-length windows onto the polished floor and illuminated a graceful stringed instrument. As if drawn to this Cariah glided over to stroke the sensual curve of the wood. Imoshen followed.

"You alone could have defended me against Jacolm's charge, Cariah. You chose not to." She tried not to sound as hurt and betrayed as she felt.

Cariah did not turn to face her; instead she looked out

through the window, her voice the merest whisper. "What would you have me do?"

"Confirm that I was not using my gifts to cheat at a foolish game of cards."

"You would have me reveal myself and risk ostracism—for what?" Cariah demanded raggedly. "Why should they believe me if they will not believe you?"

Imoshen's heart sank. She wanted to rail at Cariah, to complain at the unfairness of it all but . . . "You are right."

Cariah's shoulders slumped.

Imoshen stepped closer, placing a hand on her shoulder. "I'm sorry. I will not betray your secret."

Cariah shook her head. She pushed Imoshen away and sank onto the seat next to the harp. "You make it hard for me not to love you."

Imoshen gasped. "All I ask is that you be my friend."

A short, bitter laugh escaped Cariah. She brushed the tears from her face, then her hands traveled over the instrument's vertical strings, absently plucking them, drawing sweet notes into the air.

Imoshen watched Cariah's graceful fingers, the elegant line of her throat. "How can you hide your T'En gifts so well?"

"Years of practice."

Fraught silence hung between them. Then Cariah sighed. "My gifts are negligible so it was easy. I vowed when my mother died never to reveal the depths of my T'En inheritance. Can you imagine what it was like living in my own Stronghold, constantly watched by Father and the servants, aware that one unconscious slip would see me a prisoner, locked away as my mother had been?"

"I am sorry."

"So am I." Cariah caressed the strings. "I have only one acceptable gift and that I use sparingly."

Imoshen touched her fingers. "Play for me, Cariah. First as you would play for them, then for me alone."

Cariah met her eyes, then nodded.

Tulkhan strode down the dimly lit hall. The palace was so complex that if he did not find Imoshen soon he would not find her until she was ready to be found.

He froze as subtle T'En music drifted from the darkened room. Silently he slipped through the half-closed door. The room's occupants were too absorbed to notice him. Curious, he stepped into deep shadow.

He could see Imoshen as a tall silhouette outlined against the window, while Cariah was seated at an elegant, stringed instrument. Fingers poised, she paused, then ended the piece with a flourish. Tulkhan had learnt enough by now to know that the pauses were as important as the notes.

"This time I play for you alone," Cariah whispered. She stroked the strings with her fingers to create rippling waves of sound so sweet they flowed like water over Tulkhan's skin, bringing tears to his eyes. He felt as if she were plucking the strings of his soul.

Cariah's fingers grew still and silence followed. At last Imoshen let out her breath in a long sigh. "How can you hold it back?"

Silently Cariah looked up at Imoshen. Tulkhan could not see her face, only the back of her head.

"Something so beautiful cannot be bad," Imoshen whispered.

Cariah stood. When she spoke her voice was cool, dispassionate. "I have chosen my path."

"But is it right to make yourself out to be less than you are so that you can be accepted?"

Cariah's laughter sounded as sharp as breaking glass.

"You can talk!" Cariah flung at Imoshen.

Tulkhan saw Imoshen's shoulders stiffen. The two women confronted each other. He did not understand the point of their argument.

"I am out of my depth." Imoshen lifted her hands imploringly. "All I ask is your friendship and counsel."

Cariah shook her head slowly. The same hand which

had drawn that hauntingly beautiful music from the strings lifted to tenderly caress Imoshen's cheek. The intimacy of the touch made Tulkhan flinch. When he had suspected Imoshen of taking lovers, he had never thought to be cuckolded by a woman.

"Is that all? Do you wonder that I must refuse?"

"Cariah," Imoshen pleaded.

"No. You ask for more than I can give!" Abruptly she turned and strode towards the door, her eyes blinded by tears. Once Tulkhan had resented her, now he felt sorry for her.

When the sound of her soft footfalls faded, Tulkhan returned his attention to Imoshen. She straightened, visibly gathering her composure, before walking towards him. As she stepped into the dim shaft of light, Tulkhan moved, slamming the door closed.

As suddenly as he had moved she was gone.

While he strained to see her, he registered that familiar metallic sensation. Fear closed a cold hand around his heart. "Imoshen?"

"Tulkhan?"

He identified her tall, dark shape amidst the shadows where a moment before he could not see her. His skin prickled unpleasantly.

Silence hung between them. He felt vulnerable, exposed by the beauty of the music and the intimacy of the scene he had witnessed. When he made no move to speak, she took a step closer.

"Why are you here, General?"

He closed the distance between them and lifted his hand to cup her cheek as he had seen Cariah do. He wanted to claim her with a kiss of slow, lingering intensity, to taste her lips and savor her response.

Her hand closed over his, then she used gentle pressure to break the contact. "Don't. I cannot think when you touch me."

The admission made his blood race. "Nor I."

The rawness of his tone surprised him. He heard

Imoshen's quick intake of breath. He wanted to pursue that breath, to feel her gasp at his touch. Driven, he sought her lips. Just one kiss, he told himself.

But he knew it would never be enough when she opened at his touch, sweetly giving. She was the elixir of life, intoxicating and vital.

With a little moan Imoshen broke contact. "Why did you follow me, General?"

He knew he should warn her about Jacolm but he didn't want to destroy the intimacy of this moment. Yet questions begged to be answered. "What is there between you and the Lady Cariah?"

She turned her face from him.

"Imoshen?" he asked gently.

She sighed. "Nothing that I can share with you."

"But you share something with her? What unnatural creatures you are!"

She gave a snort of disbelief. "And the love your men share as sword-brothers is somehow more honorable?"

When he gave no answer she went to walk past him. He caught her arm, fighting the urge to pull her to him and bend her will with the force of his need for her. "What do you plot with Cariah? Answer me!"

Her eyes were dark pools in her pale face. She gave no answer, no denial.

He tightened his hold on her. "Imoshen? You tell me to trust you. How can I?"

Sadly, she mimicked his earlier action, cupping his jaw in her hand. Her lids lowered as she leant close enough to brush her lips across his. "Trust must be given." Her breath dusted his face.

He returned the kiss. "Earned, not given. I will not have secrets between us."

She pulled back. "So you say. But it is not my secret to share with you. Let me go, General."

It was on his lips to deny her. As if sensing this she twisted her arm, breaking his hold.

"We of the T'En value our word," she told him.

"You speak in riddles. You cannot expect me to trust blindly. I was ready to support you against my own man tonight—"

"That Jacolm is trouble. My honor is my own to—"

"Anything you do or say reflects on me," he told her.

"I could say the same. How would you feel if I fought your battles for you?"

He tensed. "You do. You did not even consult me before interviewing those interpreters."

Her startled look amused him despite his annoyance. For a moment she said nothing. Then she lifted her chin as if facing something unpleasant. "I see. If I have offended you, I am sorry, General Tulkhan. But I am used to making decisions and acting on them. What I did, I did for your own good."

"I could say the same. You do not know what honor means to a Ghebite man."

"And it means nothing to a Ghebite woman, to any woman?" she whispered.

He lifted his hands helplessly.

Imoshen moved to the door. As she opened it the candlelight cloaked her with its golden glow. When she looked back he wanted to kiss the furrow from her brow.

"The day after tomorrow we will take our vows, General. Bonding is no dry legal transaction. It is not an exchange of property where a man acquires a wife to act as brood mare." Emotion choked her voice. He could see tears glittering in her dark eyes. "Bonding is a joining of the souls. I only pray we will not live to regret this."

With that she was gone.

He wanted to confront her, insist that what he felt for her had nothing to do with political necessity. But how could he reassure her when he had already promised himself to keep his inner self private, shielded from her T'En powers?

A Ghebite soldier reserved his closest friendship for his

equal, his sword-brother. They faced death together on the battlefield. He trusted his sword-brother with his life. A Ghebite soldier shared something less with the wife he hardly saw; after all, she was only a woman.

Tulkhan's head reeled. Imoshen expected him to regard her as his equal. But could he share his soul with her? Would she settle for less?

Nine

IMOSHEN HID HER surprise when Tulkhan linked his arm through hers and drew her away from the others.

"In Gheeaba it is customary for the husband to give his wife a gift the day before their wedding," he said.

It was on the tip of Imoshen's tongue to correct him— she would never be his wife—but she did not want to destroy their accord.

She was aware of the disapproving stares of Woodvine and Athlyng as Tulkhan led her out of the salon. According to the old customs, bond-partners fasted and purified them-selves, abstaining from all contact from dawn the day before their bonding. But even before the Ghebite invasion, only old-fashioned people like Imoshen's family and the Keld had adhered to such customs. In the High Court this observance had been reduced to fasting from midnight the night before the bonding, and this was what Imoshen planned to do.

Tulkhan opened the door to the maproom and strode to the table, which for once was not littered with maps. Four mysterious objects were laid out there.

"First," he picked up Reothe the Builder's tome. "I wanted to thank you for supplying a translation of the pas-sages on T'Diemn's defenses. What a mind! And to think he lived four hundred years ago!"

Imoshen couldn't help smiling.

Tulkhan put the book aside and unrolled a rich velvet

cloak to reveal the longest sword she had ever seen. "I wanted you to see this. I know you think my people barbarians because we don't have written records dating back hundreds of years. But we are not ignorant. This is my grandfather's sword which was gifted to me. As you see, the scabbard is not decorated for display but the hilt . . ." He unwrapped the hand grip. It was decorated in niello with a surprisingly graceful design of a stylized rearing horse. "This is my size—a hand-and-a-half grip. I take after my grandfather, Seerkhan the Giant, or Great. In our language Giant and Great are the same word. In my grandfather's time a man's life depended on his sword and his horse. I was taught never to unsheath this sword without drawing blood. The great Akha Khan demands his tribute. Come closer. I want you to see this."

Drawn despite herself, Imoshen stepped towards him. He took her into the circle of his arms, her back to his chest. His deep voice enveloped her. She felt warm to the core.

"This sword should not be unsheathed in direct sunlight." Silently he withdrew it from the fur-lined scabbard and held it before them so that Imoshen looked along the blade. "Breathe on the blade and see Akha Khan's serpent come to life."

Imoshen took a deep breath and exhaled. As her breath moved up the blade a pattern like the variations of a serpent's skin traveled up the blade and back. She gasped in wonder and went to touch the marvel.

"No," Tulkhan hissed. "It is dedicated to Akha Khan."

Imoshen's fingers itched to stroke the gleaming blade to see if she could identify the power which animated it. "How?"

"This weapon is a work of art. Its blade was made in three parts: entwined cold, forged, then twisted and reforged. Then it was filed and burnished with infinite care. This is not the work of an unsophisticated people."

He released her to step away. His eyes met hers. She watched as he ran his finger down the blade's edge, leaving a smear of blood.

Holding Tulkhan's eyes, Imoshen placed the tip of her

sixth finger above the blade's edge. She knew she could seal a wound with her healing gift. Exerting herself, she concentrated on creating a wound. A drop of blood pooled on the pad of her finger, fell, then trickled down the gleaming metal. Tulkhan's black eyes widened. No word passed between them but they understood each other. It thrilled Imoshen.

Tulkhan cleaned the blade before replacing it in its scabbard.

"I thank you for sharing this with me," she said. "It is a gift I will treasure always."

He laughed. "Your gift is more tangible than that." With a flourish he opened the last object, a shallow chest. "This is your gift. A torque of pure gold to match my ceremonial belt."

Imoshen stared at the neck circle. Its line was elegant enough, a crescent moon. That was not what offended her. It was the subject of the filigree and niello design.

"See." Tulkhan unwrapped his ceremonial belt which was made of rectangular hinged squares of gold embossed with the same design. "Let me see the torque on you."

Imoshen opened her mouth to protest but held her tongue. Tulkhan placed the heavy gold torque around her throat, then stood back to admire the effect.

Imoshen lifted her hand to the neck circle. It felt like a yoke of servitude, binding her to Tulkhan's perceptions of a wife. She undid the clasp and removed the torque slowly, replacing it in its bed of velvet.

"What is it, Imoshen?"

"Your men deck themselves in golden jewelry—"

"It is our way. We wear our wealth on our backs. It is not so long since we were a nomadic people, old customs died hard."

Imoshen sighed. He was defensive now. "What is on the torque, General?"

Tulkhan frowned, thinking surely the design was obvious. "The great Akha Khan in the form of a black stallion."

"But what is he doing?"

"Crushing the enemies of his people." Even as Tulkhan said it he understood how this might be in bad taste considering that Imoshen's family had died on the battlefield. "It is taken from a myth where he transforms into the stallion and tramples—"

"Death and bloodshed!" She lifted the heavy torque from its resting place and held it before him, anger making her voice tight. Her island had been trampled by Akha Khan's stallion and her family all killed. How could he expect her to wear this? Tears stung her eyes. "This is exquisite workmanship, but it deals with blood and death. Is the Ghebite mind so steeped in violence that it cannot create peace and beauty for its own sake?"

"You refuse my gift?"

"I will wear your gift with honor. But I will not be your 'wife' and wear her yoke of servitude." Imoshen replaced the torque, searching his face despairingly. Suddenly she scooped up the great sword on its bed of velvet. "I value the sharing of this more than anything else!"

Her declaration warmed Tulkhan. He took the sword from her and slowly rewrapped it. "Every morning when I wake I wonder, what will Imoshen confound me with today?"

Silence hung between them, heavy with things unsaid.

Imoshen touched his arm. "Neither of us tread an easy path, General. We will be bonded and crowned on the last day of the old year. When the sun rises the day after tomorrow, it will be dawning on a new age for Fair Isle."

His hand covered hers. "I did not mean to insult you with my gift."

"It is the gifts you cannot see that I treasure most."

He shook his head. "You are a rare woman, Imoshen."

She smiled and gave him the obeisance among equals. "I will see you at the festivities this evening."

Only when the door closed behind her did Tulkhan realize she had forgotten to take the torque. He would send it to her room.

Crossing to the hearth, he stirred up the coals then sat

before the fire, resting Seerkhan's sword across his knees. His heart beat faster as he recalled Imoshen's words. The day after tomorrow the sun would rise on a new age for Fair Isle, one fraught with danger and challenge. An age he would stamp as his own!

Imoshen shifted impatiently, causing her new maid to drop the comb. "I'm sorry, Merkah."

The girl flushed, and Imoshen suspected she wasn't used to members of the royal family apologizing.

"It will be a grand feast tonight," Merkah ventured.

Imoshen nodded. This was her last evening unbonded. Tomorrow promised to be a full day with the bonding ceremony in the morning and the joint coronation after the midday meal. She longed to know whether her bonding with Tulkhan would bring peace to Fair Isle and what would become of Reothe. The temptation to do a scrying was intense but she lacked control.

And she was still no closer in her quest for knowledge of her gifts. Though the Keeper of Knowledge had provided her with a raft of ancient documents, she could find no histories of her people and no treatises on the T'En gifts. If only the T'Elegos had not been destroyed!

"There, T'Imoshen." Merkah stepped back with a pleased expression and waited expectantly.

Imoshen studied her reflection. She looked quite unlike herself. The maid had created a hairstyle worthy of the High Court. Imoshen's hair had been smoothed over padding on the crown of her head to create a fan of silver satin, while a single deep blue sapphire hung in the center of her forehead. She had argued against a diadem of zircons, preferring the simplicity of this which echoed her sapphire blue underdress.

"I look so . . . grand," Imoshen said. "Thank you." But she could see it wasn't the response Merkah had hoped for.

The girl, recommended by Kalleen, was a capable maid but Imoshen couldn't let her guard down. She longed for her old friend's company.

"You may have the rest of the evening to yourself." Imoshen rose.

"Very well, T'Imoshen." Clearly disappointed, Merkah knelt to adjust the brocade tabard, which had been embroidered with the finest thread of spun silver. It hung to Imoshen's knees over the velvet undergown.

As Merkah rose, she tripped. Imoshen caught the girl's arm, but she pulled away sharply. Just as quickly she offered an abrupt obeisance of apology. "Forgive me, my lady."

"It does not matter," Imoshen whispered. But it did. It hurt when people pulled away from her touch as if she might contaminate them.

She pretended to adjust her neckline in the full-length mirror. The truth of her position was not pleasant. In desperation the people might reach to her for reassurance, but in everyday life she was a pariah. In the Age of Discernment, enlightenment did not extend to the T'En. "You may go, Merkah. Join in the festivities."

The maid gave Imoshen the deep obeisance without meeting her eyes and silently withdrew.

Imoshen paced the room. She was ready beforehand because she had chosen not to attend the afternoon's formal entertainment. She had thought she needed time to compose herself for this evening and tomorrow, but now she was restless.

Surely it would not hurt to walk the corridors of the palace? She could pretend she was making a last-minute check on the arrangements. Sweeping out into the long gallery, she strode off energetically.

The palace of a thousand rooms was full. The Keldon nobles had all brought their own retinues, and entertainers of every kind were housed in the servants' quarters. Mainland ambassadors and nobles had been arriving steadily for the past ten days. It was a good sign, as it meant their rulers were willing to acknowledge General Tulkhan's sovereignty of Fair Isle. From conversation Imoshen learnt that the General was well known and respected. Even the ambassadors whose countries had been annexed to Gheeaba spoke well of him.

She'd had to exercise diplomacy while greeting the ambassadors from the mainland triad. When the Empress had called on these southern kingdoms to honor the old alliance, they had claimed they could not mobilize their armies against the Ghebite invasion in time. Yet now they presented themselves boldly as though their excuse was not paper thin.

Imoshen suspected Tulkhan had probably received news of his half-brother. As far as she knew Gharavan had retreated to lick his wounds. If the lack of an ambassador from his homeland troubled Tulkhan, he did not reveal it, least of all to her.

A familiar, arrogant voice echoed up the grand staircase from the marbled foyer below. Imoshen's skin went cold. Hardly daring to breathe, she peered around a column.

Kinraid the Vaygharian! The sly, manipulative traitor himself! Unbidden, she recalled those terrible days. When she had not been in her Stronghold to greet the Ghebite King and his Vaygharian advisor, they had declared her a rebel. In reality she had been abducted by one of Reothe's men, Drake, on his orders. She had escaped and returned to her Stronghold only to find the King and his Ghebites feasting in her great hall. Within a day Tulkhan had returned from the Keldon Highlands without having captured Reothe. Seeing his chance, Kinraid claimed that if the General were truly loyal to King Gharavan he would return to the Highlands at once to hunt the rebels. When the General refused to leave until spring melted the snow in the high passes, Kinraid had acted quickly. He had marched into Tulkhan's bedchamber, where Imoshen and the General lay entwined. Kinraid had laughed as his men beat Tulkhan senseless, and had looked with cruel lust on Imoshen's nakedness. But when his bare flesh had touched hers, she had seen his death. The Vaygharian would meet his end in flames of agony.

Kinraid's voice jolted her from her memories, and she looked down to see him dressed in the formal robes of the Vayghar, complete with sculptured beard and beaded hair. He was accompanied by several men in the same ornate costumes of Vayghar merchant princes. She flushed. How dare Kinraid presume on the immunity of ambassadorial status to invade her palace. The General must be warned.

Swiftly Imoshen left the upper gallery and sped to the salon. When Imoshen saw the General's familiar profile, she had to smile. He was watching a performance which she knew he would find excruciatingly boring. The audience needed an appreciation of ritualized song and dance and a knowledge of T'En history to understand the references. Since speaking with Tulkhan, she had discarded many entertainments which might exclude the Ghebites, but the mainland nobility still expected a little High T'En culture.

When she could not catch Tulkhan's eye, impatience warred with caution. It was either enter the room and disrupt the performance or get his attention by other means.

General Tulkhan was watching the play, privately marveling that anyone could keep a straight face while decked out in such a ridiculous costumes. How they balanced on one leg while completing the delicate arm movements was beyond him. When a cymbal tinkled the Keldon nobles clicked their fingers appreciatively.

Several of his men glanced his way. He bit his lip to hide a smile and thought about tomorrow's arrangements. Soon Imoshen would be his by every law known to man. Despite his impatience, dread made his heart beat like a solid drum, for no True-man had bonded with a pure T'En woman in over six hundred years. What had Imoshen the First tried to hide with her vow of celibacy?

Something stirred his senses. He felt as if silken fingers had stroked his skin. The touch was so sensual he had to swallow. Pinpricks of sensation dusted his lips. He wanted to find Imoshen and kiss her. The back of his neck tingled. Very slowly, he turned.

There she was, standing in the entrance with her intense wine-dark eyes focused on him. Damn her!

She beckoned, her expressive eyes troubled.

He sprang to his feet, weaving through the clustered

tables and chairs, heading towards her like a dog called by its master. Fury built in him.

Wharrd met his eyes, looking for an unspoken signal to accompany him. Tulkhan shook his head. He did not want the world to know the Dhamfeer had tweaked his leash!

"General," Imoshen whispered. She caught his hand and drew him with her, hastening across the wide gallery into a window embrasure where they could talk in private.

Though she radiated anger it was not directed at him.

"I've seen Kinraid," Imoshen whispered. "He dared to come here as an ambassador of Vayghar. What will we do?"

Before he could answer, the thump of booted feet on the gallery's parquetry floor interrupted them. Tulkhan moved out of the embrasure to see a self-important servant escorting five richly dressed Vaygharians, Kinraid amongst them.

He sensed Imoshen at his side and her presence warmed him. It surprised him to realize he found her support reassuring.

Kinraid stepped from the ranks and gave a formal bow of greeting. He offered a sealed scroll. "We meet again, General Tulkhan. I am ambassador to the Vayghar and these are sons of the merchant council, princes in their own right, come to celebrate your coronation."

Tulkhan accepted the scroll and broke the seal, reading it swiftly. Imoshen peered over his shoulder.

As Vayghar's official representative, Kinraid could not be refused a welcome without insulting this trading nation. The princes were there to add weight to his reputation. Tulkhan did not want to insult one of the most powerful countries on the mainland. He felt Imoshen's tense hand on the small of his back.

"Welcome, Vaygharians." He gave a small inclination of his head, the barest minimum for civility, then held Imoshen's gaze. "T'Imoshen, would you find a suitable apartment for the Vaygharian entourage, and arrange for their seating during tomorrow's ceremony?"

He knew Imoshen would understand the political

necessity of acknowledging the Vaygharians, but it was clear she didn't like it. He grasped her arm, willing her to rely on his judgment. If he sent the Vaygharians packing on the eve of his coronation, how would the other ambassadors react?

Only this morning he'd had news confirming that his half-brother was bitterly plotting revenge. It was not enough that Gharavan had inherited the extended Ghebite empire, benefiting from years of Tulkhan's faithful service. He wanted Fair Isle too.

Tulkhan feared his half-brother and with good reason. He knew the strength of the army Gharavan could raise. If he had been in the King's position he would have mobilized a massive force by calling on alliances and bringing in auxiliaries from the annexed countries. He would have struck swiftly and without mercy. Rebellion had to be put down before it could spread. Only one generation separated Gheeaba's annexed kingdoms from freedom, and they did not wear the yoke of servitude willingly.

If he did not want to see the island's fertile fields and jaunty townships reduced to rubble, Tulkhan must make the Vaygharian ambassador welcome. Politics disgusted him.

Imoshen gave the General a sharp look then turned to face the Vaygharians, giving them the formal T'En greeting. "Welcome. Come take refreshment and watch the performance while I prepare your rooms."

She escorted them into the salon then swiftly returned to Tulkhan's side. He was standing at the window, watching the swirling snow. It was almost dusk and he looked tired and depressed, as if he missed his warm homeland. Imoshen felt a tug of fellowship. She had lost her family, but in conquering Fair Isle the General had lost his family and his homeland. She wanted to ease that frown.

"I know you welcome Kinraid because of political necessity but I cannot forget—"

"Do you think I can? Because of Kinraid's lies my half-brother hates me!" Tulkhan expelled his breath in an angry sigh. "I know what Kinraid is, Imoshen. I'd rather he was here where I can watch him than have him stirring up trouble elsewhere."

"He will report back to the Ghebite King."

Tulkhan's wolfish smile made her heart lurch.

"Yes, he will report back to Gharavan. And he will tell him what I want him to know."

Imoshen felt the twin of Tulkhan's smile tug at her lips but she was still uneasy. Her hand closed around the General's arm, seeking reassurance, contact. "I don't like it."

He straightened, looking down into her face, his obsidian eyes unreadable. "Do you think I do?" He smiled grimly. "My father taught me many things, but one above all else. Keep your enemies close where you can see what they plot."

Cold fear lanced Imoshen. Was Tulkhan telling her that she was his dearest enemy, the one he would keep so close he would bed her?

Sickened by the thought she pulled away. "There are arrangements I must see to. Please excuse me, General."

Much later, as Imoshen unpinned her elaborate hairstyle she massaged her throbbing temples. There had been no opportunity to eat or relax, least of all speak privately with General Tulkhan. Earlier tonight she had observed those around her, gauging their loyalties. She was exhausted.

When she downed a tisane to ease her headache the bitter aftertaste clung to her tongue, so she poured a wine and drank that. Tonight she would need to sleep well, because tomorrow she must not falter. Imoshen stared into the fire, watching its leaping patterns.

To think, once she had imagined her bonding day would be a day of great joy and spiritual significance—the joining of her soul with Reothe's.

Dreamily she unclasped the lace tabard and laid it over the chair, followed by the rich velvet underdress. Kicking off her formal slippers, Imoshen knelt naked before the flames on the fur rug. Her hair slid across her shoulders and down her back like a silken shawl. She felt the fire's warmth caress her bare skin.

The fur was deep and so fine it enticed her to enjoy its caress. Sinking into its embrace she vaguely understood that the herb was having a strong effect, mixed with the wine on an empty stomach. She let herself drift, safe at least for now. Come tomorrow she would face the enemy.

At first her overworked mind ran on and on, replaying images like brilliant jewels—flashes of conversation, a peel of laughter, the flickering candles, the heat of sweating, perfumed bodies pressed together—then it all faded away and she felt pleasantly empty.

Her limbs grew weightless and her body became an insubstantial thing which had no hold on her. It seemed she slipped painlessly from her physical shell and she floated upwards. She turned to look down on her pale slender form, lying with such innocent abandon on the fur before the fireplace. Did she really look like that, an alabaster sculpture, her blue-veined skin like fine marble?

This incorporeal state was so peaceful she doubted she would ever feel the need to return. What did that body have to offer her but responsibilities and cruel choices? She wanted nothing but to relinquish all thought and give herself over to the warm haze which enveloped her.

"So you never felt that you truly belonged?" her companion asked.

She knew she was dreaming yet felt her leg muscles work as she strode up the slope. Around them the amber leaves of autumn fluttered down to crunch underfoot.

"Did you?" Imoshen asked Reothe. She recognized the place and time now. They were walking their horses through the woods. He had just asked her to bond with him and she had said yes.

A strange excitement animated her. Every time she looked at him her breath caught in her throat. There was something unknown in his eyes, a pre-sentiment of their joining which promised something thrilling, dangerous.

Yet she felt safe in his company. He was the one who had held back when she would have taken their kisses further. He had laughed, delighted with her response. She felt a heated blush stain her cheeks with the memory and saw his knowing smile.

Annoyed because he could read her so clearly, she turned away from him and strode on. "Don't tell me the Emperor and Empress welcomed you with open arms."

"You forget, I was only a boy of ten, orphaned by my parents' suicide. As my guardian, the Empress tried to make up for that, rearing me with her own children. Because she was open to me it was easy to win her over."

When Imoshen had first heard this she had taken it at face value, but this time she understood. Reothe was talking about finding the Empress's Key. She was the center of the palace, adored by the Emperor, revered by everyone else. Reothe was only a boy. He had to win her over to protect himself. Imoshen could almost believe it had been an instinctive thing. He was gifted indeed if he could use his T'En ability at ten years of age. Her healing gifts had not come to her until puberty.

As if thinking of it brought on her powers, a prickle of T'En awareness made her skin itch with danger. What was that smell? Tallow-dip candles?

Suddenly Reothe was beside her and she felt the hard planes of his body.

"You made a vow," he whispered hoarsely.

His hands circled her waist, bare palms on bare flesh. A familiar flash of longing ignited her body as she recognized him on a primal level. She wanted him. Why hold back? They had just agreed to bond. Her parents would oversee the betrothal ceremony . . .

But her parents were dead and this was all a lie, an impossible dream.

"No!"

Painfully, the illusion fell from her vision. Reothe still

held her but she was naked in his arms. Desperately she tried to orient herself. She was in a dimly lit cave. Plush rugs covered the ground and hung on the walls, yet the only furniture was a crudely made table, set with crystal goblets and a matching decanter of ruby wine.

"Where am I?"

Reothe laughed.

Instinctively she brought her knee up but he was already stepping back, leaving her off balance. Why wasn't she cold? They were in a warm cave. The hot springs!

"Answer me. What have you done, Reothe?"

His smile was triumphant. "I proved my theory."

"Theory? I am no theory!"

He laughed delightedly and hauled the simple lawn shirt off over his head, tossing it across to her. "Here, cover yourself if you must."

She caught the shirt, wanting to throw it back in his face. His expression told her he knew her dilemma and was amused by it. Defiantly she pulled the garment over her shoulders. His scent enveloped her. The fine material was warm from his body. It brushed her bare flesh like a caress.

Then she noticed the designs etched on his wiry chest with dried blood. Though she was not familiar with their meaning, Imoshen recognized the symbols of the Ancients.

"Your chest." She tasted the air with her tongue. "Blood and death?"

"Don't worry, it's not my own blood. I had to seal the pact."

"With a death?"

"It was necessary. The Ancients crave a little blood and death. They are a greedy lot." He smiled and she realized that this beautiful creature had no more true humanity than . . . than her.

No. She wasn't like that.

"What games have you been playing, Reothe?" Her heart thundered with fear but she would not reveal it. Planting her feet to confront him, she felt the uneven stone under the rugs. "How did I get here?"

"I brought you to me. We made our vows and we are all but bonded. Your body calls to mine."

"You killed tonight to do this!" Was she bound to him in ways she did not understand? She feared so.

"Only a snow leopard."

"Still. A creature's life force has been extinguished and to what end?"

"To unite us."

A trickle of dread made its way down her spine to settle in her belly. Was he brilliant or mad, or both?

Reothe poured two goblets of wine, holding them up to the crude candles, turning them back and forth.

"Your eyes flicker like this, red flame as dark as wine. Come, drink, Imoshen. Celebrate our bonding." The timbre of his voice stroked her senses.

She found she was standing beside him, her hand on the glass stem of the goblet, yet she didn't remember moving. Her head felt slow, her tongue thick.

"Tomorrow I make my vows with General Tulkhan, all is arranged." But it took a great effort to speak.

"No. Today you make your vows with me. You did not think I would let you bond with another, did you? We are the last of the T'En. We owe our forebears this much. And we owe it to each other."

She felt a delicious anticipation and a sense of completion as if this was always meant to be.

He raised the crystal and sipped the wine; she found her body mimicking his. The wine was tart on her tongue. Drugged?

A spurt of fear cleared her head. What would General Tulkhan think if she deserted him on their bonding day? He would never believe she had been abducted against her will. Panic spiraled through her.

"Drink," Reothe whispered.

She put the goblet down with so much haste that wine spilled across the table.

He laughed softly and took a deliberate sip of his wine. She saw it glisten on his lips but didn't see him swallow.

Somehow she knew what he intended before he moved to take her face in his hands, yet she couldn't refuse him. The touch of his lips on hers was like velvet, warm, wine-flavored kisses. And then she tasted wine on her tongue and swallowed instinctively, drinking from his mouth.

Imoshen moaned. It was the bonding in its most primitive form. In the modern ceremonies she and General Tulkhan would sip from the same cup, their lips touching the same place.

Reothe pulled away, a deep growl rising from his throat. She took an instinctive step back.

"How can you think of *him* when you're kissing me?"

She shook her head, unable to explain. "I won't do this, Reothe. I gave my word—"

"To me!" His fist hit his chest. He stared at her then shook his head and lifted a hand in entreaty. "Our vow predates your word to the General. Let's finish this now."

He leant closer, eyes closing as he inhaled her scent. When he spoke his voice was raw with need, calling up an instinctive response in her. She wanted him, had always wanted him.

"I promise it will be like nothing else, nothing you've known with him. I heard how he chose you the night of the Harvest Festival." His hands settled on her shoulders, tightening painfully. "Yet you came to me that night with his scent on your skin. Why do you torment me like this?"

Imoshen wanted to deny it. That night she had walked the battlements alone and frightened. Her need for something familiar had taken her to Reothe, but she did not know how. She had never meant to torment him. What would Reothe say if he knew . . .

"What?" His eyes flew open, alarmingly alert. The dark centers were large and flecked with the moving flames of the candles.

"I love the General." She had said the first thing that had come into her head, but even as she said it she knew it was true.

He laughed. "You can control him, you mean. You can't love less than your equal. Look!"

He raised his arm between them. Disbelievingly she saw the scar of his old bonding wound split open. A ragged gasp escaped him as blood welled to the surface, trickling freely down his inner arm.

Every instinct told Imoshen to run, yet she couldn't bring her body under control. As if in a dream she saw her arm lift between them to reveal her bonding wound to mirror his. The scar was so well healed it was almost invisible.

"You did this," he whispered. "Did you think you could erase our bonding by seamlessly knitting the skin?"

She shook her head.

He clasped his fingers through hers, palm to palm, wrist to wrist. She could feel his hot blood on the sensitive skin of her inner arm.

His eyes held hers. "Bond with me. Bond our blood, our bodies, then our minds. There is no turning back what we began that autumn."

"No."

"Part the skin, open for me."

Something shifted, warm and willing inside her.

A sharp sound escaped her. The old scar stung.

He smiled. "Your body wants me."

"No. You're doing this."

"I don't have to."

And Imoshen knew he was right. Her body had always wanted him, had recognized him before she did. She was falling into an abyss.

"As our blood mingles, so will—"

"No!" She would not say the formal bonding words.

A scream rent the air. For an instant Imoshen thought it was her own. But Reothe's startled expression told her it was as unexpected as it was unwelcome.

"Say the words!" He gave their interwoven fingers a squeeze.

"Not while there's breath in my body!"

Another scream filled the air. This time she recognized it

for what it was. A great cat's death scream. Suddenly sound permeated the cavern. Men and women yelled instructions; their boots pounded on stone as metal scraped on metal.

Reothe cursed. Dropping her hand, he flicked aside a wall-hanging, revealing a passage, and left her without a word.

Imoshen ran after him, his shirt flapping around her bare thighs. As she ran she brought her wrist to her mouth and licked the old wound. It was all she need do to make the skin knit.

Her feet carried her through a short passage and out of a torchlit opening into the night. Flaming torches did little to dispel the mist. People rushed past her. Then she heard another terrible feral scream, but this time it was the roar of attack closely followed by the ragged shrieks of someone dying in terror. She did not need to see them to know the cat was shredding its victim's belly with the claws of its powerful hind legs.

A white leopard loped out of the mist towards her. Imoshen's heart faltered. She glanced about but there were no weapons within grasp.

The beautiful beast slowed and prowled nearer, a growl trickling from its chest. It sniffed, must have smelt her fear, yet its head lifted as if it was listening to something. Then she noticed the fur under its throat. Shocked, she saw the gaping neck wound. Yet no blood dripped for it had already been spilt. A prickling sensation, part awe and part terror, traveled over her skin. If the beast was dead, what was animating it?

Instinctively she searched for the force which gave the cat life. Now that she probed she felt it, an unknown power source, angry and ancient.

Shrieks and Reothe's shouted commands told her that his people were making a stand somewhere in the mist.

The beast looked into her eyes, ancient intelligence illuminating its feline features. She knew she was in more danger from this fell creature than from a hungry snow leopard. This had to be the beast Reothe had killed to bring her here.

Despite her fear, Imoshen knelt as if in supplication and extended her hand, fingers limp. The cat stepped forward, dainty for such a large animal, and lifted its great muzzle. Jaws capable of crunching bone lightly brushed her flesh. She watched its nostrils flare as it inhaled her scent, identifying her. Then its tongue rasped across her skin.

"If you have been wronged. I will right the wrong," Imoshen offered.

The screams of the dying drove her to her feet. The cat caught her hand in the feather-light grasp of its massive jaws and led her away, its great shoulders brushing her bare thigh. With its guidance she found the defenders.

The snow cat at her side she stepped out of the heated mists into a clearing. More than a dozen people were backed up against the far cliff face by several prowling snow cats. Some swung blazing torches, others had weapons of steel. In their front ranks stood Reothe, bare chested, dressed in nothing but boots and breeches, his hair loose. Imoshen knew it was only a matter of time before the great cats brought him down.

Already he was bleeding, or was it the blood of the beasts he had slain? He held a burning brand in one hand and an axe in the other.

The snow cat let Imoshen's hand drop, then lifted its head and gave an eerie yowl. At this signal the other cats ceased their attack. As if summoned, they prowled over to join Imoshen and the great beast by her side.

Reothe's companions gasped; some made the sign to ward off evil, others dropped to their knees, heads bowed, both hands raised to their foreheads in deep obeisance.

Reothe let the weapon drop. The axe hit the stone with a dull thud. His face held hope. "Imoshen?"

"No, Reothe. I promised to right the wrong."

The great cat nudged her and she stepped forward with it at her side. She saw Reothe's eyes widen as he recognized the beast.

"I think you know what to do," she told him, though she had no idea.

Fear crawled across his face. He controlled it and handed the flaming torch to someone. Unarmed, Reothe sank to his knees to face the beast. Its head was level with his face, its jaws a mere breath from his throat. It could tear out that slender column quick as thought.

Imoshen could see the frantic flutter of Reothe's pulse. Her fingers twined through the beast's thick fur as if to restrain it. A jolt of pure energy traveled up her arm, almost knocking her back a step. The beast swung its head toward her, a low growl issuing from its throat, but she tightened her hold.

Why was she doing this? If the ancient ones used this beast to kill Reothe, she would be free of him. Reluctantly, Imoshen released the great cat.

It sat facing Reothe, whose eyes never left the cat's face.

He was communing with the Ancients. Had he stolen the power he needed to bring her here when he spilt the great cat's blood? Perhaps the Ancients had sent the cats to seek retribution.

Abruptly, the dead snow leopard lifted its paw and slashed Reothe's chest.

Burning streaks of pain raced down Imoshen's chest between her breasts. She staggered backwards.

Three parallel furrows appeared on Reothe's skin. For a moment they appeared bloodless, then they grew dark as the blood gathered. Reothe swayed but remained upright.

The beast lapped at the blood. Imoshen shuddered as she felt its rasping tongue on the flesh between her breasts, drinking from her life force.

She opened her eyes, suddenly unaware that she'd closed them, and saw Reothe watching her. His hands lifted to caress the fur of the great cat's head. In that instant the tension eased.

Hardly able to believe they had been released so lightly, Imoshen watched the life force leave the cat's body. Slowly, it crumpled to lie dead at Reothe's knees. He swayed and collapsed over it.

She darted forward, catching him before his head could

strike the stone. His body was limp and cold in her arms. The others stood immobile, stunned.

"Help me!"

They came, muttering fearfully. Between them, they carried Reothe back to his cave and made up a bed. She sent someone to bring furs and whatever medicinal herbs they had.

Imoshen was not surprised to see Drake. She had not seen him since he had tried to abduct her. He told her that those present were Reothe's most trusted people. They treated her with a deference they might have shown a vision, hardly daring to stroke her sixth finger.

"It is good you are here to care for him," Drake told her.

Imoshen felt like a fraud as she arranged the furs to keep Reothe warm, and prepared a healing drink for when, if, Reothe woke.

"Leave me now, Drake."

He obeyed her without question. She did not like herself.

Numbly Imoshen knelt by the low pallet where Reothe lay, and pulled back the furs. Blood still welled from the parallel claw marks. With an instinctive knowledge she knew they were not normal wounds.

Bathing them only made it clear that the skin would not knit without her help.

She brushed the damp silver hair from Reothe's forehead. His skin was hot and she watched as fever shook his body. Calling on her healing skills she smoothed the frown from his forehead with her fingertips.

His closed eyelids quivered. What was he seeing in his mind's eye? Was the power of the Ancients stalking him in those visions?

Her heart went out to him. She did not condone what he had done, spilling the snow cat's blood to call on ancient powers, but she did admire the strength of purpose which drove him to that desperate act. He was far braver than she.

Despite her better judgment, she could not distance herself from him. He was her kinsman and the last of her kind. No one else could save him. She could not stand back and let him wander, trapped in some other plane.

Imoshen clenched her hands in fists of frustration. Here she was, untrained, floundering against something ancient and infinitely powerful. Fear left a bitter taste on her tongue, straining her nerves to fever pitch.

A shuddering breath escaped Reothe but his chest barely moved. He was fading.

She would have to do it, she had no choice.

Closing her eyes she placed her fingers over the first of the long claw marks, willing the skin to knit. The hairs on her body rose in protest. A strange taste filled her mouth, making her teeth ache. Reothe's body tensed under her hands, his skin slippery with a sheen of sweat. An answering sweat broke out on her body, making her shiver despite the steamy air of the cave. She could feel the phantom claw mark on her own flesh burn as it closed in time with Reothe's visible wound.

With the sealing of each long welt she felt a path of itching pain etch itself down her chest. The very air grew heavy with tension. This simple healing act strained her concentration until her body felt taut as a drawn bow. Still she forced the last wound to close, ignoring her own parallel pain to the last.

When this was completed something snapped inside her, as if a taut bow's string had been released, and she felt light-headed, almost dizzy with relief.

Now the air held nothing out of the ordinary. She parted the shirt's fine material to reveal the pale flesh between her breasts. It was unmarked. To the naked eye her skin was flawless. Yet she could still feel the wounds stinging.

A sigh escaped Reothe. He seemed to be deeply asleep. Sitting back on her heels, she studied his chest. Purple ridges rose where before the cuts had welled with blood. She suspected he would carry those scars till the day he died, just as she would carry their invisible twins.

He was lying so still. Before his skin had felt too hot, now it was cold. Instinct told her to warm him with her own body heat. But she feared if she willingly lay down beside him, he would own her body and soul.

Leaning forward, she touched her lips to his closed lids in a silent benediction. Then she pulled the furs over him and rose to go.

Leaving him helpless hurt her more than she cared to admit. The urge to sink down beside him and wrap her body around his was almost overwhelming.

In desperation, Imoshen turned and walked from the cave. She did not look back. When she stepped outside the sky was already growing light, though the torches still burned.

"Will he live, T'Imoshen?" Drake asked anxiously.

Reothe's people watched her expectantly. What could she say? She had healed his body but what toll would Reothe pay for trafficking with the Ancients?

Suddenly their faces ignited with joy and Imoshen felt a presence behind her.

"T'Reothe," his followers whispered reverently, greeting him in the old tongue with phrases she had never heard spoken aloud. It sounded like a litany.

Imoshen stiffened, unable to move, unable even to turn and face him. She had underestimated Reothe. Frozen with fear, she sensed his approach.

"See," he whispered. His breath caressed the back of her neck, his words rubbed her senses like warm velvet. "We are already bound." His arms slid around her shoulders and she felt his hard thighs on her buttocks, his chest against her shoulders. "You tamed the ancient ones, you saved my followers and then me."

His people dropped to their knees one by one, giving the obeisance reserved for the Emperor and Empress, both hands going to their foreheads. Only Drake dared to lift his head and drink in their presence.

Reothe's words wove an insidious spell. "They love us. They will die for us."

Disgust overwhelmed Imoshen. It was wrong to manipulate the innocent love of a desperate people.

Reothe tightened his hold on her, his voice deeply

persuasive. "They want to worship something, Imoshen. It is in their nature. Why not us? We are the last pure T'En, our gifts are the true source of the Church's power. For too long the Church has sought to destroy us—"

"No." But the word was a plea and she despised herself for her weakness.

"Together we could—"

She dropped into a crouch to escape his tender embrace and malevolent words. Throwing her weight forward she took several steps then spun to face him. Her rapid movement made the light material of his shirt caress her body. His scent filled her nostrils, a mockingly intimate reminder.

She tore off the shirt and threw it at his feet. "I won't be a part of it, Reothe."

He smiled and looked up as the birds sang to greet the sunrise. "Your bonding day dawns. Do you think the Ghebite General will forgive you for abandoning him?"

Frustration filled Imoshen. Tulkhan was never this devious. He always tried to meet her halfway. He listened and learned. Suddenly her longing for him was a physical ache. She lifted her hand to parallel streaks of pain between her breasts, discovering she could feel with her blind fingertips what she could not see with her eyes. Scar tissue.

"I did not ask to come here," she whispered. Calling on the power of the Ancients she raked her flesh, drawing blood along those scar lines. "Release me!"

Dimly she heard a shout and saw Reothe dart after her, but he was much weaker than he pretended and he fell to his knees. Desperately he surged forward with his arms outstretched to her.

Her heart contracted and she gasped with sharp dismay at the depth of her feelings for him. Fearful lest his touch undo her resolve, she turned to run and tripped.

Ten

IMOSHEN'S HANDS AND knees stung as she tripped over a rug and hit the polished wood. A cry of pain escaped her. She felt dizzy, a little sick, and very frightened. Where was she?

That male smell? General Tulkhan! A disbelieving joy flooded her. The Ancients had answered her plea.

"Come to murder me in my sleep?" Tulkhan asked softly as he watched Imoshen spin with feral grace to face him.

Tulkhan had been sitting in the chair by his bedchamber window staring out at the cold winter's dawn, comparing it to other humid dawns in his homeland, which he doubted he would ever see again, when the room had grown oppressive.

Even the air had taken on a strange tang, making him aware of unseen danger. He had been about to draw his weapon when, with a palpable release of tension, the Dhamfeer had appeared naked and disoriented. She was bleeding from three parallel lines on her chest.

Now she stared at him as if she didn't believe she'd heard him correctly. What other excuse did she have for appearing unannounced in his bedroom? Tension fed by weeks of frustration thrummed through his body. "Either you are here to kill me or to bed me. Which is it?"

With understanding came anger and Imoshen stalked toward him, magnificently furious. Her long hair hung around her body like a cloak. Every instinct told him to flee those fierce, T'En eyes. It was only by exerting his will that he remained outwardly impervious.

"You seek to provoke me, Tulkhan. Haven't I proved my loyalty to you time and time again?"

He stared up into her face. With a jolt he noted the tears which shimmered unshed in her eyes.

"Then why are you here?"

Her hands trembled as she pushed the hair from her face, muttering under her breath. He didn't need to understand High T'En to know she was cursing him.

Spinning on her heel she stalked off, all wounded dignity despite her nakedness. He was on his feet before he knew it, lunging forward to catch her around the waist. Her skin was icy cold. She arched against him, her body an exclamation of silent fury. The wiry strength in her surprised him, but she was half a head shorter and did not have his muscle.

Anticipating her attempt to drop out of his grasp he lifted her off her feet, still writhing. Then he spun and threw her onto the bed. She twisted in the air like a cat, landing on her hands and knees, her hair splaying around her in an arc.

A shiver of instinctive awe rippled through him in response to her Otherness. She had never looked more Dhamfeer.

He tore at his vest. It was an elaborate brocade garment and the thin laces snapped easily.

Her eyes widened. "What are you doing?"

He didn't bother to answer. The vest hit the floor.

She scurried across the bed but he tackled her before her feet could hit the ground on the far side.

They twisted, wrestling.

It struck Tulkhan that she did not mean to harm him. She used her strength only to repulse him, forbearing to deliver the killing or maiming blows to his eyes or throat.

By the time she lay beneath him, both were breathing hard with exertion, their faces only a hand's breadth apart.

"This is a lie," he said and lowered his head to inhale her

scent. It hit him like a physical thing. When he went on, his voice was hoarse. "You could have blinded me and escaped. You are here beneath me because it is where you want to be."

She gave a wordless moan and lifted her face to his. He felt her smooth cheek on his throat, her soft parted lips as she traced the length of his jaw with her tongue. An involuntary shudder of pure desire went through him, triggering an answering shudder in her. His heart rate lifted another notch.

"Imoshen." Her name was an invocation, drawn from him against his will.

His lips sought hers and instead he found a cheek wet with tears. Stunned, he shifted his weight onto his elbows and studied her tense face. What he saw made him smile. Her eyes were fierce, denying the tears on her cheeks and the trembling of her chin.

Silently he sat up so that she was free to climb off the bed, but she threw herself forward into his arms. There was no mistaking the sincerity of her embrace as she wound her arms around him. He smelt fire and blood in her hair. "Where have you been this night, Imoshen?"

She shook her head, either unable or unwilling to answer.

He cradled her against his chest, dragging the covers over her cold limbs.

"What—"

"Don't ask."

There was such sorrow in her voice he could not pry. So instead, he held her close until the trembling ceased.

Tulkhan realized he was whispering Ghebite endearments, things his mother used to croon to him, things he'd long forgotten. But now he recalled his mother's hands on him and her loving touch when he was too young to leave her side to live in the men's lodge. How strange that finding Imoshen had forced him to face his mother's loss, and in facing it, he had found her again.

Imoshen pulled away from him, brushing the tears from her cheeks. The light from the open window had grown stronger and Tulkhan knew the servants would be coming soon. They must not find her in his chambers.

When he went to warn her she placed her fingers to his lips. "Hush."

There were smudges of exhaustion in the shadows beneath her eyes. Why did she look so haunted?

"We have little time," she whispered. "Know this, Tulkhan of the Ghebites. I will bond with you this day."

He had to smile. All of Fair Isle knew that.

"No." Her face was serious. She took his hand, placing his palm on her chest where he felt her heart beating strongly. "I bond with you, here and now. I swear it. We don't need the Church or a thousand nobles to witness this. It is between you and I."

Tulkhan understood. The utter simplicity of Imoshen's vow went straight to his core.

He lifted her free hand, kissing her sixth finger. What was that scent?

He held her eyes. "Know this, Imoshen of the T'En. I will bond with you from this day forward."

Silently she eased her fingers from his to slip her hand inside his shirt. He felt her cold palm over his heart. His own hand rested on her chest, mirroring the gesture. It felt as if he held her rapidly beating heart in his hand. And, as she looked into his eyes, he felt his heart's rhythm change until their two hearts beat as one, resonant and strong.

Imoshen nodded once as if satisfied, then slid off the bed. "I must go." But she hesitated, looking down at him.

At that moment she seemed fragile. Tulkhan didn't want to part now, to spend the rest of the day looking at her, unable to touch, unable to know this intimacy until the last ceremony was over late tonight.

A noise in the hallway alerted him. "Be careful, the servants come."

A sweet, sad smile illuminated her face. "They will not see me."

He knew it was true. He was mad to love a Dhamfeer.

·   ·   ·

The day of the Midwinters Feast dawned bright and cold, as Kalleen and Cariah helped Imoshen prepare for the bonding ceremony.

"There!" Cariah stepped back to admire Imoshen's hair. A circlet of gold studded with yellow amethysts sat on her brow, and a thin gold net set with amethysts at every joint held her heavy hair in place. A second outfit was laid out on her bed for the coronation this afternoon.

Imoshen adjusted Tulkhan's bonding gift. "The weight of this torque will give me a headache by midday."

Kalleen smoothed her slim hands over Imoshen's gown, which was made of exquisite gold lace over an underdress of black satin. "You are lucky you are tall. The babe does not show yet."

"Does *everyone* know?" Imoshen asked ruefully.

Kalleen wrinkled her nose. "It is the right and proper way to go to your bonding, rich with child, my lady."

Imoshen wriggled to ease the tension in her shoulders. Kalleen still addressed her as "my lady," only now it sounded like a term of endearment.

After this day she would be the *Empress* she supposed, though by Ghebite custom, General Tulkhan would accept the kingship, which in turn made her his queen. Imoshen grimaced. She did not feel royal. She felt dizzy with trepidation.

"Your hands are so cold." Kalleen rubbed them between hers and blew on the icy fingers. "What is it?"

Imoshen shrugged. She felt Cariah's sharp eyes on her. She had washed Reothe's scent from her skin, but he remained in her thoughts. It felt as if she had left a piece of herself behind in that camp amidst the hot pools. No matter how she rationalized it, she had hated to leave Reothe. Yet she believed it was for the best. For all his talk of equality, Reothe threatened to dominate her in ways Tulkhan did not. She felt as if she had abandoned her younger, naive self when she had abandoned Reothe last night.

But this very morning Tulkhan had sworn to bond with

her, and she knew he would stand true to his oath. Yet as the day progressed he was sure to draw away from her. If only she could get close to him, intimately close. She knew that if she could slip into his mind when he slipped into her body, she could imprint herself on him and . . . But no, that would not be right. What good was love if it was not freely given?

"What troubles you, Imoshen?" Cariah whispered.

"Tulkhan does not love me!" It was out before she could stop herself.

"He wants you," Kalleen said. "I've seen the way he looks at you. You are to be bonded—"

"You speak of bonding as in the old way of the country folk," Cariah corrected. "In bondings of state, the best you can hope for is companionship, and if you are very lucky a little fondness. Don't despair, Imoshen, love may follow, especially since his body pulls him to you. Make use of this."

Cariah's old-empire tone made Imoshen flinch. "My parents raised me with the old values. Their bonding went beyond the flesh to their souls. From what I know of life in the Empress's court, I'm glad my family avoided it."

"You can't avoid your responsibilities," Cariah said.

"Enough, Cariah!" Kalleen squeezed Imoshen's hands. "It will be for the best. I have seen how Wharrd has changed since we were bonded. The General will grow to love you."

Imoshen sighed. "I am being foolish. Forgive me. As Cariah says, this is a bonding of state. Sometimes when I look into the General's eyes I think that as much as he desires me, he also hates me."

Kalleen and Cariah exchanged swift glances, their silence damning. Imoshen stifled her dismay. The murmur of the approaching noblewomen who would be escorting her to the great hall filled the pause.

"They come," Cariah said. "Stand tall. Don't let them suspect."

Kalleen hugged Imoshen. "I wish you happiness. You have been so good to me."

The women entered and for the rest of the day Imoshen knew she would have no peace.

For Imoshen, the bonding ceremony felt unreal, almost as if it were happening to someone else. For one thing it went on longer than was traditional, because both Churches played a role. The Cadre performed his with bad grace, having been relegated to giving his blessing before the Beatific oversaw the giving of vows in the manner of a Fair Isle bonding.

Standing next to her, Tulkhan seemed alien and distant in his barbarian splendor. He wore the ceremonial belt over a red velvet tunic with black sable trim. His long hair fell free down his back and two plaits hung from his temples, threaded with fine gold beads.

The two of them clasped hands and the Beatific tied a slender red ribbon around their wrists. Imoshen recalled how Reothe had used the old form of bonding, cutting their skin and pressing their wrists together. When their blood mingled she had refused to make the vow. With the words unsaid they were not bonded by the laws of the Church. Yet her unruly body had responded to Reothe by breaking the old bonding scar. She shuddered.

Hands still joined, they accepted the bonding chalice. Imoshen offered it to Tulkhan. When he had taken a sip, he offered it to her, turning it so that her lips touched where his had. The memory of drinking from Reothe's lips made her dizzy. Resolutely she banished him from her thoughts.

The Beatific retrieved the bonding chalice, then the moment came for Imoshen to make her vow to Tulkhan, before the gathered nobles and town officials. It was a relief to say the words. This final step was irrevocable. It freed her from Reothe's claim. It must!

There was still the long noon feast and then the coronation ceremony to be endured, but tonight when she lay with General Tulkhan it would erase all thought of her once-betrothed.

As the pale winter sun set on the great dome of the Basilica, Tulkhan and Imoshen faced the Beatific on their knees, ready to accept the coronation symbols of the Emperor and Empress.

They had crossed the square to the Basilica as suppliants, barefoot and bareheaded, but after the ceremony they would be transported in the coronation chariot as befitted their new roles.

It was this which troubled General Tulkhan. The ornate coronation made him deeply uncomfortable. He was sure the Keldon nobles considered him a barbarian upstart, and with all this pomp and ceremony he felt himself drawing away from his own men. He wished this T'En rite over. But first, Imoshen must be accepted by the Orb before she could be Arbiter of Truth.

With deep reverence, the Beatific donned gloves so that her flesh did not defile the relic. She unlocked a delicate cage and withdrew the Orb. According to Imoshen, it came from the land beyond the dawn sun. Tulkhan stared at the fragile glass and wondered cynically how many times it had been replaced with an identical glass bauble in six hundred years of journeys and battles.

Imoshen seemed nervous. Her face was paler than usual and she wore old-empire makeup which heightened her T'En characteristics. The torque he had given her was nowhere in evidence, indeed her whole outfit was different from the gold and black of this morning's bonding ceremony. Now she wore a white underdress overlaid with fine silver lace. Her hair was loose on her shoulders like a satin cloak, and her head, like his, was bare, ready to accept the crown.

Her eyes closed briefly as she prepared herself. The tang of her T'En gift registered on Tulkhan's tongue, making him wonder about the source of the Orb's power.

Imoshen raised her arms, hands cupped to receive the Orb. It left the Beatific's grasp, falling into Imoshen's. The instant her bare fingers touched the Orb's surface it flared brightly, surprising Tulkhan and making him question his earlier cynicism. A gasp of reverence escaped the masses gathered behind them. The Orb responded to Imoshen's T'En blood.

The Beatific returned the Orb to its resting place. Then she turned to the couple, ready to finalize the coronation. An awed silence fell as the Beatific raised the twin crowns for public blessing.

Stiff with inactivity, Tulkhan waited impatiently with Imoshen at his side. Self-derision twisted within him. Whether he called himself king or prince, he would never be as respected as the rulers of the old empire. He ground his teeth.

"What is it?" Imoshen mouthed softly, though she continued looking straight ahead.

"I can't do it." His own words surprised him. "I won't claim to be something I'm not."

"What do you mean?" Startled, Imoshen turned to him.

The Beatific stepped toward them, her assistant carrying the twin crowns on their bed of velvet.

Revulsion stirred in Tulkhan. "I'm no king. I'm a soldier!"

"If you can lead an army, you can lead an island."

Tulkhan knew she was right. Suddenly he rose to his feet, pulling Imoshen with him. The Beatific took a step back, her expression a mixture of annoyance and confusion.

"Trust me?" Tulkhan asked Imoshen.

She searched his eyes, then smiled. "Yes."

He felt a corresponding smile ignite him and faced the crowd.

"I am not your emperor and I never will be." His words carried, echoing in the great dome. Not surprisingly, a murmur of confusion greeted his announcement. He lifted his free hand, signaling for silence. "I am not the King of the Ghebites. I am simply a soldier, first son of a king's second wife. I claim no royal privilege for myself. I am a general. I will place no one, whether they be noble, guildmaster, Fair

Isle farmer, or Ghebite soldier, above the other." The investiture of his men returned to him. "Like my lord commanders, I am here to serve Fair Isle."

He paused to study the sea of faces, their expressions ranging from outrage to astonishment. Certain factions would not approve. The Keldon nobles for one, but he had already acknowledged their rights and the laws of their Church.

"I declare myself Protector General of Fair Isle, and this is Imoshen, Lady Protector of the People." He took Imoshen's hand, placing it along his forearm so that her fingers draped over his.

A tentative cheer broke from the ranks of his men, telling him his instinct had been right about them. The people of Fair Isle were harder to read. A furious whispering broke out in the crowd as they debated his repudiation of the emperorship.

Imoshen's fingers tightened on his. He looked to see anger, but pure joy suffused her features.

"Signal the musicians and choir," Imoshen ordered over her shoulder to the Beatific. "We will dispense the coins and make our triumphal ride around the square now."

"The Vow of Expiation!" the Beatific hissed. "You must give that vow or negate the bonding and coronation!"

"I had not forgotten," Imoshen whispered, still facing the crowd.

Tulkhan squeezed her hand as the choir began their rehearsed piece, their voices soaring high into the great dome like streams of living sound.

"Are you disappointed?" Tulkhan asked under cover of their song.

Imoshen smiled. "No, Protector General. You have confirmed my faith in you in a most unexpected way."

"Good." He smiled, enjoying her approval.

They stepped off the dais, making their stately way down the aisle under the center of the dome. There, inset in the floor, was an ancient circle of stone, so old its engravings were almost worn away.

Before everyone, Imoshen sank to her knees and placed her left hand in the impression on the stone. Her six fingers fit the indentations perfectly.

As she gave her Vow of Expiation, promising to serve the people of Fair Isle without fear or favor, Tulkhan noted the intense expression on the face of the man opposite him. Dressed in a dark mulberry tabard, his garnet eyes glittered as they fixed on Imoshen's bent head.

For a moment Tulkhan could not remember who the man was. Then it came to him. Murgon, leader of the Tractarians, the branch of the Church dedicated to hunting down rogue T'En.

Imoshen came to her feet and the choir resumed their paean of praise. At the doors of the Basilica, two acolytes knelt to help Imoshen and Tulkhan slide their feet into their shoes. They had entered the Basilica barefoot and bareheaded; they left it wearing the mantle of their office. The crowns, however, remained on their bed of velvet.

"If only the pomp of position could be escaped as easily as the crowns and titles," Imoshen whispered, as if aware of his thoughts.

Tulkhan wanted to laugh. But she was right. There were still hours of formality ahead of them as they presided over the coronation feast, where they would sign the charter giving the three largest banks royal endorsement.

When they stepped outside, the crowd greeted them with song. Along the steps of the Basilica, two lines of people formed an honor guard. They were high-ranking nobles, Tulkhan's men amongst them, town officials, and ordinary citizens chosen by lot.

The acolytes handed Tulkhan and Imoshen their chests of newly minted coins. Imoshen's profile graced one side, his the other. It was dated six hundred seventeen, though the new year did not officially start until tomorrow.

"Time to share our good fortune," Imoshen said. "These coins will be collectors items in years to come."

They distributed the coins and accepted endless congratulations. At last the empty chests were returned to the acolytes and Tulkhan and Imoshen stepped into the open coronation chariot.

The square was packed with residents of T'Diemn and outlying farms, all come to witness this historical occasion. The chariot made its slow, stately way 'round the square, its two horses led by a groom. Then it came to a stop directly in front of the palace's grand entrance, where two tall towers stood like arrogant sentinels.

Imoshen's hand covered his. "Now you will see the display I promised."

A wizened little man scurried towards them, passing several objects to Imoshen.

"I always wanted to launch one of these things," she confided as she pulled on a leather glove and took the cylinder in a pair of tongs.

It didn't look particularly inspiring. Tulkhan had expected jewels and gold.

The little man opened his coal pouch and blew on it to quicken the flame, warning, "Take care to hold it away from your body, Empress."

Imoshen dipped the cylinder's wick in the flame. It sparked into life immediately, brighter than striking a flint. A tail of fire shot from the cylinder and it leapt from Imoshen's hands into the air. Rapid as an escaped bird, it arced across the sky, trailing sparks of light, only to burst star-bright above the palace.

Tulkhan blinked, stunned by the afterimage as much as by the improbability of what he had seen. But the crowd was not surprised. They cheered delightedly then grew expectantly quiet.

"Watch the towers," Imoshen whispered. She stripped the glove from her hand and returned it to the little man.

Tulkhan frowned. A spark flared on the nearest tower, followed by another. The crowd gasped as waterfalls of living sparks poured from the tower tops.

"The palace will burn to the ground!" Tulkhan muttered.

"Not at all. Members of the Pyrolate Guild spend years

learning their craft. Surely you've heard of the T'En fountains of light?"

Tulkhan had, but he had discounted them just as he had the rumors of the Dhamfeer powers. He stared in awe, as from every tower fountains of golden light poured down, illuminating the palace. The crowded square was utterly silent. "What are they made of?"

"Naturally the guild keeps their knowledge secret. But they are quite harmless."

Tulkhan marveled. How could Imoshen be so casual? "I will inspect the apparatus that makes these fountains and that starbird you shot into the sky."

Imoshen laughed softly. "You would have to convince the Master Pyrolate himself, and that would be no easy task. When they are apprenticed they take a vow of secrecy."

She pulled him around to face her, pressing her strong body against him. Fey laughter danced in her eyes. "Kiss me under the fountains of golden light, General."

So General Tulkhan of the Ghebites claimed Imoshen, last princess of the T'En, savoring the impossibility of the moment.

As the coronation feast wound down, Tulkhan stretched, easing the tension in his shoulders. Imoshen was his now by every law of man, and by god he wanted her.

"A word, Protector General?"

Tulkhan turned to see the self-important Ghebite priest. He contained his annoyance and stepped back so that their conversation would be more private. "Yes, Cadre?"

The smaller man glanced over his shoulder at Imoshen who was playing an elaborate game with a young Keldon noble.

The complexity and variety of games played by the people of Fair Isle never ceased to amaze Tulkhan. He supposed they had to find some way to amuse themselves. Too much peace, he thought sourly.

"Did you know she holds the records of all property ownership?"

Tulkhan grimaced. Obviously the Cadre was not talking about Imoshen. "The T'En Church has always held the records."

"It is run by a woman!"

"It is their way."

"It is not *our* way!"

Tulkhan looked down at his indignant priest. "And this is not our land. But we will make it so."

"Then relegate the Beatific to a lesser function. Give me the task and I will reorganize their Church."

Tulkhan almost laughed. "Why should they give up what they have?"

The Cadre stiffened. "Half of them are women; *only* women!"

This time Tulkhan did laugh. He gazed at Imoshen who was now performing an elaborate sequence of movements which could have been a dance. "There is no *only*!"

Anger hardened the Cadre's features. "You let your lust rule your head!"

"You let your anger rule your tongue!" Tulkhan snapped. The Cadre made to apologize but he waved the priest aside. "No. Go now. We will speak again later."

Tulkhan folded his arms and leant against the wall. Obscured by shadows, he observed the game and the purpose finally struck him. Imoshen and her opponent were performing a series of dance movements. At the end of each sequence they added another movement. The two competitors had to remember the whole sequence, perform it, and add to it each time. The first one to make a mistake lost.

He wished the game would end so he could lead Imoshen away. They had done their duty. Didn't she want him as badly as he wanted her?

"Protector General?"

"Beatific." He straightened, cloaking his uneasiness.

She returned his acknowledgment with the elaborate obeisance reserved for Empress and Emperor. Was she mocking him or did she seek reassurance because he had been speaking with the Cadre?

But she said nothing. Instead her gaze followed his, and he realized he had looked past her to Imoshen.

"T'Imoshen is at her most charming. Unfortunately, it is an illusion. Forgive me, I am going to speak plainly. You are a Ghebite and a True-man. Do not be lulled into a false sense of security. Imoshen is not one of us. The T'En are both more and less than True-people."

Tulkhan did not want to hear this tonight. He wanted that part of Imoshen which was only too real and womanly, her quicksilver passion. But he had to placate the head of the T'En Church. He met the Beatific's eyes expecting her to give another vague warning about Imoshen's gifts. What could she possibly say that he hadn't already thought of in the dark, lonely nights?

"The flame burns bright attracting the moth, but if it ventures too close it will be consumed. You may think you can warm yourself at Imoshen's fires and escape unscathed. But the T'En work their way beneath your guard. Believe me, I know." The Beatific's hand closed on his arm. Her smile was luminous with painful self-knowledge. "Reothe and I were lovers. He coached me, helped me attain this position."

Tulkhan was stunned. A married Ghebite woman would face death if she admitted this. An unmarried Ghebite woman would kill herself if defiled by a man.

"I went to hear Reothe debate in the great library of the Halls of Learning. His passion for knowledge and truth was inspiring. I was fascinated by the brilliance of his mind. It drew me with such intensity I had to walk away." She shook her head wryly. "I think that was why he first pursued me. It annoyed him to have someone walk out while he was speaking. When he came after me I should have been on my guard, but I lied to myself. He was only seventeen; I was nearly ten years older. I let myself believe I could enjoy him and remain aloof." She sighed. Tulkhan did not want to hear this, yet he was captivated. "At that time I was working my way up through the Church hierarchy. Knowing what I know now, I believe he saw ability in me and wanted a lever on the Church for the future. Reothe plans for the long term, you see, and he is utterly ruthless." She held Tulkhan's eyes. "He was under the Empress's protection, related by blood to her and her heirs, but that was not enough for him."

Tulkhan said nothing. He suspected the Beatific would continue until she got the reaction she wanted from him.

"You know that he and the Empress's heir, Ysanna, were lovers. Reothe wanted control of the royal family." The Beatific shrugged. "The Empress loved him when he came to her as a tragic youth. She reared him with her own children. Ysanna played off her suitors against Reothe. Could they sail, ride, hunt, or write poetry as well as he? He never committed himself, for there were those who did not wish to see him as the future Empress's bond-partner. When he asked Imoshen to bond with him it was the lesser of two evils, or so they thought." She fixed troubled eyes on him. "You don't know what the T'En can do. With every touch they cement their hold on you, slipping insidiously into your mind, sifting for what they can use to further their own ends."

Tulkhan nodded once, reluctantly. This time when he looked into the Beatific's face, he understood that despite everything, she still felt for Reothe.

"What better way to control someone than through love?" she whispered.

Something twisted inside him. Hadn't Imoshen said the very same thing? "She is not like that." It was an instinctive denial.

The Beatific smiled tolerantly. "Imoshen is T'En. They protect themselves. Reothe was a youth in a palace of intrigue, searching for a way to ensure his safety. You can forgive them anything. I know I did."

Tulkhan sensed movement. The game had broken up and Imoshen was coming towards them, laughter dancing in her eyes. He watched that joy turn to wariness as she read his expression.

Before he could move, the Beatific glided forward, spoke softly to Imoshen, then made a formal obeisance and left.

Imoshen paused a little beyond touching distance. "Well, General?"

"Protector General."

She eyed him thoughtfully. He could tell she was trying to understand him. A True-woman would have tried to read his face and stance; Imoshen resorted to her gift. The overflow of her power made his skin crawl, yet he still wanted her.

"Bed." The word left his lips unbidden.

"Yes."

Eleven

IN A BLUR they slipped away unnoticed. Tulkhan knew
Imoshen was cloaking them but he did not care. A madness was upon him.

The passage was long and echoed with the night's rev-
elry. The servants were absent from their posts, even the
Stronghold Guard.

Imoshen felt light-headed. Her feet seemed to fly over
the glossy parquetry floor. She could see the same strange
excitement in Tulkhan's eyes. It was heaven to escape the
confines of their official roles. She had waited too long for
this.

Suddenly, she could wait no longer. With a wordless cry
of challenge, she took to her heels. She heard the General
give chase and laughed, increasing her speed.

Habit led her to her own bedchamber, even though they
should have entered the grand suite reserved for the Emperor
and Empress.

There was no fire or light in her room. She sprang
to one side of the door and pressed her back against the
wood panel. Her heart thundered, echoing the rapid thud of
Tulkhan's boots.

He thrust the door open and charged in, stepping out
of the shaft of light immediately. She saw his body grow still
as he listened for her. He was the perfect warrior, poised for
the hunt. She could not resist baiting him.

Silently she slipped her shoes from her feet, then slammed the door shut and tossed the shoes to different ends of the room, presenting Tulkhan with three sources of movement.

She heard him spin, heard his muffled curse.

With a laugh, she sprang on his back. He staggered under the impact before regaining his balance.

She held an imaginary knife to his throat. "Yield, you are my captive, General!"

"Never!" He threw her over his shoulder, halting her fall at the last moment so that she landed lightly, but his imaginary blade stayed at her throat. "The assassin is dead!"

"I thought we were past this!" Imoshen heard his angry chuckle. Instinctively, she clasped his bare arm, seeking his motivation.

The General sprang away, muttering Ghebite curses. She heard him walk towards the fireplace where the makings of a fire had been prepared but not lit. In a moment he had struck the spark and ignited the tinder.

She rolled into a crouch and watched as he lit the candles on the mantelpiece. "What did the Beatific say to you?"

The broad planes of his Ghebite features were illuminated by the flickering flames, but his expression revealed nothing. Looking down at her, his dark eyes were hooded, cloaking his expression even further. Again Imoshen felt the urge to touch him and discover his thoughts.

"It is time I made one thing clear," he said.

She felt uneasy but kept her tone light. "And what would that be, General?"

"We are no longer captor and captive. Come here."

Though she was prepared for a battle of wits, her treacherous body was preparing for him. Every caress of her satin underdress was a foretaste of his touch.

She could sense the ephemeral but impregnable layers of his formidable will shutting her out. "Speak, General."

He grimaced. "Why don't you touch me and learn what you want to know?"

"You don't like when I do that."

"No. Yet I can't live without touching you."

It was a raw admission. Something inside her clenched in response.

"I know. It is the same with me." Heat stung her cheeks. It was hard admitting this to Tulkhan when he was so distant. She would much rather embrace him and let him feel how much she wanted him.

"You say you already carry my child. I need never touch you again. I could walk from this room and our bonding would be nothing but a marriage of state," he told her, yet his voice vibrated with repressed passion.

Pride made Imoshen school her features and call up an amused smile. "You could try but I doubt it would be feasible."

"No. These weeks have proven that. I could not see you every day and want you as I do. Not without . . ."

Triumph flashed through her and he ground to a halt, visibly angered.

"Then you'll just have to accept me for what I am, General."

"No! Either you vow never to invade my mind and use your T'En gifts on me, or I will turn my back on you." His expression was implacable. "I will have you escorted to the Beatific. Surrounded by a thousand priests and watched over by the Tractarians, the rebels won't be able to touch you or use you. The people will think you safe and I won't be tortured with the constant reminder of your presence!"

"Murgon's Tractarians!" How she hated those priests, betrayers of their own kind. A deep anger coalesced in her. Was she such a loathsome creature that she must be shut away from the light of day? She wanted to strike the General, to make him suffer the same pain she endured.

Instinctively she weighed the odds. Physically he might be stronger than her, but was his will equal to hers? If it came down to this, only one of them would survive, and she would never give up.

Yet . . . she could not bring herself to hurt him. The thought of causing General Tulkhan pain caused her pain.

Her feelings for him made her weak and she despised herself for opening her heart to this Ghebite.

Imoshen sucked in her breath, feeling the rush of air chill her teeth and tongue. How had it come to this?

"Do you understand?" he demanded. "I will not have the privacy of my mind invaded."

She nodded, numbly. Yes, she understood that fear only too well. It was why she feared Reothe. But she did not seek to manipulate Tulkhan and he should know this. It was the threat of incarceration which cut deepest. The General would use her own people against her!

"You misjudge me, Tulkhan," she said, hardly able to speak for the knot of sorrow which filled her throat. "I might have offered such a vow freely. But—"

"But?"

She wanted to defy him, to declare that she would not be bullied. She wanted him to back down. With a flash of insight she understood what she really wanted was for him to accept her without reservation. But he was a Ghebite, a True-man with all the limitations of his birth and culture.

"Imoshen?" The word was barely audible. "I will not be your puppet."

Then she understood his deepest fear, and in understanding it was able to reach inside herself for a deeper compassion. "You underestimate yourself and me. If it will satisfy you, I promise not to invade your mind except in an emergency. But I won't let you come to harm if I can save you."

When she held his eyes Imoshen thought she saw a flash of remorse.

"You would swear to this?" he asked finally.

She nodded.

He took her hand to place it palm down over her belly. "Swear on this life."

Imoshen felt an odd little flame inside her. "I swear on the life of my . . . our unborn child not to use the mind-touch on you, except in an emergency."

"Or any other T'En gift—no compulsions, no tricks of any sort," he prodded.

Imoshen gave a moan of protest.

Tulkhan felt it like a knife slicing his soul. He had not thought it would cost him so dearly. He could see he had hurt her by devaluing her trust. With this vow he had reduced what they might have shared. But he had to have peace of mind. "Well?"

"You are denying what I am!"

"If I cannot trust you, I will not touch you." He steeled himself against her pain. "The choice is yours!"

It was a bluff, but Imoshen could not know that. He had no choice where she was concerned. She was a compulsion which drove him to madness.

"You would have me deny myself to be with you? Is that truly what you want?" Her tortured eyes searched his face.

He wanted to tell her no, that she was everything to him and the rest of Fair Isle could rot. But even now he could not be sure that this feeling wasn't prompted by some T'En trick. "Make this vow or there can be nothing between us."

"How do you know I will not say the words then break my vow?" Unshed tears glittered in her eyes.

"If your word meant so little you would give it more freely."

She blinked with surprise, freeing the tears, which ran down her cheeks. "You know me so well yet you insist on this?"

He wanted to kiss the tears from her face, to pull her down to the fur before the fire. He wanted to tell her with his body what he could not admit.

"I will make this vow, General." Imoshen shuddered. "But until the day you free me from it, it will stand between us!"

Despite the warmth of the fire, a shiver passed over his skin. He could not imagine a day when he would willingly lay himself open to her T'En gifts. "The vow?"

"I vow on the life of our unborn child not to use my T'En gifts on you, except in dire emergency." Her lips twisted in a parody of a smile. "Will that satisfy you, General Tulkhan?"

He could feel the anger vibrating in her. His body was totally attuned to hers and he sensed the power building.

"You are angry with me. I'll leave you alone tonight." He raised her hand and brushed his lips across her inner wrist. It was a gesture he had seen the Keld use, one which could be formal, or very intimate.

Every instinct screamed at him to stay, but he made himself walk away. When the time came, he wanted theirs to be a joyous union.

"Tulkhan!"

He turned to see her standing before the fire in her finery, her face taut, tear tracks in her ceremonial makeup. He waited.

"Would you have me beg?" The words were torn from her.

Her desperation called to something primal inside him. Yes, he wanted her to beg for him, to welcome him. He was greedy for her.

She lifted one hand in supplication.

When he approached, she turned away, unwilling to reveal her naked need. He took her shoulders in his hands, feeling the tension in her body. An answering tension ignited him.

He noticed that the delicate lace of her overdress had torn and silently he lifted her thick hair to undo the lacing at the back of her neck. The silver tabard slipped from her shoulders and fell to her feet, glittering in the ruddy firelight. When he released her hair it ran through his fingers like silk. Unable to stop himself, he stroked it, feeling the tension drain from her. Gradually she relaxed into him, her back pressed to his chest.

His arms slid around her body, pressing her closer so that she could feel his growing need. Her hips melded against his, her welcome unmistakable.

A spasm of naked desire made him arch in response.

"The body's needs are powerful," she whispered; but he had no time for words.

Imoshen intended to hold herself in reserve. Deep

inside her, a little knot of cold resentment burned to be expressed, but when he tilted her face to his with such infinite tenderness, and his lips claimed hers, she experienced a rush of completion.

The love she wanted to deny welled up, swamping her defenses so that she gave herself utterly to the moment, luxuriating in his ardor.

Eagerly she turned within the circle of his arms to slide her hands inside his shirt, exulting in his hot flesh, the hard planes of his chest. His great heart hammered, pacing her own.

Impatiently she tore at the lacing of his shirt, shrugging it over his shoulders to reveal his coppery skin, criss-crossed by the fine silver scars of long healed wounds. To think he might have taken a fatal wound and she would never have known him.

Suddenly he was unutterably precious, as necessary to her as the very breath she took. The moment was luminous in its intensity.

His callused hands closed on her, rasping across her shoulders as he fought to undo the ties of her underdress. In a fever of desire she came to his aid and they discarded their formal garments. To meet flesh to flesh was the ultimate imperative.

When her gown fell to pool at her feet, he stepped back, a ragged gasp on his lips. Suddenly shy, she felt his gaze on her like a physical thing illuminating her. Hardly able to breathe, she dared raise her eyes to his. Naked need suffused his features.

Wordlessly she opened her arms to him and he came to her. She pulled him down before the fireplace, accepting him even as she sank into the fur. There was nothing but this moment, nothing but this man.

Much later as they lay on the furs before the fire, it struck Tulkhan that they had chosen to consummate their marriage in primitive surroundings, ignoring the royal chambers, rich with every decoration and comfort.

"Why do you smile?" Imoshen's skin was flushed, only a smudge of color remained of her formal makeup, and her hair lay damp and knotted, a riot of pale silk.

Tulkhan shook his head slowly and she blushed. Their lovemaking couldn't have been more perfect. Recalling it made him feel almost reverential. How could two people know such ecstasy in the union of their bodies and yet be strangers?

All this long day and for the long weeks before he had waited for this night. Replete at last, the tension drained from him.

Imoshen heard Tulkhan's breathing grow deep and even. Propping her weight on one elbow, she watched him as he succumbed to sleep.

Relaxed like this, he looked much younger. His dark hair mingled with the dark fur. Drawn, she leant closer to feel his warm breath on her face. With each exhalation she inhaled his breath, willing him to become a part of her. A delicious languor stole over her body as she absorbed his being, focusing on his essence. A tingling awareness of their two separate entities surfaced in her mind's eye and she . . .

Cold reality shocked her from this pleasant intimacy. She had vowed not to use her T'En gifts. Reluctantly she relinquished the sweet contact. She hadn't meant to bind him to her. It had been an instinctive act.

Pulling away, she studied the perfection of his sleeping profile. When had his broad cheekbones and coppery skin become her ideal of male beauty? It had been a gradual thing, a shift in her perception.

A little worm of anger writhed within her. How dare he threaten her! She searched her mind for the trigger and re-called the General's closed face when she approached him as he stood with the Beatific.

What had the Beatific told Tulkhan?

He stirred in his sleep. She could trawl his sleeping mind without his knowledge. Why stop there? Why not plant ideas, compulsions, even suspicions which she could later use against him?

Bitter self-knowledge shook her. It would be easy to make the attempt and far too easy to justify her actions. After all, she was only protecting them both from the Beatific's machinations.

She fought the urge to use her gifts, trembling with the effort. Finally the compulsion eased.

No wonder General Tulkhan did not trust her; she hardly trusted herself!

She sat up and hugged her knees, looking into the dying flames. It appeared she and the General were destined to share the kind of bonding True-people shared, one that went deep on a physical level, but excluded the mind-touch. Was it enough?

He wanted her. He made her body sing. She even suspected General Tulkhan could grow to love her. But he expected her to live a half-life. Could she be satisfied with that?

No.

Imoshen knew with utter certainty that she had to have it all. Tulkhan had to not only accept her T'En gifts, he had to embrace them, or she would grow to despise him and herself. Unlike Cariah, she could not be less than she was.

Tulkhan wished he could have slipped away with Imoshen as Wharrd had done with Kalleen, to forge their bonding in private, but royal bondings required celebration and duty never ceased.

He watched Imoshen perform the elaborate wine-pouring ceremony. In front of each person stood a small porcelain cup, decorated with delicate High T'En symbols. The spiced wine steamed on the still air. It was time to speak.

When Imoshen caught his eye, hers held a warning. Since their bonding, there had been little time to discuss the Causare Council and now he faced its delegates—Woodvine, Athlyng, Fairban, and others; leaders of the greater and lesser noble families of the Keldon Highlands.

He had not denied them their request for a formal
meeting, choosing to greet them in his maproom. They sat
around the large circular table, their features reflected in its
glossy surface, their wine untouched.

Imoshen lifted her porcelain cup with high court formality and took a sip. Everyone followed suit. Tulkhan rolled
the wine around on his tongue. It was sweet and spicy, not
really to his taste. He put the cup aside.

"We have been patient, Protector General," Fairban
began.

"Not a word of dissension has passed our lips before the
mainland spies," Woodvine said. "When will you recall the
Causare Council?"

Old Athlyng lifted a hand. "There are those among us
with hot heads who would see everything achieved before
spring. Fair Isle was not established overnight. Give us a sign
that you—"

"I have spoken with my lord commanders," Tulkhan
said. "They understand the idea of this Council, though it
goes by a different name in Gheeaba. The Causare Council
will reconvene but with some changes."

There was uneasy muttering.

"Have you no say in this?" Woodvine demanded of
Imoshen. "Will women be forbidden to take their seat on
the Council?"

Imoshen placed her palms flat on the table to each side
of her wine. "In keeping with custom, so that all voices will
be heard equally, there will be a new Causare Council consisting of equal representatives from the old empire and the
new. Six of the General's lord commanders will take their
seats in the Cors. You must select from your ranks six—"

"You jest!" Woodvine exploded.

Tulkhan met Imoshen's eyes as the Keld argued against
this restriction. He had deliberately selected his most trusted
men, those who could be relied on to keep a cool head. Not
only would they have to debate matters of state with their
recent enemies, but some of those enemies were sure to be
female. To Imoshen it was simply an accepted custom, to his

men it was an insult. He could trust no more than six. Besides, he wanted the Causare Council to be a controllable size.

Argument raged around the table.

When Imoshen came to her feet, voices faded.

Tulkhan watched her lift one hand, elegant as an unfurling fan.

"Six people from the old empire." She lifted the other hand. "Six from the new." She lowered her hands, palms open. Her brilliant mulberry eyes met theirs in turn. "Think on it."

It was two weeks after midwinter and the frozen lake had been pronounced safe for skating. This was the last evening of formal entertainments, for which Imoshen was deeply grateful. It would be a relief to bid farewell to the majority of the mainland visitors tomorrow. Only the ambassadors and their aides would remain. Imoshen wanted those who left Fair Isle to report that the new Ghebite overlords had not destroyed famed T'En culture, so she and Cariah had organized tonight's farewell ice ballet.

Kalleen caught Imoshen's arm as she spun past, laughing. Her wooden skates skidded out from under her, dragging them both off their feet. Being a farm girl, Kalleen had learnt to skate on the village pond, but this had not involved the fancy performance step she had just tried to execute.

Perched on the bank overlooking the lake, the musicians played, as the sedate nobles circled studiously in pairs, avoiding Imoshen and Kalleen, which made it seem all the more ridiculous.

Most of the Ghebite commanders had refused the chance to learn to skate. They sat in the large tent at one end of the lake, drinking and watching the festivities.

Kalleen gave Wharrd a wave, unworried by the disapproval radiating from the other skaters. Imoshen wished she could forget her role as Lady Protector of Fair Isle and play silly village games.

Her stomach rumbled. Hot food was being prepared in potbellied stoves on the bank. The tangy aroma drifted on the slight breeze that stirred the multicolored lanterns.

Cariah laughed as she swooped in, turning her skates to slow her advance. "You are shocking my sisters, Kalleen!"

Imoshen wondered if Cariah was obliquely censuring the Lady Protector of Fair Isle.

Kalleen rolled her eyes. "I won't pretend to be something I'm not and spoil my fun!"

"We don't all have that luxury," Cariah snapped, her meaning all too clear.

Imoshen winced and came to her feet. "Have I overstepped the mark?"

Cariah glanced around impatiently. "There are some who would resent your behavior if you sat in the tent and did nothing. Life's too short to worry about people like that!"

"Help me up," Kalleen commanded imperiously.

Imoshen laughed. What would she do without Kalleen and Cariah to lend a breath of sanity? If only she could mend the rift with Cariah. Together they pulled the smaller woman upright, steadying her.

Imoshen noticed General Tulkhan's large form weaving towards her through the circling promenaders, and her body quickened at the sight of him.

"The entertainers are ready," Tulkhan said, coming to a stop with surprising grace.

"Then we mustn't keep them waiting." Imoshen lifted her arm to link with his.

"I'd better take my place." Cariah slipped away.

The musicians ceased their playing and the skaters made their way over to the tent. The flap had been rolled up to give them a view of the lake and the floor was covered with rugs and low tables. Tonight they followed the old custom of reclining on rugs and pillows.

Imoshen sank down and slipped off her skates. It disappointed her to note that, though the ambassadorial parties and mainland nobles mixed freely with both the Keldon nobles and the Ghebites, the two groups she most wanted to mingle were stolidly refusing to do so.

A hush drew her attention. Dancing skaters, each carrying flowering fountains of light, formed a sinuous weaving snake which whirled in time to the growing tempo of the music. Imoshen stole a look at the General. He was entranced.

Lord Fairban leant forward proudly. "Here comes my Cariah."

She swept across the lake, moving with fluid grace.

Imoshen's heart swelled with pride. Cariah skated smoothly past the tent, turning in a large arc which allowed her time to jump, spin, and land again. Against a backdrop of sparkling light fountains, she performed the ice ballet. It was a display that few could equal.

Once again, Cariah was benefiting from her unacknowledged T'En gifts; while Imoshen experienced the twice-edged sword of hers. But she intended to live up to the tenets of the T'Enchiridion. In serving the True-people of Fair Isle she hoped to win their trust and acceptance. One day, people like Cariah would not need to hide their gifts.

When the dance finished the audience applauded rapturously, and this time Imoshen did not find the rowdy appreciation of the Ghebites embarrassing.

As the entertainers moved off, servants sailed across the ice with the food. Imoshen couldn't help wondering what would happen if one of them lost their balance. The whole lot would come down, tripping each other up as food went everywhere.

A smile tugged at her lips and she caught Tulkhan's eye. When he grinned she knew he had been thinking the same thing. A rush of warmth swept through her. It was a relief to know he shared her unruly sense of humor.

There was a mild stir as Cariah joined them. She bestowed a fond kiss on her father's bald head and sank gracefully onto the cushions, midway between the Keld and Ghebites.

As those around her congratulated her, Imoshen watched Cariah throw back her head and laugh. Several of Tulkhan's commanders vied for her attention. Sahorrd played a game with her hand, making a point of discovering her sixth finger.

"You have T'En blood in your family," Imoshen spoke to Lord Fairban.

"On my bond-partner's side. Three beautiful girls she gave me, but only my eldest takes after her. Did you hear?" he beamed at Imoshen. "Cariah has been accepted into the Thespers' Guild as a full member?"

"Your daughter belongs to a guild?" Tulkhan remarked. "But she is the daughter of a nobleman."

Imoshen knew that the General was was not trying to offend Lord Fairban, his reaction stemmed from genuine confusion.

"Acceptance into the Thespers' Guild is conditional on talent and ability. Anyone can learn to make shoes, and only chance dictates whether you are born into the nobility. But very few people are truly creative. To be accepted by one of the creative guilds is a great honor," she told Tulkhan gently.

"I see." He looked at Lord Fairban. "My apologies. Things are different in Gheeaba. An artist is a craftsman hired to do a job, nothing more."

The old man's lips thinned and Imoshen realized the General's apology had only served to further offend him. Tulkhan's dark eyes met hers with a silent question, but she shrugged almost imperceptibly. Intolerance stemmed from both sides. At least the General was trying.

The lavish meal continued. In between courses, ice-skating clowns performed. This was more to the Ghebites' taste. At Cariah's insistence, several of the Ghebite commanders sang in their native language.

Imoshen guessed from Tulkhan's expression that the words were rather crude, but since most of it was not understood by the gathered nobles, it did not matter. When the meal finished, people left their places to mingle. Kalleen joined Imoshen and Cariah, pouring herself another wine, saying, "Those Ghebites seem to think a female incapable of conversation!"

Imoshen smiled. "I'm sure Wharrd does not think so."

"Then why is he with the Ghebite men and not here with me?"

There was a grain of truth in Kalleen's complaint. Imoshen felt uneasy. Kalleen had been raised to hold dear the old values. She would take it hard if her bonding was reduced to the shallow parody Imoshen had witnessed in the high court.

Cariah sipped her wine and indicated the young Ghebites who were betting on the outcome of an arm-wrestling match.

"Such physical creatures," Cariah purred. "Which one will I take to my bed tonight?"

Imoshen studied the men, amused. "Aren't they a little . . . ?"

"Crude?" Cariah suggested. "Yes, but most enthusiastic. The tall one, Sahorrd, is very intense. The hairy one has amazing stamina, and Jacolm is extremely well endowed."

Kalleen tilted her head. "Why not all three?"

Imoshen gave a little shriek of delighted horror.

Cariah's laughter rippled above the noise in the tent like the song of a beautiful bird. The Ghebites looked over. Imoshen had to hide a smile.

Cariah patted Kalleen's arm. "You are a girl after my own heart. But now I must decide whether to have them one after the other, or all three at once—"

"Imoshen?" Tulkhan snapped.

She sat up, startled by his tone. His glowering expression did nothing to reassure her as he held out his hand. She placed hers in his and he hauled her upright with such vigor that she fell against his chest.

"Come watch the dancers."

It was an order. Resentment rose in her. He bundled her out onto the ice and around the side of the tent where he rounded on her. "Don't let me catch you talking of bedding three men!"

She laughed at the absurdity of it. "What is it to you, General? Cariah is not bonded. She can pick and choose. It is the custom for a woman to—"

"It is not a Ghebite custom!"

"Are they not Ghebite men she is bedding?" Imoshen asked innocently.

"It is different for a woman."

"Different? How so?"

He pulled her to him. She could feel his need for her and it triggered a sweet flash of desire, spiced by irritation. "Imoshen!"

"Don't Ghebite women enjoy bedding their men?" she prodded.

"You are in need of a lesson!" he growled.

"Are you my tutor?"

His hands tightened.

With a laugh, she let her weight drop and broke his hold. Darting past him she ran across the ice behind the tent. He was right at her heels. Driving her legs she ploughed up the snow-laden bank. He tackled her, knocking her to the ground, and they rolled down the far side of the bank into a hollow, pillowed by deep snow.

Wordlessly he pinned her beneath him, seeking her lips. Imoshen returned his kiss with equal fervor, her heart soaring. Their bonding could not fail. It was too good, too rich. If only he would accept her T'En self.

Desperation drove her passion.

When his lips left hers she could not resist teasing. "Aren't you glad I'm not a sighing, long-suffering Ghebite maid?"

"By the gods, yes!"

She laughed, reaching for him. He tensed as she freed him.

"Your hands are cold."

A laugh bubbled out of her.

The brocade tabard parted. As was the custom, her gathered trousers had no center seam. Bundled in their thick garments only the barest minimum of their flesh met, but it was enough. They writhed in the snow, eager, flushed with their mutual need. It was a delicious, stolen moment.

When Tulkhan could think clearly again, he straightened his clothes, watching Imoshen rise and expertly arrange hers.

"There is much to be said for the way women dress in Fair Isle," he told her.

She laughed and offered him her hand. He wanted to pull her back down into the snow, but they would soon be missed. They ploughed down the bank, pausing in the lee of the tent to make final adjustments.

"Do I look presentable?" Imoshen asked.

Her cheeks were flushed and her lips were swollen by his kisses.

"You look bedable," he told her.

She thumped his chest with a good deal of force before returning to the tent.

He still wanted her. Tulkhan was grateful for the thick overjacket. He waited a few minutes then joined the others.

"I thought I would find you here," Tulkhan announced.

Imoshen gave a guilty start. She had escaped to the library after fulfilling her official duties. It had been a day for leave-taking. The mainland nobles had sailed with the morning tide, leaving only the ambassadors and their servants. The Keldon nobles would stay on to avoid the difficult travel over snowbound passes. By mid-morning Wharrd and Kalleen had made their farewells.

Kalleen had promised to return in time for the baby's birth but Imoshen did not know how many T'En traits Tulkhan's son had inherited. The longer his birth was delayed the more T'En he would be. She sighed. That was another subject the books failed to reveal.

"Yes, General?" she said, making the title an endearment.

"Three more of the stable boys are down with winter fever," he told her, though she could tell by his tone that this was not why he had come.

"I'll see to them. By the way, Lord Athlyng has been talking to me. He has advised the Keldon nobles to accept the new Causare Council. Telling them to select only six representatives was a master stroke. They will be fighting amongst themselves for the privilege." She smiled. "Have you heard from Fairban or Woodvine?"

"Not yet. There is something . . ."

She waited but he did not continue. "What is it, General?"

But he didn't answer immediately, picking at the binding of the book until she pushed it away to save it from his aimless fingering.

"It's the Lady Cariah. You will have to speak with her," Tulkhan said at last.

"I thought she was doing a very good job of bringing the Keldon nobles and town dignitaries together with your men. The younger, more flexible members have struck up friendships."

Tulkhan grimaced uncomfortably. "It's her lovers."

Imoshen bit her bottom lip to keep from smiling. For such a passionate man, Tulkhan was strangely prudish. "Surely that is her own business?"

"Not when it comes to my men."

"Surely that is their business?"

He frowned. "Then you won't do anything?"

"There is nothing I can do."

He sighed and slid a formal invitation across the table. "The Beatific wants me to take a seat at the next Intercession Day, but I know nothing of T'En laws."

Imoshen chose her words with care. "We have a fair system of laws, different, I gather, from the system you have in Gheeaba. If disputes between guilds or individuals cannot be settled by priestly mediation on Intercession Day, both parties appeal to the Emperor and Empress. We would be called upon to arbitrate." It was actually the Empress who was final arbiter, but Imoshen decided not to bring this up. "You should familiarize yourself with the laws of possession and inheritance to begin with."

"More chicken scrawl?" He gave a mock sigh.

Imoshen swallowed. The familiar teasing note in his voice warmed her. "I could teach you."

Tulkhan rolled his eyes. "Taught by a woman!" he complained. "In Gheeaba women don't read or write."

She stiffened.

"Don't be angry with me, Imoshen. I did not make the rules."

"You Ghebite men have a lot to answer for!"

He gave her a disarming smile. "Here I am, at your mercy. Use me."

His meaning was clear. Imoshen felt a smile tug at her lips.

"Very well." She slid out the sheet of notepaper and dipped the scriber in the ink. "The first letter of the T'En alphabet is shaped like this."

Tulkhan groaned, but sat at her side to study. Imoshen felt the warmth of his body seep through her clothing. It was only by exercising great self-discipline that she continued the lesson.

These were the moments she savored—when there was no one to observe or judge them and their differences faded. Even teaching Tulkhan the T'En alphabet was a sinful pleasure she hugged to herself before she had to relinquish him once again to palace politics.

Twelve

I DON'T KNOW what they expect me to do." Lord Fairban was genuinely distressed. "My daughter has already refused them both. Surely it is her decision?"

Imoshen smiled, for this was obvious. "Then forget it. Cariah has her status as an independent noblewoman not to mention the support of the Thespers' Guild. No one can force her to do anything against her will. Even if she were a poor farm girl, the choice of bond-partner would be hers alone."

Lord Fairban nodded but he didn't look convinced. Imoshen felt impatient. What did he expect her to do?

She pushed that thought aside as unworthy. The old lord had turned to her, the least she could do was consider the situation, carefully, but it was hard to think clearly. Late into the night and again since dawn she had been tending the sick. A debilitating winter fever had swept through the servants and begun to work its way through the nobles. She supposed it was inevitable, considering the number of people inhabiting the palace. To save her own strength she had used her healing gifts only on the worst afflicted, relying on basic herbal lore for the majority of cases. Even so she felt drained, fragile.

Finally, to escape the confines of the sickroom, she had slipped away to the balcony overlooking the courtyard, where she knew the Ghebites would be practicing their swordsmanship.

She had wanted to lose herself in the secret vice of admiring General Tulkhan, but she had not been allowed this indulgence, for Lord Fairban had approached her. She wished the old lord would take himself and his troubles away and let her enjoy the General's unconscious display in peace.

The Ghebites were stripped to the waist and their gleaming bodies steamed in the cold. Imoshen felt her gaze irresistibly drawn to Tulkhan. He was downing a drink in between bouts and she longed to go down and challenge him. Maybe later when the men left she would slip down, tie up her formal skirts, and ask him again to train her in the use of Ghebite weapons.

Sword practice was one of the endless Ghebite customs designed to exclude and confine women. She suspected these traditions were designed for the express purpose of bonding the males closer. In a society where a man's only equal was another male, it was no surprise to see that the relationships men shared went beyond mere friendship, like sword-brothers. King Gharavan had only been following the custom when he took the Vaygharian as his lover.

She would have found it all quite fascinating if understanding the Ghebites had not been a matter of life and death for her people.

The timbre of the fighting changed, piercing Imoshen's abstraction. There was trouble. General Tulkhan intervened. The two men bristled at each other like rabid dogs.

"That's them," Lord Fairban whispered, and Imoshen jumped. She had forgotten him. "Sahorrd saw me last night. He said he wanted to marry Cariah. I told him that bonding was not a matter to bring up with me, that he had to ask her. If she accepted him, we three could discuss the joining of their estates. Then later that same night Jacolm came to me with the same request."

"But Cariah refused them both," Imoshen said. She wasn't surprised. Bonding with a jealous Ghebite male would severely restrict Cariah's freedom.

Raised voices filled the courtyard, echoing off the walls. Imoshen caught Cariah's name, butchered by the soldier's harsh accents. Tulkhan strode between the two men. She half expected him to knock some sense into them, but instead a heated discussion followed.

"If Cariah has refused them both, why are they still arguing?" Imoshen asked Lord Fairban. He had no answer. As she watched, a decision seemed to be reached. "The General is sending for something or someone."

While they waited, Jacolm and Sahorrd were led to opposite ends of the courtyard by their companions.

Tulkhan strode over to stand below Imoshen. "There will be a duel. Send for the Lady Cariah of Fairban. She should be present to greet the winner."

"I will find her," Lord Fairban said.

He stepped back from Tulkhan's view, turning anxiously to Imoshen.

"Do it," she whispered. "I swear no harm will come to her."

When he had gone she leant over the balcony, speaking only for Tulkhan's ears. "What is the problem, General?"

He grimaced. "Cariah has come between Sahorrd and Jacolm. If they hadn't been sword-brothers it might not be so bad, but they are each determined to have her."

"Surely that is her decision. Stop this before—"

"Be sensible, Imoshen. I cannot ask a man to dishonor himself before his brothers-at-arms!"

Imoshen opened her mouth to speak, but a man approached Tulkhan.

"Ahh, the dueling swords. No lectures now, Imoshen. I have no choice." Tulkhan went over to his men.

Annoyed with his dismissal, Imoshen watched Sahorrd and Jacolm select their weapons. As much as she wanted to, she knew she should not intervene. She only hoped the men could work off their ill feelings without too much bloodshed.

With formal signals the Ghebites touched the tips of their weapons, bowed, then stepped back, waiting grimly.

Imoshen stiffened. Those were wicked weapons. Surely this was no more than a fight to first blood.

"Imoshen?" Cariah said as she approached, graceful even when hurrying. Her father hung back, perhaps reluctant to bear witness.

"Lady Cariah!" Tulkhan called.

Imoshen looked down into the courtyard to see both men give Cariah a formal salute, then fall into fighting stance.

"What—?" Cariah began but her words were drowned as the men leapt at one another, their swords ringing. She gasped, stepping closer to Imoshen. "More sword practice? Why was I called?"

"Not practice. A duel."

"The fools!"

"They fight over you, like dogs over a bone." Imoshen could not keep the scorn from her voice.

Metal scraped on metal, obscenely loud in the charged silence.

"Surely it is not to the death?" Cariah whispered uneasily.

"I trust not," Imoshen answered. "The General will stop them before it gets to that point."

Cariah's hand closed over Imoshen's, telegraphing her distress.

"What do they hope to gain by this display? It will not make me change my mind," Cariah muttered.

"Perhaps if they shed a little blood it would ease their hot heads," Imoshen suggested. She heard Lord Fairban shift uneasily and glanced at him. His mouth was grim, and he winced as the sound of screeching swords echoed off the courtyard walls.

Just then the old man cried, "One of them is down!"

Imoshen's gaze flew to the courtyard and a sickening certainty swept her. For Sahorrd and his sword-brother this was a fight to the death.

Time slowed agonizingly. Down on one knee, Sahorrd lunged under his opponent's guard, aiming a killing blow to

Jacolm's exposed upper thigh. But Jacolm leapt back to avoid
the fatal strike, missing his chance to finish the bout.

"One of them is going to die." Imoshen had not meant
to speak aloud.

"Can you tell which one?" Cariah demanded.

Imoshen did not know. She studied the duelists, wondering whether foretelling death was part of her gift.

A subtle shift passed over her sight as she searched for
signs. The strangely graceful movements of the fighting men
slowed and the ring of metal on metal sang, lingering on the
air in visible arcs of sound.

"Imoshen?" Cariah pleaded, her voice rustling across
Imoshen's perception.

"I . . ." She shrugged helplessly. Both men were surrounded by an aura of vibrating air but what this meant she
could not tell.

"T'Imoshen?" Cariah pressed, resorting to formality in
her desperation.

Imoshen met her eyes. In that fleeting glimpse she saw
the same aura around Cariah's beautiful face. Fear clutched
her.

"What is it? What did you see?" Cariah demanded.

A man's hoarse scream rent the air.

Stunned, Imoshen looked down to see Sahorrd on the
ground clutching his belly. She knew without examining
him that it was a fatal wound. Even with her skills she could
not stem that much blood, repair those damaged organs.

Cariah gasped Sahorrd's name, her face suddenly pale.

Tulkhan stepped forward and took the weapon from
Jacolm, who stood frozen. He did not resist when his
General led him toward their balcony and lifted his arm in a
sign of victory.

"Jacolm will see you, Lord Fairban, to claim your
daughter," the General announced.

The old man shook his head, looking to Imoshen to explain the misunderstanding, but it was Cariah who answered.

"My father has no say in this. It is my decision and I

won't have him!" Her voice rose with fury. "You killed without cause, Jacolm. Murderer!"

Imoshen dragged Cariah into the shadows of the balcony out of the sight of the men below. "Quiet. Think what you do!"

But Cariah was beyond thought. Her furious voice carried into the courtyard below. "I despise them all. Ghebite barbarians!"

"That may be so, but we are at their mercy," Imoshen hissed, finally reaching Cariah through her grief. She slid her arm around the woman's shoulders to support her, then walked to the balustrade to face the Ghebites.

"The Lady Cariah of Fairban has already refused both men, as is her right," Imoshen told them. "In Fair Isle we respect the free will of the individual. This duel changes nothing!"

Even as she said this, Imoshen felt a flare of heat and the force of Cariah's fury made her body tremble. It was a strangely seductive sensation. It called to her, wooing her with its dark passion. She wanted to bathe in such rage. Startled, Imoshen dropped Cariah's arm, stepping away from her.

The General glared up at them as though demanding Imoshen recall her words. In a flash of revelation she understood that to do so would deny Cariah, and every woman of Fair Isle, the right to choose her bond-partner. It would relegate them to possessions like the Ghebite women who were given in "marriage" to consolidate house-lines.

"Jacolm fought for her." Tulkhan's voice sounded forced, as if he was trying to maintain a reasonable tone. "She belongs—"

"I am not a prize!" Cariah snapped.

Tulkhan indicated the body. "A man lies dead!"

"By whose hand?" Imoshen asked, heart in her mouth. She would not see Cariah blamed for Sahorrd's death.

With an inarticulate cry Cariah ran along the balcony and through the far door.

There was stunned silence then one of the Ghebites yelled, "A man lies dead because of that bitch!"

"No! He lies dead because he would not respect her choice." But Imoshen's voice could not be heard above the furious shouts of the Ghebites, and even if they had listened, she doubted they would understand.

Wordlessly, General Tulkhan shook his head and turned away to rejoin his men. Only Jacolm remained, staring unseeing up at Imoshen. Her heart filled with a cold foreboding.

In his agitation Lord Fairban clutched Imoshen's arm, drawing her into the shadows. "You should have stopped them!"

Impatiently Imoshen indicated the courtyard where the Ghebites seethed like a simmering pot about to boil over. "How could I stop that?"

"But you are the T'En Empress!"

"To them I am a nothing but a hated Dhamfeer, a female at that!" Imoshen heard the bitter edge to her voice and saw him register the truth of her words.

"Barbarians . . ."

"We must salvage the situation. Come, my lord. A man lies dead and the proper words must be said over his body." She took the old man's arm. "Sahorrd's death arose from a misunderstanding and the Ghebites will realize this when their heads are cooler." Her words sounded hollow even to her own ears.

Imoshen rested her forehead on the windowpane, relishing the feel of the cold glass on her skin. The Empress's rooms were designed to promote peace and serenity. Today this did nothing for her.

Her eyes ached with each heartbeat. Her skin felt fragile. She knew she was coming down with the same ague which had struck so many of the others and she had a fever-breaking tisane ready to take but she was too weary to move.

Since the duel this morning, the palace had been in ferment. Several altercations had broken out in the entertainment wing as Keldon nobles and Ghebites argued over who was at fault. It had taken great diplomacy on Imoshen's part to soothe their self-righteous anger. At last she had retreated to her rooms too disheartened and weary to move. It was growing dark and according to Ghebite custom the words for the dead had to be said before dusk. No matter how tired she was, she had to attend the ceremony for Sahorrd to show proper respect.

Someone scratched at the door, then entered before Imoshen could summon the strength to deny them.

"I must speak with you," Cariah began. "I keep asking myself if I am to blame . . ." She stopped, her shoulders sagging with sudden despair. "I am heartsore and want nothing more than to be alone. I have come to ask whether I should retreat to my estates."

"If you left now it would be seen as an admission of guilt, when all you have done is insist on your rights."

Cariah sighed. "My guildmaster agrees with you. He advised me to stay. And so I must." She managed a stiff smile. "Even though all my instincts tell me to run. I feel threatened by every whisper, every look. Those Ghebites would kill me with a glance, if they could."

Imoshen slid her arm around Cariah's shoulder, offering wordless comfort. Without meaning to, she inhaled the scent of Cariah's hair. She could smell her pain and felt an instinctive urge to ease it. "We must not reveal any sign of weakness. I will stand by you."

Cariah shuddered. "It is the whispering and watching. I cannot stand it."

"You feel the force of their emotions. It is your T'En gift. When this is over you and I can—"

Cariah pulled away. "I feel nothing." She met Imoshen's eyes. "You frighten me with such talk. A part of me wants to run from you, too."

Imoshen felt as if she had been delivered a physical blow. She turned away in pain. If Cariah, who was more T'En than most, could still fear her, what hope was there for others to accept her, love her?

"Jacolm! Why did he kill Sahorrd?" Cariah cried suddenly. "He loved him."

"Who knows what love means to them?" Imoshen muttered, then winced to hear her callous words.

Cariah resumed pacing. "I should have handled it differently."

Imoshen restrained her impatience. "If you cannot say no to a Ghebite male, then what chance have other women, women who are not independently wealthy with the connections of a noble family, women who do not have the power of a guild behind them? Do not berate yourself, Cariah. There is more to this than simply you, Jacolm, and Sahorrd. The right of all the women of Fair Isle to control their lives is at stake."

"I did not think . . ."

"Go now."

"Forgive me, T'Imoshen, you see further than I." Cariah gave a formal obeisance and Imoshen was aware of a subtle shift in the balance of their relationship.

When Cariah retreated, closing the door softly behind her, Imoshen stared unseeing into the flames. It was too cruel—Cariah, of all people, feared her. She felt overwhelmed by the escalation of events. Everything was unraveling.

Her muscles ached with the onset of the fever and she added more wood to the fire to warm her cold bones.

The door swung open and Tulkhan strode in without so much as a word of greeting. Imoshen straightened. He vibrated with repressed anger. A little dart of despair pierced her and she turned away from him.

"At least look at me, Imoshen!" Tulkhan's voice was raw. She turned to face him.

"Get this woman to accept Jacolm."

A bitter laugh escaped her.

He cursed. "Is it so impossible?"

"What do you think?" She stared across the room at him, a cultural chasm between them. "Cariah has already rejected both men."

Tulkhan gave an exasperated grimace. "She would have his name—"

Imoshen snorted. "She has her own name."

". . . his protection."

"She needs no protection. She is a respected member of the Thespers' Guild and a property holder in her own right. Why should she ally herself with Jacolm, or any man, unless she wants to?"

"Then why did she lie with him, with them both?"

Imoshen had to laugh. "Why do you think? Don't your Ghebite women enjoy bedding their men?"

Tulkhan flushed; Imoshen shook her head in wonder. "Why did they have to duel—"

He made an impatient gesture. "You don't understand what honor means to us." But she could see in his care-worn face the grief he felt.

Imoshen's head throbbed and her throat felt tight. She could hardly think and there was still Sahorrd's burial ceremony to endure. "Please leave. I will dress now. In Fair Isle we wear our finest clothes to honor the dead but I don't want to offend your people. What should I wear to honor Sahorrd?"

He shook his head in wonder. "Imoshen."

"What?"

"The Cadre would be horrified to see a woman at a man's—"

"I see." Anger made her voice hard but this was not the moment to make her stand. "My people will expect me to do the right thing. Someone from Fair Isle must be present to honor Sahorrd in death." There was only one male of equal rank to her, and she could hardly ask Reothe. "With emotions running the way they are, I cannot ask any of the Keldon nobles. The Beatific would be ideal if she were not a woman."

"Murgon the Tractarian," Tulkhan suggested.

Her first impulse was to deny the man this honor. Of all Church officials he was the last person she wished to represent her. It would elevate his importance in the eyes of the Ghebites.

"You have a better suggestion?" Tulkhan pressed.

She sighed. "I will write a missive to the Beatific, appointing him as my delegate. Wording it without offending her will be a challenge."

Tulkhan gave her a wry smile and hope stirred within Imoshen.

"You see, all it takes is a little compromise," Tulkhan said. "If you would but speak with Cariah—"

"Enough! What you call compromise would see the women of Fair Isle reduced to property. I will not do it." Imoshen's rage drained away, leaving her dizzy. She reached for the mantelpiece and missed.

Startled, Tulkhan caught her, swinging her up into his arms. Her skin branded his. Remorse stirred him. "You are sick."

"The Beatific," Imoshen mumbled. "I must—"

"I will speak with her. You should be in bed."

". . . trust you to think that," she whispered.

He grinned and carried her into the bedchamber. "Can I get you something?"

Imoshen frowned at him, her eyes glassy with fever as she lay back on the pillow. "Bring the tisane."

Imoshen appeared to be asleep when he returned to the bed but she roused herself enough to drain the medicine.

He sat on the bed next to her, pulling the covers up.

She brushed his hands away. "I can do that."

"I know. But I want to."

A tear slipped down Imoshen's cheek. "Oh, General. Everything has gone wrong and I try so hard. . . ."

"We both do." He pushed her fever-damp hair from her forehead.

Imoshen fought to open her eyes.

"Sleep."

"But—"

"There is always tomorrow, Imoshen. For once, trust me."

Her hand felt for his and her six fingers closed around his five. Tulkhan held her hand until she slept.

"General Tulkhan?" Lord Fairban approached anxiously.

Tulkhan had spent a restless night going over and over the events surrounding Sahorrd's death, wondering if he could have acted otherwise.

"Fairban." Tulkhan tensed. Why couldn't this man control his daughter? Then he flushed as he imagined Imoshen's mocking laughter. He was thinking like a Ghebite. Learning the T'En alphabet was not enough. He had to understand the way the people thought.

"The Master of the Thespers' Guild tells me my daughter is missing. She did not meet with him this morning as arranged and her sisters have not seen her." Lord Fairban began reasonably, but his voice gained intensity as he spoke. "Unless she has taken refuge with T'Imoshen, I fear for her safety. Where is your man Jacolm?"

Tulkhan ground his teeth as he saw the Vaygharians enter the room. Everyone was looking his way, making no pretense of polite conversation. The fatal duel and Cariah's subsequent rejection of the winner had provided the court with a feast of speculation.

"Commander Peirs?" Tulkhan called his trusted veteran. "Send for Jacolm."

To maintain the appearance of normalcy, Tulkhan joined in a game of chance, but his gaze kept returning to the doorway. When he caught sight of Peirs he rose and the others made no pretense of continuing the game.

Peirs gave a formal salute.

"Well, man?" Tulkhan snapped, then winced.

"Jacolm cannot be found. His bed has not been slept in and his—"

Lord Fairban cursed.

Tulkhan signaled for silence. "Peirs, organize a search of the palace, then the grounds. Locate Jacolm's horse and kit."

"I checked. Untouched. The kit is still in his room."

Lord Fairban paled. "If that Ghebite has—"

"Get moving!" Tulkhan rounded on his men, who hurried away. The Keld watched him silently. Though no one spoke, he could almost sense them withdrawing from him.

Tulkhan ran his hand through his hair. He needed to find Cariah and Jacolm before the worst could happen. The implications rocked him. In desperation he thought of Imoshen and the scrying platter. Without a word he strode from the room, heading for their chambers. Every servant he passed avoided his eyes.

Imoshen would understand the need to use her gifts just this once. He only hoped she was well enough.

The new maid gave a gasp of surprise when he threw the door open.

"Where is she?"

The girl glanced to the door of the Empress's bedchamber.

He strode past her and thrust the door open. The bed was empty.

"You look for me, General?"

He spun to see Imoshen's blanket-shrouded form rise from the rug before the fire. Two bright spots of color burned in her white cheeks. Her pale beauty glowed with the inner furnace of a fever.

"You are no better."

"What's wrong?"

Suddenly he didn't want to tell her.

"Is it Cariah?" Imoshen's voice was a croak.

"She's missing."

"And the Ghebite?"

"Jacolm's missing too."

"He has abducted her?"

"His horse and kit are still here."

Imoshen clutched the back of the chair for support.

He tried to reassure her. "I have men searching the palace."

She sank to her knees before the fire. "It's my fault. She wanted to run but I told her to stay!"

"No, it's my fault. I should have foreseen Jacolm's reaction. What man could face such disgrace?"

"What disgrace?"

Tulkhan had no time to explain. He crossed the room, lifting Imoshen to her feet. "We must find them before it's too late. Are you well enough to do a scrying?"

She stiffened. "You insisted that I never use—"

"Lives are at stake."

"So you would use my T'En gifts when it suits you?"

"Yes!" Why was she hesitating?

"If I do this, what stops you from having me locked away like some unclean thing?"

"Have done with this!" He heard the maid's gasp. "You, girl. I know you're listening at the door. Bring the scrying plate!"

Imoshen closed her eyes and stood absolutely still. Tulkhan's hands tingled. A prickling sensation ran up his arms. Shocked, he released her flesh, stepping back sharply.

"So you don't need the scrying plate?"

"Focus. The Aayel said it was all a matter of discipline and focus. I dread . . ." Imoshen grimaced in concentration. "They are not in the palace buildings. It is very hard, people are running everywhere. There is so much tension."

"Search the grounds."

"I am."

Merkah returned with the plate, but Tulkhan waved her away. "Go, and keep out."

"I find no bright points of life, only—" Imoshen's knees buckled and she staggered. Tulkhan caught her. In that instant a wave of nausea swept over him. Roiling, dark emotions blotted his vision.

Imoshen moaned. "Heated fever dreams. The taste of death on my tongue—"

Tulkhan cursed. She was delirious. He should call for the maid and have her put Imoshen to bed.

"Now I understand the visions," Imoshen moaned. "I thought them feverish nightmares but it was Cariah trying to reach me."

"What do you mean?" Tulkhan demanded.

Imoshen shook her head and pushed past him.

Tulkhan watched her unsteady passage across the room. "Where do you think you're going?"

"I must face this."

He strode after her, sweeping her off her feet, blanket and all. "You can barely walk."

For once she did not resist him. "The place I sense lies beyond the lake. You can't carry me that far."

"We'll ride."

By the time they had entered the stables, they were accompanied by half the court, including Fairban and his two younger daughters.

"Saddle my horse," Tulkhan called to a stableboy, ignoring all demands for an explanation. He stepped up into the saddle and held out his arm to Imoshen. She clasped his forearm, put a bare foot on his boot, and was hauled up into his arms.

Her face was starkly pale. Her eyes glittered strangely and even with the blanket between them he could feel the overflow of her T'En gifts, rolling off her skin like heat radiating from a blacksmith's forge. It made his heart race. And though he knew it probably damned his soul for all eternity, he realized that he liked the sensation.

Imoshen guided them out beyond the ornamental gardens to the lake and the woods.

"That way." Eyes closed, Imoshen led them unerringly through the winter-bare trees.

They slowed to pick their way over the treacherous ground, hollows hidden by deep drifts.

"Which way now?" Tulkhan asked. The others had caught up with them, and were floundering through the thick snow.

She flinched. "You have to ask?"

Then he saw a dark patch already half buried by the lightly falling snow.

Imoshen twisted from his arms and half fell from the mount. Barefoot she staggered through the drifts. He threw his leg over the saddle. When he caught up with her she was on her knees before the figures.

They could have been entwined in a lovers' embrace. Snow dusted their heads and clothes. Cariah lay in Jacolm's arms, her face swollen and distorted.

Tulkhan knew Jacolm had strangled her, then cradled her body while he cut his wrists right up to the elbow. His blood soaked them both, a great, black stain.

"Poor Jacolm," Tulkhan whispered. "He could not live with the dishonor. He loved her—"

"Love?" Imoshen sprang to her feet, flinging the blanket off. She wore nothing but a thin shift and her hair was loose. Already a crown of powder-fine snow clung to her head, her lashes.

"Love?" Imoshen repeated. "Love does not kill what it cannot have!"

Lord Fairban leapt down from his mount with a keening cry of pain. His sobbing daughters waded through the snow to his side, trying to restrain him.

"Cariah!" he moaned, beside himself with grief.

Tulkhan looked over their heads to a contingent of his men awaiting his orders. They would have to bring the bodies in and prepare them for burial. Which Church would claim precedence, or would it be to each their own?

It was a nightmare.

"You!" Lord Fairban spun to accuse Tulkhan. "You could have stopped this. She had already turned them down. It did not have to come to this!"

"The moment she turned them down it led to this! Don't you understand? Jacolm could not face the disgrace. No Ghebite could!" Tulkhan felt his voice vibrate with anger. Why couldn't these people see? As much as he loathed the pointless loss of life, he understood it.

Lord Fairban launched himself at Tulkhan's throat. The General caught the old man's clawed hands, turning them aside. Deranged by grief, Lord Fairban fought with manic fury, while Tulkhan fought only to keep him at arm's length.

Even in his prime, the smaller man would never had been a match for him.

Lord Fairban's daughters and servants surged forward to restrain the old man. The Ghebites barreled into the melee, pushing people down into the snow and drawing their weapons. Tulkhan bellowed instructions, ordering them to put away their swords, but his voice was drowned by the screams. Soon blood would be shed and the precarious peace shattered.

Frantically Tulkhan searched the crowd for Imoshen's fair head, fearing she would be struck down and accidentally killed, or left lying unconscious in the snow. In her feverish state the chill would be enough to kill her.

He thrust people aside, vaguely aware that Lord Fairban was being dragged away by three Ghebites. In the midst of the wrestling bodies Tulkhan saw Imoshen, a solitary figure kneeling before the corpses.

Just as he darted forward to comfort her, a woman cannoned into him. The force of the impact sent him to his knees and he barely saved them both from falling under the hooves of the frantic horse.

Imoshen was staring at the dead lovers, seeing minute details. Unbidden, she relived the moments before their deaths. At first Cariah had argued but Jacolm would not listen, then Imoshen knew Cariah's terror when she realized he meant to kill her. She experienced her friend's battle for life and her defeat. She perceived Cariah's soul which raged impotently, unable to leave the site of her murder.

At the same time she felt the Ghebite commander's utter despair. He had killed his best friend and sword-brother, only to be publicly humiliated by the woman he adored. Even as he strangled her, he told her he loved her. But, dishonored, he had no choice. Jacolm's soul had departed with his acceptance of death.

Imoshen's heart swelled with ferocious pity. Despair settled upon her like a great stone. Her grief was not only for those present, it was for all her people and for Tulkhan's men too.

In her heightened state, Imoshen could feel everyone fighting behind her, a seething mass of True-people. Their anger, fueled by loss, rose like a great tide of torment, threatening to engulf her. Their swirling passion drummed on her consciousness, almost overpowering her with its force. Channeling, she used it to empower her T'En gifts.

As Imoshen stroked Cariah's sixth finger, she watched the young woman's features settle into a peaceful pose, all trace of violent death eradicated. Now Cariah lay in Jacolm's arms as if embraced. Dusted with snow, they were an island of stillness in a sea of emotion.

Cariah's impatient soul ate into Imoshen's awareness, demanding justice, demanding acknowledgment. The words for the dead spilled from Imoshen's desperate lips. This time she would not be bluffed by the Parakletos; this time she would bind them to her will. Anger filled her throat so that the words choked before they were born. It did not matter, the words had only to form in her mind and the Parakletos came. Eagerly.

She had no fear, she was a instrument for the rage of those present. Emotion impossible to contain consumed her. Her heart was stone. Stone was immortal, a timeless memorial, and the Parakletos were her stonemasons. Their purpose appeased Cariah's tortured soul, and with appeasement came acceptance. Their task completed, the Parakletos returned to death's shadow and Cariah's soul accompanied them.

Tulkhan felt a great pressure inside his head, a roaring which drowned all noise, then something snapped and he staggered, dizzy with relief. Around him grappling bodies parted, some dropping to their knees. One woman stood staring blankly.

Thrusting past disoriented people, he strode to Imoshen's side. At his touch she fell sideways into a snowdrift, as stiff and still as a corpse. Horrified, he dropped to his knees and pulled her into his arms. Her skin was cold, her lips blue. He was terrified he had lost her.

"Imoshen!"

Remorse seared him. Desperate, he lifted her in his arms

and carried her towards the horses. Strange. A few moments ago the others had been intent on wreaking vengeance; now they stood stunned as if their desperate emotions had turned to smoke.

He handed Imoshen's unconscious form to Peirs and climbed into the saddle. "Pass her up." Tulkhan focused on taking her weight, arranging her comfortably across his thighs and wrapping her in the blanket someone had retrieved from the snow. He shouldn't have asked this of her. He nodded to Peirs. "Bring the bodies in and have them prepared for burial."

"No!" Cariah's youngest sister cried. "It cannot be!"

"What now?" Peirs muttered.

"See for yourself." The girl stumbled back and her sister moved forward, accompanied by curious servants.

There was silence as they inspected the bodies. Suddenly the servant called on the T'En for protection.

"Frozen like stone," Cariah's sister marveled.

"What curse is this?" Peirs asked uneasily.

"I can't move my Lady Cariah. She has turned to stone," the servant cried, close to panic.

"Impossible!"

"Frozen, that's all," Peirs said, going to inspect the bodies himself.

Their startled comments washed over Tulkhan. But even as the others sought to satisfy their curiosity a strange certainty settled around his heart. Imoshen's flesh had been as cold as stone when he touched her, and smooth as marble.

The others fell back as he urged his horse forward.

Silently, Tulkhan looked down at the bodies, trapped forever in a stone-cold embrace. Even the dusting of snow had been transformed. A knife turned in Tulkhan's stomach. Imoshen had ensured Cariah and Jacolm would be a perpetual reminder of his failure to understand.

"White marble," he whispered, recognizing the stone.

Someone cursed. Cariah's youngest sister declared it a miracle. Lord Fairban muttered something in High T'En. As he spoke, the others fell silent, turning to Tulkhan and the unconscious Imoshen.

The General's arms tightened around her and his mount shifted uneasily, sensing the animosity and fear. Tulkhan watched them draw back, uniting against the unknown. Even the Keld averted their faces, lifting their left hands to their eyes then upwards, deflecting the evil so that it passed over them.

His own men stared at him, their faces filled with such awe and dread that Tulkhan sensed that if he wasn't holding Imoshen safely in his arms, they might have leapt on her and torn her apart. Years of command told him he had to seize the moment.

He raised his voice, indicating the stone lovers. "This will be a permanent reminder to us all. They have paid the price for our failure to understand each other. Let there be no more lives lost so pointlessly."

Then he rode away as if he did not expect a knife in his back. Yet he knew that only years of Ghebite discipline on the battlefield, and the nobles' natural awe of the T'En restrained the crowd from turning on him and Imoshen like a pack of wolves.

Thirteen

TULKHAN'S HANDS SHOOK as he gripped the reins. What had Imoshen been thinking? A familiar suspicion crossed his mind. More than once he had wondered whether the T'En gifts were more of a reflex than a learned skill.

He glanced down into her still face. Her pallor was worse than usual, but it was the blueness of her lips which made his heart falter. This time she had overreached herself.

The outbuildings of the royal palace lay just ahead. Stableboys and servants ran forward to hold the General's horse as he dropped to the ground with Imoshen in his arms, his knees protesting.

Around him people clamored for news. He gave the servants only a brief explanation as he entered the palace.

Striding down the long gallery with Imoshen in his arms, Tulkhan called for the fire to be built up in their chambers and the bed heated. He ordered a warm bath drawn immediately. He had to bring the color back to Imoshen's cheeks.

He kicked the bedchamber door open and placed her gently on the bed. The maid appeared at his side, her wide eyes fixed on Imoshen's unconscious form with a mixture of awe and horror. Suddenly Tulkhan feared for Imoshen's safety. This girl was not Kalleen. What if she was urged by someone, the Vaygharians perhaps, to smother Imoshen while she lay helpless?

"Is she dying?" Merkah whispered.

"No, merely exhausted," he said, hoping it was true. "Leave us."

When she was gone, he placed his cheek against Imoshen's mouth, trying to detect her breath. He felt nothing. Desperate, he tore open her thin shift and laid his face on her pale breast. For an agonizing moment he heard nothing, then he felt a slow single beat and nothing more. What had happened to her out there in the snow?

A servant entered to tell Tulkhan the bath was ready. He would let no one care for Imoshen but himself. He stripped her single garment and lowered her limp form into the warm water. Though it did bring a little color to her flesh, it did not wake her.

Before the water could cool he carried her to the bed and tucked her between blankets which held warmed stones. Then he took her hands between his and waited.

By dusk that evening he had not left Imoshen's side and she had not stirred. If anything she seemed even less responsive. He was sweating with the heat of the room, but Imoshen's skin was like porcelain, cool and lifeless.

The Ghebite bone-setter who had trained at Wharrd's side had already been there and gone. His skill was in the art of sewing up wounds. This was no True-man injury.

Tulkhan pressed the heels of his hands to his aching eyes as he waited for the Beatific to send a priest trained in the arts of healing. Someone scratched at the door and he rose hopefully. But it was the Beatific herself who entered.

"General Tulkhan," she greeted him softly. Her alert gaze went past him to Imoshen's still form, and she approached the bed slowly, as if drawn against her will. Gingerly she laid a hand on Imoshen's pale cheek.

"Have you ever seen anything like this?" he whispered, desperate for a word of comfort.

"No. How could I? The pure T'En have almost died out. And even when they lived, they kept the use and extent of their gifts a closely guarded secret." The Beatific met his eyes. He sensed she was studying him, weighing up possibilities. "If she does not wake soon, she will die. Maybe the babe is already dead. It is for the best. No pure T'En woman—"

"The babe!" How could he have forgotten his son? He was so consumed with Imoshen that he had not considered the child's welfare.

He sank onto the side of the bed. His son was probably dead but he felt nothing. All his being was focused on Imoshen.

In that moment he knew she had come to mean more to him than life itself. The child she carried was his hold on the future, on Fair Isle, yet he would give it all up if Imoshen would only wake.

The Beatific opened her arms and pressed his forehead on her breast, offering wordless comfort.

He pulled away, whispering, "Sahorrd, Jacolm, and Cariah, all dead. I did not think, did not foresee. And now this."

The Beatific made a soothing noise and he looked up into her handsome face. Her hazel eyes glowed with compassion. She understood. Hadn't she confessed to loving Reothe against her better judgment?

"This is a T'En illness, General. It needs a gifted T'En to bring her back."

"Reothe!" The name escaped Tulkhan with all the hatred he felt for the rebel leader.

The Beatific stepped back as Tulkhan rose impatiently. He paced to the fire. If he were to invite Reothe into the palace to help Imoshen, what chance had he, a mere True-man, against a Dhamfeer male? Reothe had mastered his T'En gifts to such an extent that he could deliver death with a single touch. Tulkhan shuddered, recalling how one of his men had died after delivering a message from Reothe, just as the rebel leader had said he would.

Frustration raged through Tulkhan. He might as well hand Fair Isle and Imoshen over to Reothe right now!

But if he hesitated she might die, and with her his unborn child. He could not contemplate such loss.

"General Tulkhan?"

"I take it you can get word to Reothe?" He knew he was asking her to implicate herself. He'd suspected all along that the Beatific was playing a double game by currying favor with both him and the rebel leader, while looking to the future to secure her power base.

Her golden eyes widened and she spoke slowly, as though surprised he would contemplate calling on his sworn enemy. "It might be possible. I have people who watch and report. But it would not be safe to invite Reothe here. Better to let nature take its course. No, listen!" She caught Tulkhan's shirt in her hands, as if her woman's strength might sway him. "You cannot sacrifice everything you have achieved for her. Already Imoshen has betrayed you. I heard she was at Reothe's camp the night before you were bonded."

"What?"

The Beatific flinched as he grasped her shoulders.

Tulkhan released his vicelike grip almost immediately, already regretting his slip. He would not be manipulated. "Rumor, mere speculation."

"Not necessarily." She worked her shoulders gingerly and looked up at him, gauging his reaction. "The country people say she was with Reothe till dawn. They claim she saved his life after he was mauled by a snow leopard."

Tulkhan recalled Imoshen's sudden appearance in his bedchamber, naked and disoriented.

"There is more," the Beatific continued. "It is said Imoshen and Reothe planned to lead a surprise attack on the palace, to strike while you were in disarray. If Reothe were to march into T'Diemn with Imoshen at his side, the people would lay down arms and join him. Only your Ghebite soldiers would remain loyal."

It was nothing but the bitter truth. The strategist in Tulkhan knew that he should let Imoshen die.

What chance had he if Imoshen and Reothe united against him? He would never hold Fair Isle alone. Already this accursed island had robbed him of his father and his half-brother.

He looked across at Imoshen's pale, still form on the bed. How he longed to trust her!

Unable to stand still, he paced the room, aware of the Beatific's eyes upon him. Perhaps this woman hoped to gain from Imoshen's death. Did she imagine he would turn to her for comfort? Never! Yet, without Imoshen, he would need the Beatific's support to hold Fair Isle. . . .

He found himself standing over the bed, staring down at Imoshen. Full dark had fallen and he hadn't lit more candles. She appeared pale even against the white covers. He sensed that the longer she stayed in this state, the harder it would be to rouse her. He had to make a decision.

"Leave us."

"General Tulkhan?"

"Just go!" He wanted time alone with his thoughts. "I will call you when I am ready."

Silently the Beatific retreated.

He lit the candles methodically. Then he returned to the bed and stripped the sweat-dampened shirt from his back, removing his boots. Clad only in his breeches, he slipped beneath the covers, rolling the warming stones onto the floor.

Despite the stone's residual heat, Imoshen's flesh was cold and her body limp. With infinite gentleness Tulkhan slid his arm under her shoulders so that she lay draped across his body, her face cradled in the crook of his neck. He guided her still hand to his lips and kissed her fingers, even her sixth finger. Pain twisted inside him.

He rubbed her wrist across his lips, inhaling her sweet scent.

Odd. He lifted her hand to study her left wrist. Why had he never noticed that pale scar before? It was barely visible yet . . . He pressed her inner wrist to his lips, feeling the thin ridge of flesh where the skin had knitted. The scar felt more visible than it looked. Perhaps this was because her skin was so fine.

Imoshen was dying, and he should let her die, even though his heart railed against it. Tears stung his eyes. A great knot of sadness swelled inside his chest.

Her cold body leached the warmth from him despite the many blankets. His eyes closed as a terrible weariness overcame him. His thoughts grew blurred and slow. It was a cruel choice. He wanted her to live. . . .

Sleep, then decide.

Drifting away, he felt nothing but a deep abiding sorrow. He had come too far to lose it all like this. He sensed oblivion calling and welcomed it.

Tulkhan woke with a start. The huge fire he had built up had burned down to glowing embers, and the candles had guttered into wax. He had not meant to sleep so long. He sensed he would have slept longer but something had woken him.

His body screamed a warning. Through half-closed lids he watched the air at the end of the bed shimmer. A figure took shape in the flickering candlelight.

Fear froze Tulkhan's limbs. His breath caught in his throat.

The last T'En warrior stood studying the two figures in the bed, his features unreadable.

Tulkhan kept his eyes mere slits, hoping Reothe would not realize he was awake. Had the Beatific betrayed him? If she had sent a messenger to Reothe, he could not have arrived so soon unless he was just outside the city gates.

"I can tell you are aware of me," Reothe whispered softly. "How does it feel to lie helpless?"

As he said this Tulkhan discovered he was paralyzed.

Reothe laughed softly. "Your fear is sweet. I could drink it down in one gulp. Don't look so horrified. You hold Imoshen in your arms and yet you don't know her true nature? Her gifts grow, living off all of you, the fears and hopes of so many little lives. The T'En serve True-men and women because you serve us."

He fell silent for a heartbeat, then a sweet smile illuminated his face. "I can feel the Beatific in the next room. She plots to console you once Imoshen dies. She desires you, admires your virility. But if I were to go to her now, she would take me into her arms, her body, her heart. It is the fate of you who call yourselves True-people to serve the T'En for love."

Tulkhan raged against the truth he heard in Reothe's words.

"How?" His voice was a mere creak, but at least he had spoken. "How are you here? Now?"

Reothe tensed, studying him. "You are a determined creature. I could enjoy your resistance for a long time before overcoming you."

Terror clogged Tulkhan's throat as Reothe walked around the bed to crouch at his side, bringing their faces level. He could not protect himself, let alone Imoshen, from this alien creature.

"You want to know how I come to be here?" he asked, then smiled. "You called me. Ironic, isn't it?"

Tulkhan couldn't move his head. He could only see his tormentor from the corner of his eyes. The strain made his head ache and distorted his vision so that the fire's embers seemed to flicker through Reothe's features.

"Called you? Never!" he gasped.

"But you did. You see, Imoshen and I are bound, betrothed in the old way. Earlier today I sensed a dimming in Imoshen's life force. When you touched our bonding scar you called me." Reothe paused, observing Tulkhan's face. "Didn't she tell you? The night before she was to bond with you, she joined with me. We mingled our blood, our breath to complete what we had begun last autumn. See." He held his left arm out to reveal a scar that matched Imoshen's. "Everything she has ever shared with you was meant for me."

Tulkhan· could not believe it. Would not!

"Deny this." Reothe turned Imoshen's left wrist to Tulkhan's face. "She may knit the scar seamlessly. She may cloak its very existence from you but that cannot change what is!"

Before this day he had never noticed the scar. Imoshen had been hiding it. Was she tricking him, playing some deep, double game? She couldn't be, she had come to him so openly; yet, perhaps she wasn't even aware . . . No. He could not believe . . .

"This is too sweet!" Reothe crowed. "You tear yourself apart. Let me ease your pain."

If Tulkhan could have moved he would have screamed, but his body was not his to command. He could only lie writhing in mental torment as Reothe spread the fingers of his left hand over Tulkhan's face.

Instinctively the General closed his eyes to protect them, but instead of flesh on his skin, six cool points caressed his senses. Soothingly they sank deeper into his awareness, siphoning off the terror which threatened to engulf his sanity. He was aware of a sense of Otherness which was Reothe. It was not unpleasant, just . . . different.

He knew he should be terrified, but fear was a distant memory. When the presence that was Reothe retreated, he was almost sorry to lose contact. He had never experienced the intimate presence of another being like that. As he opened his eyes he was aware of a cruel separation. Until this moment he had never known how truly alone he was.

Reothe rose to stand beside the bed. A delighted laugh escaped him as he pulled back the covers.

"See what you have done for me. I grow more substantial on your emotions."

Now Tulkhan understood that this Reothe was only a projection. There was something chillingly innocent in the T'En warrior's delight. It was as if he was so far removed from a True-man that the rules Tulkhan lived by could not affect him.

One part of the General knew he should be mortified to lie defenseless before his most dangerous enemy, but the mind-touch had left him strangely distanced; he could only watch as Reothe studied the way his body entwined with Imoshen's.

Reothe's six-fingered hand glided over Imoshen's thigh. His touch was proprietorial. Instinctive resentment flooded

Tulkhan, yet an equal and opposite surge of hope filled him. Could Reothe help?

"Ask for any reward, anything." Tulkhan's words were a breathy whisper.

"Anything?" Reothe leant closer, as though fascinated despite himself. "There is nothing you can give me, True-man. Mere-man. By this time next winter I will have this palace, Imoshen, and Fair Isle. You are merely holding it in safekeeping for me." His hand passed over Tulkhan's face to rest on Imoshen's temple. A frown settled between Reothe's narrow brows. "Why did you delay so long? I may be too late to escort her from death's shadow."

"But you will try?"

Reothe gave a short laugh, his eyes as sharp as the jewels they resembled. He searched Tulkhan's face. "Did you know she saved my life the last time we were together?"

Tulkhan wanted to deny this. Reothe's satisfied smile told him the Dhamfeer was enjoying his reaction. Instinctively he tried to control his emotions. But how could he bluff Reothe when the T'En could sense his feelings, possibly even catch a whisper of his thoughts?

With what he had learned of Reothe during the mind-touch, Tulkhan understood that every word was a weapon designed to wound him. He recalled the old nursery rhyme about Dhamfeers and tried to steel himself against Reothe's cunning.

"The bond Imoshen and I share is of an older, deeper making than yours, *Ghebite*." Reothe made the word an insult. "One day she will look into your True-man eyes and realize what you are, and that her place is with me. I will save her, not for you, but for that day. And when it happens you will remember this moment."

Tulkhan closed his eyes. It felt as though Reothe were revealing a greater truth, something Tulkhan had always known but refused to acknowledge. Yet Tulkhan did not believe in fate, did not believe Imoshen was fated to be with Reothe. A man made his own future.

"You may feel a little pain. I haven't done this before," Reothe warned.

Tulkhan met Reothe's eyes and read something he didn't want to acknowledge. Instead of mocking cynicism, he saw the naked soul of a man who knowingly faced death, and for this he felt a grudging respect.

The Dhamfeer was insubstantial now. Narrow parallel scars ran down his chest, weeping fresh blood. Had Reothe been wounded when he arrived? Tulkhan couldn't remember. The glowing coals of the dying fire flickered through Reothe's body as if he was consumed from within.

One part of Tulkhan wanted to shrink from the contact as Reothe stretched on the bed beside him. He felt the T'En male's intense questioning gaze.

"What?" Tulkhan mumbled.

Those insubstantial fingers pressed his lips closed.

"Pray to your gods that I succeed, Ghebite, because if I fail, you lose us both and possibly your own life, too, since I am going to anchor myself to you. Concentrate on that burning candle, do not let it go. Ignore me even if you find what I do disturbing."

Tulkhan wanted to watch, to know what was happening, but the words triggered a compulsion and his gaze focused on the flame at the end of the bed. He was fleetingly aware of Reothe's presence at his side and then his insubstantial body moving over Tulkhan's own, settling atop Imoshen's unconscious form.

Then the candle flame blurred and Tulkhan's heart pounded in his chest. Lightness filled his body so that he felt dizzy and vague. Fear closed around his raging heart. He must not lose sight of that flame. If he did they were all lost.

He was aware of a heaviness filling Imoshen's body, then heat flashed through her limbs. She gasped as if in pain. Hope soared in him, sinking once again as she returned to the dreamless state which had captured her.

The flame flickered and separated to become two points of light. Like the reflective eyes of a great, white cat, they stalked him. Terror filled Tulkhan's chest. He could not scream, could not defend himself. Sweat broke out on his skin.

Malignant intelligence pursued him. He wanted to close his eyes to deny approaching death, but perversely he knew to break contact was to die. He dared not even blink. His eyes burned and his breath passed through his parched throat in short sharp gasps.

Abruptly the twin flames broke into a thousand sparkles like sunlight on water, blinding him.

Tulkhan opened his eyes to find the room dark except for the dim glow of the fire's coals. The candles had all burned out. He felt so weak he could hardly move. But Imoshen lay warm in his arms, her body sculpted around his, pliable and dear to him. With a rush of joy he recalled how they would lie entwined like this after making love.

Experimentally he lifted a hand to stroke her upper back. Her skin no longer had that marble-smooth feel. Hope flared within him, giving him renewed strength.

"Imoshen?" Rising on one elbow, he cradled her face in his free hand. "Answer me, Imoshen."

She frowned and Tulkhan's heart soared. Whatever Reothe had done, it had succeeded. Imoshen was waking.

Trembling with relief he sat up, gathering her warm, breathing body to his. Pure joy illuminated his soul. His fingers entwined in her hair as he cradled her face, kissing her temple, the hollow under her jaw.

The soft sound of protest she made in her throat was a blessing. He laughed, feeling tears on his cheeks. "Imoshen," he breathed, seeking her lips. She had come back to him.

Her mouth moved under his, her breath mingled with his. He could drink from her lips forever. He felt her smile.

Relief made him light-headed. He looked down into her face to see her familiar features, but her wine-dark eyes mocked him. The sad smile was not hers.

Cold certainty closed around Tulkhan's gut. "No!"

He pushed her from him, repulsed. The intelligence watching him from Imoshen's eyes was not hers.

The room spun. He had to clutch the bed frame to

steady himself. Still reeling he watched Reothe's insubstantial form rise from Imoshen's body. As his spectral form rose above her she sank onto the bed.

Then Tulkhan saw two people—the sleeping form of Imoshen, with Reothe, who was hardly more than a wraith, kneeling over her.

Tulkhan could barely summon the strength to swallow. What he had witnessed this night was something no True-man should know. Yet he could not look away as Reothe stroked Imoshen's face. His incorporeal fingers failed to brush a strand of hair from her lips. Tulkhan watched him dip his head, pressing his pale lips to hers.

It was too intimate a gesture for another to witness. He had to look away. When he looked back Reothe had turned to him, his face a deadly mask. Tulkhan scrambled off the bed and backed away, his legs hardly able to support him. He wished for a weapon, though he knew it would do no good.

As the Dhamfeer stalked toward him, one part of his terrified mind noted that the bed and Imoshen's sleeping form could be seen quite clearly through Reothe. Perhaps the T'En's gifts were wearing thin with use. He hoped so. It would be a relief to know the creature had limitations.

Reothe stopped before him. "I have braved the Parakletos, searching death's shadow to find her and bring her back."

Tulkhan barely breathed. "I thank you."

"I didn't do it for you."

"I know."

Reothe turned to gaze at Imoshen. He said something in High T'En. It sounded like poetry or a line from a song.

The Dhamfeer returned his attention to Tulkhan, a lingering smile in his alien eyes. It was a smile that held painful self-knowledge. "You do not ask. It means, *'Those we love have the greatest power to wound us.'* "

"Reothe." Tulkhan went to touch him, but his hand slipped through his body. "Can't we find a middle ground?"

"You would compromise?" Reothe shook his head ruefully. "You don't want to deal with me, True-man. I have already bargained away my soul."

He lifted his face as though looking for something beyond Tulkhan. The Dhamfeer winced as the slashes across his chest deepened and the blood ran freely.

Even so, Tulkhan felt there was something in Reothe, something he recognized because something similar lived in him. It didn't have to be this way. He went to tell the last T'En warrior this, but Reothe was gone.

Stunned, Tulkhan searched the empty room. His senses told him that it was free of T'En influences.

Wearily he went to the bed. It was the darkest part of the night, the time when sick folk died and babies were born, the predawn of a winter's night.

As though waking naturally, Imoshen rolled over and stretched. When her eyes opened, she smiled as if recalling a pleasant dream. He made an involuntary sound in his throat as she looked at him.

There was no recognition.

Had Reothe stolen Imoshen's memory? But no, now she recognized him. As memory returned her face grew haunted.

She sat up abruptly. "Jacolm and Cariah!"

Tulkhan flinched. He had hoped to see pleasure light her face, not sorrow. Were they destined to bring each other nothing but pain?

Questions burned to be asked, but tonight he was not sure he could face the answers, so he held back.

Imoshen drew a quick breath, then winced. Her chest hurt. Every muscle in her body ached as if she had been tested to the full extent of her physical endurance. The last thing she recalled was kneeling in the snow before the bodies of Cariah and Jacolm and beginning the words for the dead.

"How did I get here?"

"I carried you. You've been unconscious all day and most of the night."

She saw Tulkhan watching her closely. He looked very weary and she could sense a difference in him, as if he had been touched by something beyond a True-man's understanding. "What haven't you told me?"

He shrugged as if he did not know where to start.

"You're tired, come to bed." But he made no move to join her. "What is it, Tulkhan?"

"You hide things from me."

His expression alarmed her. "Why do you look at me like that?"

He sank onto the bed and she ached for him to take her in his arms.

"You turned the bodies of Cariah and Jacolm to stone."

"Impossible!" But even as she said it, she knew it was true.

"It nearly killed you. When I brought you back here you were as cold as stone."

She shuddered and reached for him but he did not respond. "Why won't you hold me?"

"Why don't you ask how it is that you still live?"

She shook her head, drawing back to study his face. His eyes held a deep, glittering anger which frightened her.

He snatched her left hand and turned the arm over, inspecting her wrist, then held it up for her to see.

"You say you do not use your tricks on me, then why is the bonding scar you share with Reothe hidden again?"

Imoshen frowned. The fingers of her free hand traced the scars left by the snow leopard's claws. The night Reothe had drawn on the Ancients to abduct her she had raked her chest, demanding the old powers return her to the palace. The small wounds made by her fingernails had healed because they were of a physical origin, but no True-man could see marks made by the Ancients. It seemed when she had urged her wrist to heal she had been unconsciously cloaking the bonding scar from Tulkhan. "The scar is not what it appears. . . ."

Tulkhan grew pale and he dropped her wrist. "Now that you admit it, I can see it again."

"I don't mean to hide things from you."

"Were you in Reothe's camp the night before his bonding? Did you save his life."

Imoshen's skin went cold and she opened her mouth to deny it but could not lie.

"Answer me!" Tulkhan caught her shoulders, shaking her.

Tears stung her eyes.

Suddenly he released her. "I must be mad!"

She drew into herself, seared by his derision. Deep sobs shook her. The General would never trust her.

"Imoshen," he moaned and pulled her into his arms. "I thought you were dead!"

She felt his lips on her forehead, sensed his relief. "I don't understand. Why does it hurt when I breathe? What happened here this night?"

Tulkhan looked down, unwilling to reveal that he had been useless while Reothe had risked his life to save her. Before he could confess, Imoshen leant forward and licked his throat.

Her eyes widened. "I can taste Reothe on your skin."

"He was here."

"He couldn't have been. It would take days for him to ride here."

"He didn't ride. He wasn't here in body." Tulkhan shrugged. He didn't have the words. "Reothe said he felt your life force dim, that you were bound to him in some T'En way. It was he who saved you. I . . . I could do nothing for you."

Imoshen quivered, and Tulkhan recognized her reaction as fear.

"Reothe said that I am only holding you in safekeeping," Tulkhan continued bitterly, "until he is ready to claim you."

"You mustn't listen to him." Imoshen's breath caressed his throat. Then he felt her hands on him, needful and urgent. As her lips moved on his flesh the knot of failure which had wound so tight inside him gradually eased. "Reothe can tell the absolute truth and make it sound like a lie so that you doubt your own judgment."

Tulkhan wanted to ask her if she could do the same. But

the warmth of her breath on his skin was overwhelming. It drowned all caution. The need in her was great, calling up an answering urgency in him. He wanted only to bury himself inside her, to forget everything but her touch. She was a balm to his bruised soul.

"How could you give your bonding vows to me when you already had this?" He grasped her left wrist.

Imoshen gave a little gasp. "Reothe cut our wrists before I could stop him. When he tried to say the words to complete the vow I refused." She searched Tulkhan's face. "I have been true to you. I swear."

He wanted to believe her. "I must be mad."

He felt as if Reothe had stolen something intangible. Only Imoshen's touch eased his hollowness. He had nearly lost Imoshen tonight, and if Reothe could be believed, he would not have her for long. The knowledge added poignancy to their lovemaking. Every touch was a discovery, the foundation of a memory.

Fourteen

WHEN IMOSHEN WOKE late the next morning, the bed was empty, though the scent of their passion still clung to her skin. Every movement was an effort as she forced her trembling body to perform the simple act of dressing.

She had searched her mind, but there was no memory of Reothe's presence. Tulkhan had told her how Reothe had risked death's shadow and the wrath of the Parakletos to save her. She was beholden him and she hated it.

"T'Imoshen," Merkah cried. "You are up and dressed. Why didn't you send for me?"

"Where is the General?"

"He left word that you were to go to him once you were ready."

Imoshen nodded. Her arms hurt so much she could not lift them above her head. She asked Merkah to do her hair and sat before the mirror.

As the maid set about her task she beamed. "It was such a surprise when the General told us you had recovered. The Beatific could not believe it! She was sure the baby would be dead—"

Imoshen gasped.

Merkah's startled eyes met Imoshen's in the mirror.

"I suppose it is common knowledge, or it will be soon."

Imoshen's hand closed over her belly, suddenly afraid that the fragile life had been extinguished while she lay unconscious.

Stiffly she came to her feet.

Merkah hurried to open the door.

"Where is General Tulkhan?" Imoshen asked.

Before Merkah could reply, a grey mist enveloped Imoshen's vision. She felt her legs buckle and, when she could think clearly again, found herself sitting on the floor.

"Stay here, I will bring a healer," the girl urged.

"Nonsense. I'm fine." But Imoshen came to her feet slowly and waited a moment to be sure. She didn't have time for physical weakness. "Now, where is the General?"

Merkah hesitated. "I will go with you."

"Very well."

As they walked through the palace galleries, Imoshen noted there were very few servants, and the few she did see slipped away quickly. "Where is everyone?"

"In the woods, viewing the beautiful stone lovers. Half the city has been through the palace grounds today, the queue runs right out the gate." Merkah paused by a window. "You can see it from here."

Imoshen peered over her maid's shoulder. A dark line snaked across the white snow.

They walked on in silence. Imoshen had her evidence. Until this moment she had not fully believed Tulkhan. She really had turned the dead lovers to stone. Not only had she failed Cariah, she had unwittingly revealed gifts that would only encourage True-people to fear her.

"Here we are." The maid scratched on a door panel.

At the sound of Tulkhan's deep voice Imoshen's face grew hot, the memory of their urgent lovemaking fresh in her mind. She lifted her chin and walked in. The General stood behind a large table covered with maps. Wine bottles, goblets, and several ink wells held the curling edges flat.

Merkah shut the door as she withdrew.

"Yes?" Imoshen let the tip of her tongue rest on her upper lip, tasting the air. Someone who didn't like her had been in this room recently.

When Tulkhan's eyes met hers they were cold, and the planes of his face were tight with tension. She did not understand why he had distanced himself from her.

"I have lain awake for hours thinking. You did not deny that you have been to Reothe's camp. Tell me where it is."

Imoshen's heart sank.

"You say I have your loyalty," Tulkhan persisted. "Prove it. Point out his camp."

She looked down at the maps. "That was three weeks ago. If Reothe is half the tactician I believe him to be, he will have moved by now."

Tulkhan did not seem disappointed. He slid something out from under a map and tossed it onto the table before her. The silver platter spun and settled heavily. "Then do a scrying to locate his camp."

Imoshen looked at the plate's dull surface. It was the scrying platter she had inherited from the Aayel. It annoyed her to think Tulkhan had asked Merkah to take it while her mistress slept. "You made me vow not to use my gifts."

"I'm making an exception. Do it!"

Pain unfurled inside Imoshen. He wanted to use her as a tool to locate and kill, but he had shut himself away from her. How could this be the man who had held her so tenderly last night?

"If you refuse I will—"

"Lock me up?" Imoshen whispered. "Steal my child and wall me inside the palace somewhere, leaving me to starve to death?"

Tulkhan looked shocked. "Do you really believe that of me?"

Imoshen shook her head and picked up the scrying plate. The skin of her fingers crawled with distaste. Gingerly she lifted them to her face and inhaled. "The Vaygharian has been here. Is that why you doubt me, Tulkhan? Have you forgotten so soon that he poisoned your half-brother's mind."

"I can see through Kinraid's maneuvering. Besides, he is not the only source of my information." His obsidian eyes narrowed. "Just do the scrying, Imoshen. Think of it as a test. I would be a fool to have such a tool at my disposal and not use it."

"I can't."

"You mean *won't*."

"No. I can't. The Aayel tried to explain it to me once but I did not know enough to understand her. You probably won't understand me but I am going to try to explain." She sighed. "Reothe is more versed in his gifts. I am just discovering mine. Scrying is not an exact science. If I were to pick up that plate and try to locate Reothe, I might succeed too well. I don't want to give him access to my mind." She shivered, hugging her body. "I won't do it. Please . . . I'm afraid."

Tulkhan rubbed his jaw thoughtfully. "Let me see if I have this right. You and he are both sorcerous creatures."

"No, we're—"

"That is the Ghebite word for someone who manipulates powers a True-person can't. I will call you anything I like." When Imoshen did not argue he continued. "But even though you both use the T'En gifts, you are weaker than he. Are you telling me I have allied myself with the weaker of the two sorcerers?"

Imoshen nodded. She was merely a child where her skills were concerned.

The General studied her. Once again she was aware of his keen intelligence.

"What's to stop you from turning your back on me and joining Reothe?" Tulkhan asked. "He shares your heritage. Last night he risked his life to save you. He was your betrothed by choice and . . . he loves you."

Imoshen felt her cheeks grow hot. She did not attempt to deny Tulkhan's assessment.

"So why stay here, Imoshen? Are you playing a double game, passing information to Reothe? Did you go to him the night before our bonding then come back to me with false promises on your lips? Why do you persist in this farce?"

She heard the raw pain in his voice and she ached to re-assure him. But he would not let her approach him. Had Reothe somehow cunningly planted doubts in Tulkhan's mind?

She felt too weary for subterfuge. "The night before our joining, Reothe made a pact with the Ancients. He sacrificed a snow leopard to appease their greed and drew me to him. I had no choice in the matter. Returning to you was my choice."

General Tulkhan was patently unconvinced.

She tucked her scrying plate under her arm, determined and defiant. "I am going to the library. You can place a guard on me if you choose. Though what the palace servants will think of that, I can't imagine. I am true to you, General Tulkhan. If there is a seed of doubt, it lives in you, not me!"

Why wouldn't the man die? Tulkhan's sword arm ached. His breath rasped in his throat. And still the man kept coming. Every killing blow Tulkhan struck was ineffective while his own body grew steadily weaker. Sweat stung his eyes. The swordsman hadn't been this hard to beat the first time he had killed him. With a jolt Tulkhan realized this was a dream. He was reliving his first battlefield kill.

At seventeen Tulkhan had sent this man to his grave without a thought.

Suddenly he slipped on the bloodied ground, going down on one knee, which he hadn't done in real life. He took a sword strike under his arm above the armor. The blade ran deep into his chest, burning, searing all the way. Each breath became agony and grew more shallow as he drowned in his own blood.

Propped on one elbow he stared up at his opponent, silhouetted against the sun. The swordsman pulled off his helmet. Reothe?

Tulkhan woke gasping, drenched with sweat, his heart racing. When he rolled to his feet his knees threatened to give way. Staggering, he crossed the room to the window and threw it open. The smell of death and despair clogged his nostrils. He felt utterly hollow.

He heard Imoshen moan in the room beyond and stifled the impulse to go to her. To lie in her arms now would be bliss, but each time he did, he felt the bonds of passion bind him ever closer to her. Tulkhan could not forget the moment Reothe had revealed the bonding scar he shared with Imoshen.

Last night he had let himself believe her denials, but excuses sprang too easily to Imoshen's lips. And today when she had refused to discover Reothe's camp, Tulkhan had vowed to stay out of her bed. Instead he had placed a blanket before the fireplace in the Emperor's private chamber.

Tulkhan strode to the fireplace to stir up the coals, and keep back the night. Somehow he knew this feeling of despair was Reothe's doing and that he must fight it with every breath he took.

Imoshen roused herself from a doze. It was the day before the Spring Festival, though the snow still lay thick on the ground. She blinked and remembered that she had been working through the plans for the feast before she drifted off.

The scratching came again. Imoshen did not recognize the comb's metal tone.

She rubbed her face and straightened her hair. "Come in."

Lord Fairban's youngest daughter entered. "T'Imoshen."

"Lady Miryma." Imoshen came to her feet. She and Miryma were the same age, but they were worlds apart. This woman was the youngest child of an indulgent father, while Imoshen carried the weight of Fair Isle on her shoulders.

Like the rest of the Keldon nobles, the Fairbans were preparing to return to their estates now that the worst of the snows had melted.

"My father wishes to speak with you before he leaves," Miryma said.

"I would be honored."

"You'll need a cloak. Father wants to speak somewhere private."

Imoshen did not like the sound of that. She thought Lord Fairban had become reconciled, as much as was possible, to Cariah's death.

She followed the young woman through the palace, out into the formal gardens.

"This is as far as I go. Father waits for you in the center of the maze," Miryma said.

Imoshen thanked her and moved on. The air was still, crisp, and cold. Ideal for carrying sound. She heard the horn and the baying of the dogs. The Ghebites were hunting in the woods again. She wondered with disgust what animal they had flushed out this time. They had just about hunted all game from the formal woods. There was even talk of freeing some of the animals from the menagerie, which would be cruel indeed since these were rare animals, presented to the palace as gifts and bred over generations.

When Imoshen entered the center of the snow-shrouded maze Lord Fairban spun to face her. She could tell by the furrowed snow that he had been pacing.

At the sight of her he grew still. He had aged since Cariah died. A steely determination defined his face as he studied her.

She waited, then prompted him. Her feet were starting to go numb. "I have come in answer to your summons, Lord Fairban."

He indicated the stone seat and brushed last night's snowfall from its surface.

"Come, T'Imoshen. I have been made spokesman and it is time we revealed our plans to you."

Imoshen's heart sank. "Continue."

"This may be painful for you, but I must speak plainly. You are nothing but a tool to the Ghebite General, a prize of war to be used to cement his hold on this island. Even the child you carry is more important for his hold on Fair Isle than yours. He needs you. You do not need him."

Imoshen raised an eyebrow. It seemed everyone knew of her pregnancy.

Lord Fairban nodded to himself. "I came to see this Ghebite General and I must admit I was favorably impressed. Tulkhan is a good man, for a Ghebite. But events have proved that we can never live with them. They are primitives."

He took her hand, patting it kindly. A wave of sincerity washed over Imoshen. Lord Fairban believed what he was about to say.

"There are others who feel the same way. We want to see you and Reothe in the palace. If the royal family had been pure T'En as they were meant to be, Fair Isle would never have fallen to the Ghebite invaders."

Imoshen was swamped by his vision of a future with a powerful T'En ruling class who protected the True-people of Fair Isle. She withdrew her hands from his, too dismayed to speak.

He appeared unaware of this. "When I go south I will make contact with T'Reothe, aid him. When he is ready, we will march into T'Diemn where you will be waiting for him."

Imoshen dared not reveal how she really felt. If she objected to his plans, Lord Fairban would become her enemy, for he must surely know that the information he had just revealed would result in his death and the destruction of all his associates.

"I knew you were biding your time, playing out the charade until the moment of confrontation," he continued, pleased with his sagacity. "My daughters and I leave immediately after the festival tomorrow. It is time the Keld made a stand."

"Lord Fairban, I urge caution."

"No need. I know your hands are tied for now. But when the moment is right you will strike a telling blow for Fair Isle, turning the invaders to stone!"

Imoshen slumped on the low seat, feeling the cold seep through her cloak and gown.

"My Cariah admired you, Imoshen. I have lost a daughter. You have lost your family. Let my daughters be your sisters, let me stand in place of your father."

Stunned, she could only stare at him. He radiated absolute faith in her and she knew his heart was good. Imoshen was horrified. What could she do? She did not want to be the death of Cariah's father and the annihilation of what remained of Fair Isle's old nobility.

"I will leave first," he advised. "You wait a while, then follow me out. There are spies everywhere."

Imoshen watched him go, then buried her face in her hands. To think it had come to this. Her head spun with the implications. The Keldon nobles believed she was capable of turning the Ghebite army to stone. They believed she and Reothe could not fail to rout the Ghebites. Naturally they would be happy to rise against the invaders. To know her own unthinking actions had triggered this development was bitter indeed.

Imoshen rose, stiff with cold and shock. She had no idea how much time had passed. In a daze of worry, she followed the footprints out of the maze. It was only when she came to the last turn that she noticed there was an extra set. A third person had stepped in her footprints but that person's stride was not as long as hers.

Imoshen's heart faltered.

Who had overheard them?

One of Tulkhan's spies? Since he no longer came to her bed she knew he had set people to watch her. Or maybe it was one of the ambassadorial groups, their keen-eyed servants were everywhere. . . .

Imoshen dropped to her knees, placing her bare hand in the snow hollow before lifting it to her nose.

She knew that stench. Vaygharians!

By tonight Kinraid would have Tulkhan's ear, planting his poison to grow and fester. If only the General would let her touch him. She knew if she could lie naked next to him, she could ease his doubts and soothe his fears.

But she wouldn't get the chance. Frustration welled in

her. She didn't want to betray Tulkhan. Somehow she had to convince him of that while protecting Lord Fairban.

The horn sounded again.

Inhaling, Imoshen tasted the hunting blood lust of the Ghebite men carried to her on the breeze. Tulkhan was with them. Without another thought she took to her heels, running towards the woods.

A heaviness in her lower belly reminded her of the baby's presence but did not slow her. However, it was harder going when she entered the woods where the snowdrifts had piled up. She concentrated on finding Tulkhan. Something was being hunted through the woods. The tang of male excitement hung on the air. Its unpleasant aftertaste sat on the back of Imoshen's tongue.

She ran on, letting instinct guide her. Soon she found herself on a rise, hunting the hunters. They were on horseback moving parallel to her. The thick woods slowed their pace.

She identified the General's broad shoulders amongst the hunters. He didn't want her to use her powers but she had to make him come to her. Everywhere she turned, people were trying to drive a wedge of mistrust between them, and she had to forestall their wicked whispers.

Tulkhan shifted in the saddle. He had the strangest feeling, a prickling sensation on the back of his neck which told him he was being watched. He looked up the rise. A cloaked figure stepped from the trees and looked down at him. He knew that pale form, those dark eyes.

An emotion which was equal parts dread and fascination gripped him. Right at this moment Imoshen looked completely Other, wreathed in a T'En mystique. Yet none of his men seemed to notice her.

Tulkhan shuddered. Was he aware of her because he had been touched by both Imoshen and Reothe? It seemed he was growing sensitive to their gifts, vulnerable.

Anger warred with an urgency which was not his own. He realized she was calling him and he fought the compulsion to go to her. But it was overwhelming. Confronting her was the only way to escape her pull. He let the others ride on past him and turned his mount to the rise where she waited. Her red cloak was obscenely bright against the white snow, a splash of fresh crimson blood.

At last he faced Imoshen who looked up at him, her chest rising and falling as if she had been running.

"Well?" he demanded, not bothering to dismount.

She would have stepped forward, but stopped when he jerked the horse's reins and the creature sidled away.

"I have news of a plot to aid Reothe," she said.

It was so unexpected he snorted. "Why tell me?"

She flinched. "They will tell you that I am part of it and I'm not. Don't let them do this to us, Tulkhan!"

The pain in her words lanced through his anger, but he maintained his distance. If he let his guard down she would claim his soul, and he suspected it was only a matter of time before Reothe's prophecy was fulfilled. Since the night the rebel leader had saved Imoshen, Tulkhan's dreams had been filled with visions of his own death.

He was growing to believe he would never rule Fair Isle, never live to see his son grow to manhood. It was all a shallow dream. The blood of his Ghebite companions would enrich the soil of Fair Isle and his memory would be a tavern jest, no more.

"So tell me about this plot," he said coldly.

"Why should I betray my own people? It's obvious you despise me!" Imoshen turned, her red cloak swinging in a defiant arc as she darted away through the silver trunks.

Tulkhan urged his horse forward and pursued her. Imoshen was hampered by knee-deep snow. He took his time catching up to her, letting her know who was in control. As she looked over her shoulder, he caught a flash of something in her eyes and wondered if he wasn't playing into her hands.

Annoyed, he closed the distance between them. Coming abreast of her he leaned out, caught her cloak, and pulled her off her feet. She twisted and writhed, resisting him with surprising strength. Either he had to let her go or leap from the horse. Swinging his leg over the saddle, he threw himself forward. They went down in a tangle of limbs as the horse galloped on.

Cursing, Tulkhan caught a flash of Imoshen's furious eyes before he hit the snow, pinning her body facedown under his in the cushioning snow. Only by tensing his muscles was he able to stop her from flipping him off.

She muttered something hard and angry under her breath.

He hugged her to his chest, pinning her arms. "So who is in on this plot?"

She arched in silent protest, then the fight seemed to go out of her and she melted into the curves of his body. Without warning he felt the liquid heat of desire flow through his limbs.

"Don't try to distract me!"

"I do nothing. If you lust after me, it is your response!" She wriggled against the evidence of his desire.

"Don't tell me you don't know what you do."

She laughed bitterly. "If you could think with your head for a change, you'd ask yourself why I came out here to warn you!"

"Trick me, you mean. Do you think to win my trust with half-lies?"

"You are a . . . a Ghebite dog!" she spat, panting with anger. "All rutting and—"

He laughed. "Is that the best you can do?"

"Tulkhan, listen. Because of what happened to Cariah and Jacolm, the Keld prepare to support Reothe. When he leads them to invade the city they will call on me to join them. They expect me to turn you and your army to stone."

"As if you could! You'd die trying."

"It is enough that they *think* I can do it."

"Who thinks this?" He tightened his hold on her. "Who, Imoshen? Name them and I will have them arrested, their lands confiscated—"

"That's right," she gasped. "That will certainly make the others trust you!"

"What do you expect me to do?"

No answer.

"Well?"

She remained obstinately silent.

At last he loosened his hold, allowing her to sit up and face him.

"The nobles plot to overthrow me." He tried again. "What would you have me do, Imoshen?"

"I don't know!"

The despair in her voice touched him. "Imoshen?"

She shook her head, brushing impatiently at her tears. "So much is against us, General. Sometimes I . . ." A sob escaped her.

He gathered her to him. Her tears were salty on his lips, her breath hot on his skin. How could Imoshen's touch be a traitorous lie?

Earnestly she pulled away. "We must be strong in ourselves, strong in each other for the sake of our people, and for . . ." She took his hand, guiding it to her belly where he felt a small, firm swelling.

It was his child, nestled safely within her. She smiled, almost shyly. A deep joy flooded him. He kissed the tears from her cheeks. It seemed to him that all his life had led to this moment in the pristine cold air on the ridge with Imoshen in his arms.

She returned his embrace with fierce passion. Tulkhan didn't want to go back to the palace, to his advisors who argued that Imoshen would be his downfall. He wanted her now, but that would mean laying himself open to her. He could not think for the urgency of his need.

Suddenly she froze.

"What?"

"It can't be!" She sniffed the air and her eyes widened. "What were you hunting?"

"A big white cat. My men let it out of the—"

"A snow leopard?" Her nose wrinkled as if she was smelling the predator's rank scent.

He sniffed, then tensed, for he could also smell it now.

"Move slowly," Imoshen advised.

Tulkhan rolled to his feet, searching the ridge. His mount had paused a body length away. The horse rolled its eyes fearfully but did not bolt, obeying its training despite the instinct to run. Then Tulkhan saw the cat, a patch of deeper white moving through the drifts.

"It's below us, heading this way."

Imoshen came to her knees. Dragging off her cloak she rolled it round her right forearm. "Do you have a weapon?"

"Only a ceremonial spear. It is supposed to be a clean kill, man against beast—"

Imoshen muttered something derogatory in High T'En, then she was on her feet backing up the ridge. Tulkhan spoke soothingly to his horse as he collected its dangling reins.

"Could we outride the cat?" he asked.

"Not two of us on a single mount through heavy drifts."

"Then mount up," he urged. "I'll stay and distract it."

"No."

"Imoshen, don't argue. I'll have the spear."

She laughed. "I'd like to see you tackle a snow cat with a spear. I've seen what they can do!"

"You'll get on the horse, Imoshen. You have to, you can't risk the child."

"Of course!" she snarled, her wine-dark eyes burning with resentment. "I keep forgetting. That is all I am to you, a brood mare."

He caught her around the waist, intending to lift her onto the horse. The sudden action startled the beast and it reared, knocking them both to the ground. The impact of its shod hoof struck his thigh with impossible force. His leg crumpled under him. A groan escaped his clenched teeth.

Imoshen scrambled out of his grasp. Her eyes searched his face as her hands felt his leg. "The bone is not broken but—"

Angry with himself, he pushed her away, struggling to one knee. His leg muscle protested as he tried to stand. In a few days he would have nothing but a limp and a fading bruise, but he didn't have a few days. "Get on the horse, Imoshen. Leave me."

"No." She met his gaze steadily. "I will not leave you."

The horse wheeled, its body trembling with fright. Tulkhan called it softly, but the beast danced away, taking the spear with it. Cursing, he removed his cloak and wound it around his forearm.

When Imoshen slid her shoulder under his, grasping him around the waist, he knew a moment of sheer frustration. Here he was without a weapon, injured, unable to defend himself or Imoshen.

"This way," she urged.

Each time his injured leg took even a little weight, the sweat of pain broke out on his forehead. The trees thinned out as they approached the crest where his mount waited. It whickered nervously. Behind it was only sky.

"Wait here." Imoshen guided him to a small building where he let his weight sink onto the single step.

As protection the structure was useless. It consisted of a roof supported by only a circle of elegant columns. Tulkhan could just imagine the courtiers of the old empire trekking through the woods to this lookout to enjoy the view while servants brought them food and entertainment. What a strange idle world the T'En had created, where form outdid substance.

"Is there some way down?" Even he could hear the strain in his voice.

Imoshen darted to the cliff edge to peer over the drop. "There's no path down. The river lies below but there's a wide patch of broken rocks, we'd never make it if we jumped—"

"Good. I don't want to jump. I can't swim."

She padded back to him, grinning ruefully. Crouching, she covered his hand with hers. "We're trapped, General."

"You should have taken the horse when you could!"

She smiled fondly. "As if I would."

"Heal me."

Her eyebrows drew together in a frown.

"It is an emergency. I'm not asking you to break your vow."

He saw her nostrils quiver as she inhaled angrily. "Does this mean you accept the T'En side of me!"

"Not now, Imoshen. Heal me," he urged. "Then at least I can defend us from the great cat."

"You set it free to kill it for sport. It is only doing what wild cats do, following its nature." Her garnet eyes narrowed. "You would have me deny my nature yet use me when it suits you."

In that moment Imoshen looked so Other that Tulkhan fought an instinctive surge of fear. Then he noticed the horse had drawn closer. "Get my spear."

She looked down the slope to the snow leopard. "There it is. The perfect killing weapon."

The beast had crept into the open where it crouched in the snow, so still it was almost invisible.

"When it charges you won't see it coming," Imoshen whispered as though fascinated.

"If you will not heal me, at least escape. Get on the horse and flee. It will come after me. I'm the easier prey."

She studied him sadly. "It's kill or be killed with you, isn't it?"

"Imoshen!"

But she ignored him, stepping forward to meet the cat.

"No, Imoshen!" Panic welled in him as she unwound her cloak, letting it unroll from her arm. "Imoshen!" With a groan he struggled to his feet. But the short rest in the cold had made his injured muscle seize up, and he could not stand. He fell to one knee, helpless and furious. "Imoshen, I forbid it!"

Her soft, mocking laugh hung in the air between them, reminding him forcibly of Reothe.

She stepped forward to meet the cat.

He wanted to howl with frustration at his impotence. His eyes sought the shape of the white cat in the snow. He couldn't find it. The beast had moved.

Imoshen's hands rose to her neck. When the sharp rent

of tearing material cut the air, the cat answered with a scream of its own. The primal sound elicited an equally primal response in Tulkhan. The sweat of fear rose on his skin, chilling him to the core.

A helpless groan escaped him as Imoshen dropped to her knees, baring her breasts to the beast, her head thrown back, arms outspread.

Desperate, Tulkhan slewed his weight around. Whispering softly, he called his mount. He dug his hands into the saddle girth, using it to pull himself upright. The spear was strapped firmly in place. His fingers fumbled with it. He expected at any instant to hear Imoshen's scream as the cat attacked. His blood roared in his ears.

Clumsily, because he was holding on to the horse's saddle to stand, he turned and hefted the spear in his hand, praying for one clean throw.

Too late, the beast was on her.

No. What was it doing?

Stunned, Tulkhan tried to make sense of what he saw. The great, white head of the leopard was nuzzling Imoshen's neck. Then it stepped back and sat looking at her for all the world like a tamed pet.

She rose unsteadily to her feet, her hand sinking into the winter-thick fur at the cat's neck.

When she turned a gasp escaped him.

Between her small breasts were three parallel streaks, claw marks welling with blood. One part of his mind told him he had seen this before. But he could only think that she had somehow tamed the cat.

She lifted a trembling hand to her throat. "I promised safe passage for it and its mate out of the city."

"You talk to animals now?"

She stared at him with Otherworldly eyes, impervious to his humor. "You must not let your men kill it. I cannot go back on a promise."

A promise to a snow cat? The horn sounded and he heard the baying of the dogs.

"Get on your horse, Tulkhan."

"I don't think I can."

"Try." Imoshen came up the slope to join him. "I'll help."

There was a strong smell of predator on her hands. The scent triggered a memory, he had smelt it on her once before. He frowned as he recalled that it was on the morning she had suddenly appeared in his bedchamber. Those marks were the same as the ones Reothe carried on his chest.

"What does this mean?" He took her by the shoulder.

She shook her head. "Up."

With a grunt of pain he swung his bad leg over the horse's back. "I can't stop the dogs, Imoshen. They act on instinct."

Even now he could see the pack heading up the rise toward them. The sun broke through the low clouds, bathing them with its ethereal silver glow.

Imoshen stood at his side. She picked up her cloak and swung it over her shoulders, covering her bare breasts. The great cat came to her and sat at her feet. Tulkhan felt his horse shudder with fear.

The horses and men followed the dogs, crashing up the slope. Tulkhan expected the dogs to attack but they slunk back and forth at the edge of the tree line, howling eerily, not daring to come closer.

The Ghebites pulled their horses to a halt and looked across the open ridge top. At that moment Tulkhan knew he was no longer one of them. Because of what he had experienced with Reothe and what he felt for Imoshen he had taken a step across an invisible line. He might jest and hunt with his men, but in his heart he would walk alone for he had been touched by the T'En.

"General?" one of his men called uncertainly. "Are you—?"

"I am unhurt. The hunt is over."

"Witch!" someone hissed.

Tulkhan raised his voice. "My horse threw me, kicked me in the leg. Imoshen tamed the cat."

A round of uneasy comments greeted this.

"She's in league with the evil one!" someone cried.

Tulkhan thought he detected a Vaygharian accent.

"There is no evil one." Imoshen spoke softly, yet her clear voice carried. "Only the evil in men's hearts."

Tulkhan grimaced. Trust Imoshen to speak the truth his men did not want to hear.

Their muttering grew louder.

"The hunt is over. Go back to the stables." Tulkhan urged his horse forward, eager to break up the group before they resorted to violence.

Imoshen walked beside his horse, her head level with his knee. The cat matched her step, never leaving her side.

It was a long trek back to the stables. Imoshen and Tulkhan parted company from the hunters at the ornamental lake and made their way to the menagerie.

When the keepers saw their snow leopard returned unharmed, they wept with joy. Tulkhan knew a moment's shame to think that he and his men had been ready to kill the animal for sport.

Following Imoshen's instructions, the keepers prepared the menagerie's barred cart and she climbed into the cage with both snow leopards.

"We will take the cats beyond the farms on the outskirts of town before setting them free. They will make their way into the highlands," Imoshen told Tulkhan.

He wanted to elicit her promise that she would not go south with the snow leopards, but his pride wouldn't let him. He hesitated, unsure what to say. Imoshen was right, much was against them. "Be on your guard."

A soft laugh escaped her. "You have seen what I can do and yet you tell me to be careful?"

"I know how much you risk." Risking his own arm, he slipped his fingers through the bars of the cage to grasp Imoshen's hand. "Though you refused to heal me, you did not leave me."

Imoshen's eyes narrowed. "Remember that when they come to tell you of my treachery!"

When Tulkhan returned to the palace, he discovered it

abuzz with Imoshen's latest. The servants whispered that even
T'Reothe had not seemed so T'En, that this Imoshen was
truly a Throwback to the first Imoshen.

Shape-changer, his men hissed. White hair, white cat,
white witch. It was the stuff of legend, and the Ghebite warriors were as quick as the palace servants to carry the rumors.

Fifteen

THAT EVENING IMOSHEN lay alone in her bed listening for Tulkhan's step, determined to mend the breach between them. They had grown close while escaping the snow cat, and she was sure he would open to her, but she heard him walk right past.

Throwing back the covers, she padded to the connecting door, peering through as Tulkhan made up his simple bed before the fire. She ached to go to him yet dreaded his rejection.

As he lay brooding, Tulkhan heard the softest of sounds and looked up to see Imoshen illuminated by the fire's flickering flames. For a moment he wondered if his need for her had conjured her up.

She knelt facing him. "How is your leg? Let me . . ." her hands went to his thigh but he pulled away, certain if she touched him he would be lost.

"Why do you reject me?" Tears glistened in her eyes and her hair hung loose on her shoulders so that she seemed misleadingly vulnerable.

He swallowed. "You bear the same scars on your chest as Reothe."

"Not by choice. I told you he called on the Ancients to draw me to him."

Tulkhan tore his gaze from her because to look on her would undo him. If Imoshen with all her gifts could not stand against Reothe what chance had he, a Mere-man? Truly, he was the dead man who walked and talked.

After an eternity he heard Imoshen rise and return to her room and he covered his eyes to hide his hollow soul.

Imoshen tried to pretend that it did not hurt when people would not meet her eyes. Less than three weeks had passed since she had freed the snow cats. No one had broached the subject with her, but the rumors were more damaging than direct confrontation. A challenge she could deal with. Gossip worked its harm with subtle innuendo.

Tulkhan filled his days with feverish activity and by night she heard him pacing, consumed by something she did not understand and could not ease because he held her at a distance.

"T'Imoshen?"

She glanced up to see a palace servant looking distinctly uncomfortable. The woman gave the formal bow.

"Yes?" Imoshen straightened, putting aside her reading. There was a muffled shout from the room beyond and several people shoved past the servant into the room. Imoshen's hand went to her dagger, but even as her fingers closed around the hilt she realized these people were not a threat.

". . . won't be kept out. The Empress would have seen us!" declared a stout matron.

"And so will I," Imoshen said easily, rising and approaching them.

For an instant the woman and her three companions simply stared at Imoshen.

The matron recovered first, making the deep obeisance. "It is our right to be heard."

Imoshen smiled at her belligerent tone. "Then speak. I am listening."

"For nearly three hundred years my family has lived in our home. We don't want to live anywhere else. You tell him that we don't want another house. We want—"

The others joined in noisily.

"Wait." Imoshen held up her hand. "Who is asking you to leave your homes?"

"The Ghebite General. He tears down our houses—"

"What?" Imoshen bristled. "When?"

"Right now. We were given notice the day after the Spring Festival. The Beatific said she would speak with him, but this very morning his men arrived and began—"

"I will see this for myself!"

Imoshen marched out of the palace with her escort of angry townsfolk. There were others waiting in the square. They led Imoshen through the streets of old T'Diemn.

She heard wails of distress and the sound of builders at work before she rounded the end of the lane to discover the source of the disturbance. Ghebite soldiers had moved all the families' personal belongings out of a row of houses and were demolishing the buildings.

"What is going on here?" Imoshen demanded of the first man she saw.

He flinched at her tone. "Following the General's orders."

"And where is General Tulkhan?"

He pointed and Imoshen strode forward followed by a crowd of townsfolk. Little children skipped ahead of her, shouting and calling to their friends.

She found Tulkhan standing beside someone's kitchen table which was perched incongruously on the cobbles amidst piles of pots and pans. The table was covered with large drawings, which the General was busy discussing with two men.

"Tulkhan?" Imoshen greeted him, aware as always that his Ghebite companions resented her presence. "I would speak with you, alone."

"Of course."

A boy chased his pet pig past them, calling loudly for him to come back. Several children raced after him, eager to help. Tulkhan's eyes met hers and she smiled. But she waited until Tulkhan's men moved away to speak. "Why have you thrown these people out of their homes?"

"They received notices. They'll be relocated."

"That's not what I asked. Why are you doing this?"

"I'm securing T'Diemn," Tulkhan said simply. "Take a look at this."

Imoshen glanced down at plans for T'Diemn. "What has this to do with my question? You can't turn people out of their homes!"

Tulkhan tapped the drawings. "This Reothe was an excellent engineer. See how he designed the streets of old T'Diemn so defenders could be marched to each of the four gates to hold off attackers? He also left the inside wall free of buildings so that troops could be rushed along the ring-road to reinforce a breach in the wall. But over the years people built right up against it, destroying access."

Tulkhan rolled up the plans. "I'm removing the houses which interfere with the defensive integrity of the wall."

"But they're people's homes, General. Families have lived in them for hundreds of years."

"I'll build them new homes."

"It's not the same." She could tell he did not understand. "These people are part of a whole neighborhood. They've known everyone from birth, their parents knew their neighbors' parents. You are taking more than their homes, you are taking their heritage."

"They will be generously compensated for their hardship."

"Tulkhan, gold does not solve everything. Think of the people."

"I am thinking of the people!" He rounded on her, then seemed to collect himself. "T'Diemn can't be defended as it stands, Imoshen. It is absurd to let perfectly good defensive works fall into decay because a few people built their houses in the wrong places. I am trying to make T'Diemn secure from attack. To save the city!"

"But what of all those people and their homes outside the old wall? What will become of them?"

"I'll get around to them. My engineers and I are working on that."

He looked so pleased and determined. Imoshen sighed.

"General Tulkhan, we are not at war. The rebels are contained in the Keldon Highlands. All of T'Diemn accepts you as their Protector General. Is this really necessary?"

He studied her, his face unreadable. "You stand before me, princess of a conquered people, yet you still ask this? I took Fair Isle because your people had grown complacent. No one will take Fair Isle from me!"

Imoshen flinched.

Tulkhan continued. "Soon the rebels will be raiding the fertile plains, causing trouble for my commanders who hold estates in the south." He urged her towards a lane which led directly to the old wall. A ladder stood against the stonework. "Come up and see what I plan."

She followed him onto the walls of old T'Diemn. They were wide enough for four people to walk abreast. Her ancestors had built well. To the west she could see the river gleaming in the sunshine as it wound its way through the countryside, dropping lower and lower, loch by loch, to the tidal flats and the sea. Closer still the new part of the city fell away below them, masses of pointing roofs and spires. It was a prosperous, proud city.

A complacent city?

"Look at T'Diemn sprawling before us, hopelessly underdefended. Where are the earth works, ditches, palisades? With the population and wealth of this city the townsfolk could have built defenses right around the new part. They had all last spring and summer to prepare. But no. They sat here, turning a blind eye to my approaching army."

"What approaching army are *you* preparing to defeat?" Imoshen asked.

Tulkhan frowned at her. "Have you forgotten the threat of Reothe and the Keldon nobles? This is basic warcraft, Imoshen. Bluff and counterbluff. You suffer from four hundred years of peace! Your people fought their wars offshore, territorial wars, trade wars, diplomatic wars. But ultimately what is taken by force must be held by force."

Imoshen took a calming breath. "Will you not reconsider, General? Why not build new walls around the whole of

T'Diemn? You will raise the ire of the people if you pull down their homes. Does the security of old T'Diemn outweigh the goodwill of the townsfolk?"

He shook his head sadly. "I knew you would not understand. This must be done, Imoshen. You——"

"Will you pull down the shops and homes on the fortified bridges as well? When will you stop?"

"When I think T'Diemn is defensible!"

"Then make it defensible, but don't interfere with the old city."

"That's not sensible, Imoshen. What if the outer defenses are breached? If an invading army took all of new T'Diemn, the people could retreat to the old city and hold out against their attackers."

"*If* they were attacked. You are putting all this effort into a last ditch effort. Why do you think Fair Isle *suffered* from four hundred years of peace? We used diplomacy instead of force."

"And when diplomacy no longer worked, what happened? A wise commander plans ahead. I swore to be Protector General of Fair Isle and I keep my word!"

Imoshen searched his face for any sign of softening. He looked strained and tired, but determined. "I think you are making a mistake, General. It is not the size of the defenses but the heart of the defenders which keeps the enemy at bay. If you lose the hearts of the townsfolk, you might as well open all the gates and invite Reothe in. Please reconsider."

He folded his arms, looking out over T'Diemn. "I do what I know to be right, Imoshen."

It was clear he would not be swayed and she suspected he was right. She would have to persuade her people to accept his actions.

As Imoshen climbed down the ladder Tulkhan remained, staring out over the city. Thousands of people trusted him to defend them. He could not fail them just because a few families did not want to be moved.

Tulkhan returned to the ground. As he strode out of the alley he could hear the impatient mutterings of the townsfolk and Imoshen's clear voice. If she was stirring up the people against him he would throttle her.

". . . you would come to me and cry, we have lost everything because you did not defend us." Imoshen's words reached him. He stopped, surprised. She stood there on the kitchen table, waving the rolled-up plans in one hand. "Four hundred years ago T'Reothe the Builder made our city safe from attack, but we have grown complacent. With these plans we will make T'Diemn safe from an invading army. Never again will you face the likes of King Gharavan. Never again will children and old folk be chased down the streets of T'Diemn, hunted and slaughtered.

"I congratulate those people who are giving up their homes for the good of T'Diemn. We must praise them and make them welcome in their new homes. And I thank General Tulkhan for thinking ahead and planning for the safety of everyone in T'Diemn!"

Imoshen flung her open hand in his direction and the people turned towards him. Those who were being asked to move eyed him resentfully, but others cheered. They crowded around Tulkhan so he could not move for the crush. Eventually the crowd dispersed and he was able to approach the table where Imoshen stood, leaning on both elbows to study the plans.

She straightened, greeting him with a quick smile.

"Thank you," he said, his voice meant only for her. "Even if you used your gift to sway them."

Her eyes narrowed. "You do not understand my people, General. The higher we rise the more we serve. To serve is to be elevated. I have called on these people to serve the greater good and they will do it, because not to do so would make them social outcasts."

"To what do I owe this change of heart?"

"I concede that you may be right," she told him with a grin. "T'Diemn is prosperous. We can afford to build strong defenses. It will reassure the people. The rulers of the old empire were too proud. I will not make the same mistake."

Tulkhan met her glittering eyes and knew it was true. If

he had delayed entering Fair Isle long enough for Imoshen and Reothe to be bonded and united in defense of Fair Isle, he would never have taken the island.

Imoshen offered her arm. "Walk with me, General? It is good to let the people see us united."

Tulkhan linked arms with her, but did not drop his guard. As they strolled along, pausing to speak with the people of T'Diemn, he watched Imoshen charm butcherboy and guildmaster alike.

"The people seem ready to forgive you the stone lovers and even tamed snow cats," he remarked when they were alone again.

She looked up at him, her features suddenly vulnerable. "When will you forgive me? My bed is cold and lonely. I hear you pace the Emperor's chamber. What troubles you, Tulkhan?"

But he shook his head. As much as he longed to share his fears with her, he could not.

Imoshen studied Tulkhan's design for T'Diemn's outer fortifications. She had to admire his clever use of the natural terrain, the hills and river locks.

But the defense of the capital was not concerning her now. It was midspring and Reothe's rebels threatened the fragile peace. In the weeks since the snow had melted in the Keldon passes the rebels had grown bold.

Reothe did not raid the farmers or the hardworking villagers; instead he attacked the traders whose tales of woe would be carried to the capital. The merchants who could well afford the loss squealed the loudest.

The Ghebites talked of Reothe's capture and execution, eager to avenge the deaths of their brothers-at-arms; for on three separate occasions Reothe had surrounded Ghebites on their new estates and massacred them, leaving only one man alive to tell of the attack. Reothe flaunted his ability to come and go protected by the locals.

Many of the Ghebite commanders had dispersed to lay

claim to their estates, others were prepared to accompany the General into the Keldon Highlands to answer Reothe's challenge. She knew Tulkhan must retaliate or risk losing half the ground he took last summer, but Imoshen feared Reothe would lead Tulkhan's army on a wild chase through the Keldon Highlands, picking his men off one by one.

Tulkhan strode into the room resplendent in his battle finery and her heart contracted with longing.

"We are ready to ride," the General said. "I will leave with you Peirs and a company of men to hold T'Diemn. While I am gone you must oversee the construction of the city's new defenses."

"I know what I must do." Imoshen came to her feet. "Won't you reconsider? Use me to draw Reothe out. I'll tell him I've had second thoughts, and ask him to meet me somewhere between here and the highlands. But I must be there to meet him or he will sense it is a trap. I'm willing—"

"Well, I'm not!" Tulkhan feared that once Reothe had Imoshen in his power she would succumb to the rebel leader's strange allure and renounce him. "I won't risk losing you and the child."

"Not even to hold Fair Isle?"

He held her eyes.

"Then you could lose it all!"

Tulkhan turned his hand over in supplication. "I will come back when the baby is due."

Imoshen's lips parted as if she might say something, then whispered, "You might never return!"

Silence stretched between them.

Tulkhan opened his arms and she ran to him. He felt her shoulders shake with silent sobs and he found her tear-damp lips, embracing her with all the strength in his body. If only he could put everything else aside, but that was impossible. He could not truly claim Imoshen until Reothe was dead, and he went into the highlands knowing a Mere-man could not hope to defeat a T'En warrior.

Closing himself away from her, he stepped out of her arms.

"Have you no kind word for me before you go?" Imoshen whispered, searching his face.

"I am a warrior, not a courtier." Steeling himself against her disappointment, he turned and strode out.

Imoshen stared at the place where Tulkhan had stood only a moment before. It still seemed to vibrate with the force of his personality and the things left unsaid.

Prowling to the window, she watched the men in the stable yards awaiting orders to mount up. She knew if Tulkhan were killed on the battlefield she would not be able to hold the Ghebites. No, if the General died, his commanders would turn on the island's inhabitants like ravenous wolves, breaking into factions, warring amongst themselves for the spoils. She couldn't allow this. If Tulkhan fell, she would have to ally herself with Reothe to save Fair Isle from the remaining Ghebites.

This realization frightened her. True, she feared Reothe, feared that he would try to dominate her with his superior gifts, but what frightened her most was that, in truth, she would not be averse to standing at his side—perhaps it was where she truly belonged. If Tulkhan were dead and she had done all she could to forestall another summer of war, then she would have no choice but to join the last T'En warrior. She knew that her alliance with Reothe would not be a cold political joining. And that thought was not as unwelcome as she would have liked.

Contemplation of Tulkhan's death was torture to her. Was it only last autumn that she had thought there was a right and a wrong?

The shout went up. The men were moving out.

Clasping one hand under her belly to compensate for the weight of the child, she hastened out of the room and along the gallery.

Before stepping out onto the balcony, Imoshen paused to straighten her hair and assume a regal stance. A mass of men milled before her. She watched as they formed disciplined ranks, mounted men to one side, foot soldiers to the other, all wearing purple-black cloaks. Ghebite cloaks! She

wrinkled her nose. She must speak to Tulkhan about design-
ing their own standard and colors. It did not suit her to see
his men wearing King Gharavan's colors.

The ranks of Tulkhan's men filling the square was a
grand sight, but their discipline would do them no good in
the Keldon Highlands. The rebels knew the treacherous
ravines, and cunning traps awaited them. Cavalry was useless.
Battle-trained destriers were no match for wiry mountain
ponies. Imoshen's heart twisted with pity. Few of these men
would return to T'Diemn.

When General Tulkhan rode into view she caught her
breath, already grieving for him. As he spoke to his men the
breeze carried his words over the ranks away from her. She
watched him walk his horse backwards. The trained beast
reared, dancing on its back legs. A shout went up.

Imoshen had to smile. Tulkhan loved this kind of display.

The horse dropped back down onto four legs, to pivot
in a circle, and Tulkhan caught sight of her on the balcony.
She raised her arm above her head and he returned the
salute, standing in the saddle.

Her heart swelled in her chest. She loved him but he
would never believe it. Her arm lowered and her hand settled over her belly.

He brought his closed fist to his chest over his heart,
then he flung his hand open toward her.

Her skin grew warm with the significance of his gesture.
How could he love her, knowing her as he did, knowing
how truly Other she was? Tears blurred her vision as she
lifted her hand to cover her own racing heart. Tulkhan had
grown as dear to her as the very breath she took.

The men began a Ghebite chant.

Tulkhan wheeled his horse and rode through the ranks,
leading the army through the city's streets to the fortified
bridge.

"Any word, Merkah?" Imoshen asked, as she had for the last
four weeks.

The maid looked up from her handiwork. She knew her mistress well enough now not to bother standing and making a formal bow every time Imoshen approached her. "No, T'Imoshen."

"Very well. I will be in the library." Imoshen handed Merkah her riding cloak. She had just returned from overseeing the progress of the eastern outlying defenses.

As she walked down the gallery, long slanting arrows of afternoon light filled the broad hall, making the woodwork glow. The sight should have cheered her, but she felt distant and cold, for there had been no word from Tulkhan since he sent her a short communication soon after he left, though surely she would have sensed it if he had been killed. He was due to return for Summer's Cusp Festival and stay on, for the baby could come any time after that.

What if the baby did not come? What if her son was more T'En than True-man and she continued heavily pregnant till the cusp of autumn? The child had to have a little of the General in him but she had no way of knowing how much. She had only the official records to go by, and because of the vow of chastity no other pure T'En woman had given birth in six hundred years as far as she knew.

By the time she reached the library she was panting with exertion, for the baby lay like a great summer fruit nestled in her body. The Keeper of Knowledge did not greet her as she entered. She suspected the old man was in the kitchen courtyard, arguing with the cook and drinking chilled apple cider. She could not blame him, the weather was too perfect to stay indoors.

Imoshen went to her favorite spot on the broad daybed. Spread on the low table before her were her inks and papers. She was making a list of works which were referred to in the library, but were no longer available. It was the key to a mystery which had gradually presented itself to her. Poems and treatises which everyone took for granted no longer existed. Why?

Imoshen immersed herself in her reading, cross-referencing the quotes and their sources. The movement of the fingers of light from the library windows marked the passing of time.

After a while she let the scroll fall, arched her back, and closed her eyes. She was weary. Only so much of this could stem her anxiety and then it returned.

Where was the General?

Suddenly a hand clamped over her mouth. Terror froze her limbs as a cold blade stroked her neck. Assassins? She made a protest in her throat. Her attacker increased the pressure, forcing her into the cushions.

"Quiet, Imoshen. It's only me."

Reothe's familiar voice did not reassure her. When she nodded her understanding he released her. Disbelief flooded her as she propped herself on one elbow. Reothe pushed the papers aside and perched on the low table.

"Only you? Is that meant to reassure me?" It pleased Imoshen to detect no tremor in her voice. She was rewarded with a genuine smile from Reothe. She cursed herself for caring.

Her hand slid casually across her body but Reothe beat her to it. His fingers closed around the knife hilt which she now wore strapped between her breasts for quick access.

As he withdrew the blade his eyes narrowed. "Dainty but deadly in the right hands." He did not return the weapon.

"I have to ask." She played for time, trying to guess what he wanted. His fine, silver hair was halfway down his back now and he wore clean but ancient peasant garments. He smelled of fresh herbs and dust. Dust? She must not let anything distract her. "How did you get in here?"

He laughed softly. "You forget I grew up roaming the palace. I doubt there is a secret passage I don't know. Our ancestors were great ones for intrigue. Anything built before the Age of Discernment is riddled with secret passages."

He looked thinner. His narrow features, so like her own, were more defined, as though he had been living on the edge both mentally and physically. She felt an odd sense of recognition and an unwelcome anticipation warm her body. Without intending it she felt her T'En senses flex. A strong sense of Reothe enveloped her. He was a drawn bow string, all coiled power. Her heart rate increased in response.

"Why are you here?"

A gasp escaped him. "Don't stop."

"Stop what?"

His sharp eyes met hers. "Your touch is exquisite."

"We weren't . . ." The words died on her lips. "I didn't mean to—"

"Don't." He shook his head, slipping off the table to kneel on the floor beside her. "Don't deny me, Imoshen."

She drew back, making him smile.

"Is it me you don't trust, or yourself?"

His wine-dark eyes glittered intensely, disturbingly. For all that, he was smiling and his voice sounded reasonable, even indulgent, she sensed a deep anger in him.

His gaze went to the laces on her underdress, where the swelling of her belly made the material strain. She had not bothered to have special clothes made to accommodate her growing child, relying for the most part on the all-covering tabard. Imoshen felt exposed, vulnerable, and wished she had worn one today.

"This explains much." Reothe whispered. He lifted her own knife blade.

"Reothe." Imoshen warned.

"This should have been our child, Imoshen. You hid its existence from me. I did not think you so cunning."

She shook her head, knowing only that the need to protect her child overrode everything else. Yet, when he cut the lacing she didn't protest. The material of her underdress parted, falling away to reveal the rise of her pale skin and the curve of her breasts, ripe with pregnancy. Her skin was patterned with fine blue veins like marble.

A soft sound escaped Reothe as he drew in his breath sharply. He swallowed and slipped her knife into his boot-strap. His hand hovered over her flesh. Her skin tingled in anticipation of his touch. A luxurious longing crept through her limbs.

Imoshen looked down, silently cursing herself. It was always this way with Reothe.

"What will you do if the Ghebite rejects the baby?" he asked. "It could be almost pure Dhamfeer."

"Or more True-man."

"So it is a male child."

She nodded, regretting the slip.

"I heard a rumor. They say the General can't father children," he smiled. "They are saying the baby is mine."

She flushed, trying to pull herself up but the weight of the baby made her slow. Reothe casually grasped the back of the daybed. She didn't want to come in contact with his skin so she stayed where she was, half reclining. "But you know that isn't true."

Reothe met her eyes, amused. She realized he was happy to let people believe the babe was his. Fury curled inside her. It would be the ultimate irony for Tulkhan to finally father a child and have everyone believe it wasn't his.

Reothe leaned closer and inhaled. "You smell different. I like it."

Imoshen swallowed. "Don't do this."

He nuzzled the heavy swell of her breast. "Tell me to stop."

"Stop."

She felt him smile, his cheek on her flesh. "You didn't mean it."

Despair warred with desire. The first time he had touched her he had wakened something in her, something that was his to call, and no amount of logic could sway her body's response.

His breath tickled her throat, her cheek, as he raised his head, exploring her. She felt his lips on her jaw, traveling across to her mouth. She could turn away or she could turn towards him.

She chose to do nothing.

With infinite delicacy he nibbled her mouth, his tongue brushed the crease of her lips. "Part for me."

She felt, more than heard, his words. The impulse was

there but she contained it, refused to welcome him. It would be all he needed to destroy her resolve.

A sigh escaped him and she opened her eyes to see him looking down at her, exasperated, affectionate.

"You are an annoying creature, Imoshen. How do you know that I won't take by force what you refuse me? I know you long for me."

She swallowed, making no answer, because to say anything would be to admit more than she cared to.

He leant back, ruffling papers on the table. Absently he picked one up, reading it swiftly. Imoshen wanted to stop him. Her lack of skill was a weapon he could use against her.

Reothe looked up and fixed his gaze on her. "You search for information on the T'En?"

She nodded. "Our gifts are mentioned in passing, but—"

"I know. I've already traveled the same path. I can tell you why our ancestors came here. I can reveal what has been deliberately hidden from us."

She sat up eagerly. "Yes?"

He smiled. "Come away with me now. Your Ghebite General wanders the ranges, harried by my people. We could rout him, you and I."

"And then you would share your knowledge with me?" Imoshen heard the bitterness in her voice.

"I would share *everything* with you."

His meaning was unmistakable. A rush of heady longing swept through her. The urge to go to him was almost overpowering. She fought it, desperate to keep some kind of equilibrium. When she opened her eyes, Reothe was watching her with intense fascination.

"It is only a matter of time," he told her. "The General knows it. He drives himself mad trying to deny it. Come away with me now. Put him out of his misery. He's only a Mere-man and a barbarous Ghebite, but I have to admit a certain admiration for him. Like a fish caught on the hook, he is putting up a mighty battle, but the end is inevitable. He doesn't deserve it really."

A knot twisted in Imoshen's chest.

"He saved us," Reothe said softly. "The night I came to find you wandering lost in death's shadow, he anchored us. I drew on his strength, and without it we would have both been doomed."

Fear made Imoshen's heart plunge. She had no memory of that time, but the Church taught that without the guidance of the Parakletos a soul might wander death's shadow for eternity, prey to the vengeful beings who were trapped there.

Heat stained her cheeks. "You saved me at risk to your soul, I—"

"Don't demean what we share by thanking me." Anger hardened his features.

Imoshen understood him only too well. "We share nothing!"

"You deny what you know to be true. Besides, I have the Sight. I have seen our future. I recognized you the day we met."

Dismay flooded Imoshen. "It would be so much easier if I could hate you!"

"And it would be so much easier if I could kill you." His smile was bitter.

Imoshen understood the implications immediately. If Reothe were to kill her now and plant something to implicate the Ghebites, Tulkhan's tenuous hold on the island would be shattered. Her death would smooth a path for Reothe to retake Fair Isle.

"Why don't you kill me?"

He laced his fingers through her left hand, lifting it up so that their forearms pressed together and the bonding scars touched.

Reothe pressed her knuckles to his lips. "Because I would be alone forever—"

"There are other women, countless willing women, from what I've heard!"

His smile made her wish she could have cut out her jealous tongue.

"True, and I have had many of them." He cast her a teasing glance. "But only you share the T'En heritage. For now you believe what you have with this Ghebite is enough. You might even love him a little. But he is only a Mere-man. You don't know what we could have."

"Enough, Reothe." She pushed him aside and surged to her feet, stalking away from the daybed.

"Go on, run away, Imoshen. You can't run from what you know is true."

She could feel him watching her as she paced. The late-afternoon sunlight could not dissolve the knot of cold terror which settled around her heart. She hugged her body, pulling the material of her underdress together. "Why are you here, Reothe? Why risk your life to taunt me?"

He stood across the room from her, yet she felt his presence as intimately as if his breath stroked her flesh. She knew he was using his T'En gift on her.

"Don't do that!"

"Why? Because you like it? Surely you can't have forgotten what day this is?"

She stared at him appalled. No one else had remembered.

"It's the anniversary of your birthing day," Reothe said. "Today you are eighteen and we would have been bonded."

Her eyes closed as she registered the blow, a cruel reminder of the decision she had to make.

She sensed Reothe moving towards her. When she opened her eyes the sun's rays were hitting the polished floor, casting shadows on his face. She read a calculating wariness in his features and suspected he was manipulating her feelings for him; for Tulkhan.

"I'm not going with you, Reothe, and you can't drag me kicking and screaming from the palace, no matter how many secret passages you know. Someone would notice."

Defiant words but Imoshen knew they sprang from desperation and so did he.

"I brought you a gift, Imoshen."

"I don't want anything from you."

"You'll want this. It is the last thing my parents gave me before they killed themselves." He pulled a slim volume from his jerkin. It was about half the size of the T'Enchiridion. "It belongs to the T'En."

Despite herself, Imoshen held out her hand.

Silently he joined her. The book looked unremarkable as it lay in his hand, its scuffed kidskin cover attesting to its great age.

Imoshen took it, turning the worn embossing to the light.

"T'Endomaz. The T'En laws," she translated, her heart hammering with excitement. Her fingers trembled as she turned to the title page where a name was scrawled in child-like script. "T'Ashmyr? Could it have belonged to Ashmyr the First when he was a boy?"

"He was a pure Throwback like ourselves," Reothe said.

Imoshen's mouth was so dry she could hardly speak. Could this book really date from the Age of Tribulation? Five hundred years! Reverently she turned to the first page. Disappointment made her gasp. "It's encrypted!"

"Then you don't recognize the code? I thought perhaps the Aayel had—"

"No. My parents forbade her to teach me anything about the T'En." Bitterness tore at her. "T'Endomaz. An encrypted set of laws. How do you know they are ours? This looks similar to the T'Enchiridion, which is for everyone. And Ashmyr is a popular name."

"Close your eyes, Imoshen. Hold the book in your left hand. Tell me what you feel? No, not with your T'En senses. I've tried that. It is as if someone has erased the book's past. You must rely only on your sense of touch."

She frowned but did as he said. What was she supposed to feel? He was right, to her T'En senses the book seemed blank when it should have held a sense of antiquity consider-ing its age. That in itself was suspicious.

"Feel with your fingertips," he whispered.

Then she understood. Her eyes flew open. "There are

six smooth patches on the cover. This book has been worn by the touch of a left-handed person with six fingers!"

"One of the T'En." He nodded. "It is ours, Imoshen."

"But we can't read it." She could have wept with frustration and loss.

His hands closed over hers, shutting the book. His face was suffused with evangelical passion. "I give you the T'Endomaz. I charge you to unlock the encryption and reveal our heritage."

Suddenly Imoshen was afraid of what she might learn. "No. Keep it. I don't want to be beholden to you."

She thrust the book into his hands and would have turned away but he caught her arm. His contained fury made her skin crawl.

"How can you deny what you are, Imoshen?"

Flicking free of his grasp she turned away. The swelling of her belly hit him and they both looked down.

Imoshen felt the baby kick in protest.

Reothe's free hand closed over the slope of her stomach, pressing through the gap in the material so that his flesh touched hers. There was an anticipation in him which made her teeth ache. She sucked in her breath with an audible gasp.

"Don't resist!" he hissed.

In that instant her guard was down. She felt a wave of tension roll through her body, her knees nearly gave way. The baby twisted inside her.

Imoshen swung her arms in an arc and broke all contact with him. "I won't let you hurt—"

He laughed bitterly. "You have a strange idea of me."

"I have no idea," she admitted coldly.

"Like you, I am only ensuring my survival!" he said. "Go on. Call the guards. You could have called them any time and had me arrested, had me killed attempting to escape. Ask yourself why you haven't called them!"

She drew breath to scream for the guards but he caught her to him, his free hand covered her mouth.

His laughter unnerved her. "I deserved that."

She hated him, yet recognized herself in him.

"I am going, Imoshen," he whispered. "And because I can't have you discovering my secrets, I'm going to have to do this."

"What?" The word was muffled but clear enough.

"Kiss me and find out." His hand slipped from her mouth to her throat, cradling her jaw. His fingers slid up into her hair at the back of her neck.

"Why should I?"

"Because if you resist it will be painful for both of us. I am only going to steal a few minutes from you."

He could do that? What a useful trick, one she would like to know.

Imoshen pretended to consider. "Very well."

He looked a little startled, as if he hadn't expected her to agree.

Imoshen kept her face impassive as she smiled inside. She was sure he could not do this without her discovering how. She would have all his secrets out of him . . . but no—she mustn't think, he might . . .

Lifting her face she felt his breath on her skin. And she knew at that moment she was fooling herself. She wanted to kiss Reothe, had always wanted him.

"*Imoshen,*" he whispered raggedly.

Her heart lurched.

Then his mouth was on hers and the sweetness of his touch negated all thought. It was the elixir of life, it flowed through her body, unbearably rich and fragile.

She heard his voice in her head, but his lips didn't form the words. "This is just a taste of what we could have, Imoshen. But I can't let you learn all my tricks, you're much too clever already."

Then everything faded.

Sixteen

CREAMING. SOMEONE WAS screaming and she wished they would stop.

"Get your hands off me!" Imoshen protested. She felt disoriented and nauseous with the sudden swing from deep sleep to awareness.

"T'Imoshen!" Merkah cried. "You have come back to us!"

She was lying on the daybed with a shawl thrown over her. Its silky material covered her bare breasts and that made her recall Reothe slitting the laces of her underdress. As Imoshen struggled to sit up, a book fell from her lap onto the floor. Reothe's gift.

She picked it up, tucking it under the shawl. She searched the room. A dozen Ghebites and palace servants stood clustered around something near the window. Fear gripped her. Was Reothe hurt?

"What happened?"

"He killed him," Merkah supplied unhelpfully.

Imoshen's world went grey. "Who?"

"T'Reothe killed the Keeper of the Knowledge."

"No!" Imoshen's denial was instinctive. Reothe would not do that. The Keeper was a defenseless old man. But she could not afford to defend the rebel leader. "What happened? I . . . I remember nothing."

Merkah seemed to accept this at face value. "The Keeper

was returning to his post. When he opened the door he saw Reothe with you. He was . . ." Merkah colored.

Imoshen pressed the material to her body. "Tell me, I must know."

"The Keeper says he held his face against your bare flesh."

Imoshen's hand pressed over her baby. Fear was a cold band around her heart. "Then?"

"The Keeper was at the door. He called for help. Before anyone could come, Reothe dragged him inside and killed him."

"How do you know this?" Imoshen asked.

"He told us."

"But you said he was dead."

"Almost dead."

"Is he still alive?"

"Yes, but—"

"Enough." Exasperated, Imoshen swung her legs off the daybed. Despite Merkah's protests she hurried over to the knot of men. They were lifting the old Keeper. To save the Ghebites from embarrassment she tied the shawl across her breasts.

"The shadows are too deep. Bring candles. Place him here on the table," Imoshen ordered. She noted Kinraid the Vaygharian watching her, but there was no time to curse the luck that brought him, of all men, to her rescue.

Imoshen grasped the old man's hand. Yes, he was dying, but his gaze cleared as she looked into his eyes.

"What happened?"

He smiled. "He was such a bright boy. No one else cared about the old manuscripts, but he read them all."

"Reothe?"

He nodded. Someone thrust a branch of candles onto the table, illuminating the Keeper's features.

"What happened?" Imoshen pressed. "They say Reothe hurt you?"

She searched his face, noting how one side drooped.

He'd had a seizure. Reothe had not done that, unless the surprise of seeing him had triggered it.

"I had to call for help. I didn't want . . ." He seemed to recollect himself. "Reothe grabbed me, dragged me into the room. He touched the back of my head then suddenly I had this blinding pain in my chest. I could not breathe. I knew nothing until I came around on the floor."

Imoshen nodded. "I will brew you something to drink. It will help you sleep."

But nothing would help him. As a healer, she had seen death too many times not to recognize it. Within a day or two he would have another seizure and his heart would simply stop beating.

"Before you go, Lady Protector." Kinraid appeared before her. "The men and I want to know how Reothe got in here. And how he escaped."

"I can't tell you." Imoshen knew her dislike for the Vaygharian must have been evident. "Reothe grabbed me, held something over my face, and the next thing I knew I was here with all of you."

"Then you did not see him come, or go?"

"No." It was the truth.

"Then you don't mind if we search the library?"

A protest leapt to the Keeper's blue lips and Imoshen had to smile.

"You may search, but you will not destroy or damage any of the valuable manuscripts stored here. Now I must go and brew this tonic. Have the Keeper carried to his room."

She returned to her own room with Merkah at her heels. "I must concentrate on my healing. Leave me."

As soon as the door closed she withdrew the slim volume, still warm from her body. T'Endomaz. The law of the T'En. She desperately wanted to believe it had belonged to the boy emperor, T'Ashmyr, greatest of all Throwback rulers.

What if someone stole the book before she could translate it? She strode to her chest and threw it open but it was too obvious a hiding place. Her gaze fell on the Aayel's T'Enchiridion. The book should have been burnt with her, in keeping with tradition, but Imoshen had saved it, knowing she would have to refresh her memory to say the words at the Harvest Feast the following day.

Swiftly she retrieved the T'Enchiridion. It was twice the size of the T'Endomaz. Reothe had returned her knife while she was asleep. Unsheathing her knife, she slit the inner lining of the back cover and slid the T'Endomaz inside. Unless someone inspected her copy of the T'Enchiridion they would not find it.

Reothe had given her more than a book, he had given her the key to controlling her gifts. She could not help comparing his bonding gift to Tulkhan's. How well he knew her. But she was not going to bond with Reothe. He might claim to know the future, yet the Sight was often misleading.

She had bonded with Tulkhan and nothing could change that, not even Reothe's lure of a union so powerful it would unlock the secret of her T'En gifts.

It was the talk of T'Diemn. Reothe had entered the palace unseen, seduced T'Imoshen, and killed a dozen men before disappearing in a flash of light.

It brought Tulkhan back in less than two weeks.

He returned without warning late one evening after Imoshen had already retired to her room. She was reading before the fire when he stalked in. The sight of him made her heart leap with joy then plunge in despair when she saw his expression.

Tulkhan threw his cloak and gloves on the table then strode towards Imoshen, thinking she looked more beautiful than ever with her narrow features softened by the bloom of new life. By Ghebite custom, this late in her pregnancy she would have been hidden away from all but the women of his house-line. Instead of being repelled by her changed body he wanted to run his hands all over her, to savor every ripe curve. But to touch her was to let his guard down and he must know the truth first.

"Is it true what they're saying? Did he rape you?"

She laughed and he wanted to strangle her.

"Of course not. That is a *Ghebite* custom."

Cursing, he ignored the insult. "Then you submitted willingly?"

"I was not conscious when the Keeper found me with Reothe."

"In every village or nobleman's keep, I hear the same thing," Tulkhan growled. "They are saying this was not the first time, that the babe you carry is his and you two plot to kill me when it suits you."

Imoshen came to her feet, pushing herself out of the chair. The added weight of the baby made her movements slower but no less graceful. It hurt him to look on her, knowing what was being said. According to the rumors she was sweet treachery itself.

She approached him with her hands out palm up, her face gentle and mocking. "How can you worry about what they are saying when you know you were the first and only one for me?"

He knew it was true. He caught her to him, feeling the hard swelling of the baby between them. A number of swift kicks told him his son resented the pressure. Shocked, he met Imoshen's eyes. She smiled. Any day now he would be a father. The evidence had just kicked him. A delighted laugh escaped Tulkhan.

"Our son is an active little fellow," she said. "Tell me, how many men did you lose fighting the rebels?"

The abrupt change of subject startled him. One minute she was all woman, the next she thought and spoke like a man. It unnerved him more than he cared to admit.

He shook his head wearily. "Too many died for what we achieved. Enough for me to know that you were right. The rebels hide and strike without warning, melting into the ravines so that we can't pursue them. If we do chase them, my men get separated and picked off one by one." He felt the weight of their deaths. "But I won't try your way either."

"So what will you do?"

"I am considering."

She pressed her face into his neck. Her breath was warm on his skin and his body responded to her touch. She had to twist her hips so that the baby lay to one side of them. This was his child and Reothe had stolen it from him without ever touching Imoshen!

"Why didn't you call for help?" he demanded. "We could have had him!"

He felt her sigh. "Take off your things, you smell of horse and sweat. Let me bathe you."

She moved through to the bathing room where she checked that the burner was heating and released the valve. Water steamed as it poured into the waist-high tub.

Tulkhan watched the marvel. He had not been so long in the palace that he took such things for granted, especially after weeks of living rough in the inhospitable ranges.

Imoshen approached him, ready to help him disrobe. The thought of her hands running over his soapy body made him ache to have her, despite the Ghebite stricture against such things. By rights they should not share any intimacy in the last small moon of her pregnancy. But she was deliberately distracting him. Reothe had been here in this very palace.

He caught her hands before she could touch him. "Is there something you aren't telling me?"

She looked obliquely up at him. Her expression seemed calculating, but it could have been the way the light fell on her features.

"I did not willingly invite Reothe into the palace. He grew up here. He must know of secret passages."

"He didn't just appear?"

"In a flash of light? No." She shook her head, smiling fondly at Tulkhan.

"Then he was really here. He grows arrogant."

"I don't know how Reothe slipped in and out unseen, but I'm glad he did, because it brought you back." She grinned a challenge at him, then tugged at his laces. "You will stay here now?"

"I don't know. My men are withdrawing—"

"Consolidating."

"It looks like a defeat. It stinks of defeat."

"Defeat is when you are dead," Imoshen told him. "And not before!"

"True." He smiled, admiring her spirit.

Imoshen turned her back to him. "Undo my lacings."

His heart pounded and his fingers trembled as he fumbled with the knot. Tulkhan swallowed dry mouthed.

"Wait," Imoshen whispered.

She walked over and slid the door's bolt, then turned to him and let the gown fall from her shoulders. As he drank in her splendor he understood that he would put aside the strictures of his upbringing for her. What wouldn't he do to possess her?

The following day Tulkhan stood in the maproom studying the Keldon Highlands. If he were to build fortresses to hold the two passes into that region, it would contain the rebel army's freedom of movement. He was considering the reaction of the proud Keldon nobles when his thoughts were interrupted by a servant scratching at the door.

Merkah entered with the ink and scriber he had requested.

"Close the door," Tulkhan told her.

She placed the instruments on the table.

"So?" Tulkhan prodded.

"T'Imoshen asked for word of you every day."

"Did she have any meetings with unexpected people?" The girl looked perplexed.

"Any of the Keldon nobles or their servants?"

Merkah shook her head.

"So nothing out of the ordinary happened?"

"There was that time when T'Reothe—"

"Apart from that." Idly, Tulkhan wondered what the maid hoped to achieve by spying on her mistress. Surely she realized he would never trust her, and if Imoshen ever discovered her deceit Merkah would lose her position.

"No, General."

He dismissed the girl and returned to the maps. His men expected him to lead them to victory even against overwhelming odds. But Reothe did not follow the standard rules of warfare. He attacked, then melted away, shielded by the sullen farm folk who claimed they hadn't seen him come or go. A knock on the door interrupted his thoughts.

"Yes?" he answered, expecting one of his men.

An unfamiliar servant backed in with a tray of food. "I—" Tulkhan caught sight of the man who accompanied the servant.

"Come in, Kinraid, join me." He heard the false welcome in his voice and wondered at the man he was becoming.

Twice before, the Vaygharian had brought him news. Tulkhan preferred to let Kinraid believe he had won Tulkhan's trust through his information. Besides, he would rather hear it from the snake's mouth than hear Kinraid's lies from people he trusted.

"You may leave," Tulkhan signaled the servant.

"No, he should stay. What my man has to say will concern you," Kinraid said.

Tulkhan nodded, masking his irritation. Shoving the maps aside to clear a space on the table, he sat down, stretching out his long legs. He knew he appeared casual and relaxed. It was a lie.

The little man poured wine for Tulkhan and his master.

"Speak, Kinraid." Tulkhan accepted his wine.

"The palace is riddled with secret passages," he announced. "That is how Reothe made his way in unobserved."

"So Imoshen told me."

"She also claimed to be unconscious. But my man here heard her speaking with the rebel leader."

"They spoke?" Warily he watched the two men for any sign of complicity. "Was your man able to make out what they said?"

Kinraid shook his head. "Their words were muffled by

the door, Protector General. But they spoke for a good while before the Keeper returned and caught him ravishing her."

Tulkhan looked away. The room swam before him.

"My man was one of the first into the room," Kinraid continued inexorably. "He found the Keeper on the floor and your wife appeared to be unconscious. She was almost naked. The Keeper said he caught them embracing—"

"If she was unconscious, Reothe was the one doing the embracing," Tulkhan corrected.

Kinraid's mocking silence presented a thousand possibilities to Tulkhan. Imoshen was a swift thinker. What better way to avert suspicion than to feign a faint?

"Whether she was unconscious or not," Kinraid went on, "it is clear she had the opportunity to call for help. We could have had the rebel leader arrested and awaiting you even now in the cells below!"

The vision of Reothe brought below was a pleasant one. But Tulkhan doubted that a mere prison cell could contain the T'En warrior for long.

Exasperation filled Tulkhan. How was he to defeat Reothe? No one alive today knew the extent of the Dhamfeer's gifts. No one but Imoshen.

The thought drove him to action.

"Where are you going?" Kinraid asked.

Tulkhan was filled with fury. He did not have to explain his actions to a man whose trade was treachery.

Seeing the General's expression, Kinraid stepped back abruptly and made an obeisance of apology.

The corridors were remarkably busy with servants. No, Imoshen was not in the library. No, she was not in any of the entertainment rooms, nor the kitchen or storerooms. Someone had seen her go out for a walk.

Tulkhan's boots crunched on the fine white gravel path of the palace's formal garden. What had Reothe said? The one you love has the most power to hurt you. Tulkhan felt a bitter smile twist his lips. Love. He had no time for that weakening emotion. He would be utterly calm and trick the truth from her.

There she was, through the trees. Imoshen tilted her head to study the fruit tree. According to the gardeners, this blossom-laden bush would produce masses of stone fruit. Now if she could only graft a cutting onto the fruit trees back at the Stronghold . . .

"Imoshen!"

When she turned to face Tulkhan his expression made her reel. But outwardly she maintained her calm, snapping off a twig heavy with blossom before greeting him. "I think I'll take some cuttings back to the Stronghold with me. They tell me not only is this tree exquisite in the spring, but it's an excellent fruiter."

"Imoshen!" He caught her by the shoulders. "You lied to me. You said Reothe knocked you out. But now I'm told you spoke with him."

"Your spies took this long to report that?"

He glowered and she cursed her unruly tongue.

"You lied, Imoshen!"

"I omitted to mention it. Reothe did knock me out and I don't know how he did it." That still rankled. "But not before we talked."

"What about?"

It was time for the truth. With a twist she freed her shoulders and rubbed the imprint of his anger from her skin. "It was the eighteenth anniversary of my birthing day, the day I would have been bonded to Reothe. He came to see me, to ask me to go with him."

Tulkhan blinked. She could tell he found the truth unpleasant but was not surprised.

"What was your answer?"

"I am here, aren't I?" Imoshen thumped his chest with enough force to let him know she was angry.

Tulkhan absorbed the blow but it appeared nothing would pierce his foul mood.

"Why didn't you call for help?" he demanded. "We

could have had Reothe arrested, awaiting execution even now."

"I doubt that."

"So you think a Mere-man couldn't hold one of your kind?"

Imoshen hesitated. She had never seen Tulkhan so furious. Why was he referring to his people as Mere-men? Then she recalled that Reothe had used that term. Had Reothe planted a seed of doubt in the General's mind to fester and finally destroy him?

Instinctively she lifted her hands to cup Tulkhan's face, but he caught her arms and pulled them down. His strength, fueled by rage, threatened to crush the small bones of her wrists. She gritted her teeth.

"Don't play your Dhamfeer tricks on me, Imoshen!"

"On the contrary, I think Reothe may have played a trick on you." She kept her voice even. "I was going to search for a sign of his planting doubts in your mind."

She felt him shudder with revulsion before dropping her wrists.

"I am not your enemy," she insisted.

"If you wanted to convince me of that you would have had Reothe lying in a cell when I came back."

"That is easy for you to say." A flush of warm and velvety anger rushed through her, leaving a metallic aftertaste on her tongue. She restrained the impulse to use her gift to sway him. "I am not Reothe's equal. How many of your men would have died trying to restrain him?"

"They would have died gladly for me!"

"I am not so quick to order the deaths of others!"

Tulkhan flinched.

She lifted her hands, palm up. "Tulkhan?"

"What was he doing with you naked in his arms?" The agony in his voice cut her.

"I was not naked. The laces on my underdress were cut."

Tulkhan snorted.

"I don't know what Reothe was doing. I wasn't conscious.

He used his gifts. Maybe he was planning to carry me out through the secret passage, in which case you can be glad the Keeper found us when he did."

The General stepped back from her. Imoshen saw the gulf widen between them. Only a few steps, but a chasm of misunderstanding. "Tulkhan, please?"

"Answers trip too easily off your tongue, Imoshen. I let myself believe . . . but no. From this day forward I will not be coming to your bed. I no longer trust you."

It was the worst blow. "Then you are lost because I am the only one you can trust. I love you." It was torn from her.

She saw him flinch. Was her love so terrible a thing? His rejection was a physical blow.

She almost staggered. "Tulkhan?"

He turned on his heel and walked off.

Through a blur of unshed tears Imoshen watched the stiff angle of General Tulkhan's broad shoulders as he walked away. When he rounded the corner and the blossoming trees obscured him from sight, her legs gave way and she sank onto the gravel path. The pain in her knees was nothing compared to the pain in her chest.

This was beyond repair. The General would never trust her again. By withdrawing from her he was sealing his fate, fulfilling Reothe's prophecy of his death.

She stared at the gravel. The twig had fallen unnoticed from her hands, and crushed blossoms lay all around her. They had trampled on them, destroying the fine petals. Everything she had worked and planned for might be destroyed before the tree could bloom again. If Tulkhan died, she no longer cared if she saw next spring's blossoms.

When Imoshen returned to the palace, weary and desperate to rest, she found the General in their bedchamber. Servants scurried about packing his belongings.

It was a cruel blow to have their private division witnessed by others. Imoshen met his gaze across the room.

"I will move into my old bedchamber. I stay here only

long enough to greet my son," the General informed her coldly.

Imoshen licked her lips. "Take a walk with me in the courtyard."

He would have refused but she let him see that this was not an idle request. Aware of the curious glances of the servants, Imoshen led him outside.

"Well?" he prodded when she did not speak immediately.

"I have not mentioned this before because I am not sure of things."

"No T'En riddles, Imoshen. Get to the point!"

She rounded on him. "I am not your Ghebite wife to be browbeaten!" She paused to draw a calming breath. "Let me be frank—I don't know when your son will be born. My mother carried me a full year from conception to birth. Your son is part T'En so it could take—"

"You're saying he might not be born until the Harvest Feast?"

Imoshen nodded and held Tulkhan's eyes. His Ghebite features hid his thoughts too well. "Throwbacks like myself take a full eight cycles of the small moon."

"True-men babies take around six," Tulkhan remarked. "So you are saying the longer it takes, the more T'En my son will be?"

Imoshen registered his distaste but she would not give him the pleasure of knowing how much it hurt her.

Tulkhan turned away, surprising the servants who had been openly watching them through the glass doors. He gestured angrily at them and they hurried back to their tasks.

It was already past the cusp of summer. His son should have been born any day now if he were a True-man. Tulkhan grimaced. Why had he denied the obvious? If the child was half Imoshen's he would be half T'En—an alien creature like Reothe. His boy might as well be his enemy's son.

Tulkhan strode toward the doors.

"Where are you going?" Imoshen called.

He did not answer her, but flung the door open.

"Don't bother moving my things," he told the servants. "I leave to rejoin my men."

They stared at him and then at Imoshen who had entered the chamber. Hastily recollecting themselves they made quick obeisances and left the pair alone.

Tulkhan did not want to be alone with Imoshen. Just to look on her was agony.

"You will leave me like this?" Her voice was raw.

He gave her a cold look, closing himself away from her pain. "I leave as soon as I am ready."

Imoshen allowed herself hope when she received Tulkhan's summons to the maproom, but when she saw his grim expression she knew his heart was still set hard against her.

"I've marked the passes. Are there any others?" he demanded, indicating the Keldon Highlands.

Hiding her disappointment, Imoshen studied the map. "Only those two. The Greater Pass leads directly to T'Diemn and most trade travels that way. The Lesser Pass is a longer, more difficult route and is only used by small parties. The highland ravines are steep and treacherous. Travelers might wander for days trying to find their way. What are you planning?"

"Fortifications. Once I control the passes I can monitor the comings and goings of the Keldon nobles, stop their trade. The highlands are not rich and fertile. If I have to, I can make life very harsh for the Keld. Let them choose between fresh supplies and supporting the rebels!"

Imoshen hesitated. "They are a proud people, used to austerity."

"What would you have me do, Imoshen? Repeat the mistake of your ancestor, march into one of their villages, demand they give up Reothe and his rebels? Execute the villagers until the survivors cooperate?"

She shook her head, horrified.

"That is the alternative. Unless you have changed your

mind about doing a scrying. No?" His expression was calculating. "Then we'll do what you suggested. Send Reothe a message. Tell him you'll meet him, only I will go in your stead. I'll ambush him before he can reach the rendezvous. He need never know you betrayed him."

At that moment Imoshen realized she would never betray Reothe. She might fear him and mistrust him but he was her kinsman, last of her kind. She could not lure him to his death.

"It would not work. Reothe would know if I was not waiting for him."

"I see." Grimly, Tulkhan rolled up the map. "By closing the passes I can contain the rebels' raids. That will reassure the people south of T'Diemn. I ride now." But he stood silently looking at her.

Imoshen lifted her hands. "If you would only trust me."

She winced as a bark of laughter escaped him.

"I might be a barbarian, Imoshen, but that does not mean I am a fool. Bring Reothe's head in a basket, only then will I trust you!"

Nausea roiled in her belly.

With a curse Tulkhan was gone.

She sank into the seat too stunned to think. Absently she stroked the scriber Tulkhan had been toying with, sensing his determination. If Reothe were foolish enough to bring a large force to attack the fortresses, neither side would gain. But why would Reothe wait until the fortifications were completed? Why not attack while the men were vulnerable?

Imoshen knew Tulkhan did not intend to return until the fortresses were finished and manned. This would take until autumn, maybe even early winter. She could hardly believe Tulkhan would desert her during the birth of his son, yet she had been told it was the Ghebite custom to segregate women at this "unclean" time. How she hated everything Ghebite!

Seventeen

DAYS, THEN WEEKS, passed in a kind of stupor. While Imoshen slept and ate mechanically, the baby writhed inside her as if impatient to be free. It had reached its highest point under her rib cage, and had yet to drop, so she had no relief from the pressure. She was always weary.

Imoshen was dozing, dreaming she was back at the Stronghold, where her family was celebrating the imminent birth. It would be a great event. The Aayel had been giving her wise advice on handling the contractions. Suddenly a great foreboding gripped her and she awoke, her heart hammering.

Was something going to go wrong with the birth? Why did she feel such a sense of dread?

She needed the scrying plate to help her focus. Imoshen was torn between her need to know and her fear of scrying. Then the sense of foreboding won out. She strode to her chest, the only thing that was truly hers in all the palace, and rifled through it.

Merkah should not have touched her scrying plate. Imoshen pressed it to her body, affronted. She took the plate to the bathing room and ran a little water onto it. Pricking her thumb with her dagger, she squeezed two droplets into the water. One drop of blood for her soul, one for her son's. They hit the water's surface, spreading into whirls.

The spiral of fine blood drew her gaze to the scrying

plate. It had never done that before. She'd better focus on the birth, but the reflections in the scrying plate held her captive. General Tulkhan! She saw him astride his horse, supervising the earthworks of the fortification. The ground was treacherous, the pass steep. He swung down from his mount to consult with the engineers.

Imoshen watched the breeze lift his dark hair. She wanted to touch him. It was a physical need. But she mustn't give in to it.

The water's surface shimmered. She was still looking at Tulkhan, but this time he faced death. His men fell around him, poorly protected by the half-finished fortress. Why didn't they try to defend themselves? Rebels leapt over the walls crying Reothe's name.

Reothe! Too late, she could not stop the thought. The plate already shimmered. Imoshen knew she should not look but it held an awful fascination. Reothe stood by a hot spring. He appeared to be alone except for a child of about eight. From this angle it was hard to tell if the little one was male or female.

Suddenly both of them paused and turned towards her. Reothe's eyes narrowed suspiciously. But it was the child's gaze Imoshen could not hold. They were the oldest eyes she'd ever seen. With cold shock she knew she was looking into the eyes of one of the Ancients.

Her fingers locked on the plate. She had to break the contact. With a burst of will which left her dizzy and breathless she cast the plate aside. It flew out of her hands spinning in the air and crashed straight through the stained-glass window.

The sound of the shattering glass roused her. How could she be so stupid? She was too inexperienced to scry. The foreboding must have been a forewarning of Tulkhan's death, not her baby's.

"T'Imoshen, are you hurt?" Merkah threw the door open then gasped when she saw the smashed window where lead curled like broken fingers, clasping at the empty air. "What happened?"

Imoshen had no idea what to say. She straightened. "Pack my things. Have my horse saddled. I ride out today."

"But—"

"Now!"

Merkah ducked her head. Imoshen caught a flash of resentment in the maid's face. She had been too sharp with the girl. Though she tried, she had never established with her the easy friendship she'd had with Kalleen.

Imoshen strode into her chamber where Merkah was already laying out her clothes. "No, nothing fancy. I am joining my bond-partner. I want riding clothes."

The problem was that nothing would do up over her belly. She tossed her dress aside and pulled on a pair of breeches, letting them ride under the swell of the baby. A borrowed shirt of Tulkhan's was large enough to cover her stomach. It fell to her thighs, and while it was not suitable for court, it was presentable. She took her cloak to sleep under.

"Who will be accompanying you, my lady?"

"No one. I travel faster alone." And in disguise. She did not want any of Reothe's people reporting her whereabouts to him.

She felt buoyant. If only she could reach Tulkhan in time to warn him of the attack, then he would have to believe her loyalty. If she didn't warn him, he would die.

The need to get moving consumed her.

"But my lady, you cannot go alone!"

"No? I do not need a maid, or servants. I am not incompetent!" Imoshen winced when she heard her own tone. Merkah stiffened, retreating behind a wall of offended dignity.

"I am in a hurry, Merkah," Imoshen said more gently. "Have the cook pack traveling food for me. I won't have time to hunt."

Before long she was in the stables strapping saddlebags to her horse. After a moment she sensed someone observing her. She glanced over her shoulder.

The Vaygharian. Anger fired her.

He lifted his hands in a placating gesture. "This is not wise, Lady Protector. The General ordered me to watch over you."

She made a rude noise. "I can smell a lie!"

"At least take an escort," he demurred. "A woman in your condition cannot travel alone."

Briefly she considered taking several of her Stronghold Guard but that would reveal who she was and make her vulnerable. She did not bother to reply to the Vaygharian, but took her horse's reins and prepared to walk the beast out of the stall.

The Vaygharian caught her arm.

Quick as thought she flicked free of him and drew her knife, holding it to his throat. The horse snickered uneasily, sidling away. She nearly laughed as Kinraid glanced around uneasily.

"I am only trying to serve you, Lady Protector."

"I know who you serve." She stepped closer. "I know what you are. Remember how I looked into your soul and saw your death!"

He went pale. She smelt the sweat of fear on his skin. Her lips pulled back from her teeth in a grimace of disgust. "If you are here when I get back, I will slit your throat myself!"

"That is not the way the ruler of Fair Isle treats an ambassador of Vayghar." He was on his dignity.

"No." She smiled. "It is the way I treat a traitor. General Tulkhan wants people to think he is civilized. I don't care what people think!"

She stepped away and picked up the horse's dangling reins. Silently she led her mount out. A dozen stable workers and palace servants gathered in the courtyard watching anxiously, but no one dared argue with her. She wondered who they would be serving this time next summer.

The rigors of the journey did not concern her. She had seen farm women work until the contractions started and had helped them deliver their babes on a dirt floors. Then, once the proper words were said, those women would be on their feet preparing their family's evening meal.

She had no illusions about the birth either. The powder of a pain-killing root was tucked into her traveling kit. She intended to brew a tea to sip during the worst of the pain.

Pulling the cloak over her betraying hair, Imoshen chose her way out of T'Diemn.

After four days in the saddle, Imoshen was heartily sick of riding. It was not something she would recommend to anyone in the advanced stages of pregnancy. The action of the horse's rocking on her hips triggered shooting hot pokers of pain to arc down her legs. Worse still, when she dismounted she could hardly walk.

On leaving T'Diemn she had heard a horse galloping behind her and had ridden into a grove of trees to escape pursuit. It was Crawen, leader of the Stronghold Guard, come to escort her. Imoshen was sorely tempted, but in the end she had let the woman ride by.

She had concentrated on cloaking her appearance. When she emerged on the far side of the grove, she knew the Vaygharian's spies would not recognize her. They probably would not even notice her. She had chosen the form of a wandering T'En priest, a male at that.

But maintaining the illusion required deep concentration, and once Crawen had ridden dispiritedly past her back to T'Diemn, Imoshen had let her guard slip. It had been enough to will herself unnoticed when she saw people and to keep to the lesser-used paths.

Now Imoshen's heart lifted, for by tomorrow she should see her Ghebite General. She was in the foothills of the Keldon Highlands. Here the people were distrustful of strangers, but surely they would not turn aside a weary traveler? She urged her horse towards a plume of smoke rising into the oyster-shell gleam of the dusk sky. Soon she approached the smoke's source, a crofters' cottage, built of local stone, its roof made of sod. The rich smell of simmering stew made her mouth water.

Crouched behind the bracken, Imoshen watched an old man chop wood while an old woman herded the chickens and goat in for the night. For them life was an ever-turning cycle of seasons. Imoshen almost envied them their place in the scheme of things. It looked like a safe haven for the night. Picking her way across the dim ground, she scratched on the door.

The little wizened man opened the door a crack. "What do you want?"

"Is this the way the Keld greet a weary traveler?" Imoshen concentrated on projecting a bland image.

"Plenty of strange comings and goings near here," the woman muttered from behind him. Her sharp old eyes took in Imoshen's pregnancy.

Imoshen had found her advanced pregnancy made women eager to help her. Tonight she cloaked only her T'En coloring, to attempt anything more would have been too hard to sustain for she was weary indeed.

"That infant's nearly due. Come in," the woman said.

Imoshen ducked her head to enter. "The babe has not dropped yet."

The old woman clucked under her breath, sounding for all the world like the disapproving chickens which sheltered in the far end of the cottage. The goat added its opinion.

Imoshen felt light-headed. "I can pay for food and lodging."

The woman sniffed, offended.

"As if we would take your coins!" the old man muttered.

"Thank you, Grandmother, Grandfather." Imoshen used the honorific form of address for village elders. She watched as the old woman bustled around, stirring the food on the fire. When she saw her check the bed of straw Imoshen told her, "No, Grandmother. I will sleep on the floor before the fire. I would not turn you out of your own bed."

But she did long for some warm water to wash the grime off her body. She wanted to be clean when she met General Tulkhan. It was her one vanity.

Despite the pain in her hips, Imoshen went outside to see to her horse. Everything was a chore, removing the saddle, rubbing the horse down. It appeared happy enough on a short hobble, and would have sensed predators if there were any about. For once Imoshen felt reasonably safe.

When she returned, the old woman served up a tasty stew with thick crusty bread. Imoshen ate it gratefully. Then exhaustion overtook her. She just managed to thank the old couple for their hospitality before slipping to the floor in front of the fire pit, her arms cradling her belly, her head on her saddlebag.

She was so hot, the room felt stifling. It had been her intention to wait up until the old couple went to bed, but sleep was irresistible. As she lost consciousness she felt her cloaking illusion fade and knew her true identity would be revealed. She would have to put her trust in the old people.

Her mouth tasted foul.

Imoshen tried to swallow and gagged. Someone held a cup of water to her lips. It was like sweet elixir. She drank greedily. Cruelly, they took it away before she could finish it.

It was still dark. Did she have a fever? She must remember to thank the old couple for bringing her water. At least she'd slept deeply. Since starting this journey she'd hardly been able to sleep through the night for the ache in her hips.

"Thank you." The words were a croak. "Have I been feverish?"

"No. You were drugged."

Imoshen knew that voice. She struggled to sit up. Her companion would have helped her, but she pushed his hands aside. "Why is it still dark?"

"It is the night of the following day. The old woman was free with the sleeping herb. She did not want you waking and taking your anger out on her."

Imoshen moistened her lips. "Drake, you might as well light a candle. I know who you are."

"That doesn't worry me. We were sleeping. But yes, I will make a light."

He stirred the coals in the fireplace, then coaxed a flame

from a crude candle. Imoshen smelt the burning tallow dip. She looked around. They were in the crofter's cottage, or an identical one.

"Where am I?"

"Safe in the foothills of the highlands."

So they had moved her while she was drugged. "The crofters betrayed me."

Drake laughed. "T'Reothe could see you coming across the plains to him, bright as a beacon. He sent us to warn the old couple to bring you to him."

"How?"

"We ride. Tomorrow you will join your betrothed."

"No. I meant how could he see me coming?"

Drake tilted his head. "You used your gifts to disguise yourself so that those who followed you would not discover Reothe's whereabouts. Every time you used your gifts, he sensed it."

Imoshen hung her head. She knew Reothe could sense the use of her gifts when he was nearby but if he was as sensitive as Drake claimed, he was powerful indeed. Her heart sank.

Reothe believed she had run away from the capital to come to him, not to warn the General. Or did he? If he truly believed that, he would not have ordered her drugged. Tulkhan would think she had deserted him for Reothe. Impatience gnawed at Imoshen. She must warn the General of the attack, and that meant escaping Drake for a second time. Imoshen shifted uncomfortably. "The baby presses down. Can I have some privacy?"

"You'll have to go outside like the rest of us."

As Imoshen straightened her gaze fell on her boots.

Drake noticed. "You won't need them."

Imoshen shrugged. Drake was wise not to trust her. Arching her back, she scratched her belly. The skin itched. "I'm so hungry. Is there anything to eat?"

"I'll cut some meat," he offered.

Smiling her thanks she stepped over the bodies of Drake's snoring companions and went out into the night.

The large moon was on the wane and the small moon was not in the night sky, so she knew it was not far from dawn. There was light enough for her to find a suitable bush. Her excuse to escape the cottage was genuine. The baby was sitting deeply.

By studying the stars Imoshen guessed the Greater Pass lay to the northeast, so that was the direction Drake would expect her to take. She would go south then double back. He would probably anticipate that too, but she was a country girl and knew how to hide her trail.

Hopefully Reothe had been too preoccupied to launch his attack. Drake would have been crowing if they had killed the Ghebite General already. And if she kept them fully occupied searching for her, it might buy her the time she needed to reach Tulkhan.

The enforced rest had done her aching hips good, but it was not easy picking a path barefoot through country she did not know. At first she did not mind the effort. Then her stomach rumbled and she was reminded that Drake had been cutting meat for her. Poor Drake. She hoped Reothe would not be too hard on him.

When the birds began their predawn chorus Imoshen paused to drink at a stream. The water was not as cold as she expected, which meant she was near a hot spring.

At least she moved farther from Reothe with every step. Pleased with herself she bathed her sore feet in the stream, rubbing the dirt and blood from her cuts. It was so refreshing that she would have liked to strip off and bathe her aching body but she didn't dare. They would start looking for her soon.

Slipping into the water, she waded upstream to hide her scent from her trackers. A wide, deep pool lay before her. As she stood debating whether to go through or around, the oddest sensation gripped her. The baby's head ground down to her pelvis. She could almost feel it grating on the bones, wedging itself deep. Her knees sagged and a trickle of fear floated up through her body. The baby must not come now, not when she needed to escape her pursuers.

She set off. The water was warm and so clear she could see the large, round boulders on the bottom. It was soothing and cleansed her gritty skin. When the water reached her chest she began to swim.

The first pain overtook her midway in deep water. It was so overpowering she could barely keep her head above the surface. Terror gripped her.

At last the pain slipped away, uncurling its tendrils from her body with a lover's reluctance. A burst of energy took her swiftly to the far side of the pool.

First births were generally long. Of course there were exceptions. One woman she knew had gone into labor and delivered within an hour, another had endured three days. There was no way of knowing.

She stood dripping on a rock, trying to work out her options. How far could she travel? How long did she have? The next pain rolled in like a summer thunderstorm, inexorable and intense.

Imoshen rode it. When it retreated, leaving the afterimage of its fury imprinted on her mind and body, she faced the truth. The baby was coming now. It could not wait for a better time or place.

She thought longingly of the painkiller tucked safely in her saddlebags. So much for thinking ahead. But now she had to find somewhere safe and warm. From the speed and force of the contractions she knew it would be a short, violent birth.

She also knew that the more she moved, the faster the baby would come, but she couldn't stay out here in the open. Driven by necessity, she set off upstream looking for shelter.

There was no way for her to measure the passage of time other than counting, so she took to counting between each pain and the duration of the pain and placing all these numbers in a convenient place in her head to keep track of the birthing process. It helped to think she was in control of at least one thing.

Rounding a curve in the rock wall she stared, dismayed. She had stumbled into a hot spring, a place redolent of the

Ancients. The pools held steaming water and mist hung over the narrow ravine.

Imoshen was desperate. She did not want to use a place that belonged to the Ancients.

Suddenly another contraction wracked her. They were getting harder to ride. A silent, growing terror told her that soon she would be swamped, drowned by the sensation. From experience she knew there was a point where the body took over and the mind simply had to go with it. She wanted to be safe before that point came.

Walking on rocks warmed by the hot pools, she made her way into the mist-shrouded ravine. Her damp clothes had begun to dry, but now they clung to her. A shiver shook her.

Was that a cleft in the rocks? Imoshen picked her way over slippery stones to investigate. It was the entrance to a cave. Suddenly she felt an increase in pressure and her waters broke, flooding her legs with hot fluid. Her knees almost gave way. She wanted to cry out, but bit back the sound.

Trembling, barely able to walk, she felt her way into the cave. It grew lighter and opened into a natural cavern with a central pool. A shaft of sunlight poured in through a gap in the rocks above. Steam shimmered on the water's surface. It was a beautiful place. A good place.

Imoshen felt the tightening of her muscles, a sharp clenching as if she was about to cough. Already? She panted, fighting the urge to push. Picking a spot where she could rest her back against the rock, she stripped off her sodden breeches and sank to a crouch ready for the work of birthing.

That was when she saw the creature standing in the mist, aglow with light. It was a child who was neither male nor female, the child with the ancient eyes.

Imoshen would have screamed but the urge to push gripped her. She caught her breath and went with it. The baby's head moved. There was barely time to catch her breath before the urge came again. She felt the baby move again and guessed that its head was emerging. Her skin was stretching impossibly.

Panting, she looked up. The ancient creature was still there. Not threatening, just watching.

Once more her muscles contracted. She felt her skin tear as the bloodied head emerged into her hands. By feel she searched for the cord. It wasn't around the neck.

She gulped a breath and went with the last contraction. She had intended to maneuver the infant, easing first one shoulder then the other, but her body wanted to be rid of it. The force of the push tore her further as the shoulders emerged.

Panting, she looked up. The creature was watching intently.

Then the baby's body came, slithering out at her feet into her hands. Stunned, she stared at the baby boy, hardly able to believe he was her son, very much her flesh and blood. The cord pulsed with life. For now they were still one.

He writhed in her hands, his little head turning, black hair plastered to his head.

Alarm pierced her. The Ancient was still observing her. She had to get out of here.

Imoshen lifted the baby to her chest and chewed through the cord, pinching it closed. She could not risk using her healing gift in case it drew Reothe, so she tied the cord off with a strip of material.

The baby sucked in a breath and exclaimed to the world. His mouth opened and his arms splayed out, fingers spread. Imoshen laughed.

Six fingers.

Pride stirred her. He was more T'En than True-man.

Would he ever stop yelling and look at her? She wanted to see his eyes. The hair was all Tulkhan.

Stupid man. He should have been here to greet his son. Imoshen frowned as another contraction took her. The afterbirth. It was not as painful as the baby.

True to her training, she checked that it was intact. She had no intention of dying of child-bed fever. The Aayel's T'Enchiridion remained in her saddlebags but she did not

need it to say the right words. Imoshen shivered. She would
have to find a safe place to bury her son's afterbirth then say
the words to bind his soul. But for the moment she let herself rest, leaning her head against the rock wall. It was so
good not to be in pain.

Yet even as she crouched there cradling the hot, slippery
body of her baby, her gaze never left the Ancient. What did
it want? Was it merely observing because she had entered its
sacred place? She felt a grim smile part her lips. Surely
enough blood had been spilt to satisfy it.

Birthing was a messy business. She would have liked to
wash herself and the baby in the warm pools but the presence of the Ancient oppressed her. Collecting the afterbirth
and her clothing, she rose to her knees and then to her feet.
She felt reassured by the warm bundle of life in her arms.
Keeping a watch on the creature, she headed for the cave's
entrance, walking carefully across the smooth rocks because
her center of balance had changed.

Suddenly the Ancient began moving. Making no overt
threat, it rose from the water's surface to the rock, its feet
never touching the stone. It positioned itself between her
and the patch of daylight.

Imoshen hugged her son to her chest, heart pounding so
violently she thought she might be sick. "Keep away!"

The voice was hers, but she'd never heard it sound so
feral, so full of contained violence. It frightened her.

The Ancient said nothing.

Imoshen glanced around the cave. The only other way
out was through the hole in the roof directly over the hot
pool. It would have been an impossible climb even without
the baby in her arms. She had no choice.

Though she could feel the power of the Ancient radiating like heat from an oven, she forced herself to step nearer,
edging sideways in an attempt to slip past.

It shifted to block her and extended its arms, palms
up.

A moan escaped Imoshen. "You cannot have him!"

The ancient creature lifted a hand indicating the afterbirth.

Imoshen gasped. She could not condemn her son to life without a soul. At best he would be a heartless killer, at worst dead within a day. "No. The soul must be bound to—"

In her head she heard the Aayel reciting the T'Enchiridion. Only they were not the words of birth, but the opening of the death calling. She forced them from her mind. The last thing she needed now was to call the Parakletos. But she understood the Ancients' message—they would either take her son's life force or his soul.

It was her decision.

If the Ancient had asked for her own life she would have given it willingly, but she could not bring herself to part with her child.

Tears blinded her as she handed over the afterbirth.

The Ancients had claimed her son for their own. In life he would be theirs to call on.

Tulkhan glanced up at the lookout's signal. It was just on dusk and the cooking fires were going strong. The smell of rich stew hung over the half-built fortress.

"What is it?" he yelled.

"You'd better come and see."

He didn't like that tone. Something had startled the watch.

Tulkhan strode past the nearest campfire. He was careful to hide any trace of fear. His men had to believe in him. It had seemed so simple when he believed in himself. But all the rules had changed since he had taken Imoshen's Stronghold and now he doubted everything, his own decisions most of all.

Springing lightly up the ladder he climbed onto the lookout tower. The knuckles of his right hand hurt where he had injured them working wood.

Looking down he saw Imoshen. She stood there in one of his shirts, hugging something. His heart soared. She had come to him ready to renounce Reothe. Tulkhan's first impulse was to let her in. But he checked himself. There was no horse, no sign of companions.

It could not be Imoshen. It was a trick. Reothe baited him with the illusion of Imoshen. The attack he had been expecting had begun.

"Should I open the gate, General?" the watch asked.

"No. Prepare for attack. That is not my wife."

"You fool!" Imoshen cried. "I am tired and hungry. I have walked a day and a night in bare feet through the ravines to bring you your son. Let me in!"

He had to grin. That certainly sounded like Imoshen.

"Who knows when my son is due, Shape-changer."

"Babies come when they are ready. If I don't get some food soon, I will drop!"

Tulkhan stared at Imoshen's upturned face, torn by his need to believe she was really there and the sheer impossibility of her appearance. How could it be Imoshen? She was back in the palace. She would not have come to him without attendants. In fact, he had expressly forbid it. That made him smile—forbidding Imoshen to do something was not going to stop her.

Still, he had to be sure. "How did my mother die?"

"She died alone from fever without anything to ease her passing. Now let me in, General."

It was Imoshen. Only she called him General in that fond, exasperated tone, and only she knew his secret guilt about his mother's death. "Open the gate."

Tulkhan turned and sprang lightly down the ladder, even as his men opened the makeshift gate. He darted through before it was fully open and swept Imoshen off her feet.

"Careful, you'll hurt the baby!" she warned.

He glanced down, seeing a small face, its mouth opening to launch a cry. He was shocked even though Imoshen had said she carried the babe.

"Shut the gate." He marched across the campsite, Imoshen in his arms, a squalling infant in hers. His men stopped their tasks, mouths agape. Those nearest strained to see.

"Put me down. He needs to be fed," Imoshen urged.

He let her slide to the ground by his fire. There were a hundred questions to be asked, but the baby demanded precedence, its tiny arms windmilling with frustration. That shock of dark hair stood straight up.

"He's mine!"

"Of course he's yours!" Imoshen muttered, struggling to unlace the shirt one-handed.

"You can't feed him here. My men will see!"

"I'll feed him where I please. He's hungry, and if your men don't like it they can look away. Besides, they were all babies once!"

Tulkhan saw the anger in her face but he also saw the exhaustion. "Very well."

"I don't need your permission!" Her fingers caught on the laces and she cursed, fumbling to undo a knot.

When Tulkhan took his son from her, the boy yelled so indignantly that he had to grin. He was unmistakably a Ghebite. Let Reothe try to claim him now! He turned and held the child out for his men to see. The naked bundle struggled in his hands, screaming lustily. A ragged cheer broke from his men.

"If you're quite finished?" Imoshen had knelt by the fire at his side.

He handed the baby to her and she leaned against the wall of the building behind them. Instinctively Tulkhan stepped between Imoshen and his men to shield her from their gaze. He could not help but watch as the baby turned its face to her breast, mouth open. Without any guidance from her it latched onto her nipple, sucking vigorously.

How could it be so little, yet know what to do?

"My feet," Imoshen whispered. "And food."

He knelt to look at her feet. They were covered in blood and mud. "How did you get here in this state?"

"I walked. I'll have some of that stew. I don't care if it's not ready." She kept talking as he ladled out a serving. "To escape from Reothe's people I had to leave my boots and horse behind."

"What? Reothe had you abducted from the palace? How?"

"I was on my way here. Some bread too." She accepted

a bowl of stew, scooping up the sauce with the hard bread. The baby remained tucked in the crook of her arm and both of them fed with absolute concentration.

"How long since you last ate?" Tulkhan asked.

"Evening, three days ago. This one was born yesterday just after dawn." She tore at a piece of bread with sharp white teeth, chewing vigorously. "I was coming to warn you. You won't like this but I did a scrying. I saw you fall defending this fort. I came to warn you that Reothe's going to attack."

This was what he wanted to hear, proof of her loyalty, and yet perversely he found himself wondering if she had planned this with Reothe so she could open the fortress from within when his back was turned.

"You don't believe me." Imoshen's voice sounded weary and indignant. "Why do I bother?"

He stared across the fire at her. There were bruised circles under her eyes and her gaze shimmered with unshed tears. As he watched they rolled down her cheeks, glistening in the firelight.

Before he could stop himself, he crossed the fire circle to kneel before her. He used his thumbs to brush the tears from her face.

She twisted her head to be free of his hands.

Tulkhan rubbed his jaw, feeling the bristles of the beard he hadn't bothered to remove since leaving T'Diemn. "If the scrying says I'm going to die here, what difference can warning me make?"

She shrugged. "Scrying is not an exact science. I told you that before. I am here and the baby has been born, so things are not exactly as I foresaw them in the scrying. It was one possible path and now we are on another, hopefully one which will not lead to your death. Here, hold this."

She gave him the half-eaten bowl of stew and changed the baby to the other breast. The babe protested vehemently but settled down when he found a fresh nipple.

Tulkhan had to admire his son's single-mindedness.

"My food." Imoshen held out her hand. "This is a good

spot for a fortress, but we are vulnerable to attack right now. If I were Reothe I would make a clean sweep and be rid of us altogether."

Tulkhan tried to concentrate on what she was saying. He had trouble discussing tactics with Imoshen in this situation. A Ghebite woman would never discuss such things with her husband, let alone do it while breastfeeding his son. Females were considered unclean while they were making milk, as they were when they were bleeding or pregnant. Even their normal places in the temples were forbidden to them at these times, when the priests claimed they became channels for evil spirits because of their inferior souls.

"General, are you listening to me? I didn't come all this way to die in a surprise attack." Imoshen fixed angry eyes on him.

Tulkhan concentrated on her features. Imoshen was not a channel for evil. He had seen too many different religions fail to save people to have faith in the teachings of Ghebite priests.

"Do you have people posted outside the fortifications ready to give the alarm?" she asked.

He nodded.

She looked down tenderly. The baby had fallen asleep with her nipple in his mouth. "Can I have a blanket to wrap him in?"

He took out his own blanket and laid it on the ground. She wrapped the baby and picked him up, then held him toward Tulkhan.

"What?" What was he supposed to do with a baby?

"Hold him. I want to get clean and treat my feet, then find some more clothes."

Gingerly Tulkhan took the sleeping bundle. Imoshen called for warm water and spare clothes, then climbed the central tower.

Tulkhan sank beside the fire, feasting his eyes on his two-day old son. Who would have thought? So much black hair and such perfect little features.

The baby gave a whimper, his hands splaying wide.

Tulkhan blinked and caught one little palm, the baby's fingers closing around his finger, holding on tightly.

Six fingers.

His son was half Dhamfeer. How could he not be?

Tulkhan tried to withdraw his finger. The baby's hold tightened. The boy was a determined little thing. The General felt a surge of pride. His son had not taken the full year from conception to birth but he was still half Dhamfeer. So be it.

Tulkhan leaned his head against the wall and looked up to the star-dusted sky. Their patterns were different this far south, but he had grown to know them as he traveled through Fair Isle. This was his island now and he would endure. His son was born of this land, half Ghebite, half T'En. He was the future.

With his finger encased in the firm grasp of his son, Tulkhan felt the bitter kernel of distrust, which had tainted his life for so many moons, dissolve. As it slipped from him he realized its nature and its source. Reothe had planted that self-doubt and distrust. But now it was gone and the world was his for the taking.

Imoshen made her way gingerly to the fire circle. Her feet were tender and she was still bruised and torn from the birth. When the General returned the baby, she accepted him carefully. Her breasts were tender. She had nothing in reserve for healing herself.

She just wanted to sit and hold her son. It was amazing how good it felt to hug his little body to her. Warmth from the fire seeped through her. She was tired beyond thought.

Traveling the foothills with the baby had been a test of endurance. She had hardly dared let herself stop, for fear of falling asleep and being recaptured.

It was so good to be safe at last. Through almost-closed lids, she watched Tulkhan leave the campfire to confer with his fortress commander. She had sensed something different about the General when he returned the baby to her. Tulkhan was lighter of spirit, more confident. She didn't know why, but she was relieved.

The familiar rumble of the Ghebite language hung on the air. There was something about the tone of the General's voice that she found very comforting.

"Imoshen?"

She looked up, startled. Had she dozed off?

Tulkhan offered his hand, indicating to her to stand.

"Can't we just sit?"

He sank onto his haunches with the ease of a man used to living rough. "The men are nervous, Imoshen. According to Ghebite custom a woman is unclean while she makes milk for the babe. Ordinarily no man but a woman's husband would see her for two small moons after the birth and even he would not touch her." He gave an apologetic cough. "You unsettle them."

She snorted. "Anyone would think they birthed and raised themselves!"

Tulkhan grinned. "So it may seem to you. But these men are simple soldiers. They find it hard to think differently from the way they were raised."

"You are a soldier, yet you can see things differently," she told him.

He nodded reluctantly, then with a shrug he continued. "As first son of the second wife, I have been on the outside looking in for many years." He looked up, a rueful smile lighting his eyes.

Imoshen felt a tug of recognition. She too knew what it was like to be an outcast.

Tulkhan seemed to recollect himself. "To make matters worse, they fear attack. They know you turned Jacolm and Cariah to stone and they fear the same or worse from the rebel leader. Can you tell me how Reothe will strike?"

"I can't help you. I could try to scry but Reothe would know and block me, his skills are so much greater than mine."

His disappointment was palpable.

"I am sorry, General." Regret made Imoshen abrupt. She put her free hand on his clasped hands. "This is my gift."

She brushed his knuckles, meaning to draw on the force of his own will to heal his abrasion, because she was exhausted. Strangely, she didn't have to. The food and rest must have restored her.

He lifted his hand, turning it over, flexing the fingers as he made a fist. The skin was healed perfectly.

"In time of peace it is a good gift," she told him. "But not much help at present."

"Not true." He squeezed her hand. "We may have great need of you afterwards."

Imoshen nodded, unable to bring herself to tell him that, even if Reothe allowed them an "afterwards," she doubted she had the strength to heal more than the mildest of wounds.

His knuckles brushed her cheek. "Don't let yourself worry."

It was a gentle gesture and it almost undid her. All of a sudden weariness overtook her and she fell asleep sitting up, too tired to move.

Eighteen

A SCREAM SPLIT the air, a terrible, keening note of pure terror. Imoshen pushed her hair from her eyes and struggled to sit up, her bruised body aching. All around her, men sprang up, groggy with sleep but with weapons to hand.

Tulkhan hurried around the fire to her, pulling her to her feet. She gasped as the myriad little cuts on her swollen feet split open.

"Up there, take cover." He pushed her toward the tower.

She hugged the baby to her chest. "Give me a knife. Reothe's people took mine."

He glanced into her face, startled. Imoshen cursed. Did he think she was some useless Ghebite female?

Several more screams cut the air, rising above the frantic shouts of the men.

Wordlessly Tulkhan dragged his own knife from its sheath and handed it to her.

Imoshen grasped it in one hand, then turned to dart away.

"Imoshen?"

Tulkhan's tone stopped her.

His face worked with emotion. "You came to warn me, thank you."

"Don't thank me. I probably led them here and provided the impetus for the attack."

"I don't care."

He took one step to cover the space between them and caught the back of her head in his free hand. His lips found hers in a bruising kiss. It made her heart leap. Her body recognized it for what it was.

A declaration.

She returned it with all the fervor of her long-contained passion. Tears stung her eyes. Tulkhan might take his death wound this night. She might never have a chance to hold him again. So much was against them. Yet at this moment she knew he was hers, body and soul. Fierce joy filled her. If they lived through this night she would take him in her arms and love him with every fiber of her body.

He broke first. The desire in his eyes warmed her to the core.

"Later," he promised. "If there is a later."

"There will be. There has to be!"

Then he was gone.

Imoshen climbed the ladder then pulled it up after her. There were no doors or windows on the ground floor of the tower, the fortress's last point of defense. On the next floor there were no shutters to draw across its narrow windows, no door. She scurried up the curved stairs to the floor above. Here there was no roof.

Heart pounding as the screams rose to a crescendo, she made a nest in the darkest corner and, using strips of old material, quickly cleaned the baby, then rigged a sling to tie him to her chest.

Her hands flew, but her mind moved faster. How many rebels were attacking? Which point in the half-completed fortifications had they chosen to force? What were they doing to cause those terrible screams? She knew the sounds of physical pain, this was more. This was agony of the soul.

The sweat of fear clung to her skin. No longer registering the pain of the cuts on her feet, Imoshen prepared to fight for her life and the life of her son.

She crept to a window. A pall of smoke hung over the campfires. Her nostrils stung and the back of her throat burned. This was no ordinary smoke. By the fell light the features of the men twisted in leers and grimaces of mindless terror. Some had fallen to the ground, foaming at the mouth, while others ran about slashing wildly at nothing. In their mad attacks they knocked their own men to the ground. A few simply stood and screamed.

Fear for Tulkhan made her tremble. She could see rebels forging over the ramparts, slitting throats methodically as they moved forward. Their helpless victims fell, spilling their blood on the ground. As it hit the soil the blood steamed, adding to the thick mist. It was mist, not smoke.

The Ancients!

What evil pact had Reothe offered them to overpower the fortress? Opening her T'En senses she searched for Reothe, but instead she found the Parakletos. Beautiful in their full T'En battle armor, they strode insubstantial but irresistible amidst the slaughter. Some knelt beside the dying waiting for them to gasp their last, others wrenched the dying's souls away even as they fought for life.

Sickened, Imoshen shuddered. Terror stole her breath from her chest and pinned her feet to the floor. Reothe had said the Parakletos held no power in this world. Somehow he had opened a path for them and laid a feast before them.

Imoshen dry-retched. Tears blurred her vision. Gasping, she blinked to clear her sight. Tulkhan's True-men had no defenses against the Parakletos. They appeared aware of the danger but blinded so that they did not see the rebels amidst them. Where was Tulkhan?

She identified him below her, staggering toward the base of the tower. He fell to his knees, vulnerable.

Desperate, she ran down the spiral stairs, shoved the ladder out of the floor ground, and scurried down. Tulkhan was on his knees, his head in his hands, his body hunched and shaking. She knelt next to him.

Cupping the General's head in her hands she searched his unseeing eyes. What was wrong? Then she smelt it on the mists—an overpowering terror. It stole her breath, her very sanity. But no. It was not real.

"It's not real!" she hissed. "It's an illusion!" But it wasn't. The Parakletos were real and waiting greedily to claim a man's soul. The rebels were killing for the Parakletos.

Imoshen grabbed two handfuls of Tulkhan's hair. She jerked on his head. The pain made him focus on her. Dragging in a deep breath, she blew into his mouth to drive out the poisonous mists which made him susceptible.

He pulled away from her, coughing. "Imoshen?"

Coming to her feet, she hauled him upright. "The rebels are amongst us. Your men are dying where they stand without lifting a blade."

Stunned, he looked around, then cursed and bellowed an order at the nearest man, who writhed on the ground unaware.

"He can't hear you. The mist has clouded their minds."

"Then we are lost unless you can reverse it." He spun to face her.

Imoshen shook her head. She could not do it. There were too many of them. Even if she could, they'd be killed before she had brought enough of them back to make a stand. The nearest Parakletos paused as he crouched over a dying man. T'En eyes that had seen too much horror met hers. Imoshen looked away, unable to meet his gaze.

Nearby another Parakletos wept as she watched a man die. Her eyes widened as if she recognized Imoshen, and she lifted a hand in supplication. It came to Imoshen that not all the Parakletos were cold and cruel, but they were bound by their ancient oath and tonight they served Reothe.

"Imoshen!" Tulkhan pulled her around to face him.

She dragged in a shaky breath. "You must find Reothe. Strike him down and all his work is destroyed."

Tulkhan balked as she pushed him toward the walls. "But if he can do this, how can I hope to defeat him?"

"This power will drain him. He'll be defenseless. Go after him and I'll do what I can here."

Imoshen moved off, not bothering to see if he would follow her advice. She searched for the fortress's commander.

She would bring him back first. Between them maybe they could stem the tide.

Tulkhan turned in time to see one of his men fall from the gate tower, his throat slit. Furious, he scrambled up the ladder and struck down the rebel responsible. The man fell, landing across the body of the Ghebite. Their blood mingled on the ground, steaming, bubbling.

Someone leapt on Tulkhan's back. Instinct took over. He threw the attacker over his shoulder, breaking the man's neck before his feet hit the boards. Something unseen took the man's weight from Tulkhan's arms.

Despite his unwillingness to witness what a True-man should not, Tulkhan took one last look into the fortress compound where rebels were already opening the gate. So much for their defenses. Tulkhan's lookouts had succumbed without giving a warning, and the rebels had been able to bring their ladders right up to the walls. The gate swung open. Rebels charged inside to slaughter the defenders, who were preoccupied with their terrible, dark visions.

Three men stood at Imoshen's side. Tulkhan fought the urge to go to her aid. He had to kill Reothe. He climbed down the ladder outside the fortress wall. Where was the Dhamfeer? A glowing cleft in the rock wall to the south of the pass caught his eye. The rebel leader was sheltering in a narrow, dead-end ravine, working his evil sorcery.

He ran, his feet flying over the uneven ground past a cluster of wiry mountain ponies which whickered nervously. Three rebels drew their weapons as he approached the glowing cleft. Behind them, bathed in unnatural light, Reothe knelt in a trance. Imoshen had been right. Reothe was vulnerable now.

The first bodyguard charged Tulkhan, sword raised. The General deflected the attack and went for his knife, but remembered too late that Imoshen had it. He grappled with the rebel, using the man's body to shield him from the other two. Furious with himself, Tulkhan caught the man's hand and turned his own knife back on him, throwing the rebel at the second attacker. The third darted in. There was no time for finesse. Tulkhan parried the blow, stepped inside his guard, and elbowed him in the throat, leaving him gasping his last.

The second rebel struggled free of his companion, ready to attack. It was a woman.

Tulkhan hesitated. She didn't.

She leapt forward, driving up with her weapon. He staggered back, blocking awkwardly. The uneven ground betrayed him and he went down with her on top of him. Before she could turn her blade to strike, he broke her neck. Casting her body aside, he came to his feet.

The element of surprise was gone, along with the eldritch glow. Reothe had woken from his trance, though he still seemed disoriented as he fumbled to draw his sword. His movements growing sure, he lifted the sword's point.

"She sent you, didn't she?" Reothe said, beckoning with his free hand.

"Are you really here this time?" Tulkhan slashed and was delighted to feel the impact of metal on metal as Reothe blocked.

The T'En warrior's free hand surged forward, bringing a slender knife into play. Tulkhan sprang back warily, circling his opponent. Reothe matched him step for step, a long, slender sword in one hand and a short knife in the other.

It was the T'En style of swordplay. Tulkhan regretted not testing Imoshen's skill to learn more about this technique. Though the slender sword was less able to deflect the slashing blows of his own sword, it had extra length and amazing maneuverability.

"She's playing a double game, Ghebite. Don't you realize it doesn't matter which of us lives? She will have it all in the end."

Tulkhan ignored Reothe's taunts.

He wished he had a cloak to wrap 'round his free hand or cast over Reothe to put that short dagger out of commission. He knew he could break through Reothe's defense, but not without risking the dagger.

"I took your son, you know, stole him before he was born—"

In that instant as Tulkhan tried to make sense of this, Reothe charged.

Instinct helped the General deflect the sword—his blade skidded up the shaft to strike the pummel—but he could do nothing about the knife. Twisting his body, he avoided the blow under his ribs to his heart, and took a wound in the abdomen instead.

Tulkhan's free hand closed over the knife's grip.

Reothe smiled and stepped back.

The General staggered, trying to keep his guard up. He knew that if this wound wasn't treated very soon he would bleed to death.

His hands and legs tingled. One knee gave way but he did not drop his guard.

"You are too much trouble to kill outright. I would like to stay here till you die, and watch the Parakletos take your soul, but I have to go. My people need me." Reothe studied Tulkhan's face from a safe distance, his expression strangely intent. "You can die knowing you did well, Mere-man. But you had no hope of winning."

He straightened and strode off.

Tulkhan shifted. A sharp jab of pain made him gasp. If he pulled out the blade or tried to move, it would speed up the bleeding. He could not stay here to die.

He blinked tears of pain from his eyes. The blood of the three defenders soaked the soil but there was no mist. Whatever dark sorcery Reothe had been working, it had faded when Tulkhan had distracted him.

Imoshen!

Even if she had turned the tide with the rebels, Reothe himself was coming for her. Tulkhan felt the stain of failure. Yet Reothe had said she would win no matter which of them lived. Then he heard Imoshen's voice assuring him that Reothe could tell the truth and make it sound like a lie, or a lie sound like the truth?

Tulkhan's vision blurred. He had to move. He couldn't.

He should have been there at her side to face Reothe. Despair, more painful than the knife's blade, scorched him.

Imoshen knew the moment Tulkhan confronted Reothe because the mist suddenly vanished, and with it the Parakletos. Once free of the mist's effects, the Ghebites had formed a solid core of resistance, their training coming to the fore. When the commander had asked for Tulkhan she had explained he had gone to defeat Reothe. But Tulkhan had not returned and Imoshen hid her dread.

Despite the disparity of numbers, the Ghebites held the rebels at bay. The battle could go either way. At that instant Imoshen looked up to see Reothe ride through the gate. The dawn breeze lifted his silver hair as he looked down on the struggle.

She knew as soon as the Ghebites saw him they would lose heart. If only it had been Tulkhan.

Darting forward, she pulled the commander back from the fray, pointing. "General Tulkhan has returned."

The commander's gaze followed her gesture and he saw what she willed him to see. He gave the Ghebite war cry. His men echoed it, calling Tulkhan's name and attacking with renewed vigor. The rebels faltered.

Imoshen looked up at Reothe. Even from this distance she could tell he was furious. She could almost feel the air between them crackle. Her breath caught in her throat.

Cradling the baby between her breasts, she encouraged the Ghebites. At that moment the rebels, discouraged, turned and ran. The defenders surged after them. But none of the Ghebites tried to stop Reothe as he dismounted and walked towards her.

Imoshen's stomach lurched. Her legs threatened to give way. Heart pounding, she stood her ground. The baby was a trusting being, oblivious to all threat and unaware of his vulnerability.

Reothe came to a stop within an arm's length of her. Imoshen could hardly breathe. She expected him to strike her down with one blow. She had no defenses against a T'En warrior who could barter with the Ancients and bind the

Parakletos to his will. She faced Reothe in the knowledge that now that he knew her loyalties he would kill her.

And what did it matter? Tulkhan must be dead. Otherwise Reothe would not be standing before her, eyes blazing. She had wagered everything on one throw of the dice and lost. The baby woke and struggled against her. She cradled his warm head, feeling his fragile skull under the powder-fine hair and skin.

Why did Reothe hesitate?

Perhaps he did not want to hurt the baby. How could she be so naive? He was the ultimate pragmatist. He would not hesitate to kill Tulkhan's son before the boy grew old enough to cause trouble.

A flood of fury engulfed Imoshen. No one would touch her child while there was still breath in her body. Reothe studied her, unmoving. Amidst the mass of fleeing, fighting figures, they were still.

"Very clever, Imoshen. This time you've won, but it is only a skirmish."

Tension sang through her limbs. She did not understand why he hadn't dealt her death blow.

"Tulkhan is dead," he continued. "Do you really want to stand alone against me?"

When she looked into his hard eyes she saw an image of Tulkhan bleeding but still alive. Imoshen's heart leapt with relief but she was careful to hide this from Reothe.

"Think on it, Imoshen, then come to me. I will not be so patient again."

He turned and walked unharmed through the Ghebites who were dealing with the injured rebels.

Imoshen sank to her knees, dizzy with relief. But Tulkhan lay out there, injured and alone. And if she knew Reothe, he was going back to deliver the killing blow.

Tulkhan! she cried silently, opening her T'En senses to search for him.

The merest flicker of his essence prickled on the periphery of her mind. She felt his fading strength. The General lay dying somewhere out there, without her.

As she ran out of the gate the Ghebites called after her, but she ignored them.

Tulkhan lay propped against a rocky outcropping where he could see the entrance to the narrow gully. Dawn lightened the sky so he could make out hazy shapes.

Once Reothe had secured the fortress Tulkhan expected him to send several rebels to make sure he was dead. His hand still grasped the sword but he did not raise it, preferring to save his strength. He would take at least one or two of them with him before Reothe's prediction came to pass.

He heard running boots, shouts. This was it.

But they ran on past him. He heard hoofbeats and suddenly a figure blocked the entrance. It was Reothe.

"Come to finish me yourself? I'm honored," Tulkhan grunted. He lifted the sword in greeting.

"You are a hard man to kill, Ghebite."

Stepping forward, Reothe drew his sword. Tulkhan knew the end was inevitable but he would not go quietly.

At that moment three of his own men charged through the cleft's opening. They looked from him to the rebel leader.

Reothe spun around, saw the odds, and hesitated. For an instant no one moved, then Reothe dropped his weapon and leapt. With amazing agility he scaled the almost sheer rock wall.

The Ghebites charged after him, but not one of them could climb the wall. They cursed fluently. Tulkhan looked up to see Reothe's boots disappear over the crest.

Tulkhan's men returned to him, taking in the extent of his wound. He saw from their faces that there was no hope. How had Imoshen and his men turned the tide of the attack?

Almost as if the thought had called her up, Imoshen slipped through the gap into the narrow ravine. She stepped gingerly toward him, muttering something about the stench of Ancient greed.

"We are too late. He's dying," one man told her.

"You forget who you're talking to," another said. "This Dhamfeer can heal."

When she crouched beside him Tulkhan noticed the baby asleep between her breasts.

"My son slept through it all?" he asked, his voice thick with equal measures of laughter and pain.

Imoshen smiled then inspected the General's wound. Her heart sank. There was blood on his lips, it bubbled with each breath—a very bad sign.

What could she do, exhausted as she was? She met the General's eyes. The sweat of pain stood on his greying skin but he looked at her with perfect faith. He trusted her to save him.

It was too cruel.

She took a deep breath. The stench of Reothe's sorcery was so thick she almost gagged, though the Ghebites appeared unaware of it.

Tulkhan coughed. It was a horrible sound. She could not, would not, lose him now.

She pressed her cheek to his chest where she could sense his heart laboring. The baby's weight made her back ache and she straightened.

"I failed you," Tulkhan whispered. "How did you defeat him?"

"No. You were victorious!" one of his men insisted. "When you appeared in the gateway the rebels broke and ran."

"I don't understand," Tulkhan rasped.

Panic seized Imoshen; his voice was fading.

Looking into his eyes she searched for a flicker of something she couldn't name. It was instinctive. Healing his grazed knuckles had drawn on his will, using only a small portion of her gifts, but this was a far greater healing. It would exhaust all her reserves, and this time Reothe would not willingly come to search death's shadow for her.

"When this is over, General, you must take me home."

"Of course."

"This could hurt."

"You think it doesn't hurt now."

That made her smile.

Closing her eyes, Imoshen called on the General's own fierce will. Whatever the cost, she would help him to heal himself.

It was the second hardest thing she had ever done.

Tulkhan woke from a disturbed sleep, his mind a jumble of half-remembered images—confronting Reothe, facing death, Imoshen coming to save him.

"Thirsty."

The cup that the bone-setter lifted to Tulkhan's lips held the sweetest water he had ever tasted.

That was when he looked up and saw the framework of the roof over his head, stark against an endless blue sky. Above him the men sang as they fitted wooden slates to the staves.

"Don't drop one on my head," Tulkhan tried to shout but it came out a croak. He pulled himself upright. "How long have I been asleep?"

"One day."

"Where is Imoshen?"

The man moved to one side and Tulkhan saw her asleep on a pallet in the far corner of the room.

"What, sleeping in the middle of the day?" Tulkhan laughed, rolling to his knees. The movement tugged at the pain in his chest, his muscles ached and his joints popped, but he was determined to wake her.

The man caught the General's arm, a warning in his eyes.

Tulkhan felt fear, by now a familiar companion. Forewarned, he crawled across the floor to kneel beside Imoshen. His son was asleep at her breast, her nipple still in his mouth. She lay completely still, her face pale.

He knew the signs, but this time he could not call on Reothe for help.

"How did this happen?"

"As the color came to your skin, she grew paler."

"But she is a healer. It's her T'En gift."

The man shrugged. "Maybe even she has limits. Remember, in Gheeaba a woman would not rise from her bed for one small moon after giving birth, or take on her normal duties for another moon. She would be waited on by the other wives and her baby brought to her for feeding.

"This Dhamfeer crossed the ranges barefoot. She walked a day and a night to get here. She reversed the night terrors when the fortress would have fallen—"

"Then she saved me." Tulkhan bowed his head. He had begun to expect the impossible of Imoshen.

The baby woke and opened his wine-dark eyes. His gaze traveled up Tulkhan's chest to his face. There was no greeting, no recognition in those eyes, just impassive interest.

"Here, General." The bone-setter lifted the baby. "You'll have to give him a name."

"A name?" Tulkhan had not thought of that, could not think of it when Imoshen lay so still. He would have to find a wet nurse. "Why is the baby still feeding from Imoshen?"

"The milk flows. She rouses herself to take a little food and water—"

"What!" Then it was not the same as the last time. There was hope.

As the bone-setter moved off to clean and change the baby Tulkhan grasped Imoshen's hand in his. He stroked her cheek. "Imoshen, wake up and tell me what to call our boy." Tulkhan grinned. His father would be turning in his grave. A Ghebite father always chose his son's name. "I can't call him babe forever."

He saw her lips move ever so slightly as if she would like to smile. Elation filled him. Stroking her pale hair from her forehead he leant closer.

"You can hear me. Is there anything I can do for you, get you?"

With great effort her lips formed the word, *Home.*

Tears of relief stung Tulkhan's eyes and he kissed her closed lids. "Rest easy, I will take you home."

They rigged a cover over the supply wagon and Imoshen traveled in that. Their progress was slow but Tulkhan was pleased. Every day Imoshen regained her strength and the baby grew.

The day before the Midsummer Feast they stood on the rise before T'Diemn. Tulkhan called a halt to the caravan and climbed into the wagon.

"We are home," he told Imoshen and lifted her in his arms so she could see. "There."

He watched her face as she stared across at T'Diemn. It was one of the loveliest cities he had ever seen. Its spires and turrets shimmered in the rising waves of heat.

Imoshen's face fell.

"What?"

She glanced away quickly. "The Stronghold is my home."

He understood. What could he say?

"Where is your home, General?"

He could never return to Gheeaba. He knew that now.

"My home is where you are," he said simply.

He saw her register his meaning. Her fierce hug warmed his heart.

She pulled away from him. "Since we are here we must make the best of it. The people will want to see us and our son, Ashmyr."

Imoshen had insisted they call the boy Ashmyr. She'd said T'Ashmyr had bound the island to him during the Age of Tribulation, uniting the T'En and locals alike; only the Keldon Highlands had resisted him. So Tulkhan's son was named after a T'En emperor. He did not mind.

"Do you think you should ride?" Tulkhan was uneasy. She had hardly so much as peeped outside the wagon except during their night camps.

"No. But you could carry me and I could hold the babe. The people of T'Diemn would like that."

When they arrived in the capital they received a rousing welcome. The populace was celebrating the birth of the baby and the rout of the rebels, which he was sure had grown in the telling. The townsfolk came out of their houses and shops to cheer. And they cheered loudest of all for Tulkhan's son.

"You won't reconsider?" Imoshen asked.

Tulkhan looked across at her. They were sharing a rare moment of privacy in the ornamental garden. Delicate blossoms hung from the trellis above them. It was a place of ethereal, dappled light and sweet scent.

Nothing in Ghebite society was valued for its beauty. They valued wealth, military power, but not pure aesthetics. In his brash youth he would have despised the waste of effort, but now he could only admire a culture which had time for the pursuit of beauty for beauty's sake.

"Now that we've hosted the Midsummer Festival, I must return to the south. The fortress controlling Greater Pass is almost finished, but I must complete the one sealing off the Lesser Pass before the harvest. Let the Keldon nobles winter in the ranges without fresh supplies."

"I don't like it," Imoshen stated. "It's a static defense. It gives the rebels a chance to study the fortresses, learn the patterns of your guards. In time they will spot a weakness and strike."

Tulkhan knew that. Tactically, Reothe could not let the Protector General finish the fortresses. All trade and large caravans had to use the passes. If Tulkhan succeeded in barricading the Keldon Highlands, it would be a blow to Reothe's reputation. His supporters would be prisoners in their own estates.

"I must go." He joined her on the seat. "I delayed only for the Midsummer Festival."

She looked down, playing with the baby's hands. Imoshen

never let the babe far from her side. He had noticed her waking at night to check on him.

"Your workers will be attacked," she whispered.

"I don't expect Reothe to disappoint me."

"What will you do without me?"

Tulkhan sighed. He knew that only Imoshen's gift had saved him and his men last time. Though she would say no more about that night, she often woke muttering in High T'En, her skin cold with the sweat of terror. And he recognized the High T'En word, Parakletos.

Oh, he needed Imoshen all right, but she would not leave the baby with a wet nurse.

"I won't risk you and the baby. You can defend yourself, but my son can't."

"I won't leave him behind." She rose, annoyance flushing her cheeks, and stepped into a shaft of dappled sunlight. The faint breeze played with wisps of her pale hair so that it seemed to have a life of its own. Anger and the stirring of her T'En powers exuded from her skin, making his heart race.

He ached for her but his bone-setter had warned him that there was good reason the Ghebite men did not touch their women for two small moons after the birth. His description of the injuries of an ordinary birth had horrified Tulkhan. No, he would not inflict himself on Imoshen until she was ready. But it had taken great self-restraint.

"You are my bond-partner," Imoshen told him, refusing to rise to the bait of an argument. "And though I respect your wishes, I will do what I believe to be right. I could not live with myself otherwise."

"Then we are at a deadlock," Tulkhan said and left her.

Imoshen watched him walk away. Only yesterday Ashmyr had looked into her eyes and recognized her. He had been born more than one large moon short of a full year, but she was not sure that her exertion and the danger she faced had not brought him on early. Even so, he was doing well and so was she. But while she had recovered physically, she felt more vulnerable than ever before. Reothe was so powerful he was willing to traffic with the Ancients and call on the Parakletos, at risk to his own soul. To defeat Reothe she had to discover his limitations.

The palace library was no help. She had to get into the Basilica and search the archives. Somehow she would translate the T'Endomaz and use the knowledge against Reothe. How ironic.

How cruel. He had given her the most valuable thing he possessed—his parents' last gift—and she would use it to destroy him. Tears stung her eyes. But it was her lot to face terrible choices, as it had been Imoshen the First's; she had bound her T'En warriors to her with oaths that went beyond death. How she had done this was probably told in the T'Elegos. Again Imoshen mourned its loss.

Putting such thoughts aside Imoshen stretched, arching her back. Tonight was her last night with the General. The soft tug on her nipple made her other breast run with milk. She pressed it to stop the flow. Her body tingled. She thought longingly of Tulkhan's rough hands. If only he would hold her. She was sure she could overcome whatever scruples were restraining his ardor.

Tulkhan sprawled on the bed watching Imoshen feed their son. He and his men were ready to move out. All that remained was this one night with Imoshen. He longed to hold her in his arms, but did not know if he could trust himself to do that without wanting more.

The baby fed eagerly. Tulkhan could hear him gulping milk.

He grinned. "My greedy son will get wind and keep you up all night."

"Oh?" Imoshen fixed him with teasing eyes. "So you're an expert now. I wager Ghebite men never care for their children."

"Not true." Tulkhan leaned against the headboard and linked his hands behind his head. "When I was six I left the women's quarters and joined the men's lodge. There I was reared by the men who served my father. They trained me in the arts of war, preparing me for my role as first son of the King's second wife."

He caught her watching him, her expression horrified.

"You mean you never lived with your female relatives after that? How sad."

Her reaction startled him. "Why?"

Imoshen shook her head. "No wonder Ghebite men think women are a race apart!"

She detached the drowsy baby and tucked him into the basket by their bed before moving to sit before Tulkhan. A drop of milk still clung to her nipple. He found himself staring at it, unable to think of anything else.

Imoshen rose to her knees, her breasts tantalizingly close to his face. "Are you thirsty?"

A shaft of urgent desire shot through him. Surely she wasn't suggesting . . . ? It went against everything he had been taught, yet it was so tempting. . . .

He tore his gaze from the full expanse of her creamy white breast. "Imoshen!"

She tilted her head, a smile playing about her lips.

"Is this how the women of Fair Isle act?" His voice was hoarse with the effort of denial.

Imoshen sighed and closed the bodice of her shift. "I don't know. It was never mentioned in my lessons on sharing pleasure with a man."

"You had lessons on . . . on—"

"Physical love?" Imoshen laughed. "Of course. Everyone does. At least all well-educated people. I don't know about the farmers." Her lips quirked. "I suspect their education is more practical than theoretical."

"How can you jest?" Tulkhan shifted across the bed, pulling the covers with him to hide his state. "Imoshen, that is unnatural."

"How can you say that? Didn't those men who reared you see to it that you learned how to lie with a woman?"

He could clearly remember them bringing a certain type of woman to his chamber when he was sixteen. It had been an

enjoyable lesson, one he partook of regularly until he joined
the army just after his seventeenth birthday.

Tulkhan folded his arms. "That was different."

"Different?"

For a moment he thought she was angry. Her eyes glowed
like jewels.

"Imoshen?"

"How can you deny me when it is plain for all to see
that you want me?"

The baby whimpered, responding to her tone. Imoshen
glanced into the basket, then looked back at Tulkhan.

"I don't understand you," she whispered.

He shook his head slowly. "Nor I you."

But it did not stop him wanting her.

"You will be killed," she cried suddenly. "Reothe wants
to lure you into the Highlands so he can murder you."

"What would you have me do?" Tulkhan reasoned. "If I
threaten the Keld to betray Reothe's hideout they will grow
to hate me. Yet I cannot let him undermine my hold on Fair
Isle. I have no choice."

"You go to your death!" Tears spilled down Imoshen's
cheeks. Her balled fists hit his chest, pounding, thudding in
time to his raging heart.

He caught her to him, pinning her arms against his
chest, and kissed her forehead. He had no more words.

He felt her body tremble, felt a responding shudder run
through him. He wanted her so badly.

He could feel her hot breath and the moisture of her
tears on his throat. His need to comfort her went core-deep.

"Make love to me." Her lips moved on his skin.

His arms tightened. "I can't. It would hurt you so soon
after the birth."

She laughed and pulled away from him. "I'm healed.
Besides, do you think I care about a little pain?"

"I will be careful."

She smiled and opened her arms in welcome.

Nineteen

THIS TIME WHEN the General marched out, Imoshen watched from the balcony with Ashmyr in her arms. The tenderness of her lovemaking with Tulkhan had left her aching for him, vulnerable to the slightest nuance of his voice.

Sorrow formed a hard kernel in her chest as he gave her a farewell salute. She must not think of what awaited him in the Highlands. As the last soldier disappeared from sight she turned away. There was much to keep her mind from her fears, not least of all discovering the limits of Reothe's powers.

Determinedly Imoshen made her way out of the palace and across to the Basilica. As she strolled, deliberately casual, through the great double doors with Ashmyr in her arms she was noticed by the priests. They clustered around her, delighted and honored by the visit, fussing over the baby, who watched them all with curious, unblinking eyes.

"So serious!" they laughed.

Imoshen's innocent request for a tour of the building was greeted eagerly and they were already halfway through the kitchens and storerooms when the Beatific caught up with them.

Imoshen knew the head of the T'En Church probably wished her anywhere but inside her bastion of power, yet protocol demanded she welcome T'Imoshen graciously.

"There could not possibly be anything to interest you in this section," the Beatific said. "Let me escort you."

Imoshen smiled. She knew the Beatific would not let her out of her sight, but that would not stop Imoshen meeting the Archivist and probing her mind.

"Our Basilica contains many great treasures preserved for posterity," the Beatific said smoothly, leading Imoshen away from her acolytes. "But first you must meet the leaders of each branch."

When the Beatific made a point of showing Imoshen the Tractarians' private chambers, she felt as if she had walked into a nest of snakes. One by one the mulberry-robed priests fell silent, turning to watch her. Murgon came to his feet and his gaunt face moved as he mouthed the words of welcome, but she read contempt in his eyes. Imoshen's skin prickled. This man was half T'En, yet he despised her.

"I will accompany you on the tour," Murgon said, offering his arm.

Imoshen took a step back, unable to hide her revulsion. She could not bring herself to touch him.

"That will not be necessary." The Beatific's smile finally reached her eyes.

Imoshen felt the color rise in her cheeks. Let them think her cowed by their display of force. It would make it all the easier for her to trick them.

The Beatific led her away, and after viewing countless trophies of war and tributes from long-dead mainland kingdoms, they came to the Archives.

Imoshen was careful to appear only mildly interested. The Archivist and several of her staff came forward.

"Welcome to the Archives of the Basilica, T'Imoshen," the Archivist greeted her. "I think you will find this library is even greater than the palace's."

While Imoshen pretended to admire the collection she searched for something neutral to focus their attention. A multifaceted glass sculpture was on display beneath a window. It converted pure sunlight into shafts of rainbow light.

"Fascinating. How does it do that?" The delight in her voice was genuine.

She crossed to the captive rainbow. Extending her fingers into it she watched the colors trickle over her pale skin.

"It is a prism, a child's toy." The Archivist placed a hand on the glass sculpture.

"We had no such toys in the Stronghold," Imoshen said, trying to use the tenuous connection between them to sift the woman's mind. She turned her hand over and over, feeling the light, feeling the outer edges of the Archivist's mind. She had never attempted this with so weak a link.

"That's because your Stronghold was one of the earliest built by your namesake, Imoshen the First. There was no time during the Age of Tribulation to indulge the senses. So many uprisings had to be put down."

Imoshen sensed the Beatific grow tense, but what could the woman do? Imoshen was not touching the Archivist. She had to keep the woman talking while she concentrated on finding out where the oldest cartularies were kept. They were the key to the T'Endomaz. "Because I was named after her I have always felt a kinship with Imoshen the First. It was such a shame the T'Elegos was lost when the palace burned down."

The Archivist smiled to herself. Imoshen felt her reaction as though it was her own. The Archivist felt superior because Imoshen was mistaken. The T'Elegos had not been lost. It was safely hidden in the Basilica, in this very chamber!

Imoshen's mind reeled. She froze, desperate not to reveal herself.

". . . Sardonyx's revolt of sixty-four," the Archivist was saying. "Some works predating the conquest did survive the sea journey, but they were lost to posterity along with the first Imoshen's T'Elegos. During the Age of Tribulation not only was the palace burned, but your Stronghold was sacked twice."

"What a shame," Imoshen said softly. When she felt she could hide the triumph in her heart she looked up and smiled. "I would like one of these prisms for Ashmyr when he is older. I think it would delight a child to make rainbows."

"Of course," the Beatific agreed readily. "Now, would you like to see the music wing where the choir will be rehearsing?"

Imoshen nodded, hugging her impossible discovery to herself. Joy and outrage mingled freely. She did not understand why the Church hid the T'Elegos from the people of Fair Isle but she knew she was so close to breaking the T'Endomaz encryption.

Even the arrival of Murgon and several of his Tractarians during the choir's rehearsal did not dispel her elation. They watched her suspiciously but there was nothing to see.

Despite her impatience, Imoshen bided her time until Intercession Day. It provided her best chance to slip unnoticed into the Basilica. Every fortnight the Church opened the disputation hall where anyone from a landless worker to the richest guildmaster was welcome to consult the priests trained in matters of T'En law and its interpretation.

If a disputation could not be settled, applicants then requested the assistance of a Church representative to present their case to the Empress for a decision. Consequently there was always a long line of petitioners awaiting hearings in the public rooms of the Basilica.

Late that afternoon Imoshen fed Ashmyr and strapped him between her breasts. She would have preferred to leave him safely in his little basket, but she trusted no one. The fear of the Ancients was always at the back of her mind.

Imoshen pulled up her cloak's hood and shuffled forward, blending with the crowd. She did not intend to use her gifts; that might attract Murgon and his Tractarians. Unchallenged, she moved past the public rooms packed with busy priests, each full of their own importance. Excitement powered her legs as she glided up the grand staircase. The first time she had seen its marbled balustrades she had been overwhelmed by its beauty, now she barely took in the glistening stone. Thanks to her guided tour she knew her way to the Archives, which were deserted on Intercession

Day. Her soft-soled boots carried her soundlessly across the mosaic floor.

She went straight to the false wall panel, recognizing it from the Archivist's memory. The woman had even supplied her with the knowledge to open the panel. Imoshen felt no remorse about her methods. As far as she was concerned the T'Elegos was her heritage. The Church had no right to hide it.

The baby stirred against her chest and she crooned softly under her breath as her fingers traced the design of the carved wood panel, which was inlaid with ivory and gold. In her mind's eye she saw the Archivist trip the mechanism and her hands mimicked the action. It felt exactly as the woman remembered. How strange to have the tactile memory of another person.

The panel clicked and the catch sprang open. Imoshen's heart leapt. At last she would discover the secrets her namesake had inscribed in the T'Elegos. She would know what Reothe knew, know his weaknesses as well as her own, and she would have the key to break the encryption of the T'Endomaz.

Sliding the panel across, she peered into the dusty vault. And blinked in astonishment.

Nothing?

Her heart missed a beat.

No, it could not be. The vault was empty.

Had she given herself away? Had the Beatific removed the T'Elegos?

Imoshen sank to her knees. There on the stone floor she could see the dust-rimmed outline where a single jar had stood. This corresponded with what she knew. According to legend and what she could glean from historical accounts, Imoshen the First had spent the last winter of her life working on a long scroll of vellum. She had been determined to preserve the story of the T'En travails for posterity and to honor the legendary T'En warriors who had died in her service subduing Fair Isle. Imoshen knew that the best way to preserve a single ancient scroll of vellum would be to seal it in an earthenware jar filled with oil to protect it from insects and damp.

The T'Elegos had almost been within her grasp! Imoshen's hands clenched in frustration.

Moving the jar could have been done secretly. But who would have taken it and why? Had the Beatific decided to change the hiding place? And if it wasn't the Beatific, who else would have the access and the motive? The Archivist certainly believed that the T'Elegos was still in its hiding place.

Imoshen straightened, her thigh muscles flexing with the added weight of the baby. Leaning against the wall, she stared into the empty vault. Her mind went blank and her vision blurred.

Candlelight danced on the walls. Someone stood with his back to her, rolling a heavy jar into position. He knelt to pick it up, turning toward her.

Reothe!

The vision faded.

Imoshen blinked, startled and dismayed. She had not meant to use her gift. Never before had she called up the image of an event merely by desire. But then she had never tried.

Reothe had stolen the T'Elegos! Anger stirred in Imoshen. He knew the T'Elegos had not been destroyed and he had hidden this knowledge from her. Had he removed the jar with the Beatific's approval or by subterfuge? She knew he was capable of slipping in here even more easily than she had done.

Why had no one at the Basilica discovered the loss of the T'Elegos? Imoshen had received the distinct impression from the Archivist that this document was too dangerous to read, yet too precious to destroy. For generations it had lain here, preserved in secret, keeping Imoshen the First's insights into the T'En mysteries safe from prying eyes.

Reothe must have given her the T'Endomaz knowing she could not unlock the secrets without the T'Elegos. As furious as she was with him she found it hard to believe evil of Reothe. Perhaps the T'Elegos contained information which could be used against the pure T'En.

Although she rarely came across it, there were True-people who hated the T'En. Murgon of the Tractarians for example. Imoshen suddenly felt vulnerable.

Backing out of the secret vault she closed the panel. Before she knew what she intended, she brushed the carved woodwork erasing all memory of her touch. Now no one with the T'En gift would be able to tell she had been here.

That made her stop. How had she known how to cover her tracks?

Simple logic had told her how to erase her touch. If these steps did one thing, then by reversing them she removed the traces. But before now her mind had not worked along such paths, and she had struggled to focus her meager gifts.

Softly she cursed herself—for perhaps she betrayed her presence. As far as she knew there was only one person who could trace her steps. Since when had Reothe become the enemy? When had he been other than the enemy? As for the Tractarians, they were only half T'En. Though they were trained to sense the use of the gifts, as far as she knew there was only one person who had the skill to trace her actions.

Imoshen made her way to the grand staircase. Suddenly she sensed danger. Sick dread filled her as she took in the cluster of purple-robed priests at the entrance. And there, wandering casually through the throng, was Murgon.

She had betrayed herself. Somehow these part-T'En traitors had sensed her presence. Murgon turned and looked directly at the staircase. Imoshen froze, willing herself to appear ordinary, then realized the very act itself was attracting Murgon. Terror killed all thought. Three intercession priests chose that moment to pass her, arguing loudly over a case.

Imoshen moved up the steps with them. From the balcony she looked down to see Murgon call two priests over and confer with them before heading towards the stairs.

She fled.

The Basilica was a sprawling rabbit warren and she had only a rough idea of its layout. She had to find the nearest safe exit. Opening her T'En senses she risked a quick search. The maze of passages and informal rooms assumed a three-dimensional shape in her mind as she sought for an escape route not guarded by the Tractarians.

Then she felt them questing for her. They were weak but they outnumbered her. Scattered like ants on a rubbish heap they picked their way through the dross looking for the source of power which drew them like honey. She might crush one or two but she could not stand against all of them.

Nausea rolled over her. She had endangered herself and Ashmyr for nothing. These Tractarians would find her and she had no excuse for entering the Basilica today. How the Beatific would crow!

Her T'En power rose to the surface, making her skin tingle and the familiar metallic taste collect on her tongue. She was aware of every individual tooth in her head, as well as the vast well of emotions emanating from the True-men and women in the rooms around her. Instinct told her to use her gifts to escape.

Slipping into a deserted storeroom she fought the impulse, reeling in her T'En senses, even though it left her feeling exposed. Without her gifts she could not tell where the Tractarians were, could not tell if they were closing in. Like a trapped animal she could smell her own fear.

Ashmyr stirred, whimpering in his sleep.

Leaning against the cold stone wall of the cluttered storeroom, Imoshen forced her breathing to slow down.

Lifting a trembling hand to her face she wiped the sweat from her top lip and listened intently. Far away she could hear the clatter of the great kitchen and smell the food being prepared.

The kitchen!

It was the perfect avenue of escape. The kitchen of any great establishment was always full of bustle, people coming and going, deliveries, flirting scullery maids and cheeky stable hands trying to steal freshly baked pies.

Hardly daring to think what she planned, Imoshen left the sanctuary of the storeroom. She followed the fresh scent of spices, baking meat, pickles, and preserves to the kitchen.

At any moment she could be discovered by a servant loyal to the Beatific and turned over to the Tractarians. . . .

What was she thinking? She had not been declared rogue.

No one but the Tractarians knew she was in the Basilica illegally. As long as one of them was not standing by each kitchen door she had a chance of escape.

Stepping into the shadow of a deep doorway she watched the flow of human traffic across the cavernous kitchen. With over a thousand people to be fed, the kitchen staff was an efficient army. People peeled vegetables, their heads down and hands flying over long preparation tables; others dragged loaves out of deep ovens, swinging around to slide them onto to cooling trays. The scent of the fresh bread almost made Imoshen gag. One of Murgon's priests stood by the far door. The workers averted their eyes when they passed her. Curiously, they seemed to dislike this priest. Did they dislike all Tractarians or just this one?

Heart pounding, Imoshen slipped away before the priest could sense her. Her hair, her eyes, her sixth finger all marked her for what she was. A surge of hatred for her pursuers overtook her.

Imoshen headed toward the familiar smell of soap and clean air. The laundry was deserted, the coppers emptied of their loads of washing. No one guarded this door for it led to an enclosed courtyard which contained nothing but flapping priestly garments drying in the sunshine.

A mulberry tabard caught Imoshen's eye and she suddenly had an idea. Crossing the scrubbed tiles of the laundry she entered the courtyard. No one was about. With a sharp tug she pulled a robe off the line, throwing it over her shoulders. She lifted the hood onto her head to hide her hair.

Mouth dry with fear Imoshen went inside. Now she noticed how the other priests avoided her eyes. It had not occurred to Imoshen that there would be a hierarchy within the priesthood, but under the circumstances she was grateful for it.

She crossed the floor of the busy kitchen, taking care to appear at ease with her surroundings. The Tractarian by the door met her eyes briefly. Imoshen willed herself to appear familiar, willed her son to be silent.

"No sign?" the woman asked in High T'En.

Imoshen realized they kept the old language alive to exclude others. She slipped into the language as easily as she had slipped into the Tractarian's robe. "No. I've been sent to check the carts."

"Good idea."

With one hand on Ashmyr she moved off, careful not to appear hurried. Once she entered the outer courtyard it was simple enough to follow one of the many delivery carts through the lane and out into the sunshine of old T'Diemn.

Imoshen felt light-headed with relief. This day had taught her a valuable lesson. She had more than one enemy within the T'En Church. If the Beatific was a cunning cat, Murgon was a ravening wolf, leading his pack in pursuit of her.

Walking steadily away from the Basilica she joined a crowd outside a teahouse then darted into a side lane long enough to remove the priestly robe. Without remorse she tossed it onto the rubbish a nearby shopkeeper had left burning. She stirred the coals until the material caught light. As she watched the robe burn she vowed never again to leave herself vulnerable to the Tractarians.

She had risked so much today—and for what?

Reothe had the T'Elegos. But she could wait no longer. Tulkhan was in danger and she must face the most difficult decision of her life.

Exhausted by her close escape Imoshen slept all afternoon and into the evening. Late that night she packed her traveling things. Then she debated over the wording of a message for Kalleen and Wharrd. She dared not give away her plans, but called on their friendship, asking only that they meet her at her Stronghold as soon as possible.

As she watched Ashmyr asleep in his basket tears blurred her vision. It was because she loved him so fiercely that she had to remove him from danger; for she believed the inevitable confrontation between herself and Reothe was fated to be her last.

She would not leave Tulkhan to die alone. She must stand at his side, and if by some miracle they survived, Kalleen would restore Ashmyr to her. However, if as she feared, she fell at Tulkhan's side, then Kalleen and Wharrd would know to flee Fair Isle. It demanded a lot of their friendship to ask them to raise her son, but if Reothe recaptured the island they would lose everything, their estates, their titles, and their lives.

Secreted in her family's Stronghold was a king's ransom in portable wealth. With her great-aunt she had collected and hidden it during the spring and summer of the Ghebite invasion, intending to use it to set free their relatives. Now it would be put to good use. With this wealth Kalleen and Wharrd could take Ashmyr and flee to one of the mainland kingdoms, far from Reothe's influence and the taint of the Ancients.

Safe and unknown, her boy could be raised in peace. When she saw them in person, she would tell Kalleen and Wharrd not to encourage her son to recapture Fair Isle. There was nothing to be gained by frittering away his life with fruitless revenge. No, she wished only that he be happy.

Imoshen smiled. Maybe when he grew to adulthood he would travel into the dawn sun and discover his T'En origins. But in truth she did not care what Ashmyr did as long as he grew up free of fear and Reothe. Imoshen folded the note and sealed it with a daub of wax and the pad of her sixth finger.

Unable to resist she knelt beside her sleeping son. Her heart swelled with love as she stroked his shock of fine dark hair.

"Merkah?" Imoshen looked up when the girl passed by with an armful of clothes. "I won't need anything so fancy, just my traveling things. And you'll need yours too."

"I am to come with you this time?" Merkah was still resentful.

"As far as the Stronghold. But before you finish packing, please send for Crawen."

"Yes, my lady." Merkah hurried away, eyes bright with curiosity.

Imoshen picked up her son, cradling his soft head against her cheek. She would not take him into danger. And she would only venture into danger once she knew that he was safe. If she and Tulkhan lost, she would never see Ashmyr grow up. He would never know how much she loved him. She felt his head bob against her cheek, his little mouth open, he was looking for another feed.

She held him away from her to memorize his perfect little features. Tears ran unheeded down her cheeks. He would never know what it cost her to give him away. Perhaps she should touch his unformed mind and leave a message there for him to find one day. No, she must let him be his own person. One day, Kalleen and Wharrd could tell him that his mother had given him up so that he would grow up free. She had to content herself with that.

"Crawen, my lady," Merkah announced.

Imoshen held out the message. "I want this to reach Windhaven as soon as possible. Deliver it into Kalleen's own hands."

The woman took the sealed missive. "Am I to wait for an answer?"

"No. I'm going to my Stronghold. You can escort Kalleen and Wharrd there."

Crawen smiled. "It will be good to go home."

Imoshen nodded but there was no smile in her heart.

Imoshen meant to leave early the next morning, but both she and Ashmyr woke during the night hot and fretful. Merkah talked of the spotted-fever which had swept through the children of T'Diemn. Though Imoshen had had it as a child, it appeared she was still susceptible to a milder version.

Rather than take her son on a journey when he was ill, Imoshen sat by his cot and bathed him, speaking softly to soothe him and using her gift to cool his body. All day he lay on the bed next to her, safely tucked in the crook of her body. As she tended to his needs she savored every moment, knowing she must soon give him up.

By evening he was cool and sleeping naturally. There was no sign of spots and her own fever had broken.

"Merkah?" Imoshen sat up, careful not to disturb the sleeping baby.

The maid paused as she tiptoed across the room.

"We'll leave tomorrow. There's no point in setting off this late in the day."

The girl nodded and left.

Imoshen tucked a pillow on each side of the baby then slipped into the bathing chamber to wash the weariness from her body.

Rubbing her damp hair dry, she entered the room to find Merkah beside the bed, the baby in her arms.

"He was stirring so I picked him up."

"Thank you." As Imoshen stepped forward she noted the glow of color in Merkah's cheeks. "Are you feverish?" Imoshen touched her forehead. The girl had the same fever. Strange, her mind was closed. Imoshen would not have thought Merkah had the strength of will to resist the T'En gifts. "I will mix you something—"

"No, I will use the herbs my mother used."

"I am a healer, Merkah, I know which herbs to use."

But the girl would not be swayed. Imoshen was not surprised. Some healers guarded their knowledge jealously. "Then get some rest and we will see how you are tomorrow."

But the next day Merkah was still feverish. She kept to her room, refusing Imoshen's offer of help.

Imoshen spent the day pacing impatiently. Now that her mind was made up, every day was an agony of waiting, but yet the longer she delayed the longer she had with her son.

Over the next few days Merkah's fever worsened. Imoshen could have left without her but she allowed herself the painful indulgence of prolonging this time with Ashmyr. Besides, it would take several days for her message to reach Kalleen and Wharrd, and they would need time to pack and travel to the

Stronghold. Imoshen longed to see the home she had been forced to abandon at an hour's notice last autumn.

It was a week before Merkah was finally well enough to attend to her duties, and Imoshen faced the fact that their leaving could no longer be delayed. She stared down at her sleeping son and her heart ached with love for him. She could not bear to think of giving him up but it was the only way to keep him safe.

Mid morning they set out with two servants and six of her Stronghold Guard who were happy to be returning home. Imoshen had not told them that she intended to leave them there and continue south to meet up with Tulkhan at the Lesser Pass.

They made good time and were soon into the woods. Imoshen smiled as Merkah frantically brushed away an insect which had fallen out of a tree onto her shoulder. Her maid was not a good traveler. It did not matter, Imoshen would be leaving her at the Stronghold as well.

As they traveled through the balmy summer afternoon Imoshen's heart lifted at the thought of going home. She would see how the Stronghold and the new town had fared through the winter, and show them her son. For the moment she allowed herself to think only that far ahead.

Trying to make the halfway point, the party rode late into the long summer twilight. Finally they came to the burned-out ruins of what had once been a bustling inn. Imoshen was surprised no one had taken up residence. True, there was no roof, and weeds had sprouted in the walls, but it was an ideal spot. Perhaps the people south of T'Diemn did not have the confidence to rebuild until this trouble with the rebels was settled.

Others had camped here before them and cleared out a hearth space, so they lit a fire on the stones and prepared the evening meal. Merkah seemed distracted. Twice Imoshen had to call her to bring something while she changed and fed Ashmyr.

Her companions sat back and ate their meals, talking

happily of the Stronghold, their friends, and families. Imoshen noticed Merkah sat alone, watching the darkness fearfully.

"You must not be afraid," Imoshen told her, growing exasperated with her timidity. "We are a long way from the rebel camps."

"True," one of the Stronghold Guard said. "But I have heard tales of Reothe and his people traveling far into the north while the Ghebites are busy building their fortress."

"There are many tales," Imoshen said dismissively. And there were. If you believed half of the reported sightings, Reothe would have had to fly from one end of Fair Isle to the other. "Get some sleep. We'll make an early start tomorrow."

Imoshen tucked Ashmyr into the crook of her arm and closed her eyes. The thought of losing her son haunted her. She gave up trying to sleep and reviewed her plans. Were they safe from attack?

Imoshen tried to weigh up the chances. To escape notice she had chosen to travel with a small group, and only her palace staff had known she was going. But there had been the delay due to sickness. They would have already been at their destination if first Ashmyr and herself, then Merkah, hadn't caught the fever. But she couldn't begrudge those extra days with her son.

Imoshen woke with an odd taste in her mouth. The larger moon was waxing and their campsite amidst the ruins was bathed in its silvery glow. She sniffed. The air had that strange tang which foretold a thunderstorm, yet the stars were clearly visible.

Stiff from the saddle, she struggled to her feet with the baby cradled in her arms. Her head was thick with sleep, only the sensation of something impending drove her to move. "Merkah, wake up. We must take cover."

Her maid did not stir.

Exasperated, Imoshen searched the sky. There was not a cloud to be seen. No storm. Then what . . . ?

Reothe vaulted onto the ruined stone wall directly opposite her, his silver hair glowing in the moonlight.

Twenty

YOU!" IMOSHEN HISSED. She tried to swallow, tried to warn her companions. "To arms. We are attacked!"

But her people did not stir and Reothe's people did not attack.

He jumped down into the shadows and prowled towards her, moving into the moonlight. Instinctively she covered the baby, pressing him closer to her chest. Fear closed her throat, robbing her of speech.

Frantically she kicked the nearest guard in the back. She grunted but did not wake.

"They are asleep," Reothe told her, his soft voice hanging on the still night. "And will remain that way until dawn, when they will wake to discover you have run away during the night to join me."

"No." It was a breathless denial.

He came to a stop before her and held out his hands. "Give me the baby, Imoshen."

Her heart sank. Selfish fool. If she had already given Ashmyr into Kalleen's safekeeping, she would have resisted Reothe with every fiber of her being, but as long as her son was vulnerable she dare not resist. Every contact with Reothe had confirmed that he was the master of his gifts and she the novice. She could not stand against him—better to play along with him and strike when she was sure Ashmyr would not come to harm.

Reothe smiled as she passed the sleeping baby to him. Turning Ashmyr's face to the light he studied the boy.

Imoshen could hardly think for the rushing of blood in her ears.

"So much black hair . . . but at least he is half ours," Reothe muttered. "Come, Imoshen."

He cradled the small baby against his body and held out his other hand.

She was too devastated to move.

"Bring his things and your own," Reothe ordered. "Do it, or I will walk off with him. I imagine even on his own he is enough to bring the General running—"

"I'm coming."

"I rather thought you would."

Numbly she collected their belongings. Reothe carried the baby and she followed him out of the ruins. None of her people stirred. They would assume she had gone of her own free will. Would Tulkhan believe them?

A dozen rebels mounted on wiry mountain ponies waited in the shadows of the trees. She could just make out their sturdy peasant clothes and weaponry.

Imoshen felt a lightening of the atmosphere as she stepped onto the road. As her head cleared she realized she had been betrayed. Someone had told the rebels her plans. With a sickening lurch Imoshen realized Merkah must have slipped them the herb which mimicked the fever, then taken it herself, yet Kalleen had recommended the girl.

Merkah had to be passing information for someone of influence. The Beatific. . . ?

"Wake up, Imoshen, your horse is waiting," Reothe chided.

She looked up to see him swing into his saddle. Taking the reins in one hand, he cradled the baby in his free arm.

Her empty arms protesting, Imoshen put her foot into the stirrup and swung her leg over the pony's back. She wanted to rail at Reothe, to plead with him to give back the boy, but she was in no position to bargain.

Reothe wheeled his horse. "Ride out. We will follow."

The rebels rode off and left her with their leader. Imoshen twisted in the saddle, confused. Reothe laughed and pulled a brass cylinder from inside his jerkin. He tossed it onto the grass outside the entrance to the ruin.

"What's that?"

"An invitation to your Ghebite lover."

His tone made Imoshen's skin turn to ice. Reothe was preparing a trap and she and the baby were his bait.

"What did you promise the Beatific in return for betraying me?"

But he gave nothing away. "Ride on, Imoshen."

She raged against her impotence but as long as Reothe held her son she would obey him.

During that long night Imoshen never left Reothe's side. She watched as her son slept peacefully in the arms of the man who had sworn to kill his father. A burning anger grew inside her. Not only had she been betrayed but Reothe was using her child as bait.

At first she paid no heed to the direction they rode, thinking only of escape. But then she noticed as the dawn chorus began and the sky lightened that they were headed north, not south. Trust Reothe to lay a false trail for their pursuers. They would be expecting him to return to his hideout amidst the loyal Keld.

Shortly after dawn the baby began to squall. Reothe halted and the others waited, watching.

"He must be fed," Imoshen said. She had been waiting for this. When Ashmyr was safely in her arms she would create a diversion, anything she could lay her gift on. While they were distracted she would gallop off. She had enough skills now to cloak her passage from all but Reothe, and if he followed her, well . . . she would find a way to kill him. She had to.

Reothe urged his horse closer to hers. "You are ready to feed him?"

She nodded, leaning forward. They were thigh to thigh.

She was eager to take the babe and her breasts ached in anticipation. Suddenly Reothe swung his free arm around her waist, dragging her off her mount. Frightened by the thought of him dropping Ashmyr, Imoshen twisted and clung to him.

She found herself sitting across Reothe's thighs as he passed the baby to her.

"Forgive me if I do not trust you, Imoshen," he said above Ashmyr's screams. "I want you where I can control you."

Then he laughed at her expression and urged his horse forward.

Reluctantly she undid the laces of her bodice. With the baby feeding hungrily at her breast she had no choice but to remain where she was. Reothe's arms encircled her. Holding the reins with one hand, he clasped her firmly to him with the other.

If she tried to struggle free and get to the ground, she risked dropping Ashmyr and being trampled by the rebels who rode with them.

The rocking motion of the horse and the relief of having Ashmyr in her arms again made her relax. They made their way through the deep woods, fording shallow streams where she could see every smooth stone on the riverbed.

As morning passed, Reothe made no attempt to return her to her own mount and she did not suggest it. Just holding her son was enough for now.

Her eyes felt gritty from lack of sleep. The dappled sunlight passed over them, alternately blinding her and warming her, then plunging them into a green-tinged twilight.

Her baby slept safely in her arms. She refused to sleep. She was so weary. She would not sleep.

Imoshen woke with a start, feeling something brush her face. It was dusk. Her cheeks burned when she realized she had slept in Reothe's arms. That would have amused him.

The others were already dismounted when Reothe swung

his leg over the horse, stepping down. He wound his fingers through the reins, effectively quelling any thought she had of kicking the tired horse to a gallop, and lifted one arm to help her dismount. She longed to shun the offer, but she was stiff from sitting in one position and didn't want to stumble with Ashmyr in her arms.

"Give me the baby."

"No. I must change him."

"I'll change him. You go with Selita and tend to your needs. You must be hungry."

When he said this she discovered she was ravenous. Already someone had started a fire. With great reluctance Imoshen handed her son to Reothe.

"This way." Selita was a farm girl much like Kalleen in size and coloring, but with the more pronounced Keldon accent. Imoshen could have overpowered her and escaped, but Reothe knew she wouldn't. While he held Ashmyr she would not leave the camp.

The rebel girl waited while Imoshen took the chance to refresh herself. She splashed cold water on her face and hands, willing her mind to clear. Then she looked up at the sky through the gap in the leaves, trying to get her bearings. They would have to turn south soon. The longer they stayed in the territory occupied by the Ghebites, the greater the chance of Reothe's band being captured.

When they returned, a foreign, spicy smell hung over the camp making Imoshen's stomach rumble.

Reothe sat with his back against the rock, his knees raised. The baby was wedged in an upright position, facing him. Wide awake, Ashmyr waved his arms around, tasting the air with his tongue.

Imoshen's heart turned over seeing her son so terribly vulnerable, a pawn in this endless game of power.

"Your share is there." Reothe indicated a bowl on the ground next to him.

Holding the bowl in her hands she found she could not eat, despite her hunger. "Give Ashmyr to me."

"He likes it where he is." Reothe rubbed the babe's

cheek with one knuckle. Ashmyr turned his face and sucked on the knuckle.

"I can't eat unless I hold him," Imoshen confessed.

Reothe's sharp eyes turned on her. She tried to smile but she could not hide the urgency of her feelings.

He frowned. "I did not know how strong it was."

He put his bowl aside and passed the baby to her. As she held her son, her body relaxed. Propping the bowl on her knee, she ate quickly as she fed Ashmyr, only too aware that Reothe was watching her. He seemed amused.

"Food's good," she said to distract him.

"It's a speciality of Amarillo's. He's from one of the lesser islands of the archipelago."

The cook tilted his head in her direction. Imoshen didn't want to know their names. She didn't want to grow familiar with these people whom she might have to kill.

But she nodded and smiled. "Thank you. Very good."

Reothe nodded. "Amarillo has served me since my first voyage. I bought him when his master was going to have him whipped—"

"Bought him?" Imoshen asked around a mouthful.

"Yes. Slavery is common in the archipelago. Each island preys on the others."

"I thought they made beautiful crafts, pottery, exquisite mechanical things."

"They do." Reothe glanced at her, then rolled with cat-like grace to his feet. "They also cut off their enemies' heads, shrink them, and hang them in their household temples."

As soon as Imoshen had eaten, Reothe ordered them to break camp. He held out his arms for the baby.

She handed him over, then climbed into the saddle, keeping close to Reothe's horse. Their thighs brushed.

"Such devotion," he purred. "What a pity it isn't for me."

A shiver of fear ran up Imoshen's spine.

They rode through the night, pausing at dawn for fresh horses. Imoshen watched Reothe closely but he never let her baby go, or passed him to anyone else. She had no choice but to follow his lead, still north.

Why hadn't he returned to the safety of the Keldon Highlands?

Tulkhan stood on the lookout tower of his fortress, staring down into the valley of the Lesser Pass. A single rider worked his way up the treacherous switchback path.

As the figure drew nearer, Tulkhan could see he was driving his horse at a reckless pace. His message must be urgent. Abandoning the tower, the General swung through the trapdoor and down the ladder.

"Open the gates. He's one of ours," Tulkhan ordered.

The gates eased open to let the horse and rider enter. His mount's sides were flecked with foam.

Tulkhan caught the exhausted messenger as he fell from his saddle. "What is it?"

The man thrust a cylinder into Tulkhan's hands. He tore it open, unrolling the thick paper. It was written in the common language of Fair Isle, but his mind refused to take in the meaning.

"Forgive me, General," pleaded the messenger. "Your wife . . . she ran away to join the rebel leader."

"She was abducted," Tulkhan snapped. He didn't recognize his own voice. The man flinched. "Reothe has laid down a challenge. It says here that I must meet him at Northpoint Harbor. It actually said that Imoshen and the child were with Reothe. Typically ambiguous.

"It makes no sense," the fortress commander muttered. "That's the northernmost harbor in Fair Isle, far from the rebel's territory. Why would he risk a confrontation there?"

Tulkhan shrugged. He had planned to man the fortresses in the Greater and Lesser Passes and so contain the rebels and insolent Keld. Pulling back his forces to face a threat in Fair Isle's north was an unwelcome complication. If the Keldon nobles sensed a weakness, they might join with the rest of Reothe's people and attempt to regain the capital.

In order to travel swiftly, he set off with a small band of men, planning to collect more in T'Diemn before he advanced further north. But he would not need an army.

The battle ahead was not of the physical kind.

Tulkhan ground his teeth. Imoshen was the key to Fair Isle but she was also as dear to him as the breath he took. Frustration and fear tore at him. Imoshen and his only child were in the hands of an unstable Dhamfeer warrior who would stop at nothing.

Selita peered through the steam. "Are you out of the tub already, T'Imoshen?"

Imoshen wrapped herself in the drying cloth. She was grateful for the chance to bathe in warm water, but finding herself a "guest" at Chalkcliff Abbey was disturbing. It was the largest abbey outside T'Diemn, and though the Seculate had been careful not to be seen, he was clearly aiding Reothe. Since he answered directly to the Beatific, Imoshen was left in no doubt where the leader of the T'En Church's loyalty lay.

She turned to Selita. "Your turn."

"I'll only be a moment." The girl discarded her clothes eagerly.

"Take your time." Imoshen finished drying herself, then fingercombed her damp hair as she walked into her chamber.

Reothe lay stretched across her bed playing with Ashmyr.

Making no attempt to hide her nakedness, Imoshen selected a fresh nightgown and pulled it over her head. Her hands trembled as she tightened the drawstring under her breasts then the second one at her throat. So as not to betray her nervousness, she took her time braiding her damp hair into one long plait.

Reothe watched her silently, his expression unreadable. When Selita entered the room wrapped in a cloth,

Reothe dismissed her. Imoshen wanted to protest but she held her tongue as Selita tugged on her clothes and departed.

It had been in a chamber almost identical to this one that Reothe had confronted her at Landsend Abbey. Reminding her of their vows he had urged her to join him and retake Fair Isle, but she had refused. Even as she thought this, the scar on her wrist tingled.

She hugged her left arm to her breast. "I am ready to feed the baby now."

"Come and get him."

Feeling his eyes on her, Imoshen walked stiffly across the chamber to the bed. Every nerve protested at his presence. From her pounding heart to her rapid breathing, her body recognized him.

Ashmyr lay on his back, contentedly sucking his fist. At least he had not suffered during their enforced march.

Imoshen scooped her baby up and backed away. She heard Reothe chuckling as she turned, heading for the chair by the fire.

"Is it that I am so terrible?" he asked. "Or is it that you don't trust yourself?"

She sank into the deep chair and loosened the upper drawstring, freeing her aching left breast. Ashmyr had only to feel the warm curve of her flesh on his cheek to realize what was coming. He latched onto her nipple.

"You need to ask, when you do not hesitate to threaten my child to control me?"

She heard the rustle of his clothes as he moved. Her skin prickled.

Reothe crouched down beside the chair. She looked away from him, into the baby's face.

"Don't hate me, Imoshen. I am only trying to protect what is mine."

His—as if he or anyone possessed her! She could not speak for her fury.

Reothe drew a sharp breath.

The urgent tug of the baby's sucking triggered the flow

of milk in her other breast. Before she could press her hand over the nipple to stop the flow, she felt a familiar tug.

Imoshen found Reothe's fair head at her breast. Her heart turned over. He had not pulled the material down, but between the heat of the milk and his mouth it felt as if the thin nightgown had melted away. His teeth grazed her nipple as she felt him draw on her aching flesh, triggering an arrow of sweet desire straight to her core.

A groan escaped her.

Her free hand sank into his silver hair, feeling its fine texture. She leant forward to experience that silken touch with her lips and inhale his scent. The melt began deep within her, dissolving her limbs, her will.

"No . . ."

"No?" He lifted his head, his lips glistening, his eyes hungry.

She felt her body respond, impossibly urgent. How could she expect him to understand when she didn't? "Reothe, please."

"No." He smiled. "Not till the moment is right."

A flash of anger ignited her. "I wasn't asking—"

"Yes, you were. I can feel how much you want me. It sears my senses. It always has."

She shook her head. She did not like to think what his admission revealed.

With the nail of one finger he circled the damp patch of material around her nipple. "You taste so sweet."

A clench of desire seized her. Unlike Tulkhan, Reothe would accept her for what she was. He would revel in her Otherness.

"Reothe, even if I desire you, you must know I have made a vow. I am Tulkhan's bond-partner."

"Only by necessity, and only after breaking your vows to me."

"Nevertheless, Tulkhan and I are bonded."

"Only till his death."

Her mouth went dry. "You mean to kill him."

"I won't have to. At most he would only live another

twenty years. Fifty is a good age for a True-man. But you and I have another eighty years or more." He leant closer to her, brushing her cheek with his lips. "Imoshen, don't deny what you know to be true."

She drew in a shaky breath, senses scorched by his nearness. All those years alone . . .

"You want me," Reothe whispered. His breath dusted her skin. "We would have already been together if the Ghebites hadn't chosen to launch their campaign last spring."

It was true. How different her life would have been if the Ghebites had attacked this year instead of last. Had she taken her vows with Reothe, she would have been standing by him to drive the invaders back into the sea.

"Yes, exactly," he breathed, watching her face. "Don't deny me, Imoshen."

Drawing a deep breath she met his eyes as honestly as she could. "True, I want you. I may even love you a little, Reothe. But I gave my vow to Tulkhan, as true a True-man as I have ever met. I am bonded till death parts us and I hope he lives another fifty years!"

She wanted to anger him. It was easier to keep her distance from an angry Reothe.

He lifted her free hand, stroking her bonding scar. "With me you can bond beyond death."

"No."

"I speak the truth. Test me."

He was offering to mind-touch with her.

She wanted it. It was awful to acknowledge how much. She had been so lonely, shut out by Tulkhan's resistance to her gifts.

Reothe smiled and leant closer. Imoshen gasped as she felt the first tingle of awareness brush the surface of her mind. But that forbidden fruit was too sweet to taste without risking her strength of purpose, so she shut herself away from Reothe, surprised to discover that she could.

"No. You may believe the T'En can bond beyond death, Reothe, but I do not want to end up like the Parakletos, a restless shade, bound between this world and the next. Besides, I gave my word to the General."

"You gave your word to a Ghebite, a man blinded by his upbringing, a man who does not understand your true value."

"Nevertheless, I gave the General my word."

"Under duress! Why does it always come back to this?" Reothe sprang to his feet. "Why do you find it so easy to break your word to me?"

The baby jerked in her arms, responding to his tone. She changed Ashmyr to the other breast, reminded again of Reothe's touch. Then she looked up to see him watching her, one elbow propped on the mantelpiece, a frown drawing his narrow brows together.

"You gave your word under duress, Imoshen. I know you believed you were saving our people from further warfare, but it is coming . . ." He stopped himself as if he was about to say more. "As for us. You gave your word freely to me but you cannot say the same for that Ghebite. To which of us do you owe your true loyalty?"

She pressed the fingers of her free hand to her closed eyes, weary beyond belief. Every word she said made things more tangled. With a sigh she looked up at Reothe. "There is no right, only survival."

A smile lit his face, igniting him from within.

"What?" She regarded him warily.

He crouched beside her, earnest and intense. "I'm glad you said it all comes down to survival. For I am also a pragmatist and I will do whatever I must to ensure the right outcome."

Imoshen went cold. That wasn't what she meant at all. Or was it?

Reothe stroked the baby's foot. Ashmyr's toes curled in response, eliciting a smile from the rebel leader.

There was a scratch on the door; a servant backed in carrying Imoshen's meal.

Reothe rose, stroking her cheek with casual affection. "Eat up. You will need your strength. We ride tomorrow—"

"South?" It was out before Imoshen could stop herself.

An impish smile lit Reothe's face. The more time she

spent with him, the more she realized he was not like other men. Did Tulkhan find her as fey and disturbing as she found Reothe?

"You will see." He left with a mocking grin.

The servant placed the dish on the table beside Imoshen. She dismissed him and tried the food. This time it was chicken and just as thickly spiced.

Reothe's words returned to her. He would stop at nothing to regain Fair Isle. Hadn't she vowed almost the same thing? She'd vowed that her children would rule Fair Isle. Now that seemed a hollow goal. If Tulkhan fell she would not hand Ashmyr over to Reothe to rear as his tool. She refused to live out her days as Reothe's puppet empress, with her son's life hanging in the balance. If Tulkhan fell she would have to flee Fair Isle. If Tulkhan fell . . . pain curled through her. It was impossible to imagine his brilliant mind and forceful personality obliterated. But he was as vulnerable as any True-man so she must face her worst fears.

How could she contemplate the General's death? Was she as bad as Reothe?

No. Unlike Reothe, there were things she would not sink to, such as invading people's minds against their will. But what of the Basilica's Archivist? That hadn't been against the woman's will, but it had been without her knowledge.

Imoshen sighed and licked the spoon clean. Was evil only a matter of degrees, only a matter of perspective?

According to different legends, T'Imoshen the First had been either a glorious savior of her people, or an ignoble invader who stole Fair Isle from its inhabitants.

In time to come, would Imoshen herself be regarded as a turncoat who betrayed the last of her kind, or a devoted servant of Fair Isle whose statesmanship saved the island from destruction? It all depended on who was victorious and wrote the history books.

She shivered. Reothe or Tulkhan? A True-man who had invaded a peaceful people for gain and now strove to unite them or a T'En warrior who would do anything to return the rightful rulers to power? Was there a difference?

And what of Fair Isle?

If only Reothe were totally despicable then she could hate him. But he was too much like herself. . . .

Imoshen stood with her baby snuggled in the crook of her arm. Completely trusting, Ashmyr had dozed off while she pondered their fate. A glow of pure love filled her.

Tulkhan glared at Kalleen as he tossed Imoshen's letter onto the table between them. "How can you claim you don't know what she wanted?"

The opinion of T'Diemn was divided, rumor ran rife. Half the townsfolk believed Imoshen had run off to join the rebels, the other half sided with the General, believing she had been abducted.

"I know as much as you, General Tulkhan," Kalleen bristled. "If you can read more into Imoshen's letter, let me know."

"When we arrived at the Stronghold she had already been abducted," Wharrd explained, a restraining hand on Kalleen's arm. "So we hastened to T'Diemn."

"Then I am no closer to solving the puzzle." Tulkhan retrieved the letter and smoothed the fine paper.

"What will you do, General?" Wharrd asked.

Tulkhan tucked the letter inside his jerkin. "Go after her and my son."

"But it's a trap!"

"Of course."

"I will go with you."

"And I," Kalleen spoke up.

Tulkhan saw Wharrd's face go grey. The bone-setter caught Kalleen's hands in his. "You carry our child. I can't risk losing you."

The familiarity of it made Tulkhan wince.

Kalleen smiled sadly. "If you fail I will lose everything."

Wharrd shook his head but she held his eyes obstinately.

Tulkhan knew Imoshen would do what she thought was right and he was almost certain that would not entail running away to join the rebels.

He had to believe in her. "I must organize my escort and plan my route," Tulkhan said, leaving Wharrd and Kalleen to sort out their differences alone.

He strode down the corridors of the palace, throwing open the doors to his maproom.

"General Tulkhan?" A servant paused in the other entrance. "The Beatific is here to offer her support."

He groaned inwardly. He did not doubt the Beatific was here to plant more insinuations about Imoshen's loyalty. "Send her in."

Tulkhan studied the woman as she approached the table. "Why does Reothe lure me north?" he asked abruptly.

She looked surprised. "I have no idea. I am not a tactician—"

"No?"

She had the grace to flush and look down.

Tulkhan tapped the town of Northpoint on the map, which was spread over the tabletop. "This harbor offers excellent anchorage for deep-draft ships and it is barely a day's travel from the mainland with the right wind. Why would Reothe ask me to meet him there when his noble supporters and rebel army are in the Keldon Highlands?"

"Perhaps he feels the Highlands are secure?" the Beatific hazarded.

"Could he be getting support from one of the mainland kingdoms?"

"The mainlanders support a *Dhamfeer*?" Scorn laced the Beatific's voice. "Why do you think none of them honored our alliances? They wanted to see Fair Isle humbled. And they fear the T'En."

It was all too familiar. He had once thought that way.

"That's what I suspected." He rubbed his chin, glad to be rid of the beard. "Then it comes back to *why*. What does Reothe hope to gain?"

"You are going to meet him?" The Beatific regarded him closely.

"Yes, I—"

"It is a trap."

"What Reothe doesn't know is that I have a trap of my own to spring on him." He noted the way her eyes widened but she remained otherwise impassive.

"Really?" she remarked. "How fortunate."

Tulkhan nodded and hoped the message would disturb Reothe when it reached him. His only regret was that he didn't have a trap at all—not yet anyway.

Early the next morning Tulkhan set out with a band of handpicked men and Kalleen, who could not be persuaded to stay behind. She had threatened to follow them, and in the end Wharrd had been forced to give in.

They could travel fast with only a small band. Commander Peirs was to follow as soon as he could organize a company large enough to quell any ragtag rebels Reothe might have gathered around him.

Tulkhan hoped Reothe expected him to move slowly north with his main army. In truth, he was prepared to move swiftly, strike fast, and get out quickly. At this point surprise was his only strategy.

He had lost his chance to seize the initiative by using Imoshen and the babe to lure Reothe out. In fact, the T'En warrior had turned the tables on him.

Tulkhan raged at his impotence. He would not sacrifice Imoshen and his son.

It was eight days since she had been abducted. Reothe's band might have reached Northpoint by now. The rebel leader had to be expecting support from one of the mainland kingdoms; otherwise, he would have gone to ground in the Keldon Highlands. Yet who would deal with a Dhamfeer?

Imoshen stood at the window looking down into Northpoint Harbor, where a single merchant ship lay on the glistening sea.

Ashmyr stirred and grumbled, so she padded back to him. Like her own Stronghold, the oldest part of Northpoint's defenses dated from the Age of Tribulation. Protected from

attack by the sheer cliffs below, her room at the top of the
tower was an ideal prison. Short of throwing herself to her
death, there was no escape.

The Ghebite commander who had briefly ruled
Northpoint had filled the Citadel with luxurious booty, no
doubt looted on his travels across Fair Isle. The bed was
draped with brocade hangings; jewel-bright carpets lay three
deep on the floor. Gilt-edged mirrors and paintings covered
the walls; crystal and fine porcelain littered every tabletop
and sideboard. It was so opulent it was obscene.

But he had not enjoyed the luxury for long.

She chose not to ask what had happened to him. He had
vanished along with his men. The servants were all loyal to
Reothe, and the townsfolk they had passed on their way had
seemed overjoyed to see the T'En warrior.

The baby whimpered. Imoshen picked him up.

"Can I get you anything, my lady?" Selita asked.

"The key."

Selita grinned impudently. She had overcome her initial
shyness. If the girl hadn't been her guard, Imoshen could
have grown very fond of her.

Selita lay sprawled on the rug before the unlit fireplace,
peeling a mandarin. Imoshen watched her, soothing Ashmyr
absently.

"I don't know why you are complaining," Selita remarked. "T'Reothe has forgiven you. He holds no grudge,
despite the way you've treated him. Before the Harvest Feast
you will be back in the capital as Empress of Fair Isle, and
my people's honor will be restored."

Imoshen's hand froze. The Harvest Feast was less than
two weeks away. How could Reothe hope to reverse the
Ghebites' advantage in such a short time? Her thoughts in
turmoil, Imoshen resumed rubbing Ashmyr's back gently.

Selita must have overheard something. She had said her
people's honor would be restored. She had to be talking
about the Keld. Imoshen could just imagine the stern matriarch Woodvine strapping on armor and riding into battle.
According to Fairban, the Keld were ripe for revolt. She

joined Selita and sat down, resting her back on a heavy chest. Casually she settled Ashmyr across her lap.

Selita tossed her plait over her shoulder and nudged the tray of fruit toward Imoshen.

"What pretty hair you have." Imoshen stroked the girl's braid. "I knew someone once who had just this shade of coppery hair."

It hurt her to recall Cariah. She had failed her friend. She must not fail her son or his father.

Selita rolled to a sitting position so she could face Imoshen. "Reothe said I wasn't to let you touch me. He said you would seduce me. Were you about to then?"

Imoshen shrugged innocently. "I've no idea what he meant. I don't have a fraction of the gifts he has. I'm only really good at healing. I was just going to offer to brush your hair."

She selected a mandarin and began peeling it. The skin came away easily and juice dripped down her arm.

Selita's golden eyes studied her thoughtfully. "You know, I'd trust you less if you pretended to go along with all this. But you make no pretense of wanting to be here. What do you see in this Ghebite General? Surely he can't compare with T'Reothe!"

The girl was impudence herself, but Imoshen made sure her face revealed nothing. She laughed and licked the juice off her wrist.

"What a question! What does any woman see in a man?" She offered a mandarin wedge to Selita.

The girl bit into the fruit and spoke around it. "But the General is only a Mere-man and you are pure T'En like T'Reothe. He will not bed a Mere-woman. He says it is but a pale imitation." Resentment tinged her voice. "What does he mean?"

"I've no idea." Imoshen ate a wedge. "I think he boasts!"

Selita giggled, then frowned. "You can't charm me into letting you go. I love T'Reothe. I think you're mad to refuse him."

"You can think what you like," Imoshen said. She offered

the girl another wedge, her concentration on the tenuous contact they shared. Already she could taste the mandarin's tang on Selita's tongue. "Tell me, how did you join the rebels?"

Selita hugged her knees and stared out the window. As she began her story Imoshen sifted through the upper layers of her mind, careful not to disturb the girl with her presence.

When Selita paused, Imoshen made the right noises while she continued searching for Reothe's plans. While much of Selita's mind was occupied with thoughts of Reothe, they were not the kind Imoshen found useful.

She discovered the rebel fighter resented her and was skeptical about her ability to satisfy Reothe. But it was hard to find an errant memory when the mind was thinking of other things. Perhaps she should ask Selita a question to trigger the right thought? She settled in, waiting for the right moment.

Suddenly the door swung open and Reothe stalked in. Striding across, he grabbed Selita by the arm, dragging her upright. "Get out, Lita!"

"Why? I've done nothing wrong," she gasped.

Heart thudding, Imoshen snatched up Ashmyr and scrambled to her feet.

"You little fool. She nearly had you!" He dragged the girl to the door, pushed her out, and slammed it after her.

Twenty-one

WHEN REOTHE TURNED to face Imoshen she backed off.

He advanced. "Put the baby down."

"No!" She held him closer.

"Put him down, Imoshen. You don't want him to get hurt."

She blanched. Silently she tucked her son into his basket.

"Come here."

"You can't bully me." But her heart hammered painfully as she stepped around the basket toward him.

"Closer."

"This is close enough."

A gasp escaped her as he covered the distance between them in one long stride. His hands grasped her shoulders. "That was very foolish, Imoshen. I could feel you using your gifts from the other end of the Citadel."

"Then why don't I feel you, when you use yours?" It was out before she could stop herself.

His eyes narrowed and he smiled slowly. "Why do you think? I am no novice. I cloak my gifts. Don't you try to turn Selita or anyone else into your tool. I'll feel it. I will stop you and it won't be pleasant."

Fear made her heart skip a beat. Did she want to force him to hurt her? No, better to . . .

"Good. I don't want to hurt you, Imoshen."

But she knew he would if he had to. She tried to divert him. "Whose ship is in the harbor? Why do they fly no flag? What will you do when Tulkhan gets here?"

"So many questions. Do you really expect me to answer any of them?" He tilted his head, watching her.

Imoshen noticed the tip of one of the snow leopard's scars peeping through the gap in his shirt.

"Why do your scars show when mine don't? Why did the leopard's claws mark us both when they only touched you? What price did the Ancients ask of you? Why do the Parakletos serve you when they resented serving me?"

His hands tightened on her shoulders. She thought she detected a flicker of fear in his eyes. Then he pulled her closer, till their bodies touched, thigh to thigh, her eyes level with the end of his nose.

"If you would only trust me, Imoshen. I would share my knowledge with you." His arms encircled her. She wanted to back away but she felt an irresistible pull towards him. His breath tickled her face, as his fingers stroked her hair.

His voice was rich velvet rubbing across her skin. "Trust me, Imoshen."

A soothing, sweet warmth flooded her. It would be so easy to accept his lure. He promised everything, his love and the gift of knowledge. Together they could unfold the mysteries of the T'En.

But the price was too high.

"Trust?" Bitterness tightened her throat, thinning her voice. "That is a strange thing to ask when you threaten my son, when you hide so much from me. You give and take in the same breath. How can I break the encryption of the T'Endomaz when you have the key? I know you stole the T'Elegos from the Basilica."

His eyes widened and he laughed with delight. Then he shook his head sadly. "The T'Elegos does not contain the key to the T'Endomaz."

She ignored this. "The T'Elegos is my heritage too. Where have you hidden it?"

Immediately she felt him think of the hiding place—a cavern appeared in her mind's eye. Then the thought was shut down like a door slamming closed, so that her mind reeled with the impact and everything went dark.

When the blinding pain eased she found herself lying across the bed with Reothe kneeling at her side.

"Are you all right?" he whispered.

She nodded and winced.

"I told you it would hurt if I used my gift to limit yours."

Tears stung her eyes. She would not cry in front of him. "I had to try."

"Imoshen!" The despair in his voice made her flinch. He pulled her into his arms, stroking her hair, pressing her cheek to his throat. "When will you stop fighting me?"

There was no answer to that.

She felt him lower his head and inhale her scent. "Only three more days," he whispered brokenly.

She stiffened. Three days till Tulkhan got here? Three days until Reothe murdered him?

"Reothe, I was thinking . . ." Shakily she pulled away from him to kneel on the bed, taking one of his hands in hers. "What good is Fair Isle? It is just one small island. You have ships and loyal followers. Why stay here to battle for an ungrateful land? Why not go east into the dawn sun. I've always wanted to see our homeland. There must be more like us. You could . . . Why do you look at me like that?"

His hand slipped from hers as he swung his legs off the bed and strode to the semicircle of windows. The setting sun's rays gilded his fine features and pale hair. She could see the tension in his shoulders as he gripped the sill.

"You must know the truth, Imoshen. We are outcasts. We have no homeland." He did not turn to face her and his voice vibrated with contained pain. "You know that Imoshen the First brought her people here, but you don't know there were three ships. Two did not survive the crossing.

"Our ancestors weren't refugees or brave explorers, Imoshen. There were old people, women, and children on those ships. They were outcasts, selected for their T'En traits. I have read the first Imoshen's own account of their flight and the reasons for it. Terrible things happened in the name of the T'En. The people could no longer suffer us to live. They banded against us, they offered us death or banishment."

"No! It is a lie!"

"I have read the T'Elegos, written in her own hand." He turned to her, glowing with the intensity of his emotion. "The T'En are fallen angels."

"No. You must have misinterpreted the T'Elegos. High T'En is designed to carry many shades of meaning. And even . . . even if Imoshen the First's people were banished for some reason, it has been more than six hundred years. If you were to make the journey to our homeland beyond the dawn sun, they would not deny us—"

"You don't know what I know."

"How can I when you hide everything from me? Why did you give me the T'Endomaz and where does it fit in?"

He hesitated. "I believe the T'Endomaz is the hidden lore of the T'En. During the Ages of Tribulation and Consolidation the young pure T'En left their parents at ten years of age. They were taken by a pure T'En mentor who trained them in their gifts. I believe the T'Endomaz is the very book they would have been trained from."

Imoshen moaned. "Why didn't you tell me? Why not share the T'Elegos with me? Why hide it?"

"I didn't hide it from you. The leader of the Tractarians hates me, Imoshen. I saved Imoshen the First's history from Murgon's prying eyes." He grimaced as though even the man's name tasted foul.

She could easily believe Murgon hated him. "But why?"

Reothe shuddered. "When I was a boy of ten, raw with the suicide of my parents, I was sent to the palace to be reared by the Empress. Because Murgon was four years older and related through my father, she gave me into his care. We took our lessons with the royal heirs, explored the palace and attended functions at their side. We were being groomed to become royal advisors.

"Murgon was mad for T'Ysanna and she used my adoration of her to keep him at a distance. He took out his spite on me. At first it was little cruelties which might have been accidents. But he grew bolder until I was nearly killed by a jest gone wrong. He startled my horse, causing it to throw me. The Empress must have suspected because she arranged with the Beatific to have the Church request his services.

"I thought that was the end of it. We gave him gifts and he was inducted into the priesthood. But he bided his time. The day before the Harvest Feast he forged a note from Ysanna asking me to meet her in the underground passage we had discovered below the portrait gallery. When she did not appear I tried to leave but found the door locked. What with the festivities no one missed me for two days. And then when they did begin searching they could not find me.

"I wandered alone in the dark without food or water. I tried all the false panels I could trigger until I discovered the catacombs. To be sure I could get out I wedged the entrance open with my shoe."

Imoshen's gasp made him pause, but she quickly indicated he should go on.

Reothe smiled wolfishly. "If only he knew, Murgon did me a favor. I believed I was dying. I lay on the slab like legend says T'Sardonyx did, and said the words for the dead, for my soul. The horror of it triggered my gift and I left my body behind. The Parakletos came, some curious, others resentful.

"The Parakletos found me wandering lost in death's shadow and led me back to this world. In my dealings with them I have learned all is not what it seems."

"You said they have no power in this world."

"They don't. Some are filled with a thirst for revenge and will try to steal your soul, others pity the True-men and women they escort into death's realm." He shook his head sadly. "Woe betide the caller who summons them without the will to withstand them!"

"Yet you say they were kind to you?"

His sharp eyes met hers. "Did I say kind? One day I may tell you what passed between us before they returned me to this world."

"So they returned you to the catacombs. How did you escape?"

"By then Ysanna had revealed our dangerous games and the underground passages were being searched. When they found me I had been lost for five days. The Empress was furious. But I did not reveal Murgon's role. For one thing I had no proof—Ysanna's note had disappeared—and for another Murgon had been transferred into the Tractarians. Anything I said against one of their number would have been suspect. Besides, I thought that was the end of it." Reothe grimaced. "I was wrong. When the old leader of the Tractarians died, Murgon was named the successor. He promised to make them a power once more and they loved him for it.

"For most of the Age of Discernment the Tractarians' strength had been fading. The only living pure T'En was your great-aunt and she was no threat. But with my birth they began to lobby for more resources, more priests. There is nothing like a threat to make True-men and women band together. In any other branch of the Church, Murgon's T'En characteristics would cause suspicion. He joined the Tractarians because he saw it as a route to power. As their leader he meant to discredit me.

"But when the old Beatific retired I made sure I had the new Beatific's ear. I had picked her for her potential, had been cultivating her for years." Reothe smiled across at Imoshen. "Politics. I can see you despise the power play, but you must learn to use it for your own survival as I have done. Murgon and his Tractarians fear us. What True-people fear, they destroy."

"You speak as if we were at war with True-people."

"Except for the occasional Throwback like you and I, the Church has almost succeeded in wiping us out. For centuries they've kept us in ignorance. What right did T'Abularassa have to rewrite our history? She and Imoshen the First's own daughter, the Beatific, deliberately hid the T'Elegos. They used the T'Enchiridion to bind us to serve them. I heard how you gave your Vow of Expiation. What crime have you committed that you must ask for expiation?" He stepped closer to search her face. Though he did not touch her, the force of his presence made her body thrum.

Reothe held her eyes. "Do you know how lonely it is to live in a palace full of True-people and know that while they laugh with you and love you with one breath, they could turn on you with the next and stone you to death? A decree from the Beatific is all it takes to declare one of us rogue."

So that was why he had "cultivated" the Beatific. Imoshen could understand his instinct for self-preservation. "But the last rogue T'En was stoned over a hundred years ago," she objected. "True, Murgon is a fanatic, but this is, or was, the Age of Discerment—"

"Discernment? Age of Denial more like!" Reothe exclaimed. "They thought we had died out. They had your great-aunt cowed. They claimed to be enlightened because they believed us a spent force."

Imoshen shook her head. "Who is this *They*? Besides, it is different now that the Ghebites—"

"Hate us. The Ghebites are more dangerous than you realize. They despise us because we are not True-people. And look at what they do to their own women!" He gestured in frustration. "What if the current Beatific were a man instead of a woman? What if the Beatific and the Ghebites joined forces? Who signs the decree to declare a T'En rogue? Imoshen the First chose celibacy, but who enforces the practice. The Church. The Church represents the True-people. *They* are our enemies, yours and mine."

Imoshen shook her head. Fair Isle was her home, its True-people *her* people.

Reothe prowled away. He paused by the mantelpiece, staring into the cold fireplace. "Light a fire, Imoshen."

She blinked. "Light it yourself, the flint is there."

"No. I mean *light* it."

She understood. A frisson of excitement made her skin prickle. "I don't know how."

"Oh, come now. You nearly had Selita enthralled and you weren't even touching her."

The prickling of her skin increased. She looked at the pyramid of wood arranged in the hearth. All it needed was a spark. A stinging sensation snapped behind her eyes and when she opened them little flames consumed the kindling.

Delight flooded Imoshen. She darted over, kneeling before the fire to admire her handiwork.

"Very nice," Reothe said dryly. "Now you see why they want to wipe us out."

"But it was only one little spark!"

"It only takes one spark to start a fire."

Fear chilled Imoshen's flesh. She wanted to deny the truth of his words but could not.

Reothe held her eyes. "Mere-men and women kill what they fear."

She thought of her people cast out of their homeland, then persecuted in their new island home. "I must read the T'Elegos. Are you sure you interpreted the old language correctly? Its meaning can be ambiguous."

He laughed. "Yes, my little scholar. Remember that first time you quoted High T'En to me? I wanted to hug you. But you would have run away."

"Nonsense!" But he was right. She had been wary of him, fascinated yet frightened by the force of his personality.

He sighed. "All along our timing has been out. If only you had been older, we would not have had to wait so long for our bonding. We would have been bond-partners when the Ghebites attacked. The Empress would have—"

"*Would* have, *could* have! It's too late to talk of what might have been!"

"You are right." Reothe whispered sadly.

The last of the sun's setting rays faded, casting the room into darkness except for the flames of the fire. Imoshen felt as if she had traveled a lifetime since Reothe sent Selita away.

He took one of her hands in both of his. "I promise

when all this is settled we will read the T'Elegos together. Somehow we will break the T'Endomaz's encryption. You can't stand against me, Imoshen. Stand at my side, my equal in every way."

Her heart turned over. She trembled as she pulled her hand free of his. He called her his equal yet he had deliberately kept her in ignorance. And when Reothe spoke of sharing the reins of power it was incumbent upon Tulkhan's death. She shuddered. Nothing, not even Reothe's promise of a shared T'En heritage, could make her sacrifice the father of her child.

Imoshen touched Reothe's face, felt the lean line of his jaw. "Second cousin, last of my blood kin, last of my kind, don't let this war consume you. Sail east. Provision your ships and make your way via the archipelago. You know those islands, the land beyond—"

"And you'll come with me?"

She let her hand drop, startled by the prospect.

"I jest, Imoshen. I would not ask it of you even if you said yes. It is not something to be attempted lightly. The sailors of the archipelago don't venture east. They say to go into the dawn sun is death." He gestured. "Imoshen, ask yourself, it has been six hundred years, why haven't we had visitors from the land beyond the dawn sun?"

It was a good question. She tried to read his face. "You tell me."

"I don't know," he answered with simple honesty.

"Then why don't you sail into the dawn sun? It would be a glorious adventure—"

"Don't patronize me, Imoshen. And don't try to influence me with your gift."

"I wasn't." But she was. Even as she said the words she had instinctively added a push, willing him to feel her enthusiasm.

"No?" he pressed with a half smile.

Again she felt that dangerous attraction and would have pulled away from him but he caught her hand, lifting her arm to press his bonding scar to hers.

"It is you and I against the rest, Imoshen. For the moment the Ghebites accept you. But I heard about the stone lovers. How long before they cease thinking of you as their pet Dhamfeer and begin to fear you? How long before your General smothers you in your sleep and drowns his half-Dhamfeer pup—"

"No!" She sprang away from Reothe, heart thudding. Tulkhan would never do that.

Her tone made the baby stir and cry. At the same instant there was a scratching at the door.

"Enter," Reothe called, then lowered his voice. "Don't fool yourself, Imoshen. I am your only true friend because we share the same enemies. Our goals should be the same!"

She turned away from him to retrieve Ashmyr from his basket.

"T'Imoshen's food." A servant waited with a tray.

Reothe gestured for him to enter as he lit the candles.

Imoshen wanted to send the meal away but she would need her strength for what was to come. In three days Tulkhan would arrive and somehow she had to . . .

"Bring it here, please." She sat down by the fire.

"I'm going to send Selita to you," Reothe said when the servant had left. He did not need to warn Imoshen against trying to influence the girl.

She ate slowly, methodically. Today she didn't even taste the delicious spices.

Reothe lingered. His hand brushed her shoulder. A tingle of awareness moved across her skin. It was the overflow of his T'En gift, questing for an opening, a welcome. But Imoshen closed herself away from him, knowing that he was probing for the mind-touch. It hurt her to shut him out, as much as it hurt her to know Tulkhan had shut her out. But she remained obdurate.

Grimly Reothe sighed and left.

The events of the afternoon made Imoshen's head spin. She could still see Reothe gilded by the sun, declaring they were fallen angels.

Wearily she returned the quieted baby to his basket, her

mind reeling with the implications of what she had learnt. Reothe had asked who deserved her loyalty. Tulkhan and the True-people of Fair Isle, or Reothe and the T'En? She had three days to decide.

Tulkhan estimated they would have another day's hard ride before they approached Northpoint. His people were tired. It was midafternoon and they had been riding since dawn. He was weary himself but driven by the knowledge that every step brought him closer to Imoshen and his son.

"General?" Wharrd called.

"Yes?" He knew they should stop to eat and let the horses rest, but he was loath to delay.

Wharrd said nothing, his expression eloquent.

"Very well, first likely spot we'll take a break."

He could almost feel their relief. Little Kalleen never complained and consequently none of his men dared to grumble.

"Down there?" Wharrd asked. He pointed to a single fishing hut halfway up the hillside, far above the pebbly beach.

Tulkhan recalled this place from his campaign last spring. There had been a whole village here bustling with life before his people attacked. In the first small moons of the campaign they had been brutal, wiping all resistance before them. The little fishing huts built to withstand storm had offered no protection from armed men.

Tulkhan experienced a twinge of regret. He'd had no argument with these innocent fisherfolk. He had simply decided to take Fair Isle and had unleashed his army. The island was too ripe a plum not to pluck. For the first time Tulkhan faced the unpleasant truth. Reothe stood on the moral high ground. The T'En warrior was only defending his homeland, his heritage. His betrothed? No. Tulkhan believed Imoshen loved him.

"General?" Wharrd pressed.

Tulkhan reigned in his wandering thoughts. "Very well." He turned his mount toward the beach. The others followed. He needed to approach Northpoint undetected to find out where Imoshen was being kept. A tight, well-coordinated raid might succeed in freeing her. But it was exactly what Reothe would expect of him, that or to lay siege to the town itself.

Tulkhan noticed the fisherman's boat pulled up beyond the high-tide mark. Reothe would expect an attack from the land, not from the sea. But they would need more than one boat. . . .

Imoshen paced the length of her chamber, unable to relax. Her decision was made. Fair Isle was her home and its people were her people, no matter what their race. She would continue Imoshen the First's work and see the pure T'En race accepted by the True-people.

Sometime today the General would reach Northpoint, and when he did, she would stand at his side, against Reothe.

Selita had fled after lunch, complaining of a headache. Reothe had been in twice to check on Imoshen, but refused to answer her questions. He simply satisfied himself that she was not up to anything and left. Like her, he could feel the tension in the air, the heavy foreboding of a thunderstorm about to break. It made her teeth ache.

Sensing her anxiety, Ashmyr had been fretful all day.

Imoshen stood at the windows of her prison staring down at the harbor. The evening stars dotted the emerald sky. She frowned, counting the ships. Another two had arrived with the evening tide.

She hadn't seen Reothe since midafternoon. For all she knew Tulkhan might be attempting a raid on the eastern wall of the harbor town at this very moment, their battle cries carried inland on the sea breeze.

Imoshen returned to the chair by the fire and fed herself and her son. Tonight was the best time to attempt her escape. Hopefully Tulkhan's arrival would distract Reothe and keep him too preoccupied to monitor her for the use of her gifts.

Imoshen went through her normal routine, even putting on her nightgown and sitting by the fire with Ashmyr's basket at her feet. But her body burned with restlessness.

She had to find a way of giving Tulkhan an advantage, but first she and Ashmyr had to escape Reothe. Time to test him. He was not all-powerful. He had to have a weakness.

Settling her body into the chair she forced herself to relax. Monitoring her breathing she was aware of her heartbeat slowing. Her T'En senses spread out until she could feel the servants in the lower rooms bustling about, clearing up after the evening meal.

Her perception was only minimal, just a general sense of purpose with no individual personalities rising to the surface. Could she manipulate one of these people, make that person come up here on some errand? She'd never attempted anything like this before but she was desperate.

First she had to select someone who seemed susceptible. Maybe a probe to test . . .

She felt it! The sharp flare of Reothe's perception. He was coming for her. Gasping, she retreated, reeling in her awareness until she had nothing but a True-woman's senses. She strained to hear his footfalls along the corridor. Heart pounding, she waited, dreading the inevitable confrontation.

From her brief contact she had felt the formidable strength of Reothe's will but he also seemed preoccupied.

He was already in the corridor.

Imoshen must distract him, soothe his suspicions. She began unraveling her plaits, her heart beating rapid as a snared bird's.

Reothe scratched on the door.

She had to clear her throat before she could speak. "Enter."

She glanced up, feigning calm. Reothe strode in and came to an abrupt stop before her, ignoring the baby at her feet. Waves of tension rolled off him. His narrow nostrils flared as he inhaled, his eyes narrowing. "What have you been up to?"

Though it cost her, she continued to unravel her hair, ignoring him.

"Imoshen?" he pleaded.

Startled, her gaze flew to his and connected. Why did he look so strained? All her healing instincts told her he suffered mental anguish.

"What is it?"

His lips parted, then he shook his head and strode to the fireplace. He stared into the flames, his back to her.

Imoshen came slowly to her feet. "Has General Tulkhan come?"

"Why?" He turned sharply. "Do you sense him?"

"No, I . . ." She shrugged, not about to reveal that the General had forbidden the mind-touch. In closing himself away from her he had prevented her contacting him even in an emergency like this. "No, you said three days and it has been three—"

His bitter laughter cut her short.

Unnerved, Imoshen could not read Reothe's mood, but she could sense the danger of his gifts barely restrained. She dared not provoke him.

The silence stretched between them as he stared at her. Reothe was T'En, but, tonight, vulnerable and troubled. He was . . . Other. It called to her.

A heat dawned in her center, creeping through her limbs. Imoshen felt her face flood with betraying color. Reothe's lips pulled back from his teeth. She knew he could sense her arousal.

She turned but there was nowhere to run. Still, her feet carried her to the windows. The sea breeze cooled her cheeks, lifting the loose strands of her hair.

Her hands closed on the cool wood grain of the windowsill. Across the bay each ship was a small self-contained world illuminated by lanterns. If only . . .

"No you don't!" Reothe's hands closed on her shoulders.

She could feel him down the length of her body. He radiated heat, tension, and purpose.

She focused on the bobbing lights in the bay, the sea breeze, anything but his need for her.

His breath brushed her ear.

She tilted her head to avoid it, but the melt continued deep inside her, the call of her body to his, answering his unspoken need.

His hands tightened. "Tell me to go away."

"Go away."

"Cruel, your head tells me one thing but your body tells me another." His voice rubbed across her senses like raw silk. "If the Ghebite General had not come, we would have been bonded. Life would have been sweet for us. Can't you see it, Imoshen?"

At his insistence she could. Visions appeared before her—the pair of them riding together, poring over the T'Elegos together, deciphering the T'Endomaz. A well of longing, long suppressed, opened within her. Reothe would accept her T'En self. He would put no limitations on her gifts. For him she simply was. She saw herself meeting him on the deck of a ship. She carried a small fair-haired baby, and when Reothe's arm lifted in welcome she went to him as she was meant to.

"Don't plant visions in my head!"

"Don't insult me. I see the same visions myself. Sometimes they fade and I fear one of us will die. At other times they grow so strong I forget where I am and think you are with me—"

"Don't! I don't want to know." She did not want to acknowledge his vulnerability, his need for her. It would weaken her resolve.

"We were meant for each other, Imoshen." His voice dropped. "We are the last of the T'En. It is time to save our people. I want to gather all those with T'En blood. I want to create our own T'En Hall of Learning where we develop our abilities and share what we have learnt.

"Our race would no longer be a source of anxious curiosity, worshipped in one breath and feared the next. In every village there would be a T'En healer. Every bonded couple who produced a child with T'En traits would consider themselves blessed. This is my dream and I need you to help me make it possible."

Imoshen bowed her head. The pain caused by her Otherness which had always set her apart, the unspoken jibes, the fear and awe which had come to mark her interaction with other people, all this mingled inside her. Reothe's vision would imbue her differences with a holy purpose.

"We will renew Fair Isle. It will be the renaissance of the T'En, the Age of the T'En. Do you dare to dream with me, Imoshen?"

She tried to think clearly. Instinct told her Reothe was sincere. He wanted to redeem the fallen angels, to create a golden age. But she feared the power he promised. "True-people—"

"Need us. It is in their nature to look for a higher authority. Why should we be hunted down and eradicated like vermin? I have lived on the outside too long. Join me, Imoshen. Restore the T'En."

She drew a ragged breath.

It seemed to draw his hands upward from her shoulders. His fingertips traced the line of her throat where he must have felt her pulse racing. No doubt it pleased him to know how he moved her.

She felt the heat of his body down the length of hers, knew that he desired her. The gentle pressure increased, insistent, eager, demanding.

Anger stirred in Imoshen. "I will fight with the last breath I take—"

"Why? When we both know you want me. Your T'En gifts perfume the air. I could feel your desire from across the room. Your scent intoxicates me. Even as I speak you tremble."

"With rage!" It was too much. "You bring me here against my will, hold my son to ensure my co-operation, then think I will welcome you into my bed?"

Furious, she spun to face him. His jaw clenched so tightly she could see the hard knobs of muscle. Good. Let him storm out of here in a fury. Or better yet, let him strike her so she could hate him.

He stepped back, coldly furious. "You back yourself into a dangerous corner, Imoshen. You leave me no choice."

Her heart plummeted. She glanced uneasily at the slumbering baby. But Reothe turned on his heel and stalked toward the door.

She wanted to call him, to ask what he meant to do. Biting her tongue, she contained her fears.

Before he opened the door Reothe turned to face her. "I'm placing a special lock on this door. If you try to force it I will know."

She nodded her understanding.

He stepped through the open door then looked back, an odd expression on his face. "You had your choice. Next time we speak things will stand differently between us."

The door closed and Imoshen sank to the floor, pressing the heels of her hands into her closed eyes. Reothe meant to move against her. He would capture Tulkhan and kill him while she was trapped here.

Without moving, she probed the door. Nothing disturbed her senses. If she could only identify the T'En lock Reothe had fashioned, she could disarm it. Suddenly a sharp white pain stabbed into her unshielded senses.

Tears bled from her eyes. Blood roared in her ears. Shivers shook her body. It was a force she could not escape. It chilled her to the bone. She had to get warm. Hardly able to see, Imoshen crawled to the bed and pulled the covers up.

Pain obliterated her will, leaving her anxious only to escape the pressure inside her head. She gave up the unequal fight and lay gasping on the bed, waiting for it to pass.

As abruptly as it had started, it stopped, leaving her wrung dry, too weak to lift her head. For a long time she lay there, tears seeping from her eyes onto the pillow.

She was useless. She had tried and failed.

So fragile did she feel that she dared not even probe beyond this room. Any attempt might trigger the pain.

Twenty-two

TULKHAN CLAMBERED UP the rope ladder to the deck.
He knew the merchant captain of this ship owed no
allegiance to Fair Isle; for him this would simply be a
business transaction. Once Tulkhan had hired this vessel they
were assured of an escape route. This ploy *had* to work.

He felt that familiar mixture of fear and excitement
which preceded a battle, the knowledge that he faced death
with only his wits and skill. But this time he did not face a
True-man.

Reothe was expecting an attack from the land. If Tulkhan
had been willing to wait a few more days, Commander Peirs
might have provided one and created a diversion, but the
General wanted to move before their presence was discovered.

Once their escape route was secured, Tulkhan planned
to enter Northpoint with a select band of men. The port
was full of sailors, a few extra would not be noticed.

Informants had told him Imoshen and his son were
locked in the Citadel's tower. He had even seen the light
of her window, impossibly near yet so distant. Below it
was a sheer drop to the rocks. If it had been possible he
would have scaled those sea cliffs, but he was not an accursed
Dhamfeer warrior.

Instead, he planned to infiltrate the Citadel, free
Imoshen, and slip away. He was gambling that Reothe would
be concentrating his defense on the town's perimeter, leaving

the Citadel's defenders relatively unprepared. But if his band was detected Tulkhan was prepared to fight a pitched battle back to the wharfs and escape by sea.

As his feet hit the deck a sailor greeted him in a thickly accented version of the trading tongue.

"Captain's waiting below."

Tulkhan had dealt with Lowland merchants to ensure safe passage for his army to Fair Isle, and knew he would have to haggle. Those Lowlanders had no god but gold.

He followed the sailor down the steep steps and along the narrow corridor, ducking the beams as he went. The small cabin door swung open and he stooped to step through.

The captain's chair was empty.

Before he could free his sword they jumped him. With no room to maneuver he staggered. Hands closed on his throat, others tried to wrest his half-drawn sword from his fingers. Driving himself backwards he smashed into a wall, crushing the man on his back. The pressure on his throat eased.

With an effort he shook off the one who hindered his sword arm and was about to draw it for a telling blow when a flash of blinding pain clouded his vision. He fell to his knees. His arms buckled and a boot hit his ribs as he pitched forward. His breath escaped in a helpless groan.

"Don't hurt him," a familiar voice warned. "I want him unharmed—"

"You tell *him* that," someone muttered.

Tulkhan blinked as he was rolled over. A blinding light seared his eyes, a branch of candles. No, just one candle, but Reothe held it.

"This will hurt more if you resist," he told Tulkhan conversationally.

Of course he resisted.

Reothe's free hand splayed over Tulkhan's face. He tried to keep the T'En warrior out, then he was falling through the back of his skull. Falling, falling . . .

.   .   .

Fighting nausea, Tulkhan sagged against the wall. It was cold and metal bands hurt his wrists.

Voices. Hated laughter.

". . . trust him to put up a fight," the Vaygharian said and laughed again.

Tulkhan blinked. The Vaygharian was aiding Reothe?

He tried to focus on the face opposite him. It was definitely Kinraid.

"What are you doing here?" Tulkhan's voice was raw but clear enough.

"He's aware," Kinraid announced.

Reothe stepped into view. He studied Tulkhan critically. "He'll heal in a day or two. You can tell your master I've delivered him as I promised. Now he must honor his part of the bargain. I want those mercenaries."

"You'll get them. They're waiting to sail across. With the weather and tides the way they are, it will take two days for them all to disembark."

"Then send your message."

Kinraid gave a slight bow and left.

"So you've sold me?" Tulkhan asked. "Who would want me that badly?"

"Why, King Gharavan of course. He'll try you for treason before he executes you," Reothe explained. He lifted a bowl of water sprinkled with crushed herbs. "I'm not a healer like Imoshen, but—"

"Why bother?" Fury and sorrow swamped Tulkhan. His own half-brother had colluded with this vile Dhamfeer to betray him!

Reothe shrugged and stepped closer to bathe the blood from Tulkhan's head. His hands were cool and competent. A droplet of water trickled down Tulkhan's neck and inside his jerkin.

"You nearly succeeded, True-man. I wasn't expecting an attack from the sea. Luckily my people are vigilant." Reothe pressed a dry cloth to Tulkhan's head and held it there. "You should have killed Gharavan when you had the chance—"

"Do you have a brother?"

"No."

Tulkhan grimaced. "Then don't presume to judge me."

Reothe tilted his head to study him. "You are right."

Tulkhan was taken aback. He glared at Reothe. He wanted to hate the Dhamfeer.

"Are you afraid to kill me yourself?"

"That would be a waste. You're worth more to me alive, in exchange for trained soldiers I can use to crush your leaderless men."

"Beware any mercenaries my half-brother sends. They will serve his purpose, not yours," Tulkhan snarled.

Reothe smiled. "Unlike you, I don't make the mistake of underestimating Gharavan's treachery. Mere-people are an open book to me. They come to serve me for wealth; in the end they will serve me for love. Love is more powerful than fear." He stepped back to put the bowl and cloth aside, then turned to watch Tulkhan. "No. I don't need to kill you. Besides, why should I make a martyr of you for Imoshen to mourn when your own misjudgments will be your downfall?"

Tulkhan winced, believing Imoshen would despise him. He was as good as dead.

Reothe stepped closer again. Tulkhan saw his nostrils flare as he inhaled.

"I smell no fear on you. Why don't you fear me?"

"I don't care how much you mock me." Tulkhan swallowed. Failure left a bitter taste on his tongue. Although he faced death, it wasn't his own fate he cared about. "Just don't hurt Imoshen and the boy."

Reothe almost smiled. "That is too sweet. You see, the boy already belongs to me. I touched his mind before he was born."

Tulkhan tried to hide his anguish.

He was aware of Reothe's curious gaze on him. Why was he studying him so closely, as if genuinely interested in his reactions?

"As for Imoshen . . ." This time Reothe did smile. "I can't hurt Imoshen." He saw Tulkhan did not understand.

"Have you ever wondered why the men and women of Fair Isle share everything equally, from ownership of wealth to political rights?"

Tulkhan shrugged. He didn't want a history lesson.

"Have you come across this arrangement in any other land?" Reothe persisted.

Tulkhan shook his head.

"Why are the women of your homeland slaves to their men?" Reothe asked, sounding like one of Tulkhan's childhood tutors, patient, persistent.

"Slaves?" Tulkhan stiffened. "I . . . I suppose it's because the women are not as strong as the men."

"Exactly." The T'En male watched him closely, waiting. "The strong always rule."

Surely Reothe could not mean what Tulkhan thought he meant?

"Did you think the balance of power in T'En society sprang from some obscure altruistic motive? No. Power is wielded by the powerful." Reothe stepped closer, his wine-dark eyes sparkling with inhuman amusement. "Imoshen does not know it. How could she? It was all written in the T'Elegos, but T'Abularassa hid our heritage.

"Her pure T'En cousin, Sardonyx, went rogue, demanding the information in the book be made public. There was an uprising in T'Diemn itself. The palace burned. T'Abularassa claimed the T'Elegos had been destroyed. She and the first Beatific hid it. Eventually I discovered where. An ambitious priest helped me gain access—"

"The current Beatific."

Reothe glanced at him consideringly. "Yes. She has been very useful."

Tulkhan wasn't going to let him gloat. "If Imoshen is more powerful than you, why doesn't she know it?"

"How could she?" Reothe smiled. "No one knows. Pure T'En females have always been celibate by law. I thought it was to stop them having pure T'En children, because the males of the line don't breed true with any but a pure mate."

"Imoshen told me her T'En gift was healing. She fears your gifts!"

Reothe nodded. "People fear what they don't know. But my gift is this."

He brushed his fingers on Tulkhan's forehead. The sensation was a cool breeze ruffling his thoughts, strangely refreshing, if unnerving.

"Mind skills. I can make people believe they are hurt. I can guide people to heal themselves. I can bring them what they most desire. But it is all illusion. Already Imoshen outstrips me. It has been a gamble all along to keep ahead of her. When I heard . . ." He stopped and looked at Tulkhan. "Imoshen the First forbade pure T'En females to breed because it brings on their gifts. With the growing babe the power grows. So it was they and not the men who ruled our homeland. It is that residual power which still runs our society. The Beatific, our last Empress, and the women who rule the guilds, they seek power and don't realize whom they have to thank for it. Even now, Woodvine of the Keld awaits my signal to lead the nobles against your men in T'Diemn. She is but one in a long line of strong women."

Reothe fell silent, his thoughts turned inward. Tulkhan watched him, fascinated despite himself.

"Why do you tell me all this?" Tulkhan asked.

Reothe smiled sweetly. "Because you are as good as dead, Mere-man, and I thought you would appreciate the irony of knowing you always had it within your power to destroy me, if only Imoshen had understood her own potential. It is her mistaken belief that I am more powerful than her that allows me to control her."

Victory had been within his grasp all along? Tulkhan wanted to rage at the unfairness of it all, but he shut his eyes, vowing he would not give the rebel leader the pleasure of knowing how he felt.

When he opened his eyes, he saw Reothe's frank sympathetic expression and he knew his enemy understood only too well.

"Do you like to watch me suffer?" Tulkhan snarled.

"Yes. Part of my gift is the vicarious enjoyment of emotions, the more intense the better."

"You're insane!"

"No. Just different." Reothe leant closer.

Tulkhan wished his hands were free; spread-eagled in chains he could do nothing but glare at the Dhamfeer.

"I think I have enough now. I just need one more thing, taste." With that Reothe licked Tulkhan's throat, lingering in the hollow near his ear.

Anger vibrated through the General's body.

Reothe stepped back and gave an odd little formal salute. "I thank you."

Tulkhan wanted to ask him what Reothe thanked him for, but he dreaded the answer.

"Wait," he whispered. "I have a question."

"Ask."

"The night you came to the palace and saved Imoshen . . . If you aren't as gifted as her, how did you—?"

"You ask, don't blame me if you don't understand. I have some knowledge of death's shadow." Reothe repressed a shudder as he undid the laces of his shirt. Parallel ridges scarred his chest. "I used my gift to anchor myself in you. If you only knew it, we are closer than blood kin. And I borrowed from an outside source."

"A snow leopard . . ." Tulkhan had seen those same marks on Imoshen. "But how?"

"Imoshen and I are bound in a way that you and she can never be. I have trafficked with the Ancients and compromised my principles because of you. You threw my plans into confusion." Reothe pulled the laces tight. "Power exacts a price and there will be a price to pay for regaining Fair Isle, but I'm willing to pay. My people have been persecuted too long. Imoshen and I will introduce the Golden Age of the T'En and you will be but a memory. You damned yourself the day you stepped on this island. It was already mine but I wasn't ready to move. You forced my hand."

Tulkhan said nothing.

Reothe shrugged. "Think on it, Mere-man. You were

in the wrong to invade a peaceful island. I am only redressing that wrong."

"I'll escape if I can," Tulkhan warned. "I'll tell Imoshen about her gifts and I'll see you dead!"

Reothe gave a mock bow. "I would expect no less."

Tulkhan watched him climb the ladder out of the windowless cell, taking the only light with him. Alone in the cold dark Tulkhan faced his own mortality. And he cursed the day he made Imoshen swear not to use her gifts on him.

Imoshen woke to find a hand on her mouth and a body pressed to hers in the darkness.

She recalled huddling in the bed crippled by the mental blow Reothe's lock had dealt her. Sleep must have overcome her. She glanced over to the fireplace but the baby had not stirred.

"Imoshen?"

"Tulkhan?" Her heart rejoiced in his familiar scent, the rasp of his whispered voice. "How did you get in here?"

"I slipped in by sea. They're all out watching the entrances to the town."

She nodded. That made sense, and Reothe's lock was to keep her in, not someone out. Hugging him she ran her fingers through his silky, dark hair. "I missed you so much. I never thought to see you again."

His lips were achingly familiar, his kisses so sweet. She wanted to drink him in. Tears of joy stung her eyes and slipped unheeded across her cheeks. He kissed them away, as loving and gentle as she knew he could be.

His ragged breath spoke of such longing she could only respond to his touch. An impossibly savage surge of desire ignited her. They had been parted, faced death, and now were united. It was only natural to want him like this.

"Wait, we must escape—"

"Everyone's gone, watching the roads." He caught her hand, guiding it inside his shirt. She could feel his pounding heart under her fingers. Her own heart thudded erratically.

His free hand undid the drawstring on her gown and pulled the neckline down. His palm pressed over her heart. She covered his hand with hers, just as she had done that morning when they swore their bond. She felt her heartbeat steady to thud in time with his. Words weren't necessary.

Silently she tugged at the laces of his breeches. When he moved to take over she pulled her nightgown above her head and tossed it aside, looking up to see him magnificently naked before her in the light of the larger moon.

Extending one hand she drew him down onto the bed and pulled him to her. Tomorrow they might die but tonight they had each other. She wanted him fiercely and wanted him to know it.

He hesitated. She welcomed him with a subtle tilt of her hips. When she felt him fill her a shudder of repletion shook her. His body trembled in sympathy.

It was beyond her control. Her body's needs overcame all thought. Her lips sought his, their breath mingled. The urgency in him spurred her on. If only he would let her touch his soul. She longed to make that final contact.

Threading her fingers through his hair she drew his face to hers.

"General," she whispered, "if we die tomorrow, know that I love you."

He froze. She felt his fingers dig into her shoulders. His hands moved up through her hair as his mouth took hers. It was a brutal kiss, but she welcomed it because she wanted to shut out everything else, to imprint this moment forever.

Again tears burned her eyes and her throat grew tight.

Then she felt it, the faintest whisper of cool contact, brushing the fevered plains of her mind.

Impossible. But it was there and she recognized that sentient sensation. Dawning panic took her.

Like a great blue-white sun, she felt Reothe's essence rise above the horizon of her perception. The mountains she built could not keep him out and he blazed forth across her mind, searing her with his presence.

Turning her back on that intense coolness, she tried to escape.

Wordlessly he sought her. Imoshen, let me love you.

It was a plea from the heart. It demanded nothing.

She was already caught.

A spasm of desire rolled through her. She lost the perception of where her body ended and his began. Rippling waves of passion built around them, sweeping her ever closer to the edge, driving her to clutch him as they were swept over.

When she found herself again, she clasped him close. He was her only solid point in the chaos of her heightened perception.

Stunned, she turned her face away and the tendrils of intermeshed awareness parted, prickling all over her body. At last he was just a cool, soothing presence in the dark stretches of her mind. There was no room for thought, no words for what she had experienced.

Time seemed to stretch. He demanded nothing of her, seemingly content to linger in contact. And she, who had never known the intimacy of such contact, marveled.

Was this what it was meant to be like with one of her own kind, a sharing of complete trust?

But he had tricked her.

She tried to ease away from the mental contact. He held on, passive but determined. Fear made her heart lurch and he reacted with a soft breeze allaying her fear.

"Reothe?"

He covered her lips with his fingers, cool, calming, calculating.

Calculating?

Then she felt it, the familiar pinprick as new life flared within her. It was a tiny starburst of sensation so intense she gasped.

She felt his flash of triumph. Fury engulfed her. She chased him down a long tunnel. His blazing essence escaped her and his own walls sprang up. This time she pulled back before she hurt herself. The transition was so abrupt her head reeled with impressions and nausea threatened.

"Imoshen?"

But already she had scrambled across the bed away from him.

"Imoshen, don't do this."

"You tricked me!"

"Yes. The drug was in the food, disguised by the spices. It was three days until the night you were fertile, not three days before your General arrived. His arrogant Ghebite pride won't let him accept you once he knows you carry my child."

"It was him I took in my arms, not you!"

"Not in the end."

That was true. A flood of sensation rolled over her, memories so intense she gasped. She felt raw. "So this is what you promised?"

He was a pale form glowing on the bed. In her heightened T'En state all surfaces gleamed with an inner radiance.

His hands lifted in a pleading gesture.

"You did wrong to trick me, Reothe."

"Sometimes you must do a little wrong to achieve a greater right."

She snorted, rejecting this utterly. Chaotic impressions rushed her.

"Reothe!" Imoshen pressed her hands to her closed lips, fighting nausea as her head filled with sensations. "What's happening to me? I feel strange."

His touch was reassuring. She sank into his arms and he cradled her against his chest. The unnerving sensations passed. His cool essence was so calming she had to fight to remind herself he had betrayed her.

"Oh Reothe," she whispered, "why did it have to be this way between us?"

Tulkhan lifted his head and blinked. The single candle flame seemed brilliant after the dark.

It was Reothe again, descending the ladder.

"Come to gloat?" Tulkhan tried to goad him. Anything

was better than hanging here like a piece of butchered meat waiting to be served up to his half-brother.

Reothe crossed the stone floor and stepped close, wordlessly offering the inside of his wrist to Tulkhan, holding it just below his nostrils.

"Do you smell her on my skin, Mere-man?"

As he said it, Tulkhan experienced a flash of jumbled sensations. He felt Imoshen's body under his, felt her quicksilver passion ignite.

He wanted to deny them, but the impressions were too vivid to be a lie. Devastated, he turned his face away.

"The next time you see her, know this: she carries my child. As her true mate I have awakened her T'En potential. Whatever she may have felt for you will be colored by this. Once she might have loved you, but can you bear to be pitied?"

It was the final blow. A groan escaped Tulkhan.

"Accept your fate, General," Reothe whispered, satisfaction strong in his voice. "You were outclassed."

Stepping back Reothe called, "He's ready."

Tulkhan turned to see several armed rebels descend the ladder.

"It is nearly dawn," Reothe told him. "At the Vaygharian's signal from the cliff-tower Gharavan's ships made a night crossing with the wind behind them. There is only the exchange to get through, General, then you go home to your people and die."

Suddenly Tulkhan was overwhelmed with a longing to see the brilliant sun of his homeland, the brightly dressed people in the markets, the proud Ghebite men riding at one with their horses.

When they released him Tulkhan rubbed his wrists and stretched to loosen his stiff muscles. One of the rebels moved forward with a chain but Reothe waved him off.

"There is no need. Come, General."

They walked side by side towards the ladder. Three of the rebels climbed up first. Tulkhan thought briefly of forcing Reothe to kill him, but his rebels might simply maim him, and besides, he had discovered a nub of resistance deep within him. He would not go down without a fight.

Yet why did he feel so useless?

It was Reothe's doing! It had to be.

"Climb." Reothe gestured to the ladder.

Tulkhan obeyed. When they were on the next floor the ladder was pulled up and a stone slid over the opening of the cell to create a living tomb.

He shuddered.

"Come take your place in history, General," Reothe said.

They were escorted out of the gates of Northpoint Citadel and into the township. It was the darkest part of the night, before the dawn. The small moon had already set and its larger mate was waxing. Tulkhan looked down to the bay where a low fog clung to the water. Few of the town's inhabitants were stirring.

Reothe and their escort marched silently down through the curving streets to the wharfs. Incongruously, the smell of freshly baked bread made Tulkhan's stomach rumble with hunger.

A large bonfire burned on the stones of the wharf. Reothe lifted a brand and waved. Tulkhan saw a man return the signal from the ship. He could not pick the Ghebite flag, but then the Ghebites would hardly advertise that they were supplying rebels to a Dhamfeer prince in exchange for the black sheep of their royal family.

The cruel irony of it tortured Tulkhan.

Imoshen woke from a troubled doze with a start. Ashmyr slept in her arms. The baby had woken after Reothe had slipped silently away. She had refused to speak to him, turning her face to the wall. All her perceptions of herself had been overturned, and she had felt too confused to confront him, her dearest and most dangerous enemy.

Now a sense of foreboding made her anxious. She slipped out of bed. The room looked normal. Instinct took her to the window. The bay was still dark but a bonfire burned on the wharf.

Its leaping flames drew her gaze, reminding her of something. Before she could pinpoint the memory several figures stepped in front of the bonfire. Amidst them was a broad-shouldered man, taller than the rest. Even from this distance she recognized Tulkhan.

Without a thought for the consequences she willed him to think of her.

Something cool brushed her perceptions and she realized Reothe was on the wharf with Tulkhan. The General must be Reothe's captive, yet he seemed unharmed—unarmed, yes, but not restrained. She couldn't imagine Tulkhan giving up without a fight.

It was so strange.

No time to wonder . . . this was her chance.

Eagerly Imoshen darted back to the bed to collect Ashmyr. Barefoot, her hair loose, dressed in nothing but her nightgown, she hurried to the door. With Reothe down on the wharf intent on the General, she could risk breaking his lock.

Experimentally she ran the fingers of her free hand over the door. There was nothing, no tingle, no pain waiting to cripple her mind.

Amazed, she concentrated on the mechanism within the lock chamber. Suddenly the door swung open.

There was no T'En lock keeping her in, only her belief that it existed. Hot shame flooded Imoshen. Reothe had fooled her. He must have remained outside the room ready to rebuff her first attempt on the lock, blocking it so firmly that she would not dare try again. She had played right into his hands.

Furious with herself, Imoshen ran down the dark corridor with Ashmyr in her arms. Nothing was going to stop her. No one would see her. She willed herself to move beyond the edge of the perceptions of those she passed. But there were few, for the tower rooms were almost deserted. She had no trouble finding her way out and into the township.

Tulkhan shifted as mist flowed around his boots. It drifted up from the water to creep across the wharf around him and into the streets. He had heard there were times when the buildings of Northpoint were shrouded in fog and only the Citadel tower rose above it.

He could hear the gentle slap of waves hitting the approaching boat's prow, mingled with the creak of the oars. Tulkhan watched the evidence of the boat's passage toward them. The mist swirled around it so that at times the heads of the men looked like disembodied shapes. A rope sailed up toward them and was made fast.

His captors stepped up onto the wharf.

"Kinraid!" Bitterness closed Tulkhan's throat.

The Vaygharian made a mock bow. He turned to Reothe. "Three boatloads of mercenaries are ready to disembark, and the rest when the Ghebite traitor stands on the mainland. I'll take him off your hands now."

A surge of despair gripped Tulkhan.

No! This was not his emotion. Reothe was manipulating him.

Suddenly the pall that had settled over him lifted. He heard Reothe gasp and the Vaygharian curse.

The rebels stepped back, muttering uneasily amongst themselves. Tulkhan turned to see what had startled them.

Imoshen! Fog curled its insubstantial tendrils around her. She was illuminated by an eerie inner radiance. With her silver hair loose and her white gown floating around her, she seemed to be carried on a sea of glowing mist.

The Vaygharian and his companions made the sign to ward off evil, calling on their gods to protect them. Even the rebels backed away, mouthing something in High T'En.

Tulkhan's teeth ached and his tongue registered the metallic taste of power. For an instant he thought he read fear, quickly masked, in Reothe's features.

"Imoshen." The T'En male stepped forward, his hand extended in welcome but when she made no move to accept it he let it drop. "The General was just leaving. The events of this last summer have been set to rights. Soon Fair Isle will belong to the T'En."

Tulkhan could not bear to look on Imoshen. Her choice was clear—she had renounced him for her own kind. How could he hope to stand against the last of the T'En united in purpose?

Though he felt the intensity of her gaze he shut himself away from her, too proud to let her discover the blow she had dealt him.

This accursed isle had stolen everyone he had ever loved but it would not take his self-respect. He would return to Gheeaba and restore his honor by killing his half-brother.

Imoshen shivered. Tulkhan would not meet her eyes. Reothe must have told the General she had given herself to him willingly. No wonder Tulkhan despised her, but it was not true.

Desperately she reached out for him but Tulkhan jerked away, obviously repelled by the thought of touching her.

His revulsion ate into her flesh like acid. The pain of it made her gasp and stagger. Reothe supported her, taking the baby, as a wave of dizziness swamped her vision.

All along she had known the General found her Otherness unnerving, but she had believed they could overcome that. Now she knew he did not merely hate her, he was disgusted by her.

It was cruel to learn the truth.

"Take him away," Reothe gestured to the boat.

She watched in stunned despair as Tulkhan stepped un-coerced into the boat. When he sat down the mist closed around him, shrouding all but the crown of his head from sight.

Imoshen could not believe he had repudiated her.

But he had.

The Vaygharian made to leave.

"No." Reothe stopped Kinraid. "You will stay until the

last mercenary stands on this shore. I know how the Vayghar fulfill their bargains."

Kinraid hesitated, resentment coloring his features. "So be it. Push off."

The rebels uncoiled the rope and tossed it to the boat.

"Here. Take the traitor's brat with you!" Kinraid tore the baby from Reothe's arms and threw him into the mist.

Imoshen gasped. The white cloth of Ashmyr's gown fluttered like useless wings as he sailed out and down into the fog-shrouded sea.

She screamed, calling on Tulkhan with every shred of her being to catch their son.

An ominous small splash filled the void left by her cry.

Shouts came from the boat. Men yelled. Several large splashes followed. It sounded as if the boat had overturned.

Imoshen spun to face Kinraid. Rage seared her soul.

Drawing his sword, he stood ready to fight. Behind him the bonfire roared like a rampaging beast eager to consume. Imoshen recalled her vision of his death.

"You will die by your own hand in flames of agony," she told him, hardly able to speak for the fury which closed her throat.

Terror engulfed his features. Against his will he turned to the bonfire. As though fighting every step he took, Kinraid dropped his sword and ran clumsily, leaping into the flames. His screams rose on the night, piercing, utterly abandoned.

The confrontation had taken no time at all.

Imoshen ran for the edge of the wharf. White noise rushed in her head.

Reothe caught her, absorbing the impact.

"Ashmyr's dead, Imoshen. I felt his life flicker out!"

No. She could not believe it. Frantically she twisted in Reothe's arms but he knew the T'En breaks and holds as well as she. At last he caught her body to his, using his superior strength to pin her arms.

"He's dead, Imoshen. Believe me!"

She stiffened in refusal.

"Imoshen?" He cupped her face in his hands. She felt him probe. It was too much. Instinctively she snapped back, retaliating against his intrusion, the strength of her gift unleashed by desperation. He gasped and staggered. Even as he crumpled to the wooden planks she leapt over him.

In her mind's eye she still saw Ashmyr falling with his gown flapping uselessly, still heard that terrible small splash echo over and over.

He could not be dead.

Where was he? Where should she dive?

She couldn't see the boat for the thick mist, but she could hear the splashing, the shouts from the men in the water.

"Tulkhan!" she cried, probing for him.

"Here!"

Two hands surged from the mist holding a small, still form. In the same heartbeat they sank down, hidden by the thick fog.

"Help! I can't swim!" Tulkhan called, panic edging his voice.

She recognized his fear. Her body reacted, heart pounding furiously.

Dropping to her knees, she searched the swirling mists, identifying the occasional dark shape which might have been any of the Vaygharian's men struggling to stay afloat.

"Accept me, Tulkhan. I can swim."

She closed her eyes and probed for his mind. There it was, familiar for all that it was filled with cold terror. She slipped into him, felt the baby clutched to his shoulder, their shoulder. The pair of them went under.

As cold, dark water closed over his head, panic roiled through him. She fought him for control. At last he understood and relaxed enough for her to kick, driving his strong limbs in a thrust that would bring him and Ashmyr to the surface.

She forced his free hand to form a scoop and drove his arm in an arc which carried him forward, kicking at the same time.

Now that he could feel the results he let himself go with her, trusting her to save them. It was only possible with his cooperation. She could feel his great heart raging, powered by his determination to live.

With another stroke his hand brushed the barnacle-encrusted pylon of the wharf. Desperately, he clutched it, trying to keep his head above water. The still baby was wedged safely in the crook of his neck.

Imoshen detached herself from Tulkhan's perception and crawled along to meet him. Stretching full length, she hung over the edge of the wharf, feeling through the mist. Her hands encountered Tulkhan's head, his broad shoulder.

"Give him to me."

Silently Tulkhan passed the baby's limp form to her. She brought the little body to her chest and rolled away from the edge, huddling in a crouch. In the growing dawn light she saw that the life had left Ashmyr. She probed, but not a flicker remained.

It could not be.

She would not let it be!

In desperation she tore the neckline of her gown and raked the scars of the Ancients. Fiery tendrils of pain raced down her chest, but it was nothing compared to the pain of her loss.

With all her will she called on the Ancients. Ashmyr was theirs already. She could not begin to understand their purpose, but surely they would not let him die!

Tulkhan heaved his cold, wet body over the edge of the wharf. Imoshen's tragic figure riveted his gaze. She knelt, her breasts bared. Parallel rivulets of blood stained her white skin. With her arms extended she held the limp form of their son before her.

He did not need to be in touch with her mind to share her agony. It was written clearly on her face and it mirrored his own.

"Imoshen?" Tulkhan would have gone to her but Reothe hissed a warning.

Startled, he glanced to Reothe. His skin went cold.

Blood trickled from the Dhamfeer's nostrils and ears. Even his eyes wept tears of blood. He lay sprawled on the wharf, barely able to lift his head. The rebels had deserted them.

Reothe lifted a trembling hand. "Help me."

Tulkhan found nothing incongruous in this plea. His only son was dead. Nothing mattered.

He scrambled across the wharf. Sliding an arm under Reothe's back, Tulkhan lifted the T'En warrior against his chest. Reothe's hands clutched him in a spasm of pain. A raw groan escaped him.

Reothe froze. Tulkhan followed his fixed gaze and stiffened as he recognized the same childlike being he'd seen when he had inadvertently spilled blood at an ancient site.

"The Ancients answer her summons," Reothe whispered.

Tulkhan studied the apparition which hovered in the mist above the sea. He could not bear to meet its fathomless eyes as it glided through the fog toward Imoshen.

"I don't—"

"Imoshen called on the Ancients to save Ashmyr," Reothe explained. "That much is clear even to me."

Tulkhan shuddered at Reothe's tone, equal parts fear and scorn.

An inner light suffused the Ancient, making Tulkhan squint and his eyes water. As its hands closed on his son's body he felt a surge of panic. He fought it. The boy was dead, nothing could hurt him now.

Imoshen's arms dropped to her sides. Except for the rapid rise and fall of her breasts she was utterly still. Her wine-dark eyes were fixed on the Ancient, her face naked with desperation.

Hope rose in Tulkhan's chest. He forced it down. Death could not be denied.

"Can they save him?" Tulkhan asked despite himself, unable to tear his eyes from the eerie tableau.

"For a price."

The Ancient extended a hand and touched Imoshen's closed eyelids. She shuddered visibly, took a deep breath, then gave a slight but firm nod.

Taking the baby in both hands the Ancient lifted Ashmyr's head and breathed into him. The little body jerked in a painful spasm. A grunt of sympathetic pain escaped Tulkhan but his heart raced as hope surged, closely followed by revulsion. This was not right. No one returned to life from beyond death's shadow.

It was too much for Tulkhan to grasp. He strained to see through the radiant glare which consumed Imoshen, the Ancient, and his son.

Was it possible? Would the baby's life be returned? Would the child be whole? Surely he must be tainted? Tulkhan wanted to ask Reothe for reassurance. Only by an effort of will did he hold his tongue, straining for the slightest sound.

A vibrating cry broke from the baby. Imoshen gasped, her hands lifting, pleading.

The Ancient held the baby in one arm and floated closer to Imoshen. It leant towards her until its forehead touched hers. They might have kissed. For an instant they stayed thus, then the Ancient transferred Ashmyr to Imoshen's hands and retreated.

She swayed, steadying herself with difficulty, the baby pressed to her body.

"What did it do?" Tulkhan whispered.

"I can't tell, I am as blind as you."

"Reothe?" He studied what he could see of the T'En's face. His eyes were not blank like a blind man's. Surely he did not mean his T'En gifts had been destroyed? "What happened to you?"

Reothe grimaced, raw pain and despair passing across his features. "Look!"

Imoshen now held the baby, a living, breathing child. As Tulkhan watched, the glow which had illuminated her and the Ancient faded and with it the apparition, until only Imoshen and Ashmyr remained.

She sank to her knees. Oblivious to them, she stripped the wet gown from the baby, lifting him to her breast for food and comfort.

A sliver of silver dawn light illuminated the horizon behind the town, bringing the first hint of natural color to their surroundings. Tulkhan shifted Reothe a little to ease his tense muscles. He felt the other give an involuntary shudder of pain.

Behind him he could hear voices, and guessed the rebels had drifted back and would soon find them. Quick as the thought, he slipped the knife from Reothe's waist and held it to the rebel leader's throat.

A painful laugh escaped Reothe. It scraped across Tulkhan's raw senses like salt on an open wound. But he would not falter. The T'En warrior was his bargaining tool. Tulkhan had the rebel leader where he had always wanted him—helpless. Why then did he feel no rush of victory?

"Imoshen?"

Imoshen looked up, startled to hear her name. She felt like a sword's blade forged beyond recognition by the fires of pain.

Dawn's subtle light revealed the two people dearest to her.

"Ashmyr lives." She stroked the soft dark head at her breast, joy and wonder suffusing her.

"But at what price?" Reothe whispered.

His question was an unwelcome intrusion. She glanced his way, noticing for the first time how he lay limply in Tulkhan's arms. The way the General's blade was pressed into Reothe's throat made her flinch. Cradling the baby she crept over to them.

Already Tulkhan's long, dark hair was drying in the breeze which carried the mist away. He held the knife so tightly his knuckles were white.

But it was Reothe who made her gasp. Blood had dried in painful paths where it had trickled from his nose and ears. It looked as if he had wept tears of blood.

Her heart turned over with outrage. "Who did this to you?"

His eyes closed and he gave a wordless almost imperceptible shake of his head. A rueful smile touched his lips.

When he opened his eyes the knowledge was there for her to read.

"No, impossible!" she cried. "I would not, could not, hurt you!"

Tulkhan muttered something in Gheeaban. She glanced to him and registered his pain, but there was nothing she could do.

It was a terrible burden to feel for them both.

Silently she offered Tulkhan her apology. He looked away, unable to accept it. Her heart faltered.

Dragging in a tight breath, Imoshen returned her attention to Reothe. Blood-tinged tears slid from under his closed lids.

"Are you in pain?" Imoshen touched his temple, anxious to ease his discomfort, and felt a blankness.

Tulkhan shifted, stretching his cramped muscles. "He says he is blind. His T'En gifts are gone."

Instinctively Imoshen spread her fingers over Reothe's face. She probed. His body stiffened, a guttural groan escaped him. It tore at her. Sweat broke out on her skin, making it grow chill in the dawn breeze as she searched.

"I can't find you." She could not believe the essence she had felt so acutely was dulled to a point where she could not perceive it. Gone forever? "I can't—"

"He said your gifts are greater than his," Tulkhan told her softly, almost sympathetically. "That they always have been."

"But—"

"You did this to him," Tulkhan continued, almost cruelly. "Had you but tried, you could have withstood Reothe at any time!"

Imoshen's gaze shifted from Tulkhan's remote, obsidian eyes to Reothe's pain-ravaged face.

"All bluff, Imoshen," Reothe whispered. He held her eyes silently, asking forgiveness. "A great gamble and I almost won."

His smile wrenched at her.

"Stay back!" Tulkhan barked suddenly.

Imoshen turned to see the rebels approaching, followed by a stream of townsfolk. The baby at her breast gave a soft whimper. She soothed him automatically and came to her feet to face Reothe's rebels. As they edged forward, weapons drawn, the townsfolk hung back behind them, torn between fear and curiosity.

Imoshen studied the wharf and the bay, now visible through a thin film of retreating mist. The Vaygharians in the water had slunk off like rats.

"There will be no more fighting." Imoshen met the eyes of the rebels. "Sling a sail between two poles to make a stretcher. T'Reothe is hurt. I want him carried to the Citadel."

As the rising sun chased the last of the mists away Imoshen watched the rebels work. Tulkhan sheathed the knife and released Reothe, placing him gently on the deck. The Ghebite General did not approach her when he stood. It was a painful omission.

The rebels seemed subdued, concerned for their injured leader, and obviously unsure of their own status as prisoners.

The creaking of a boat's oars made Imoshen turn.

"Wharrd comes," Tulkhan announced, then added grimly. "I must have the Vaygharian ship's captain captured before he can carry a message back to my half-brother."

He strode past her to the end of the wharf.

Tulkhan did not trust himself near Imoshen. This night he had seen into the dark depths of his soul and he did not like what he had learned. It was as the Beatific had said. A True-man forfeited much if he loved one of the T'En. Logic told him to climb into Wharrd's small boat and leave Fair Isle while he still owned his soul, but that would mean deserting his son, his only heir. Common sense told him his son was dead, that this creature Imoshen cradled was a changeling, but he could not bring himself to leave.

A spear of insight stabbed Tulkhan. Would his son grow into a being like Imoshen? Would the adult Ashmyr look upon Tulkhan with garnet eyes and scorn him as a Mere-man?

No wonder the T'En had been cast out of their home beyond the dawn sun. How could True-people live with the knowledge that Tulkhan was now privy to?

Wharrd lifted an arm and waved.

Tulkhan returned the signal automatically.

"Don't leave me, General," Imoshen whispered, suddenly at his side.

He snorted. "I have no intention of relinquishing what I have taken. And do me the courtesy of keeping out of my head, T'En."

She gasped softly. "I was not . . . I did not mean to. I need you, General Tulkhan."

"Oh?" He felt like laughing. What could Imoshen possibly need from a Mere-man like himself? "You have my son, you have Fair Isle, and now you have your betrothed, suitably chastised. What could you possibly want with me?"

He looked down into her face, illuminated by the soft morning light. She looked tired, fragile, and vulnerable. He knew his words had hurt her. The irony of it was that in hurting her, he had hurt himself, because despite everything he still loved her.

Against his better judgment he cupped her cheek, feeling the softness of her skin on his calloused palm. Wisps of her pale hair lifted in the breeze.

She turned her face into his palm and kissed him. It was the gentle gesture of a supplicant, but her eyes were as sharp as ever.

"I need you to rule Fair Isle, General Tulkhan. The people are afraid of the T'En. I need someone they trust to represent their interests."

He almost choked. "So I am to be your tool, your puppet king? Truly, I am honored."

"Don't!" It was a plea from her heart.

"Think what you ask, Imoshen. I won't be your tool, I could not live with myself."

"I know," She slid closer to him, pressing against his side. He had to acknowledge how much he craved her touch. "I don't want a public life. You are a good man, a true man. You have earned Fair Isle, General Tulkhan. Keep it. I know you will rule wisely. And—"

"Kill him!" The words were out before he knew he meant to say them. "Have Reothe executed."

He felt her stiffen as the boat with his supporters bobbed nearer.

"I can't do that."

"Why not?"

"He is the last of my kind. I can no more kill him than you could order your half-brother's death. Remember what you said to me when I advised you to kill him?" Sorrow made her eyes luminously intense. "You said if you could kill that easily, I would be dead. Now I give you the same answer. There have been moments when I could have taken another path, one that would have led to your death, but I did not. Don't ask me to kill Reothe."

"Then banish him."

"I need Reothe. He has knowledge of the T'En which I must have for my own peace of mind. And for the time being he is harmless."

Tulkhan laughed bitterly. "We should stone him now while we can!"

He looked into her eyes, seeing the knowledge there. They both knew that, with Imoshen untutored in her T'En legacy, if Reothe should regain his gifts he would be too powerful and cunning to contain. She did not attempt to deny this but offered Tulkhan a rueful smile.

"Reothe is the last of my kin."

"And the father of your child?" It cost Tulkhan to ask it. She nodded, searching his face. He waited for an explanation, a plea for forgiveness, but she said nothing.

"Imoshen, tell me he took you against your will. Offer me cold comfort."

A rope snaked up through the air towards them. Tulkhan caught it on reflex and made it fast. As he straightened he met Imoshen's gaze. A charged silence hung between them. Then Wharrd and the Ghebites clambered up onto the wharf, demanding an explanation, and the moment was lost.

Imoshen stepped back as Tulkhan moved forward to lift Kalleen onto the wharf. In a few moments he was surrounded by his own people. They greeted him exuberantly, knowing only that the rebel leader lay strapped to a litter unable to move, while their General stood with Imoshen at his side, apparently victorious.

The irony of it was bitter. Yet he could not help but smile and accept their heartfelt congratulations. They had feared for his life. They had stood by him when all was lost and he had worked a miracle. He was their legendary General Tulkhan, a man capable of pulling victory from the jaws of defeat. Fair Isle was his and they shared a golden future.

Not one of them knew he was bound by chains of love to a creature more dangerous than his worst nightmare. He met Imoshen's eyes above their heads and saw only her Otherness. Her expression reminded him of Reothe.

In that moment Tulkhan realized they were all her tools.

Imoshen slipped away from the celebrating Ghebites. Their hearty joy grated on her raw emotions. But Kalleen darted after her, hugging her, a thousand questions on her lips. When she attempted to take the sleeping baby, Imoshen would not part with him.

Ashmyr was more precious to her than life itself.

Returning her friend's hug Imoshen felt the rush of new life illuminating Kalleen and smiled, though the sudden expansion of her T'En gifts startled her.

Kalleen wrinkled her nose as she studied Imoshen. "What is it, Imoshen? You look . . . different."

Tears stung Imoshen's eyes. Kalleen grasped her arm impulsively, offering comfort.

Imoshen blinked the tears away and shook her head, dredging up a smile of reassurance. "I need you to go to the Citadel. Have chambers prepared and food laid out. Tell them the General has triumphed and is reconciled with the T'En. The rebels must not panic. There will be no retaliation, no executions."

Kalleen nodded and called Wharrd to her side to explain what was to be done.

Imoshen left them. She crossed to where Reothe lay strapped to the makeshift stretcher, and knelt down beside him. The rebels stepped back to a respectful distance.

She touched his cheek, feeling the crust of dried blood. "Are you in pain?"

He grimaced. "What does it matter? I have lost and I'm as blind as a Mere-man. Kill me now before I recover, because I will not rest until I have restored the T'En."

She placed the fingers of her free hand on his forehead, concentrating on easing his pain. When his fine features relaxed she let her hand drop.

"I don't want to kill you, Reothe."

He turned his face away from her. Sadness settled in her core. Tulkhan had withdrawn from her, and now Reothe.

"I am alone and frightened by what I've learned this night, Reothe. I thought I could shut the T'En gifts away and use them only when I chose. But . . ."

She caught him watching her.

"What did you promise the Ancients?" he asked.

"What did *you* promise them?" she countered.

Knowledge sat heavily on his face but he would not answer.

Imoshen sighed. "All I ever wanted was to ensure my survival and that of my child."

"What will you do with me, Imoshen?" Reothe whispered.

Tulkhan joined them and Imoshen came to her feet. Rebels and townsfolk watched uneasily, fearing purges and executions.

Imoshen raised her voice. "People of Fair Isle, listen. Tell the rebels who hide under your beds that there will be no more killing. Fair Isle has seen enough death. We take T'Reothe to the Citadel, our honored guest."

Four of them came forward to lift the litter as Imoshen turned to Tulkhan, extending her hand. For a moment she thought he would refuse to touch her, but he raised his arm and she closed her fingers over his.

She wanted to reassure him but he was too remote from

her now. He had made his acceptance of her conditional on Reothe's death, and she could not order the execution of the last T'En warrior. Reothe had a vision for the future of the T'En race and it was a vision which inspired her. Reothe was her other half, closer than a lover or a brother. Without Reothe to anchor her gifts, she doubted she would survive, and she was afraid of what she might become.

No wonder the T'En were so unstable.

Pain curled around Imoshen's heart. To think it had come to this.

Last autumn when General Tulkhan's forces had prepared to storm the Stronghold, it had all seemed so simple—death or honor. Every decision she had made had been with the best of intentions. She wished she had never opened the Pandora's box of her T'En gifts. But here was Ashmyr in her arms and another life growing inside her, and she could not turn back the passage of events which had led her here.

Imoshen lifted her chin and prepared to face the township.

In the growing light of a new day they made a slow, stately procession through winding streets to the Citadel. The shopkeepers stood in the doorways; solemn and wide-eyed children watched history unfold.

The smell of freshly baked bread made Imoshen's stomach rumble. She veered toward a baker's apprentice who had run to the front of the shop. He brushed flour from his apron as he balanced a tray of fresh loaves, hot from the oven.

Imoshen's mouth watered. She met his awed eyes. "May I?"

The baker nodded proudly.

"Best in all Northpoint," the man announced. "Take as many as you want."

"Thank you." Imoshen took one and tore into it. Warm, crusty bread melted in her mouth. She grinned. "Excellent!"

The baker beamed and his apprentice cheered. The crowd surged forward, first one then another stroked her hair or touched her sixth finger.

"*T'Imoshen*" they whispered reverently, their relief and pleasure evident. She tried not to think how easily their feelings for her could turn to hatred.

With the baker's consent Imoshen offered a loaf to the General.

Tulkhan's fingers closed on the bread and his mouth moistened in anticipation. He looked into Imoshen's eyes with rueful understanding. She had done it again. With a simple gesture she had won the people over.

Was it by design or pure luck? It did not matter.

He tore a chunk from the loaf and ate it, giving the baker his compliments before they resumed their journey.

Imoshen's gaze met his. "It appears you have won, General."

He looked into the eyes of the creature he should despise but she was the woman he adored. "Appearances can be deceptive, T'Imoshen."

She linked her free arm with his. Here she was, co-ruler of Fair Isle with the Ghebite General to do her bidding and her T'En prince, Reothe, too weak to resist her. To all appearances she was triumphant.

Yet even without using her gift she foresaw trouble. She was surrounded by enemies, the Beatific, Murgon's Tractarians, the mainland spies, Reothe's rebels, and the vengeful Ghebite King. . . .

She was T'Imoshen, the last of the T'En, and she would carry on the work of her namesake. She would see Fair Isle united, her race accepted, and peace and prosperity for all her people.

ABOUT THE AUTHOR

CORY DANIELLS lives by the bay in Brisbane, Australia, with her husband and six children. With more than twenty children's books and numerous short stories published, she set out to combine her two loves, fantasy and romance, in the T'En Trilogy.

She holds a black belt in Tae Kwon Do and is currently learning Aikido and Iaido, the Japanese martial art of swordplay.

**LOOK FOR THE STUNNING CONCLUSION TO
THE T'EN TRILOGY IN SUMMER 2002. . . .**

Reothe gestured to himself. "You did this. You could
have turned your gifts on me at any time."

But Imoshen did not dare unleash the powers he seemed
so sure of. At least for the moment they were equal. His
abilities were crippled and hers untutored. "How could I
suspect my true potential when everyone believes the males
are more powerful than the females? You hid the T'Elegos. It
is as much my birthright as yours!"

"You have only to ask and I will share *everything* with
you."

She fought a heady rush of desire. He promised so much
more than the knowledge of their T'En legacy. But her
choice was made. "I'm sorry, Reothe. I must stand by my
vow to Tulkhan."

"You surrendered to save your life, Imoshen. Your vow to
me is of an older making and sprang from your own free
will."

"Our betrothal belongs to a lost future."

"I have the Sight. I've glimpsed many futures. I believe we
can claim the future we want. Look at your left wrist."

A sharp sting made her gasp and she covered her wrist.
But she could not deny that the bonding scar they both
shared had split open.

Shortly after General Tulkhan accepted her surrender,
Reothe had come to her at Landsend Abbey. He had offered
to help her escape, but she had already given the General
her word, and the people of Fair Isle relied on her to smooth
the transition of power. Before she could explain this, Reothe
had cut their wrists to begin the bonding ceremony. But
she had refused to complete the oath. In Landsend Abbey, she
had made the decision to follow her head, not her heart;
now just over a year later, she hoped it had been the right
decision. Imoshen gritted her teeth as blood welled between
her fingers.

"Imoshen?" The tone of Reothe's voice made her look up, just as he raised his left arm. A thin trickle of blood seeped from the wound across his wrist. "I told you once it would stop bleeding on the day we were properly joined. We have shared our bodies and our minds, yet you still refuse me. This might not be a perfect future, but it is all we have, and I will not give it up!"

*In a world of treachery and magic,
a warrior princess must face an unknown future—
while her past comes back to haunt her....*

Fair Isle was once a lush and lovely land, renowned
for its wealth and elegance. Now its fields lie blackened
by barbarian Ghebite conquerors who despise
its traditions of female freedom—and fear its captive
young empress, Imoshen. One of the last
pure T'En—legendary for their subtle enchantments
and fearsome beauty—Imoshen's magical nature is
just beginning to emerge as this new era dawns on Fair
Isle. Now, pregnant with Ghebite leader Tulkhan's
child, she must battle to save both her land and her new
union from being torn apart by suspicion and fear.

Despite their clashing cultures, Tulkhan stirs in Imoshen
a quicksilver passion, an all-consuming attraction
that trembles on the brink of love. But as Imoshen tries
to resist the urge to give in to this powerful longing,
an older bond—and more sacred lust—tempts her.
For she cannot forget her youthful betrothal to her
kinsman Reothe, the last T'En warrior, a proud and
sorcerous renegade who now seeks to reclaim
Fair Isle—and Imoshen as well....

US $5.99 / $8.99 CAN

ISBN 0-553-58100-7

58100

0 76783 00599 0

S